Roswell G Horr

Comments on Current Questions

Big issues of an off year; silver, the tariff, tin plates, the commercial

marine, reciprocity

Roswell G Horr

Comments on Current Questions
Big issues of an off year; silver, the tariff, tin plates, the commercial marine, reciprocity

ISBN/EAN: 9783337419615

Printed in Europe, USA, Canada, Australia, Japan

Cover: Foto ©Andreas Hilbeck / pixelio.de

More available books at **www.hansebooks.com**

THE TRIBUNE MONTHLY.

VOL. III.   JULY, 1891.   NO. 7.

BIG ISSUES OF AN OFF YEAR.

EX-CONGRESSMAN HORR'S COMMENTS

—ON—

CURRENT QUESTIONS.

SILVER —THE TARIFF—TIN PLATES—THE COMMERCIAL MARINE —RECIPROCITY.

LIBRARY OF TRIBUNE EXTRAS.

$2 a Year.   Single Copies, 25 Cents.

THE TRIBUNE ASSOCIATION,
NEW-YORK.

BIG ISSUES OF AN OFF YEAR.

SILVER—THE TARIFF—TIN PLATES--THE COMMERCIAL MARINE—RECIPROCITY.

SHORT TALKS WITH VOTERS.

THE WORST OF MONOPOLIES.

With 400 votes against 300 the Ohio Democratic Convention adopted a free-coinage platform. The opposition was not weak in argument nor uncertain of purpose, and yet when outvoted it accepted the platform which 300 delegates held dangerous to the country and unjust to its millions of working people. It was well said by one speaker that the voters of Ohio had no occasion to sacrifice their own prosperity in order to enrich the few millionaire mine-owners of silver States. Nevertheless, the millionaires had their way, and under pretence of assailing monopolies they committed the Democrats of Ohio to support the worst and most hurtful of all monopolies. This same Democratic Convention denounced without measure the new Protective Tariff, on the ground that it oppressed the people for the benefit of capitalists engaged in favored industries. But no other industry ever has been petted and favored as the mining of silver would be if the policy of the Ohio Democrats should prevail.

The convention thinks it an outrage that a duty is placed on raw wool and on tin plates. But suppose Congress had provided that every pound of wool produced in the country should be purchased by the Government at a price nearly 30 cents per pound above its market value, and should be stored in public warehouses, and that legal-tender notes should be given to the producers which all other citizens should be compelled by law to accept in full satisfaction of all debts or claims. That would be indeed an outrageous burden, and yet it is precisely what the Democrats of Ohio propose to do for the benefit of the millionaire mine-owners, while they bitterly oppose any attempt to secure a better market for the products of 5,000,000 farms.

Suppose Congress had enacted that every pound of tin plates produced in this country should be purchased by Government, and in addition all the tin plates that any foreigners might see fit to send hither, and that legal-tender notes should be given for the entire quantity at such a rate that instead of $30,000,000 it should cost over $40,000,000. Would there not be strong reason for denouncing such a plunder of the many for the benefit of the few? But the same Democratic Convention which rants and raves about the duty on tin plates solemnly resolves that Government must pay about one-third more than the market price for all the silver that may be delivered to it, so that the yearly product of American mines, which is now worth about $51,000,000 in market value, shall be sold to the Government for $72,000,000 or more. The new tariff has not a single provision which would take from the people half as much money for any purpose whatever as the Free-Coinage bill would take from them for the benefit of the few owners of silver mines.

The wool duty, according to the declaration of the candidate nominated for Governor by the Democrats of Ohio, has made wool cheaper than it was before. If he were less of a demagogue and more of a student, he would probably be aware that woollen goods cost no more now than they did before the new tariff was enacted, and that not only because the foreign importers have reduced the cost of goods as much as the new tariff added to the duty, but also because the American manufacturers themselves sell at prices as low or lower than were charged six months ago. The pretence that the people are burdened is simply false and fraudulent, but if it were true, all the loss that could be imposed upon them by duties on woollen goods would be insignificant, compared with the direct loss alone which the free coinage of silver would involve. Pretending to oppose monopolies and legislation for the benefit of individuals, the Democrats of Ohio have committed themselves to the worst and most mischievous of all forms of legislation against the public welfare and for the benefit of a small class of citizens.

WAGES AND LIVING.

The tariff question turns at last mainly upon the condition of the working people. One would suppose it an easy matter to show, as the experience of almost every middle-aged man tells him, that there has been a great improvement during the last thirty years in this respect. But memories are treacherous. The habits of to-day have too often blotted out altogether recollections of the experiences of other years. The man who lives to-day in comfort, earning good wages as a mechanic or artisan, often fails to remember what his actual circumstances were when he began active life, or if he remembers, attributes the difference rather to his own rise in the world than to any change in the general condition of the wage-earner.

Hence it is that detailed information on this point always comes to the mind as a sort of revelation, surprising and to many scarcely credible. There are not a few who have this feeling, as they peruse the statements made in a recent article by "The Boston Commercial Bulletin" on the condition of the working people half a century ago. It first quotes a letter from an old cotton-mill superintendent:

The hours of work were then from 5 a. m. to 7 or 7:30 p. m., with 30 minutes for breakfast and 45 minutes for dinner. Women to a greater extent than now were employed; children of tender years were numerous in the mills. The pay of the ordinary day laborer was 75 cents, and spinners on hand mules rarely averaged $1 for fourteen hours of toil. The work of the weavers was exacting and tiresome in the extreme, and 66 2-3 cents per day was above the average pay.

In comparison with these figures "The Commercial Bulletin" says:

The compensation of a wage-worker shows a marked increase. The women of the weaveroom now average $8 per week of sixty hours, and the men $10 a week, while mule spinners average from $11 to $12. The wages of masons, carpenters, painters and other out-

door laborers have doubled within the last fifty years, and their hours of labor materially lessened.

Thus it is clear that the wage-earner has a far greater purchasing power than he had in former times. The question need not here be discussed whether wages are as high, even now, as they ought to be, or whether hours of labor ought to be still further reduced. The question is whether the conditions in this country have been such as to benefit the wage-earners, and as respects wages received the statements given by the paper above quoted correspond with all other evidence attainable. But as to the mode of living in working families the same journal says:

The meat brought on to the table of the wage-worker of that day was pork. Coffee, tea, milk and sugar were used sparingly, and molasses was almost invariably used for sweetening. Satinet for winter wear and nankeen for summer use were the garments of men and boys alike. Cowhide covered the feet of the boys in winter. During the other months they went barefoot. Their winter garments included neither undershirts nor overcoats, but the woollen comforters served instead. Calico was the ordinary dress for women, and but few varied therefrom even on Sunday. In the tenements stoves were unknown, carpets were beyond the occupant's means, and the walls were unadorned with paper or pictures. Chairs were of wood only. The feather bed was usually for the comfort of the parents, and the younger members slept on straw. One room served for their sitting-room, dining-room and kitchen, and the garret was rarely separated by a partition. The rug before each bed was of braided woollen rags. These operatives, it must be remembered, were native American men and women who came from country towns.

It is scarcely necessary to add anything by way of strengthening the contrast which these statements so forcibly make. He who has visited any of the manufacturing towns of New-England, though it be for only a day, is well aware that the ordinary condition of the working people is now far from that described so graphically in the foregoing extract. The journal from which these statements are quoted says with truth:

The operative's house, with its modern conveniences, unknown to the manor house of the first half of the century, and alike productive of health and comfort, though of much higher rental, demands no greater percentage of his earnings than did that of an earlier day. In all else the cost of living has not materially increased, manufactured goods consumed in the families being materially lower in price. Whatever difference there is in some of the living expenses is accounted for by the improved quality of goods purchased. The luxuries of a few years ago are the necessaries of to-day.

It is not intended to imply that the whole change, wonderful as it has been, is due to any single cause. But no one who investigates with care can fail to be convinced that the large proportion of it is due to that American policy which has defended the working people of this country against direct competition with the laborers of other lands. It has enabled them to ask and employers to pay a much higher rate of wages for labor, and at the same time has placed within their reach substantially all the necessaries of life at a much lower cost than they formerly paid. It is for this reason that the intelligent and thrifty workingmen of mature age are almost without exception hearty believers in the American policy of Protection, and ready to do their utmost to prevent its overthrow.

SQUARING THE CIRCLE.

The Democratic party is rallying around the old standard of Free Trade. Last year there was only one leader of the party in Ohio who ventured to proclaim himself a Free Trader without equivocation and reserve. This year the State Convention condemns Protection as an iniquitous policy, favors "a tariff levied for the sole purpose of producing a revenue sufficient to defray the legitimate expenses of the Government economically administered," and calls for a graded income tax. A tariff for revenue only was what the Democratic National platform demanded in 1876 and 1880. This is what the Ohio Democrats now want, but being mindful of the fact that England with its revenue tariff is compelled to tax incomes, it adopts that feature of the Free-Trade system. By demanding the imposition of the income tax, they emphasize in the most practical way their absolute conversion to Free Trade. In fact, they virtually revive the tariff plank of the Democratic National Conventions in 1856 and 1860, which declared :

The time has come for the people of the United States to declare themselves in favor of free seas and progressive free trade throughout the world, and by solemn manifestations to place their moral influence at the side of their successful example.

A revenue tariff and taxation of incomes not only embodies the free-trade ideas of England, but also revives the revenue system of the Confederate States when they were the Solid South in rebellion. The secessionists were Free Traders. In the constitution adopted by the Confederate States the powers conferred upon Congress excluded Protection. Free Trade was made the foundation of the Confederacy as shown by the following extract from the definition of the legislative powers :

To lay and collect taxes, duties, imposts and excises for revenue necessary to pay the debts, provide for the common defence, and carry on the government of the Confederate States ; but no bounties shall be granted from the Treasury ; nor shall any duties or taxes on importations from foreign nations be laid to promote or foster any branch of industry ; and all duties, imposts and excises shall be uniform throughout the Confederate States.—(Confederate Constitution.)

The Ohio Democrats have thus squared the circle of their historic past. By declaring themselves to be opposed to the "iniquitous" policy of Protection and to be in favor of a tariff for revenue only and of the imposition of income taxes, they return bag and baggage to the Free-Trade lines of the Buchanan, Breckinridge and Douglas conventions, and support with the moral influence and example the traditions of the Confederate Congress. Our friends in Ohio have the advantage of knowing exactly where the enemy is encamped.

INCOME-TAXATION AND FREE TRADE.

"The Sun," in that spirit of courageous independence which is characteristic of that well-conducted Democratic journal, condemns the inconsistency of its party in Ohio in opposing "all class legislation" and favoring at the same time a graded income tax. It describes an income tax as class legislation of the worst sort, since that system divides the community into the honest and the dishonest, and imposes at once a tariff on integrity and a bounty on perjury. It shows that in 1870, when the tax was still in force as a war measure, it was paid by one adult male out of every thirty. That "The Sun" considers a complete demonstration of its character as class legislation. The demand of the Ohio Democrats for a graded or unequal income tax it denounces as a clamor for "a final outrage in the way of class legislation," since it "would divide the free and equal citizens of the United States into various classes ; one class paying nothing, another class paying 5 per cent, another paying 10 per cent, another paying into the Treasury half of their incomes, and so on up to the class which suffers an absolute confiscation of the earnings of its skill, intelligence, energy and accumulated savings."

This is all true and cannot be controverted. In the attempt to pull the wool over the eyes of the Farmers' Alliance fanatics the Ohio Democrats have stultified themselves and condemned themselves out of their own mouths. Not only have they committed themselves to class legislation on a tremendous scale, but they have also invited unpopularity by demanding a revival of the most odious methods of war taxation—methods which, as "The Sun" justly remarks, cannot be enforced without the establishment of "a system of inquisition and espionage repugnant to American ideas and abhorrent to the free citizen."

The Ohio Democrats, however, while convicted of folly in opposing and favoring class legislation in the same breath, are consistent from another point of view. They have recorded their rancorous hostility, not to the McKinley Act alone, but to the whole policy of Protection. They want a tariff for revenue only, and as little of that as possible : and foreseeing that the expenditures for National administration and for payment of interest on the war debt must be met in some way, they fall back upon the English plan of taxing incomes with communistic modifications. What they want is Free Trade, and they are logical enough to couple with it a system of filling the National exchequer grounded upon English methods. The Republicans throughout the country are under pressing obligations to the Ohio Democrats. National issues were defined at Cleveland in the sharpest possible way.

THE OCEAN MAIL ACT.

The Postmaster-General's proposals for ocean mail service will inevitably be received with coolness and uncertainty by the steamship companies and vessel-owners now in the carrying trade under the American flag. These interests were disappointed by the failure of the Navigation Bounty bill. and they have not yet adapted themselves to the requirements of the Ocean Mail Service Act. Of the two measures, the first offered immediate relief to the shipping interests, which had been suffering from several decades of National neglect and from the active competition of foreign subsidized lines, while the second was a creative measure designed to increase the efficiency of the American steamship service already in existence and to promote the establishment of new lines. If the first measure had been adopted there would have been a quick and enthusiastic response from all the corporations now struggling for existence against untoward conditions. The act which was passed will compel them to make large investments of capital in the building of new ships before they can derive substantial benefits from it. It may also subject them to competition from new interests to be created by it. It is less of a relief measure, but offers encouragement for active measures on their part for improving their service. The letter published on another page brings out these points with lucidity and force.

It will be natural under these circumstances for the American lines forming a remnant of a once-powerful commercial marine to be exceedingly cautious and deliberate before committing themselves to the new policy, and earnestly striving to avail themselves of the opportunities opened to them. There are some considerations, however, which ought to have great weight in influencing their decisions after their managers have had sufficient leisure for reflecting upon the situation. The measure which their representatives and the shipping leagues advocated was based upon the system of navigation bounties adopted by France and Italy. While that policy has been useful in developing the commercial marine of each of those countries, the results have been somewhat disappointing, and have excited abroad some controversy respecting the practical efficiency of the methods adopted. Indeed, it will be apparent to any one who closely studies the commercial statistics of those nations that more beneficial results have accompanied the direct payment of steamship subsidies when that system has continued without reference to the bounties. The German and English Governments are employing the latter system to a very large extent, and it may be said to be the preferred method of promoting the development of commerce now in operation in maritime Europe. The new Shipping Act is grounded upon the best and most satisfactory experience of competing nations. It is, therefore, less open to criticism in this country from political opponents than the Bounty bill would have been, and is more likely to remain in force for a long period.

This inherent probability of permanence is an element to be considered by shipping interests seeking to enlarge their investments and to increase their business. They require a reasonable degree of assurance that the new policy is not a tentative measure liable to be modified and counteracted by hostile legislation. The payment of navigation bounties was a French and Italian expedient, not sanctioned by American practice. The policy of converting the mail service into an agency for the development of shipping interests was adopted under Democratic Administrations before the Civil War, and has been sanctioned by maritime Europe. The new act is grounded upon principles which insure its permanency and thereby invite the confidence of investors. The most rigorous economist cannot find fault with it, for it is evident that it will cost less for the Government to create an auxiliary navy of high speed by paying well for mail transportation than it will to continue indefinitely the construction of fast cruisers for the navy. The new act, while it was weakened by the amendments offered to it in the House, remains a logical and creative measure, and will yield in due time a large increase of transportation facilities under the American flag.

OCEAN MAIL PROPOSALS.

The Postmaster-General's circular inviting bids for ocean mail service marks the beginning of a new policy which aims to restore the American flag to the seas. The details of the recent act passed by Congress have been exhaustively considered, and comprehensive action has been taken to carry out the intent of the legislation. The Postmaster-General has had a most difficult duty to discharge, and he has succeeded admirably in opening up the whole subject on such broad lines as to test the practical value of the act. The circular may be regarded as tentative in its effects. It is designed to call in proposals for a fast ocean mail service in American bottoms from six Atlantic, four Gulf and three Pacific ports. and to improve postal communications with Europe, South America, the West Indies. Central America, Australia, China and Japan. The Postmaster-General has acted upon the principle that the first work to be accomplished is to ascertain practically what can be done under the provisions of the act. By inviting proposals for mail service in the broadest possible way he appeals strongly to American enterprise and capital to take advantage of the new law and to supply the Nation with an improved and largely developed commercial marine on the high seas.

We have described this circular as the beginning of a new policy. It would have been more accurate to term it a reversion to the enlightened Democratic policy which prevailed before the Civil War—that of making the mail service a medium for the development of shipping interests. In 1855 under a Democratic Administration the amount paid for mail service to vessels sailing under the American flag was $1,936,715, and there was not a year of that decade of Democratic Congresses when considerably more than $1,000,000 was not expended for that purpose—often nearer $2,000,-000 than $1,000,000. When Mr. Vilas took it upon himself to veto an act of Congress passed for the relief of shipping interests, and to cut down the amount paid to American vessels for mail service to the beggarly sum of $43,319, he was not acting as an old-time Democrat. The Republican policy of converting the postal service into an active agency for promoting the development of the American carrying trade is one which has been repeatedly sanctioned in the past by Democratic Congresses. It is one that can heartily be supported by all Americans on broad, patriotic grounds.

The United States during the last two years has been asserting its dignity as a continental and maritime Power. An international conference has been held at Washington in order to facilitate continental exchanges of produce and manufactures. A second conference attended by representatives of the maritime Powers has effected in the same capital a revision of the rules of the sea. The Government is now offering in the Reciprocity policy a large measure of unrestricted trade to the Southern republics on the basis of equitable exchange. Another year will witness the dedication of the World's Fair held in commemoration of the greatest maritime exploit in history and the largest exhibit of the industries and products of the American Continent that has ever been collected. All these great transactions have required an immediate and radical change of policy respecting the commercial marine. That must first be restored, and then the promise of two brilliant years of American diplomacy and of the development of the export trade as the result of Reciprocity conventions, the World's Fair, and of a vast increase of National prestige, will be fulfilled. President Harrison and the Postmaster-General are in hearty sympathy with the shipping legislation of the last Con-

gress, and are making an earnest and broadminded effort to carry out an enlightened policy. The appeal made to old-time mercantile energy and maritime pride ought not to be neglected.

GOVERNOR CAMPBELL'S ERROR.

The speech of Governor Campbell, of Ohio, upon his renomination was intended to make the tariff the leading question of the campaign. State issues he was willing to consider subordinate and comparatively unimportant, as he well might. The silver question he was willing to ignore, his followers being almost equally divided thereon. But he imagined that the tariff question was one on which his supporters would be united and zealous.

It is a pity that Governor Campbell did not inform himself as to the facts before he ventured into speech. If he had done so, he would not have been so ready to charge that the tariff had burdened and plundered the people. It ought to have occurred to him that, if he had any excuse for saying that wool had been cheaper since the new tariff was enacted than before, there had been no additional burden imposed by that duty, and the circumstances as to other products might have been substantially the same. But it pleases some men to speak first and look into facts afterward. In that way, no doubt, he came to make some assertions about the tariff which have no sort of relation to the facts. It is not true that imported products generally have been rendered more costly by the new duties. On the contrary, though most articles have not been changed in price at all, it will probably astonish the Governor to find that nine-tenths of those which have in any way altered in price have declined. He will search a long while, and probably without success even then, if he tries to discover any class of articles which command a higher price than a year ago. Some of the reasons he may not be able to comprehend, and others he will obstinately refuse to admit, but it may be profitable to mention a few of them, nevertheless.

This country has been the most important and profitable customer of foreign producers in many branches of industry. When it was proposed by means of higher duties to stop undue dependence upon foreign production, the manufacturers abroad saw that they were obliged to give up the American market, or to sacrifice the whole or a part of their profits. In scores of cases already known they have reduced their selling price fully as much as the addition to the duties, and are now delivering goods at exactly the same prices duty paid that they charged before the new tariff went into effect. This is the explanation of increased or unchanged imports of important classes of goods in spite of the higher duties now imposed. In some products the foreign manufacturers have been helped by a remarkable decline in cost of raw materials. But this decline has not been accidental. A material part of the whole world's supply had been taken for many years to meet the American demand. The new duties threatened to cut off that demand. The foreign manufacturers thereupon named the figures which they could afford to pay for the materials, in view of the new duties, and producers found themselves forced to take those prices or to lose a great part of their market. It is a literal fact that the threatened withdrawal of American custom has put down prices of some important products all over the Western World.

Governor Campbell had better look into these things before he talks again. He will find that in a really astonishing number of cases foreigners have been obliged to pay the whole of the new duties imposed by the McKinley Tariff bill for the privilege of selling at all in the American market. It will puzzle him to show that these duties have in any way or to any extent proved a burden to American consumers.

THE LEAGUE AT WORK.

With Mr. Clarkson's return the active campaign of the National League will begin. Its opportunities are great and manifest. The important campaigns this fall happen to be in those States where the League is strong already, and where it has given proof of its utility in awakening public interest and in organizing its members for hard work. In New-York, Ohio and Iowa especially, where the results of the elections will be highly significant, it possesses a great army of energetic workers who only need to be infused with the zeal which distinguishes its president. Mr. Clarkson succeeds in nothing more quickly and certainly than in inspiring others with his own courage and force. His knowledge of the situation in the West will enable him to render the League with its peculiar methods of work highly effectual in counteracting the influence of the Farmers' Alliance. Nothing in the history of the development of that organization offers proof that its strength is drawn from the impossible plans which ambitious politicians have persuaded it to assume. Primarily it is the result of the social instinct. Undoubtedly, the farmers generally have felt that their profits were lower than they ought to be, and have been disposed to listen with an inclining ear to any scheme that promised higher values and freer money. But unlimited coinage and the Sub-Treasury scheme are not the cause of their present association. They are rather a result of it. The farmers organized largely from class sympathy and under a social compact for self-defence against combinations intended to advance the prices of machinery, freights and other necessities, and to depress the price of

fruits and grain. Their political movement was a later undertaking into which they were borne and driven by demagogues.

Although the last elections were far from showing that the average farmer has identified himself with any of the wild schemes officially advocated by the Alliance, they did show that the organization was dangerously strong in half a dozen States whose continued fidelity to Republican policies is most important. The Republican League better than any available influence is competent to draw the farmers of Iowa, Minnesota, Kansas and Ohio back into their relations with the Republican party. By close and complete organization, which shall include every citizen whose inclinations are toward Republican principles, by the maintenance of club-rooms constantly open for discussion and friendly intercourse, by frank debate in open meetings where the interchange of views shall be invited freely, and by such a thorough distribution of Republican newspapers as will insure to every voter the opportunity of understanding the aims of the party and the results of its administration and legislation, a force can be exerted upon public opinion which will inevitably bring out many thousands of Republican ballots that might otherwise be lost. The League movement promises great advantages and deserves the hearty support of all who wish Republican policies sustained.

MORE TRADE AND LESS TAXES.

According to Senator Carlisle, whatever the McKinley bill did or did not, it was sure to cause an increase of taxation and a decrease of importation. The Senator obtained this result by arguing that the duties being generally increased, importation naturally would fall off, but not so much as to prevent the heavier rates of duty from drawing a larger revenue than ever from the people's pockets. There are several points in which the Senator's statement was weak, but the chief was in its blind disregard of the free-list. Like his fellow Free Traders, he never thinks of the free list. His speeches had no room for the fact that it provided a free importation 10 per cent greater than that of the Mills bill, including goods imported in 1889 to the value of $365,406,000, on which the people had paid taxes of more than $65,000,000.

It is possible to obtain now a fairly good idea of the influence which the new tariff is exerting on revenues and importations. The McKinley bill went into effect on October 6, 1890. Taking the seven months beginning with the following December and ending with last June, it is seen that the total importation of merchandise amounted to $493,437,678, as against $471,025,966 in the same months of the year preceding, and the revenues from those imports in the period embraced in 1890-'91 amounted to $113,126,076 14, as against $136,033,381 69 in the period of 1889-'90. At the same time our exports of domestic produce have greatly increased, amounting to $510,021,807 during the seven months specified in 1890-'91, as against $482,155,402 during the same months of the year before. These are facts—hard, unyielding facts—and they send Mr. Carlisle's speculations to the ground. The precise figures of revenue and importation during each of the months mentioned are shown in the following table. The figures are official:

Months.	Imports of Mdse. 1889-'90.	Imports of Mdse. 1890-'91.	Customs Revenue. 1889-'90.	Customs Revenue. 1890-'91.
December	$50,896,414	$60,402,331	$15,825,107 32	$16,104,553 09
January	63,225,032	62,300,683	21,743,305 83	23,807,053 06
February	58,253,001	65,970,569	18,966,305 50	14,564,140 72
March	67,170,507	77,634,836	20,004,765 82	15,373,522 85
April	71,002,140	81,275,106	19,807,406 60	12,591,090 18
May	70,138,040	71,093,623	17,618,409 08	11,995,141 77
June	75,434,042	73,451,529	21,641,827 53	14,166,745 47
Totals	$471,025,956	$495,437,648	$136,033,381 60	$113,126,076 14

The effect of this table is crushing upon the Free Traders. It shows how accurate and faithful were the representations made by the authors of the McKinley bill as to its effects, and how utterly mistaken were those offered by its opponents. Trade is freer than ever. Revenues are smaller. We do more business and we pay less taxes. The free importation of 1889-'90 in the total indicated above was $161,589,912. That of 1890-'91 was $241,130,314. In other words, access to such needed foreign goods as they do not or cannot themselves produce is less hindered to the people than ever before, while foreign goods competing with their own are held back that theirs may have the first chance in their markets. So long as racial lines, political divisions and industrial inequalities remain to mark off one

nation from another this must be the policy of a well-ordered community.

BUILD UP THE LEAGUE.

From every point of view it is important to the success of the Republican campaign in New-York this fall that the Convention of League Clubs which is to be held at Syracuse on August 5 should be largely attended. In Ohio the League, working in perfect harmony with the regular organization, as everywhere it should and must work, is giving a remarkable impetus to the Republican campaign. The League movement has never extended so far in New-York as in some of the other large States, but it is powerful and can readily be made much more so. The work done by President McAlpin and his associates in the Executive Committee of the State League has insured a large and enthusiastic convention. By so much as its size is increased, its efficiency in promoting party interests will increase too. It ought to draw together 2,000 delegates. Between now and August 5 many clubs may be formed if our friends in the country districts will act upon the suggestions contained in the letters that have been so extensively addressed to them by Colonel McAlpin. It is a common American experience that volunteers make the best soldiers. That is one of the theories of free government. It should operate to render the League sufficiently strong and well organized to carry every election precinct where a fair fighting chance can be found.

It is gratifying to know that the regular party organization has encouraged and assisted Colonel McAlpin's work. The party leaders in almost every county are active in promoting the formation of clubs, and are lending the benefits of their experience toward solving the difficulties which in country districts especially stand in the way of political association. There is no length to which they should not go in a work so promising. They should let it be distinctly known that they look with interest and satisfaction at every movement which gives strength to Republican prospects. Practically, the only difficulty encountered anywhere in this State or in others to embarrass the progress of the League is the fear on the part of conservative politicians that it may in some way bring about a division of forces, a clash of party interests and internal friction. The danger of this has nowhere been realized, and the idea is one that should be constantly guarded against.

Republicans should remember that the political scales in this State hang very evenly. A slight influence one way or the other means success or disaster. The extension of these League Clubs is not a slight influence but a great one, far more than enough if it be wisely directed to insure the recovery of every branch of the State government.

A PRACTICAL TEST FOR VOTERS.

DEMOCRATIC LIES OF THE LAST CANVASS EXPOSED.

PRICES IN 1890.

EFFECTS OF THE TARIFF TESTED—RETAIL PRICES LAST SEPTEMBER AND IN 1891.

From The New-York Tribune, February 2, 1891.

The course of prices in 1890 was strongly influenced by two distinct causes, the effects of which it is not easy to distinguish. Expectation of silver coinage caused a rise early in the year, but that advance was aided to some extent by news that much winter wheat had been killed. Again, in August, a marked advance accompanied the purchases of silver and the rise in its price, but at that time also the certainty of a great loss of corn, oats and wheat had a powerful influence. These were the forces which substantially controlled the movements of the year. The new Tariff bill, about the influence of which there was so much talk, had no appreciable influence whatever, as will presently appear.

The same quantities, proportioned to their actual consumption in this country, of several hundred articles, including those which represent more than nine-tenths of the entire cost of living, which cost at wholesale prices in New-York $100 05 at the end of 1887, and declined to $94 38 at the end of 1888, and further declined to $90 29 at the end of 1889, continued to fall until February 26, 1890, when the cost of the same articles and quantities was only $87 64. Then began the first rise prompted by expectation of silver coinage and speculation in breadstuffs. But the movement in wheat, corn and oats, and the actual scarcity of potatoes incident to the season, caused more than three-quarters of the entire advance. The highest point reached in the spring was $91 64 1-2, on April 22, and the advance from February 26 was $4, while the difference in cost of the above named articles alone accounted for $3 06 of that advance. The changes in other prices were therefore comparatively unimportant. But for the stimulus given to speculation in breadstuffs by prospects of monetary expansion, the rise in that class of articles would probably not have been so great.

A decline then followed to the lowest point for the year, May 27, which was but $87 34. Up to this time the naturally prevailing tendency was that which had ruled ever since the beginning of 1888, and it was helped at that season by prospects of remarkably abundant crops, except

for wheat and some kinds of fruit which it was known the previous winter and spring had cut off. Moreover, after May 27 the upward movement was so gradual that as late as June 30 the aggregate cost of the same articles and quantities was only $89 14 1-2, so that during the first half of the year, excepting the temporary effects of silver agitation and the influence of a short wheat crop, unusually low prices prevailed.

Then came the rapid rise in July and August, when it was expected that the Silver bill, which was to go into full effect on August 13, would swiftly and greatly expand the currency. At the same time, the extent of injury to corn and oats and to spring wheat became known. The advance in cost was over $2 50 in July, and from August 6 to August 27 it was $3 11, so that the aggregate cost of the same articles and quantities on the latter date was $94 89 1-2. In three months prices had mounted almost 9 per cent. Some reaction naturally followed when it was seen that the Silver bill did not have the expected effect, and by September 3, in only one week, the aggregate of prices had dropped 1 1-2 per cent, but the later advance then began, which continued until near the close of the year. The highest prices for all commodities were made on December 5, when the aggregate was $98 45, but the subsequent reaction was not great, and the year closed with a renewed upward tendency, the same articles and quantities costing on December 31 $98 36 1-2.

These figures relate to wholesale prices only, and the rapid advance during the last quarter was not due to the tariff, but directly to failure of crops and speculation in the products of which the supply was short. Included in the aggregate for September 3 are quantities of wheat, corn, oats, potatoes, butter, eggs and apples which cost just $5 04 1-2 more on December 5 than on September 3, while the rise in the aggregate of all commodities as above stated was but $5 10. Unless it be maintained that wholesale prices of these commodities were lifted by new duties, the influence of those duties upon wholesale prices generally must be pronounced practically nil. There were other and sufficient reasons for these advances. Butter and eggs always rise as the winter comes on. Apples and potatoes were extraordinarily scarce. The loss of 600,000,000 bushels of corn, of 200,000,000 bushels of oats, and 100,000,000 bushels of wheat, was assuredly enough, with the active speculation thereby excited, to account for their advance. The following table shows the aggregate cost of all commodities included, but arranged in classes, "other food" embracing sugar, molasses, liquors, coffee, tea, rice, fish, salt and spices; the "metal products" embracing coal and petroleum; and the miscellaneous articles including lumber, brick and all building materials, turpentine, linseed-oil, hemp, paper, glass, soap, many varieties of paints, fertilizers, and about sixty kinds of chemicals and drugs. The cost of the same articles and quantities in each class at the beginning of each year since 1879 is shown in comparison as follows:

	Breadstuffs.	Meats.	Dairy and Garden.	Other Food.
1879............	$10 41½	$7 50½	$13 61½	$11 36½
1880............	22 06	9 20½	14 01½	11 37½
1881............	19 74	9 75	17 31½	11 66½
1882............	23 40	10 63	17 85	11 00
1883............	20 81	10 80½	17 00	11 75
1884............	10 89½	10 52	13 88½	10 41
1885............	10 34½	9 43	14 20½	8 95
1886............	16 11½	8 84½	14 80	9 09½
1887............	15 32½	8 53½	14 55½	9 15
1888............	18 56½	8 92	14 48	10 34
1889............	16 10½	8 51	13 72½	10 35
1890............	13 75	7 62	12 96	9 93½
1891............	19 72½	7 62½	16 31½	10 22

	Clothing.	Metal Products.	Miscellaneous commodities.	Total.
1879............	$16 91	$14 06½	$13 05	$92 65½
1880............	20 62	24 07	10 91	119 08½
1881............	18 71	19 25½	17 77	113 80½
1882............	18 77½	20 50	16 63½	119 45
1883............	18 08½	18 92	17 25	113 92
1884............	17 08	16 67½	15 12½	103 79½
1885............	16 00	14 97½	14 15½	91 19
1886............	15 42½	14 57½	14 13	92 97½
1887............	15 02	15 88½	15 29½	91 94½
1888............	15 29	17 33	14 58	100 05
1889............	14 71	16 34½	14 57½	94 38
1890............	14 64½	16 21	15 11	90 29
1891............	14 38½	15 87½	14 22	98 90½

Here it appears that in breadstuffs, and in dairy and garden products, occurred more than the entire advance in prices from January 1, 1890, to January 1, 1891, while meats and other food were substantially unchanged, and clothing, metal products, and the miscellaneous articles were, on the whole, lower. As the three latter classes include articles which are chiefly affected by the tariff, the fact that these were lower for each class at the end of 1890 than at the beginning, notwithstanding an important rise in the cost of other products, will appear to fair-minded inquirers entirely conclusive.

But it was not wholesale prices, some will object, that were immediately or especially affected by the tariff. The claim was made during the late political contest that retail dealers had raised prices of "every necessary and comfort of life." The falsehood had its effect, but it is worth while to know that it was a falsehood. The Tribune has caused an investigation to be made of retail prices in the most important branches of trade in this city, the results of which are given in full in the following columns. The tables show actual selling prices on September 1, more than a month before the new tariff went into effect, and when it was very generally believed that the bill would not pass, in comparison with present retail prices, after the new duties have been in force for more than three months. The results may be briefly stated. Out of 951 quotations obtained, only ninety, or less than one in ten, were found to have been changed in any way, upward or downward, since September 1. This fact alone, if there were nothing to add, completely disposes of the falsehood so industriously circulated for political purposes. But again, just half, or forty-

five, of the changes reported, are reductions in price, while of the advances reported in only an equal number of cases by far the larger part are due to causes with which the tariff has nothing to do.

Out of 298 quotations obtained from four of the best known dealers in groceries and canned goods twenty-two show lower prices now than on September 1, namely for sugar, flour, lard, certain fruits and olives; twenty show higher prices, namely, for eggs, imported bacon, and olives, butter, coffee, corn and oatmeal, potatoes and starch; and 256 show no change whatever! In the latter class are all the quotations for canned goods, which, it is said, were enormously advanced to consumers. The rise in eggs and butter is incident to the season, and the advances in corn and oatmeal and potatoes needs nothing but the short crops to explain them, while, if American workmen suffer because they pay more for imported bacon or olives or starch, the fact is not generally known.

The aggregate of all prices quoted was $105 11 in September, and is now $104 35 for the same articles. But a more accurate mode is to reckon 100 cents spent for each article quoted in September, and the corresponding cost of the same quantity in January, and on that basis $298 would buy in September what cost $298 51 in January, the net advance being only a sixth of 1 per cent.

Out of 276 quotations of boots and shoes, from several dealers, only one reports any advance whatever in prices. The others report thirteen changes out of 240 quotations, the changes being all reductions in price. But the one dealer reports sixteen changes out of thirty-six quotations, the changes being all advances. Including all the quotations given the ratio of cost would be such that $276 in September would buy what $277 97 would buy in January. But presumably the buyers who have their eyes open do not search long for the one place where prices have advanced.

Out of 202 quotations of hardware, tools and implements only seven have advanced at all, four of these quotations being for Disston saws, two for imported trowels, and one for boxwood rules. All other quotations are not changed. If American workingmen are supposed to buy as freely of imported trowels as of American, the latter being cheaper, the same articles which would have cost $202 in all kinds of hardware in September would cost in January $202 83, an advance of less than half of one per cent.

In glassware and cutlery only five quotations out of forty-eight show any advance, and those are for articles not of common use, excepting the larger sizes of window glass. The smaller sizes are unchanged, and nearly all table ware and household goods. The combination of American workers and manufacturers to control the price of window glass is the obvious explanation, and the duties have not been so changed as to alter their power in the least. In this class $48 in September would buy as much as $48 65 in January, an advance of 1.5 per cent.

Out of 128 quotations of clothing, underwear,

blankets, cotton goods, table linen and carpets, changes are found in only nineteen, of which there are reductions in seven quotations for clothing, one of blankets and one grade of carpets, nine in all, while there are advances in five quotations for underwear, in three for table linen, one of carpets and one of cotton goods. In all articles quoted of this class, $128 in September would buy only as much as $127 41 would buy now. But this statement is exceedingly incomplete, as perusal of the detailed reports will show, because of a vast number and variety of articles of which no exact quotations are given, though prices are shown to have been much reduced. This is particularly the case with the great variety of "ready-made" clothing, and a large share of the grades of woollen cloth most generally worn.

Confining the statement, however, to those articles only of which definite quotations are given and giving equal importance to the more costly imported goods where those of American make are cheaper, or to the reports of the single dealer who is alone in advancing prices of boots and shoes, the aggregate cost of 951 articles quoted for September would buy the same articles at retail now for $954 37, an advance of only 3-10 of 1 per cent. This is the fact about retail prices, it must be remembered, at a time when there has been an advance of nearly 6 per cent in the wholesale prices of all commodities, though exclusively because of the rise in breadstuffs and in dairy and garden products. If proper addition should be made for the great variety of articles of clothing which are now selling at lower prices than in September, and for other articles of which reports are given but definite quotations are not obtained, there would undoubtedly be found a small decline rather than any advance in the average of retail prices.   W. M. G.

PRICES IN DETAIL.

The following tables and quoted remarks show the prevailing prices of to-day in representative houses, as compared with those of September:

GLASSWARE AND CUTLERY.

E. J. DENNING & CO.

Prices, Sept. 1, 1890.		Prices, Jan. 15, 1891.
35- 75 per doz	....Tumblers....Per doz.,	35- 73
$5 00-12 00 per doz	....Forks......Per doz.,	$5 00-12 00
5 00-12 00 per doz	....Knives ....Per doz.,	5 00-12 00
1 40 per doz	..Cups, Saucers...Per doz.,	85- 1 40
9 25-15 50	....Dinner set (127 pieces)..	9 25-15 50
66- 1 25 per doz	....Goblets......Per doz.,	66- 1 25

O'NEILL'S.

Sept. 1, 1890.		Jan. 15, 1891.
35- 97 per doz	....Tumblers....Per doz.,	35- 97
$4 30- 5 00 per doz	....Forks......Per doz.,	$4 30- 5 00
4 30- 5 00 per doz	......Knives ....Per doz.,	4 30- 5 00
1 30- 4 97 per doz	Cups and Saucers Per doz.,	1 30- 4 97
11 07-38 00	....Dinner set (127 pieces)......	11 07-38 00

OLIVER McGURKIN.

Sept. 1, 1890.		Jan. 15, 1891.
35-$4 00 per doz	....Tumblers ....Per doz.,	35-$4 00
50- 5 00 per doz	....Goblets ....Per doz.,	50- 5 00
60- 4 00 per doz	..Forks, col'd han. Per doz.,	60- 4 00
$1 00- 6 00 per doz	Knives, col'd han. Per doz.,	$1 00- 6 00
1 20- 5 00 per doz	..Cups and saucers..Per doz.,	1 20- 5 00
4 30- 5 00 per doz	....Plates......Per doz.,	60- 4 50
10 00-35 00	..Dinner sets (125 pieces, decorated)...	10 00-35 00

This house says that the McKinley bill has raised the price on American china a little, but the retail price is not changed.

JOHN PARKE.

Sept. 1, 1890.		Jan. 15, 1891.
75-$1 20 per doz	....Tumblers....per dozen,	75-$1 20
$4 50- 5 50 per doz	....Forks......per dozen,	$5 00- 6 00
1 00- 1 50 per doz	....Cups......per dozen,	1 00- 1 50
1 00- 1 50 per doz	....Saucers....per dozen,	1 00- 1 50
8 00-20 00	....Dinner set (125 pieces)....	8 00-20 00
4 50- 5 00 per doz	....Knives.....per doz.,	5 00- 6 00

MENS' UNDERWEAR.

E. J. DENNING.

Sept. 1, 1890.		Jan. 15, 1891.
$ 13-$ 25 each	....Collars, 4-ply....	$ 13-$ 25
25- 40 pair	....Cuffs........	25- 40
75- 1 25	......Shirts.......	75- 1 25
	(Cotton) drawers (all imported).	
2 75- 3 25	........(Woollen) drawers......	2 75- 3 25
25- 1 50	........(Cotton) hosiery......	25- 1 50
35- 1 75	....(Woollen) hosiery (all imported)..	35- 1 75
1 75- 2 95	....(Cotton) undershirts.....	1 75- 2 95
2 75- 3 25	....(Woollen) undershirts....	2 75- 3 25

O'NEILL'S.

Sept. 1, 1890.		Jan. 15, 1891.
$ 20-$ 25 each	....Collars, 4-ply....each	$ 20-$ 25
15- 25 pair	...... Cuffs ....pair	15- 25
75- 1 00	......Shirts	75- 1 00
50- 50	....Drawers (cotton)...	55- 80
85- 2 00	....Drawers (woollen)....	85- 2 00
25- 40	....Hosiery (cotton)....	31- 55
24- 75	....Hosiery (woollen)....	24- 75
	....Undershirts (cotton).....	
38- 75	....Undershirts (woollen)....	38- 75

This firm says that American manufacturers have taken advantage of the Tariff bill and have used it to raise prices but the retailers have not raised prices to the public except in a few cases. Shirt muslin, 5 to 12½ cents a yard, same as before September 1. Sheetings, 15 to 35 cents a yard; mostly the same as before, but a few grades slightly cheaper. Cotton ginghams, lower grades, 3 and 10 cents, the same as formerly; better grades, 18 and 20 cents, an advance of 2½ per cent. Sateens, 10, 12½, 18, 20 cents, same as formerly. Imported goods, about 10 per cent higher than formerly.

BRILL BROTHERS.

Sept. 1, 1890.		Jan. 15, 1891.
10- 20 each	....Collars, 4-ply ....each,	10- 20
11- 25 pair	....Cuffs, 4-ply .....pair,	11- 25
69-$2 50	......Shirts	69-$2 50
15- 50	....Drawers (cotton)....	15- 50
98- 4 50	....Drawers (woollen)....	98- 4 50
15-	....Hosiery (Balbriggan)..	15- 50
10- 1 00	....Hosiery (woollen).....	10- 1 00
48- 1 98	....Undershirts (cotton).....	48- 1 98
98- 4 50	....Undershirts (woollen).....	98- 4 50

COTTON GOODS.

MACY & CO., Isidor Straus—Selling prices of cotton goods have not changed since fall. The reason is we had a stock on hand. New goods cost more, and will have to be sold higher. Advances will be from 5 to 7½ per cent on most domestic cotton goods. We are selling some new goods at same prices as in the fall, but are losing money on them, and it is only a question of time when the rise must come.

WOOLLEN PIECE GOODS.

BROWNING & WARD—Domestic goods have not yet increased in price, owing to the stock for next spring having been bought last summer. For next fall's goods there is a prospective advance of 5 per cent on the better classes and 10 per cent on the cheaper grades.

HENRY HENRICI—Domestic woollens have not changed since September 1, but there is a prospect of about 5 per cent advance for next fall.

TABLE LINEN AND BLANKETS

E. J. DENNING & CO.

Sept. 1, 1890.		Jan. 15, 1891.
40-$2 00 per yard	..Table cloths (imported)...	40-$2 00
$1 00- 6 00 per doz	....Napkins (imported)......	$1 00- 6 00
3 75-12 50	............Blankets............	2 00-12 30

O'NEILL'S.

Sept. 1, 1890.		Jan. 15, 1891.
35-$1 00 per yard	..Table cloths....	35- 69
82½-$1 50-$1 85 per doz	....Napkins...	90- $1 50-$1 85
2 00- 2 50- 3 00	......Blankets $2 00-	1 50- 3 00

CARPETS.

W. & J. SLOANE.

Sept. 1, 1890.		Jan. 15, 1891.
30- 85 per yard	....Ingrains....per yard	50- 85
$1 00-$1 50 per yard	....Brussels....per yard	$1 00-$1 50
1 25- 1 50 per yard	..Moquettes...per yard	1 25- 1 50
1 25- 1 50 per yard	....Velvets....per yard	1 25- 1 50
1 75- 2 75 per yard	....Wiltons....per yard	1 75- 2 75
3 00- 5 00 per yard	..Axminsters....per yard	3 00- 5 00

(W. & J. Sloane furthermore authorized the statement that in the ordinary run of carpets the prices in the coming spring will be substantially the same as they were last spring (1890), the only change being the variations in prices of special patterns and special lines of imported rugs, but their variations in prices will be no greater than they have been every year.)

E. J. DENNING & CO.

Sept. 1, 1890.		Jan. 15, 1891.
75 one price only	Ingrains	one price only 75
$1 25 one price only	Brussels	one price only $1 25
1 50- 1 60	Moquettes	1 50- 1 60
1 25 one price only	Velvets	one price only 1 25
2 25 one price only	Wiltons	one price only 2 25
1 85- 2 00	Axminsters	1 85- 2 00

J. & J. DOBSON.

Sept. 1, 1890.		Jan. 15, 1891.
$ 25-$ 75 per yard	Ingrains	per yard $ 25-$ 75
90- 1 35 per yard	Brussels	per yard 90- 1 35
1 35- 1 00 per yard	Moquettes	per yard 1 35- 1 00
1 00- 1 35 per yard	Velvets	per yard 1 00- 1 35
1 85- 2 25 per yard	Wiltons	per yard 1 85- 2 25
2 50- 4 50 per yard	Axminsters	per yard 2 75- 4 50

SHEPPARD KNAPP & CO.

Sept. 1, 1890.		Jan. 15, 1891.
$ 50-$ 75 per yard	Ingrains	per yard, $ 50-$ 75
90- 1 25 per yard	Brussels	per yard, 90 1 25
1 25- 1 50 per yard	Moquettes	per yard, 1 25- 1 50
1 00- 1 50 per yard	Velvets	per yard, 1 00- 1 50
1 75- 2 00 per yard	Wiltons	per yard, 1 50- 2 00
1 50- 2 00 per yard	Axminsters	per yard, 1 50- 2 00

TOOLS.

PATTERSON BROTHERS.

Sept. 1, 1890.		Jan. 16, 1891.
$ 50-$ 80	Axes	$ 50-$ 80
50- 80	Hatchets	50- 80
50- 80	Trowels	50- 80
1 10- 1 35	Brade's English Bricklayers	1 10- 1 35
45- 75	American Bricklayers	45- 75
90- 1 25	American Plasterers	90- 1 25
20- 40	American Pointing	20- 40
14- 65	Bit Braces	14- 65
5 per lb.	Cut Nails per lb.	5
5- 6 per lb.	Finishing Cut Nails per lb.	5- 6
6 per lb.	Wire Cut Nails per lb.	6
6- 15	Files (three-cornered)	6- 15
10- 50	Rules, Boxwood	10- 50
40	Squares, Iron	40
75- 2 50	Squares, Steel	75- 2 50
90 $1 75	Saws	90-$1 75
$1 25-$2 25	Disston's	$1 25-$2 25
75	Buck Saws	75
5- 50	Tack hammers	5- 50
50- 95	Steel hammers, best	50- 95
16	Masons' hammers, ∂ lb.	10
	Planes.	
90	Wooden jack	90
$2 60	Iron jack	$2 60
75	Wood smoothing	75
$2 10	Iron smoothing	$2 10
5- 15	Gimlets	5- 15
	Screws.	
12	Good ⅝ inch screws ∂ gross	12
28	Good 1¼ inch screws ∂ gross	28

Mr. Patterson said: "The only things in our line affected to any extent by the McKinley bill are cutlery, by which I mean pocket and carving knives, razors and similar things imported from Sheffield, England. The effect of the bill will be to bring American goods of this class forward."

J. H. DRAKE'S SONS.

Sept. 1, 1890.		Jan. 16, 1891.
	Axes	$1 00-$2 00
	Hatchets	20- 1 00
	Adzes	1 00- 2 00
	Trowels:	
$0 90-$1 50	Brades' English Bricklayers'	1 05- 1 70
50- 1 00	American Bricklayers'	50- 1 00
75- 1 25	Plasterers'	75- 1 25
	Pointing	
3- 5	Cut nails, per lb.	3- 5
4- 6	Finishing nails, per lb.	4- 6
10	Wire nails, per lb.	10
50- 100	Augers	50- 1 00
5- 15	Files (3 square)	5- 15
8- 50	Rules	8- 50
25	Squares (iron)	25
50- 2 00	Squares (steel)	50- 2 00
1 00- 2 00	Disston's hand saws	1 10- 1 75
65- 1 50	Buck saws	75- 1 75
25- 75	Chisels	25- 75
5- 30	Tack hammers	5- 30
15- 25	Iron hammers	15- 25
35- 1 00	Steel hammers	35- 1 00
75- 80	Jack planes	75- 80
2 00	Iron planes	2 00
1 50	Iron and wood planes	1 50
00	Iron planes, smoothing	00
1 10	Iron and wood planes, smoothing	1 10
5- 10	Gimlets	5- 10
25 2 00	Braces	25- 2 00
	Screws:	
3- 5	¾ inch to 1¼ inch, per dozen	3- 5
5- 25	1¼ inch to 6 inch, per dozen	5- 25

WHITE, VAN GLAHN & CO.

This firm's prices were identical with those of J. H. Drake's Sons, except in the following items:

6- 10	Wire nails	6- 10
50- 1 00	Buck saws	50- 1 00

HALL, GREPPEN & CO.

Sept. 1, 1890.		Jan. 16, 1891.
50- 1 00	Axes	75- 1 25
50- 1 00	Hatchets	30- 75
1 25	Adzes	1 25
1 00	Bricklayers' trowels (Brades, Eng.)	1 25
1 00	Bricklayers' trowels, American	75- 1 00
1 00	Pointing trowels, American	25- 40
	Nails:	
4	Cut nails, lb.	4
5	Wire nails, lb.	5
1 00- 1 75	Saws	1 00- 1 75
75- 1 00	Buck saws	75- 1 00
11	Chisels, ¼-inch	14
60	Chisels, 2-inch	60
50- 75	Hammers, steel	50- 75
5- 25	Iron hammers, tack	5- 25
25- 50	Iron hammers	25- 50
50- 1 50	Wood planes from sm'th'g to fore	50- 1 50
25- 5 00	Iron planes from sm'th'g to fore	25- 5 00
5	Tacks, per paper	5

KUGLER & WOLLENS.

Sept. 1, 1890.		Jan. 16, 1891.
75-$1 50	Axes	75-$1 50
50- 1 25	Hatchets	50- 1 25
1 25- 1 50	Adzes	125- 1 50
85- 1 10	Trowels, bricklayers' Eng. brades	85- 1 10
75	Trowels, bricklayers', American	75- 1 10
25- 40	Trowels, pointing	25- 40
75- 1 35	Trowels, plastering	75- 1 35
4	Cut nails, lb.	4
5	Finishing nails, lb.	5
5	Wire nails, lb.	5
18	Augers, ½-inch	18
85	Augers, 1½-inch	85
10	Gimlets	10
40- 90	Braces	40- 90
1 60- 1 75- 1 90	Ratchets	1 60- 1 75- 1 90
8	Rules, boxwood	10
60- 85	Squares	60- 85
1 45- 1 50	White beech planes, German	1 45- 1 50
	(Used by German cabinet makers.)	
4 and 5	Jacks	4 and 5
11- 2 50	Screws, per gross, accord'g to size	11- 2 50

WILLIAM H. UNCKRICH.

Sept. 1, 1890.		Jan. 10, 1891.
50-$1 00	Axes	50-$1 00
40- 75	Hatchets	40- 75
$1 50- 3 00	Adzes	1 50- 3 00
75- 1 50	Trowels, bricklayers'	75- 1 50
	(No English used.)	
75- 1 50	Trowels, plasterers'	75- 1 50
15- 35	Trowels, pointing	15- 35
4	Cut nails (average price per lb)	4
5	Finishing nails (average price per lb).	5
6	Wire nails (average price per lb)	6
75	Augurs	75
7- 30	Rules (boxwood)	7- 30
25	Squares, iron	25
65	Squares, steel	65
1 50	Saws (average price)	1 50
25-50- 1 00	Buck saws	25 50- 1 00
18	Chisels, ¼-inch	18
22	Chisels, ½-inch	22
28	Chisels, ¾-inch	28
32	Chisels, 1-inch	32
50	Chisels, 1½-inch	50
70	Chisels, 2-inch	70
50	Hammers, steel	50
5- 25	Tack and iron hammers	5- 25
75	Jack planes	75
1 75	Iron planes	1 75
1 00	White beech jack	1 00
65	White beech smoothing	65
5	Tacks, per paper	5
7	Gimlets	7
50- 1 50	Braces	50- 1 50
3	Screws, ⅜-inch up to 1-inch, per dozen	3
6	Above ⅜, ordinary sizes	6

SHOES.

ALFRED J. CAMMEYER.

Sept. 1, 1890.		Jan. 16, 1891.
$5 00-$7 00	Ladies' Fr. kid Louis XV heels, H.S.	$5 00-$7 00
5 00	Same, P. L. tips	5 00
5 00	Cloth top, P. L., H. S.	5 00
3 50	P. L. foxed, Fr. kid tops	3 50
5 00	P.L. Samp., Kang. tops, P.L. tip, H.S.	5 00
4 00	Straight-goat foxed, kid top, goat tip.	4 00
4 00	Fr. kid Waukenphast, P.L. tip, H.S.	4 00
2 50- 5 00	Kid button, P. L. tips, H. S.	2 50- 5 00
1 50	Gaiters	1 00
1 60- 6 00	Kid shoes, button, common-sense	1 60- 6 00
3 00- 3 50	Kid-foxed Kangaroo, kid top, H. S.	3 00- 3 50
1 90	Kid-foxed Kangaroo, kid top, H. S.	1 90
	Low shoes and slippers:	
3 00- 4 00	P. L. Oxfords	3 00- 4 00
3 00- 3 50	French kid Oxfords	3 00- 3 50
1 50- 3 00	Kid Oxfords	1 50- 3 00
1 25- 3 50	Kid Oxfords, box toe	1 25- 3 50
1 00- 3 50	Opera slippers	1 00- 3 50
	Misses':	
1 50- 3 50	Soolma kid, straight goat, Curacoa kid, button, spring heels	150- 3 50
1 50- 2 50	Kid button, P. L. tips	1 50- 2 50

2 50..Kangaroo top, straight goat foxed,
spring heels 2 50
1 50- 3 50.........Kid common-sense.......... 1 50- 3 50
1 00- 1 50.Child's button. Am. kid, Fr. kid.. 1 00- 1 50
25- 1 00...................Infants'............. 25- 1 00

Men's:
6 00- 7 00...........French calf, H. S...... 5 00- 7 00
2 50- 4 50.........American calf. H. S. welt. 2 50- 4 50
5 00- 7 00...............Cork sole, H. S...... 5 00- 7 00
5 00- 6 00.............P. L. cloth tops, E. S. 5 00- 6 00
6 00- 6 00.French calf, lace, H. S. double sole 5 00- 6 00
4 00 ....American calf, H. S... 4 00
2 50- 7 00 ....Calf Waukenphast, H. S...... 2 50- 7 00
6 00- 8 00.........French calf, H. S. boots.. 6 00- 8 00
5 00- 6 00..American calf. H. S., boots.... 5 00- 6,00

Slippers:
2 00- 2 50.................Real alligator...... 2 00- 2 50
1 00- 2 50..................Goat opera......... 1 00- 2 50
1 00-30 00.............Embroidered opera..... 1 00-30 00
1 50- 2 00...................Pumps, P. L....... 1 50- 2 00

Boys':
4 00 ....Calf, H. S......... 4 00
3 00 ....Calf, H. S......... 3 00
1 75 ....Veal calf........... 1 75
2 00- 3 00..........American calf. welt..... 2 00- 3 00
4 00 ....P. L. (dress)....... 4 00
2 00- 4 50.................Waukenphast......... 2 00- 4 50
1 75- 2 00...............P. L. Oxford......... 1 75- 2 00
1 50 ....P. L. pumps......... 1 50
2 00 ....Slippers, alligator... 2 00
90- 1 50...........Goat slippers (opera)..... 90- 1 30
1 00 ....Arctics............. 1 00
35- 50....................Rubbers............. 35- 50
1 25 ....Men's Arctics........ 1 25
75 ....Men's rubbers........ 75
60 ....Men's sandals........ 60
35- 50.............Men's im. sandals....... 35- 50
25- 75.................Ladies' rubbers...... 25- 75
1 25- 1 75.................Ladies' Arctics.... 1 25- 1 75
30- 75...................Misses' rubbers..... 30- 75
1 25- 1 50................Misses' Arctics..... 1 25- 1 50

"You may say," said Mr. Cammeyer, "that this talk
about the McKinley bill increasing the price of shoes is all
rot. They are going to be lower instead of higher. If
any manufacturer should say to me, 'I am going to raise
prices,' I would say to him, 'Let me have your portrait to
hang in my office. It would be a curiosity.'"

EDWARD DAY.

Sept. 1, 1890.	Women's:	1891 and 1892.
1 50- 2 50	.........Am. kid, button, M. S......	1 50- 2 50
3 50- 5 00	.......Imported French kid, M. S.	3 50- 5 00
3 50- 5 00	.......Imported French kid, H. S.	3 50- 5 00
1 25- 2 50	..........Am. kid. Oxfords......	1 25- 2 50
2 50- 4 00	.......French kid. Oxfords......	2 50- 4 00
25- 50	..................Rubbers..........	25- 50
1 25- 3 50	.......Black kid slippers......	1 25- 3 50

Misses':
1 25- 2 50.........Kid, button and lace...... 1 25- 2 50
20- 35.................Rubbers............. 20- 35

Men's:
1 75- 3 00...........Am. calf, M. S......... 1 75- 3 00
4 00- 5 00...........Am. calf, H. S......... 4 00- 5 00
6 50- 8 00.........French calf, H. S....... 5 50- 8 00
2 50- 4 50...............P. L. shoes........ 2 50- 4 50
60- 80...................Rubbers.......... 50- 75
1 00- 1 50...................Arctics........ 1 00- 1 50

Slippers:
2 50- 4 00..........Gentlemen's alligator,... 2 50- 4 00
1 00- 2 00.............Imitation alligator.. 1 00- 2 00
1 25- 2 50..................Goat, opera..... 1 25- 2 50
75- 2 50...........Embroidered, opera..... 75- 2 50
1 00- 1 50.................Felt slipper.... 1 00- 1 50

Youths':
1 15- 2 00..........Am. calf, M. S......... 1 15- 2 00

Boys':
1 50- 2 50..........Am. calf, M. S......... 1 50- 2 50

(Mr. Day said: "Shoes are not only as cheap as they
were in September, but orders are now being placed for
next winter at lower rates than last year. There is a
tremendous home competition among manufacturers. Retailers are going to get better shoes next year for less
money. I keep a sign up which says, 'On account of the
McKinley bill we can sell 60-cent rubbers for 40 cents.'")

B. NATHAN.

Sept. 1, 1890.	Women's:	Jan. 16, 1891.
$3 50-$8 00	.................French kid...........	$3 50-$8 00
1 90- 5 00	................Dongola kid...........	1 90- 5 00
5 00- 9 00	...............Patent leather.........	5 00- 9 00
27- 85	....................Rubbers...........	27- 85
2 00	..............High button Arctics.......	2 00
2 25- 6 00	..........French calf Oxfords........	2 25- 6 00
2 85- 7 00	........Patent leather Oxfords.......	2 85- 7 00
1 35	.................White kid slippers.......	1 35
3 50	....................Satin slippers.......	2 85
1 25- 3 50	.........Black French kid...........	1 25- 3 50

Misses':
$ 25 ....French kid........... $ 25

---

2 00- 3 00	.................Dongola kid.........	2 00- 3 00
3 50	...............Patent leather shoes......	3 50
27- 45	.................Rubbers............	27- 45
2 00	....................Arctics	2 00

Men's:
2 85- 5 00..........American calf, M. S..... 2 85- 5 00
4 00- 5 00..........American calf, M. S..... 4 00- 5 00
5 00- 8 00............French calf, H. S...... 5 00- 8 00
4 35- 9 00.........Patent leather shoes..... 4 35- 9 00
50- 1 50...................Rubbers.......... 50- 1 50
1 25- 2 00...................Arctics......... 1 25- 2 00

Slippers:
2 50- 3 50.............Genuine alligator..... 2 50- 3 50
1 39 ....Imitation alligator.... 1 39
1 39- 2 00................Goat, opera........ 1 50- 2 00
1 39 ....Embroidered opera...... 89
1 25- 2 00...............Felt slippers...... 1 25- 2 00

Boys':
2 00 ....American calf, M. S.... 2 00
4 00 ....French calf, H. S..... 4 00
5 00 ....Patent leather shoes.... 5 00

L. M. HIRSCH.

Sept. 1, 1890.		Jan. 16, 1891.
$3 75	.......Women's imported French kid....	$3 75
3 50- 4 50	.....Women's imported French kid....	3 50- 4 50
1 50- 3 00	.............Women's Dongola	1 50- 3 00
2 65- 3 98	..Women's 1st qual. kid, P. L. tips...	2 65- 3 98
2 65	.........Women's French kid, P. L. tips..	2 00
2 89	................Women's P. L. Oxfords.....	2 50
2 35	.........Women's French kid Oxfords.....	1 89
1 75	..............Women's P. L. slippers.....	1 25- 1 35
1 75	........Women's white kid slippers.....	1 75
1 75	.......Misses' French kid, 1st quality...	1 35- 1 50
1 00	................Misses' pebble goat.......	1 00
2 35	.................Misses' P. L. vamp.......	2 35
1 75	....Misses' straight goat, spring heel...	1 50

Boys' shoes:
1 25 ....Veal calf, M. S...... 1 25
1 50 ....American calf, M. S...... 1 50
2 00 ....French calf, M. S...... 2 00

Youths' shoes:
1 00 ....Veal calf, M. S....... 1 00
90 ....Split calf, M. S...... 90
1 50 ....French calf, M. S...... 1 00
1 75- 2 00...........French calf, hand sewed... 1 75- 2 00
1 50- 1 75.........American calf, hand sewed... 1 50- 1 75

Men's shoes:
1 00- 2 00.........American calf, M. S...... 1 00- 2 00
2 50- 3 50............French calf, M. S...... 2 50- 3 50
2 50- 3 75...........American calf, M. S..... 2 50- 3 75
3 50- 4 50............French calf, H. S...... 3 50- 4 60

Men's slippers:
59- 80.................Imitation alligator... 59- 89
1 50- 2 50..............Genuine alligator..... 1 05- 2 50
75- 1 25..................Goat opera......... 75- 1 25
39- 1 50...............Embroidered opera..... 39- 1 50
25- 50...................Felt slippers...... 25- 60
18- 35.................Women's rubbers...... 18- 35
50- 75.................Women's arctics...... 50- 75
20 ....Children's rubbers..... 20
25 ....Misses' rubbers....... 25
50- 75...................Misses' arctics...... 50- 75
35- 50..................Men's rubbers........ 35- 50
75- 1 00.................Men's arctics........ 75- 1 00

(Mr. Hirsch's superintendent said: "We are reducing
prices on all lines of shoes, and shall continue to do so
until our spring trade sets in. Mr. Hirsch laughs at any
one who tries to scare him about the McKinley bill.")

S. COHN & BROTHER.

Sept. 1, 1890.		Jan. 16, 1891.
$3 50	................Women's French kid.......	$4 00
2 00	...............Women's Dongola kid.......	2 25
2 50	..............Women's Dongola kid.......	2 75
2 50	............Women's Dongola P. L. tip....	2 75
5 00	..............Women's kid, first quality...	6 80
4 00- 4 50	.........Women's French kid, P. L. tip...	6 00- 5 50
4 00	..........Women's French kid, plain toe...	4 00
2 75	..............Women's bright Dongola.....	3 00
3 25	..............Women's bright Dongola.....	3 25
3 50	..............Women's P. L. Oxford ties...	3 00
3 50	................Women's French kid........	3 00
1 75	................Women's P. L. slippers.....	1 00
1 25	.................Women's white kid........	1 35
2 75	................Misses' French kid........	3 00
2 00	...............Misses' Dongola kid........	2 25
2 00	...............Misses' straight goat......	2 25
2 00	.............Misses' P. L. vamp..........	2 00
1 50	(Dongola) Misses P. L. tip spring heel...	2 50
1 75	................Misses' plain Dongola......	2 00
2 00	.................Misses' plain Dongola.....	2 00
2 00	................Misses' straight goat......	2 00
2 50	...............Misses' straight goat......	2 50

Boys' shoes:
1 50 ....Veal calf, machine sewed... 1 50
2 00 ....American calf, machine sewed... 2 00
2 50 ....American calf, hand sewed... 2 50
3 50 ....French calf, hand sewed... 3 50

Men's shoes:
2 00 ....American calf, machine sewed... 2 00
3 00 ....American calf, hand sewed... 3 00
4 50 ....French calf, machine sewed... 5 50
6 00 ....French calf, hand sewed... 6 00

Men's slippers.

2 00	....Imitation alligator............	1 00
1 00- 2 50	............Goat opera............	1 00- 2 50
2 25- 3 50	............Genuine alligator.......	2 25- 3 50
1 00- 3 00	....Embroidered opera............	1 00- 3 00
1 00- 1 50	....Felt slippers............	1 00- 1 50

(Mr. Cohn said that he had increased the price of women's and misses' shoes, owing to the fact that leather was higher. He was found to be the only dealer who had marked his shoes higher than they were on September 1.)

GROCERIES.

PARK & TILFORD.

Sept. 1, 1890.		Jan. 10, 1891.
	Canned Goods:	
25	....Salmon, 1 lb case............	20
25	....Lobster, 1 lb case............	25
28	....Shrimps, 1 lb case............	28
22	....Corned beef, 2 lb case.......	22
40	....Corned beef, 4 lb case.......	40
	Sardines:	
38	....Boneless, ½ lb tins...........	38
28	....Boneless, ¼ lb tins...........	28
30	....Boneless, ½ lb tins...........	30
25	....Bones, ½ lb tins............	25
18	....Bones, ¼ lb tins............	18
17	....Ferris's hams............	15
80	....Smoked beef tongues, each....	75
	Bacon:	
35	....Irish bacon, per lb...........	38
38	....English Wiltshire, per lb.....	40
	Cheese:	
15	....American mild cream, per lb....	15
25	....American dairy, per lb........	25
1 00	....Edam, each............	1 00
	Lard:	
33	....3 lb pails............	35
55	....5 lb pails............	50
1 10	....10 lb pails............	1 00
	Butter:	
Jan., 1890.		**Jan. 10, '91.**
30	....Creamery, per lb............	35
50	....Fancy Phila., ½ lb prints, per lb	55
80	Fancy Darlington, ½ lb prints, per lb	60
	Coffees:	
34	....Roasted Java............	30
30	....Roasted Mocha............	30
30	....Roasted Maracaibo............	30
30	....Roasted Rio............	30
Firm handles no unroasted.		
	Sugar:	
55	....Cut loaf, pkg. 7 lb............	52
55	....Crushed, pkg. 7 lb............	52
53	....Powdered, pkg. 7 lb............	52
50	....Granulated, pkg. 7 lb.........	50
48	....White A, pkg. 7 lb............	47
46	....Extra C, pkg. 7 lb............	45
	Flour:	
7 25	....Pillsbury, per bbl............	6 50
4 00	....Pillsbury, per half bbl.......	3 50
90	....Pillsbury, bag, one-eighth bbl..	85
7 00	....Pianta, per bbl............	6 50
7 25	....Washburn's gold medal, per bbl..	6 50
	Meal:	
20	....Yellow and white, 7 lb........	20
28	....Graham flour, 7 lb............	28
25	....Rye, 7 lb............	25
6	....Oatmeal (Akron), per lb......	5
7 00	....Oatmeal (Akron), per bbl......	8 00
1 35	....Irish oatmeal, 14-lb tins.....	1 35
10	....Scotch oatmeal, 1-lb paper....	10
90	....Buckwheat flour, per bag of 25 lb.	90
30	....Buckwheat flour, per 7-lb bag....	30
	Potatoes:	
3 50	....Potatoes, per bbl..............	4 50
1 30	....Potatoes, per basket............	1 65
45	....Potatoes, per peck............	60
28	....Eggs, per dozen............	35
	Teas:	
30, 40, 60, 80	....Oolong, per lb............	30, 40, 60, 80
75	....Oolong (Formosa), per lb......	75
30, 40, 50, 75, 90.	English breakfast, per lb.	30, 40, 50, 75, 90
1 00	....Hyson, per lb............	1 00
50, 75, 81	....Young Hyson, per lb........	50, 75, 81
1 00	....Gunpowder, per lb............	1 00
50, 75, 81	....Japan, per lb............	50, 75, 81
1 00	....Orange Pekoe, per lb........	1 00
1 25	....Flowery Pekoe, per lb........	1 25
	Canned vegetables:	
35	..Asparagus, Oyster Bay, No. 3 tins..	35
15	..Lima beans, No. 2 tins........	15
10	..String beans, No. 2 tins........	10
25	..Stringless beans, No. 2 tins....	25
18- 25	..Corn, No. 2 tins........	12, 13 & 15
12, 13 & 15		
15, 25 & 28	..Peas, No. 2 tins........	15, 25 & 28
25-	..Peas, French............	25- 30
30		
10	..Pumpkin, No. 2 tins............	10
15	..Succotash, No. 2 tins............	15
12	..Tomatoes, No. 3 tins............	12

	Starch:	
55	..Kingsford's silver gloss, 6-lb box..	55
90	..Kingsford's silver gloss, 12-lb box..	56
7	..Kingsford's silver gloss, 12-lb box, lb	7½
9	..Kingsford's cornstarch, per lb....	9
	From California:	
35	..Apricots, No. 3 tins.........	35
35	..White cherries, No. 3 tins....	33
35	..Black cherries, No. 3 tins....	35
35	..Egg plums............	35
35	..Green gages............	35
35	..Nectarines............	35
35	..Peaches............	35- 40
37	..Bartlett pears............	35
45	..Apples, gallon cans...........	45
15	..Blackberries, No. 2 tins......	15
18	..Blueberries, No. 2 tins......	13
20	..Damson plums, No. 2 tins....	20
30	..Pineapples, No. 2 tins........	30
40	..Pineapples, No. 3 cans........	40
32	..Quinces, No. 3 cans........	32
30	..Raspberries, No. 2 cans......	30
30	..Strawberries, No. 2 cans......	30
	Olives.	
25	..De Lucques (bottles)...........	25
25	..Marinees (bottles)...........	25
	Gordon & Dilworth's ½-gal. jars.	
1 25	..Queen olives............	1 25
55	..Queen olives, 27 oz. bottles....	55
44	..Queen olives, pt. bottles........	40
	Crackers:	
20	..Bents, per lb............	20
12	..Butter, per lb............	12
10	..Soda, per lb............	10
35	..Soda wafers, 2 lb can........	35
35	..Milk wafers, 2 lb can........	35
25	..Bottles Shrewsbury's catsup....	25

(Joseph Park said: "It is hard to base any calculations this year on certain things in our line, such as apples, butter, potatoes and eggs. Eggs are, of course, higher and scarcer than last year at this time, owing to the cold weather. They were naturally cheaper in September than now. The apple crop was almost a failure last year. So were potatoes. I think that much good potato land in Northern New-York, which has not been cultivated for years, will be tilled this spring. Butter is of course higher than it was in September, but is no higher than it was last January. We have to rely on California for most of our canned fruit.")

ACKER, MERRALL & CONDIT—Prices like Park & Tilford's. A member of the firm said: "The McKinley bill has made no perceptible change in our retail prices for groceries, canned goods and flour. Wines, cigars and liquors—the imported brands—have been raised by the bill. Starch, which is on the free list, is higher now than in September. We are Free Traders here. By an arrangement, our prices are the same as those of Messrs. Park & Tilford."

A. T. ALBRO.

Sept. 1, 1890.		Jan. 16, 1891.
18- 25-	....Salmon, No. 1 tins........	18- 25
18-	....Lobster, No. 1 tins........	18-
30-	....Shrimp, No. 1 tins........	30-
25-	....Corned beef, No. 2 tins......	25-
	Sardines.	
35-	....Boneless, ½-lb can........	35-
18-	....Boneless, ¼-lb can........	18-
	Hams.	
15-	....Niagara and Baltimore, lb....	15-
10-	..Bacon, Niagara and Baltimore, lb.	10-
90-	..Smoked beef tongues, each....	80-
14-	..American mild cheese, per lb....	14-
25-	....English dairy, per lb........	25-
1 00-	....Edam, each............	1 00-
	Lard.	
35-	....3-lb pails............	35-
55-	....5-lb pails............	55-
1 00-	....10-lb pails............	1 00-
	Butter.	
35-	....Creamery, per lb............	35-
40-	..Darlington, ½-lb prints, per lb....	40-
	Coffee.	
35-	....Roast Java............	35-
36-	....Roast Mocha............	36-
32-	....Roast Maracaibo............	32-
27-	..Unroasted Maracaibo........	27-
30-	..Unroasted Java........	30-
31-	..Unroasted Mocha........	31-
	Sugar.	
56-	....Cut loaf, 7 lb............	52-
56-	....Crushed, 7 lb............	52-
54-	....Powdered, 7 lb............	50-
50-	....Granulated, 7 lb............	46-
48-	....White A, 7 lb............	44-

Flour.

44-	Extra C, 7 ℔	42-
7 00-	Pillsbury, bbl	6 50-
3 65-	Pillsbury, ½ bbl	3 50-
90-	Pillsbury, ⅛ bbl	85-
16-	Yellow and white meal, 7 ℔	10-

Graham Flour.

7 00-	Extra quality, bbl	7 00-
85-	Extra quality, ⅛ bbl	85-
28-	Extra quality, 7 ℔	28-
6 00-	Rye flour, bbl	6 00-
75-	Rye flour, ⅛ bbl	75-
25-	Rye flour, 7 ℔	25-
5-	Oatmeal, Akron, ℔	5-
8-	Oatmeal, Akron, 200-℔ bbl	8-
1 35-	Oatmeal, Irish, 14-℔ cans	1 35-
10-	Oatmeal, Scotch, ℔ papers	10-
75-	Flour, buckwheat, 25-℔ bags	75-
27- 28	Eggs	34-

Teas.

30, 40, 50, 60, 80	Oolong	30, 40, 50, 60, 80
50, 75, 1 00	Oolong, Formosa	50, 75, 1 00
30- 90	English breakfast	30- 90
30, 50, 60, 80, 1 00	Young Hyson	30, 50, 60, 80, 1 00
80- 1 00	Gunpowder	80- 1 00
40, 60, 80	Japan	40, 60, 80
35	Oyster Bay asparagus, No. 3 tins	35
18	Lima beans, No. 2 tins	18
25	Stringless beans, No. 2 tins	25
15	Corn, No. 2 tins	15
18	Peas (domestic), No. 2 tins	18
30	Peas (French), No. 2 tins	30
18	Pumpkin, No. 3 tins	18
18	Succotash, No. 2 tins	18
12	Tomatoes, No. 3 tins	12

Catsup, Shrewsbury.

45	Quart bottles	45
25	Pint bottles	25
18	½ pint bottles	18

Fruits.

30	Apricots, No. 3 tins	30
38	White cherries, No. 3 tins	38
38	Black cherries, No. 3 tins	23
23	Egg plums, No. 2 tins	23
23	Green gages, No. 2 tins	23
25- 38	Peaches, No. 3 tins	25- 38
35	Pears, Bartlett, No. 3 tins	35
30	Apples, 4-quart cans	30
23	Damson plums, No. 2 cans	23
28	Pineapples, No. 2 cans	28
30	Quinces, No. 3 cans	30
28	Raspberries, No. 2 cans	28
30	Strawberries, No. 2 cans	30

Olives.

25	Crescent, small bottles	25

Gordon & Dilworth's.

$1 10	Queen, 2-quart jars	$1 20
50	Queen, 1½-pint jars	55

Crackers.

20	Bent's water, ℔	20
12	Butter, ℔	12
10	Soda, ℔	10
35	Soda wafers, 2-℔ cans	35
35	Milk crackers, 2-℔ cans	35

JACKSON & CO.

Sept. 1, 1890.		Jan. 15, 1891.
35	Strawberries, No. 2 cans	35
35	Quinces, No. 3 cans	35
35	Damson plums, No. 3 cans	35
35	Pineapples, No. 2 cans	35
40	Imported olives, pints	40
60	Imported olives, quarts	60
35	Apricots, No. 3 cans	35
38	White cherries, No. 3 cans	38
35	Egg plums, No. 3 cans	35
35	Green gages, No. 3 cans	35
40	Peaches, No. 3 cans	40
38	Bartlett pears, No. 3 cans	38
35	Oyster Bay asparagus, No. 3 cans	35
20	Lima Beans, No. 2 cans	20
25	String beans, No. 2 cans	25
15- 18	Corn, No. 2 cans	15- 18
18, 20, 30	Peas, No. 2 cans	18, 20, 30
20, 22, 25, 30	Peas, French, No. 2 cans	20, 22, 25, 30
20	Succotash, No. 2 cans	20
13- 15	Tomatoes, No. 3 cans	13- 15

Teas:

40, 60, 80	Formosa Oolong	40, 60, 80
50, 70, 90	English Breakfast	50, 70, 90
40, 60, 80	Young Hyson	40, 60, 80
80	Gunpowder	80
80	Japan (uncolored)	80

Flour.

6 50	Pillsbury, bbl	6 50
6 75	Jones & Co.'s, bbl	6 75
20	Yellow and white meal, 7 ℔	20
30	Graham flour, 7 ℔	30
30	Rye flour, 7 ℔	30
40	Akron oatmeal	40
60	Irish oatmeal	60
10	Scotch, 1 ℔ paper	10
30	Buckwheat flour, 7 ℔	30
4 50	Potatoes, bbl	4 50
1 35	Potatoes, basket	1 35
60	Potatoes, peck	60
35	Eggs, ordinary, per doz	35
48	Eggs, extra fresh	48
8	Starch, laundry, per ℔	8
10	Starch, corn, per ℔	10
54	Sugar, cut, 7 ℔	55
52	Sugar, crushed, 7 ℔	52
48	Sugar, White A, 7 ℔	48
52	Sugar, powdered, 7 ℔	52
50	Sugar, granulated, 7 ℔	50
40	Sugar, Extra C, 7 ℔	46
36	Coffee, Roast Java	36
36	Coffee, Roast Mocha	36
34	Coffee, green Mocha	34
32	Coffee, Green Java	32
55- 1 00	Lard, 5 and 10 ℔ tins	55- 1 00
35	Creamery butter	35
60	Butter, Philadelphia, 1-℔ prints	60
84	Butter, Darlington, ½-℔ prints	80

Cheese.

18-	American mild cream, ℔	18-
30-	English dairy, ℔	30-
1 10-	Edam, each	1 10-
25-	Salmon, No. 2 tins	25-
25-	Lobster, No. 2 tins	25-
30-	Shrimps, No. 2 tins	30-
25-	Corn beef, No. 2 tins	25-
20-	Boneless sardines, ¼-℔ tins	20-
35-	Boneless sardines, ½-℔ tins	35-
17-	Ferris's hams, ℔	17-
10-	Baltimore bacon, ℔	10-
19-	Smoked beef tongues, ℔	19-

FURNITURE.

B. M. COWPERTHWAIT & CO.

Sept. 1, 1890.		Jan. 15, 1891.
$3 25-	Lounges	$3 50-
8 50-	Couches	9 00-
11 50-	Sofas	12 00-
15 50-	Turkish chairs	16 00-
7 50-	Easy chairs	8 00-
19 00-	Window chairs	20 00-
14 00-	Reclining chairs	15 00-
13 00-	Settees	14 00-
3 75-	Rattan chairs	4 00-
3 75-	Rattan rockers	4 00-
4 50-	Ladies' desks	5 00-
3 00-	Wall cabinets	3 00-
2 80-	Piano stools	3 00-
1 65-	Whatnots	1 75-
9 50-	Mantle mirrors	10 00-
90-	Looking glasses	1 00-
2 80-	Polished top tables	3 00-
2 80-	Marble top tables	3 00-
3 50-	Fancy brass tables	3 75-
1 40-	Clocks in marble, iron, walnut and cherry	1 50-
3 80-	Parlor stoves	4 00-
2 80	Extension tables	3 00
7 50	Sofa tables	8 00
1 65	Leaf tables	1 75
3 50	Side tables	4 00
7 50- $300	Sideboards	8 00- $300
90	Cane dining chairs	1 00
1 80	Leather dining chairs	2 00
4 75	Sofas, couches, lounges, in leather, rep, haircloth and carpet, etc.	5 00
90	Wood top tables	1 00
4 80	Refrigerators	5 00
4 50	Stoves and ranges	5 00
11 00- 300	Chamber suits, marble and wood tops	$12 00- 300
28 00	Armoires	30 00
4 50	Wardrobes	5 00
4 50	Chiffoniers	5 00
1 40	Washstands	1 50
47 00- 250	Cabinet folding beds	50 00- 250
1 90	Bedsteads	2 00
6 00	Dressing bureau	6 50
95	Bedroom tables	1 00
11 00	Painted suits	12 00
3 80	Iron bedsteads	4 00
50	Looking glasses	50
2 80	Bureaus	3 00
9 50	Bed sofas, couches and lounges	10 00
1 40	Upholstered folding cots	1 50
75	Wood and canvas cots	75
9 50	Ladies' work tables	10 00
1 45	Fancy chairs and rockers	1 50
3 80	Rattan chairs and rockers	4 00
75	Cane chairs and rockers	75
90	Spring beds	1 00
9 50	Hair matresses	10 00
7 50	Wool mattresses	8 00
5 50	Cotton mattresses	6 00
5 50	Husk mattresses	6 00
95	Straw mattresses	1 00
1 90	Excelsior mattresses	2 00
2 80	Jute top mattresses	3 00
4 50	Flock top mattresses	5 00
5 50	Fibre hair mattresses	6 00
90	Blankets and comfortables	1 00
1 90	Axminster, Moquette	2 00
90	Body Brussels	1 00
85	3 ply ingrain	90

(These quotations are bottom prices, running up according to grade of goods.)

FLINT & CO—Prices have not changed any, and if

there is any change it will not be felt before next fall.

BAUMANN BROS.—Prices have practically not changed since September 1. Any slight changes there have been were downward.

JOSHUA GREGG—Prices of furniture have not varied at all.

READY-MADE CLOTHES.

HACKETT, CARHART & CO.—Prices are so far reduced from what they were last fall that no proper idea of the market value could be formed. Selling away down on account of the lateness of the season. Indications are that the retail prices next fall will be the same as last fall. Domestic wool cloth has not yet increased in price. Indications are that it will rise a trifle by next fall, but that will not affect the retail price of clothing.

ROGERS, PEET & CO.—Prices have not changed any since September 1. The reason is that material for goods now being sold was bought last spring. Material for next spring's goods was bought last summer, and consequently spring clothing will not be any higher. They are now buying material for next fall and winter, and indications are that they will then have to charge from one to three dollars more for the better class of suits. Cheaper grades of clothing, however, will not change in price. Clothes made from imported cloths will cost from 5 to 7½ per cent more, but the advance will not be felt in the retail trade before next fall.

RAYMOND & CO.—Men's suits that were from $12 to $35 are now from $10 to $30. Boys' suits that were from $5 to $14 are now from $4 to $12. Overcoats:

	Sept. 1.	Jan. 15.
	$25 00	$15 00
	25 00	20 00
	20 00	16 00

Reductions are owing to lateness of season. Some spring goods will be a trifle higher to dealers, but not to consumers. In regard to foreign goods prices are being reduced in Europe, so that goods will be about the same in this country as formerly.

NOW FOR TIN PLATES.

WHY THE NEW DUTIES WERE LEVIED AND WHAT THEY HAVE DONE.

THEY HAVE BEEN ANTICIPATED BY REMARK-ABLE EXHIBITIONS OF AMERICAN ENTER-PRISE WHICH LEAVE NO DOUBT OF THE SUCCESSFUL ESTABLISHMENT OF THE NEW INDUSTRY.

With a singular fatuity the Free-Trade advocates have consolidated their opposition to the new Tariff bill upon its tin-plate provisions. They have, however, this excuse for their policy, that if they are forced to admit that a new industry of immense proportions has been created here by the tariff they are robbed of their only effectual argument against Protection. When the McKinley bill went into effect the American people were consumers of 737,735,029 pounds of tin plates annually, and not a single pound of them was made or tinned in the United States. They had cost the people at the foreign price in 1890 $23,074,214, and during the period of twenty-five years ending with 1889 the tremendous sum of $320,037,362 had gone from America to England for tin plates.

There is nothing essentially difficult in the manufacture of tin plates. As a present mechanical problem it is utterly insignificant. It consists, first, in the manufacture of bar steel. That, of course, is now of no account in the problem, for any plant that is capable of producing steel rails is

capable also of producing steel bars, and the finest steel rails in the world are made here to the annual amount of 2,111,544 net tons in 1890. There are a score of American manufacturers who can produce all the bar steel required to make all the steel plates necessary to supply the entire American demand for tin plates, and at least three such manufacturers, Carnegie, Phipps & Co., of Pittsburg; the Pennsylvania Steel Company, of Harrisburg, and the Welman Iron and Steel Company, of Chester, have given notice that they are now equipped to make steel bars. So far as any inequality that may exist between them and British steel barmakers is concerned, it is obvious that they stand, with regard to the making of steel bars for tin plates, precisely where they stand with regard to the making of other forms of bar steel, so that as they have competed triumphantly with foreign producers in these other forms, they can as easily compete in steel bar making for the tin trade.

There is no difficulty, then, about the first and chief step in the tin-plate industry—the manufacture of the bar steel from which the steel plates, thereafter to be coated with tin, are to be rolled. The second step is the rolling process, and that, too, is already solved. It was a principal argument of those who opposed the new tin-plate duties that there were no black plates made here of the kind used in tin-plate making, and they asked what was to be gained by increasing the duties on the tinned product when its base was wholly wanting. These persons overlooked the fact that fine qualities of sheet iron and sheet steel used in the production of fine kitchen utensils and galvanized iron (which is simply a sheet of soft steel coated with zinc) were already made in this country in enormous quantities, and that the plants capable of making them needed but slight additional equipment to roll the finer qualities of steel sheets used for tin plates. The American product of sheet iron and sheet steel for roofing, galvanizing and domestic purposes, such as the making of stovepipe, coalhods, breadpans, etc., already amounts to quite 200,000 tons, a productive value of not less than $15,000,000. Some slight changes were made by the McKinley Act in the tariff on sheet steel for the especial purpose of rendering our iron and steel workers competent to go ahead with the manufacture of that particular quality of steel sheet used for tinned plates, and as many as four firms—Jennings Brothers & Co., of Pittsburg; the St. Louis Stamping Company; P. H. Laufman & Co., of Apollo, Penn., and the United States Iron and Tin-Plate Co., of Demmler, Penn.—are now producing such plates. There are certainly as many as sixteen or twenty other establishments to which their production is perfectly easy, and which of course will produce as the demand for them increases.

Getting down at last to the real question that confronts those who advocate the policy of making our own tin plates and of saving to our own labor and capital the enormously profitable trade which has hitherto gone unchallenged to England, it is found to consist of nothing whatever beyond the possibility of our being able to coat with tin a home product of steel already provided or safely guaranteed. How much of a question this is any one can judge for himself. It is impossible to imagine a simpler process than the coating of black plates with tin. It is the work of thirty minutes. The plates are washed in sulphuric acid to get out all imperfections, and then in clear water. They are rubbed with sand to render their surfaces smooth, and are dipped in palm-oil, which serves as a flux. Then they are dipped in tin, sometimes in one pot of metal and sometimes in two or three, and then they are allowed to become cold and are rubbed down. That done, the tinned plate is ready to be assorted, packed and sold.

What there is in this process to discourage American ingenuity it is difficult to perceive. What there is in the way it has to be done to discourage American labor is quite another matter. From beginning to end it is a manual process. The plant is simple, and wholly inexpensive. There is a pot of acid, another of water, another of oil and two or three of metal, a box of sand, a box of sawdust and a sheepskin rubber. That is the sum and substance of a tin-plate factory and the product of the factory is great or small in direct proportion to the number of these sets of pots contained within it. Each set, however, must have seven workmen, and they must do all the work by hand. They must soak the plates in the acid by hand. They must wash them in water by hand. They must rub them smooth and dry by hand. They must dip them in oil by hand and in the metals by hand. They must rub them down by hand. The entire process is one of manual labor. There is a machine consisting of a series of rollers, which, after the plates are coated, is used to make their surfaces bright and smooth, but the function of this thing is to scrape off the metal, not to put it on, or, in other words, to economize tin at the expense of the quality of the plate. It is not used at all in the manufacture of the best quality of tin plates either for roofing or domestic purposes. Its one object is to cheapen the manufacture by reducing the thickness of the coating and by so much as it is used the plate is deteriorated. But except for this machine, the process of tin-plate making is a process of human labor. The problem, as it really exists, relates to the rate of wages paid abroad and the rate demanded here.

In Wales all labor is cheap. The best mechanics receive wages that no American employer would think of proposing. Female labor is also extensively used in the tin-plate factories and it is half as cheap again as the cheap male labor. It being perfectly clear that there is no climatic or mechanical difficulty in the way of our providing ourselves with our own tin-plates, that we already produce the bar steel and are equipped to roll this kind of sheet steel as we now roll other kinds, and that the difficulty relates to wages, and to nothing else, here, then, is the question: Is it worth while to be taxing foreign plates heavily to give our manufacturers the chance to take our market?

It is admitted that there would be a fair opportunity for controversy here if we were obtaining as consumers the benefit of the cheap labor of Wales. But that is not the fact. On the contrary, although we take fully three-fourths of the entire output of the Welsh factories, although they exist only for this market, they are selling their product here at a price greatly in excess of its fair value, and the chief argument of those American metal-workers who desired Congress to increase the tin-plate duty so that they could manufacture here was that they would be able, notwithstanding their increased expense in wages, to sell at even lower rates than the foreign product was bringing in the summer of 1889. Their proposition to the American people, reduced to its simplest terms, was this: You are now buying 360,-000 tons of foreign tin-plate annually, on which there is only a revenue duty; in 1889 you paid for this product, including the duties, $28,281,-668; all that went to employ foreign labor and to sustain foreign industry; you paid for the iron and steel imported in those plates much more than you paid our protected steel-workers for the iron and steel used in domestic steel rails and sheet steel; you received, as consumers, no benefits from the cheap labor employed in making these plates and tinning them, but they cost you as much as if they had been made at the American rate of wages; your three-quart coffee-pot that cost you 25 cents cost the British maker less than 11 cents: your pint tin-cups that cost you 5 cents cost him less than 2; your twelve-quart dishpan that cost you 35 cents cost him less than 14; he charged the American workingman 50 cents for a dinner kettle that cost him only 12 cents, and these comparisons fairly illustrate the difference throughout the tin-plate trade between what his goods cost him and what he got for them from the American public. We ask you, then, that a high tariff be levied on his products, and we will make such products here; we will increase the American consumption of American iron-ore by 1,000,000 tons annually, of limestone 300,000 tons, of coal and coke 2,000,000 tons, of pigiron 400,000 tons, of lead 5,500,000 pounds, of tallow and oil 13,000,000 pounds, of sulphuric acid 40,000,000 pounds, and of lumber 12,000,000 feet; we will employ 35,000 American workingmen, and pay them $20,000,000 in wages, and we will sell you tinware cheaper than you get it to-day; we will do this substantially within a period of six years from the date of the new tariff, or, if we fail, you can take the increased duty away; it can do you no great harm meanwhile, for the foreign tin-plate-maker is already charging you prices so much greater than his expenses that he can have no honest pretext for a further increase, and if he makes a further increase it will prove all the more conclusively that we should build up this industry at home, and subject those who supply its product to that same form of competition which has reduced the price of galvanized iron sheets from 7 3-4 cents a pound in 1880 to 4 1-4 cents in 1889, of cut nails from $3 68 per keg in 1880 to $1 60 in April, 1891; of steel rails from $67 25 per ton in 1880 to $29 25 in 1889, $31 75 in 1890, while all this time, and, indeed, for fifty years, the price of tin-plate has remained at about the same figures, $6 in May, 1880, $4 25 in June, 1889, $5 05 in June, 1891.

These were the arguments that convinced Congress of the wisdom of transforming the tin-plate duty from a revenue duty to a protective duty. Certainly, if the desirability of protection can be admitted at all, it must be in these circumstances. The facts being conceded, it is possible to hold with regard to them only one of two positions—either that the duty should be raised or the American rate of wages should be levelled to the European scale. The principles which apply here apply in all trades, and if it is proper to abandon the tin-plate industry to foreigners merely because, paying lower wages, they can produce cheaper we, who take three-fourths of their produce, obtain no benefit from their cheaper production, then, of course, every other industry should be abandoned for the same reason, or we should accept the conditions of their free competition and reduce our labor with our tariff. Congress did not take the free-trade view. It raised the tariff, providing that the new rates should go into effect on July 1, 1891, and that if by July 1, 1897, the product of domestic plates in any year between those dates has not equalled one-third the amount of the plates imported in any year between those dates, tin-plate on October 1 following should go on the free list. Nothing could be fairer than this, and its fairness will be admitted by such Free-Traders as are not essentially incapable of seeing more than one side of a question. It simply affords American metal-workers the chance to see what they can do.

The new tariff has not yet gone into effect, but already the free-trade press is crying out with a funny air of triumph, and as if the whole controversy as to our power of production under the new law had been settled before it has been so much as opened, that no American tin-plates are now being made except for the purpose of political show. This is not true, but what if it were? If the challenge thrown out by the new law is accepted, and if the Free-Traders are willing to stand or fall—as certainly the Protectionists are—upon the issue, it can scarcely be pretended that the time to test the law's efficacy is before it has gone into operation! The proper time is fixed in the law—on July 1, 1897. If by that time nothing has been accomplished, Protectionists will be compelled to admit that something has gone wrong.

They are not alarmed, however, at the prospect. American enterprise has already accomplished a remarkable work. To make light of it is to be silly, to deny it is to be dishonest, and to claim that American skill is unequal to the task is to insult the most inventive and successfully industrial nation on the globe. American tin plates are already selling in the open market—not in large quantities, of course, nor in great varieties, but sufficiently to satisfy their manufacturers that they can easily and profitably produce at current prices. Several of the manufacturers now at work are themselves enormous consumers of tin plates, a fact which has stimulated them to make haste in establishing their works. They are themselves using their entire product, and would do so were it many times greater than it now is, but this of course does not affect the practical point that they are commercially producing. Such establishments are the St. Louis Stamping Company, Norton Brothers, of Chicago, and Somers Brothers, of Brooklyn, all of whom are now tinning plates and building mills to roll their black plates from the steel bars. The United States Iron and Tin Plate Company, of Demmler, Penn., P. H. Laufman & Co., of Apollo, Penn., Fleming, Hamilton & Co., of Pittsburg, Marshall Brothers & Co., of Philadelphia, and the large importing house of N. & G. Taylor, in the same city, have all erected plants and are now successfully producing for the open market. That their output is small in comparison with the country's demand goes without saying, but in view of all the circumstances it is encouragingly large. To suppose that these firms, all of whom are wealthy and long-established metal-workers, are going into this business for fun or to gratify Mr. McKinley and the Republican Congress is sheer idiocy. They propose to make money, and for that end are embarking or preparing to embark in large expenditures of capital for rolling mills and tinning plants.

The work that has been done by N. & G. Taylor, who are particularly mentioned here only because of their relation to the tin-plate trade as great importers, sufficiently illustrates what each of the other American producers has accomplished and is making ready to accomplish. The house of the Messrs. Taylor is ninety years old, rich, most thoroughly respected, conservative and successful. It has been importing tin plates for the open market for more than half a century, and does a business in them to-day of more than $1,000,000 a year. There is nothing about the manufacture of tin plates that to the Messrs. Taylor is a mystery, for the great bulk of their importations is made, that is, rolled and tinned, according to formulas which they have themselves prepared at their Philadelphia establishment. Their Welsh agents, therefore, are simply mechanics who put into effect what the Messrs. Taylor by careful experiment have found to be the best methods of rolling the steel and coating it. They now propose to give themselves the benefit of their own intelligent devices, and to become American manufacturers rather than foreign importers. They have already erected one complete tinning plant, from which they are turning into their stock about forty boxes (112 sheets to the box) of 20x28 roofing tin plates daily. They are constructing a second plant to duplicate this product, and are rapidly pushing forward plans to erect a mill wherein they will make their own steel plates and tin them. They are perfectly satisfied of their ability to make all grades of bright or dull plates at prices below the ruling prices when the McKinley bill went into effect. The statements of such a firm as this are a sufficient answer to the stupid jeers of the Free-Trade organs, and encouraging if not conclusive evidence that the new law is wise, that it will result in the saving each year of at least $30,000,000 to American labor and to American producers of steel, lead, coal, lumber and other commodities, and that it will as surely reduce the price of tin plates as similar laws have reduced the price of other forms of steel.

L. E. Q.

PROTECTION AND SILVER.

EX-CONGRESSMAN HORR'S COMMENTS, ON CURRENT QUESTIONS.

FARMERS AND THE TARIFF.

A WORD OF EXPLANATION.

PROTECTION FOR US THE SCIENCE OF SELF-
DEFENCE—ROSWELL G. HORR OUTLINES
HIS PLANS AND PURPOSES.

It may be proper for me to outline briefly the work I am going to try to do for The Tribune the coming year. My purpose is to write a series of articles upon the various phases of the economic system known as the American system of levying tariff duties.

My aim will be, among other things, to give a plain, honest statement of the history of tariff legislation in this country from the foundation of the Government down to the present time; also to present an accurate statement of how the several tariff bills have affected the business of the country, and how they have worked in the cases of actual application. I shall also answer some of the falsehoods which so confused the public mind during the last campaign. In doing this, permit me to state that I am a firm believer in the doctrine of Protection; that I have great admiration for what I believe it has done heretofore in building up the vast industries of the United States, and great faith in what it will do in the future for our common country, if carefully and wisely followed to its logical and practical results. My aim will be to state the position of both parties, fairly and accurately, and in language that cannot be misunderstood.

My whole life has been spent in work of some kind, but more especially among men who till the soil and manufacture the goods produced in this Nation. I have visited and personally inspected more than two hundred different shops, factories and mines in twenty-five different States of the Union; have examined into their workings, their needs and their possibilities; and have, in the last six years, travelled over one hundred and fifty thousand miles among the farms and shops of this country. I have endeavored to learn something of the condition of the farmer, the mechanic and the laboring men, who constitute the great bulk of the population of this Nation. I am fully satisfied that the men who labor in the United States to-day, whether they work on farms, in shops or factories, or in mines, are the best fed, the best clothed, the best schooled, and of course the best paid of any men doing similar work on the face of the earth. I believe that nowhere else in the world is labor more honored and more dignified than it is here in the United States.

We should all strive to keep this ascendancy, and to improve the condition of the farmer and artisan in every way possible. To do this that system must be the best which promises the largest and most constant employment for all our people, and which insures them the most ample pay for such employment. Plenty of work and good wages will always insure prosperity to any people. Good prices for the products of the farm is only another form of stating good wages for the farmers.

My opinion is also very clear that the financial and business progress of the United States, for the last thirty years, is without a parallel among the nations of the world. It seems to me that this wonderful growth and prosperity are due largely to our system of so levying duties as to take care of our own country, and so as to build up our own industries, and protect the men who work for a living on our own farms, in our own shops and factories, and in our multitude of mines. Now, if it shall turn out, upon careful examination, that our present system of protective duties has led up to a greater growth of our entire country and to more general prosperity among our people than anywhere else blesses the human race, then we will all be slow to seek a change or demand any untried experiment.

I am not unmindful of the fact that I enter upon this work at a time when the cohorts of Free Trade are flushed with a temporary victory, when the Free Traders of the Old World are joining their cry of anguish over their prospective loss of our markets to the shouts of their friends and allies on this side of the ocean. Yet, believing as I do most firmly and sincerely, that to adopt the theories of the foreign manufacturers and their importing agents in this country would bring disaster to our own people and end in ruin to the business interests of the United States; I say, believing this, my time and energy shall be devoted to a persistent effort to avert such a catastrophe.

It is also proposed that I shall answer any questions, propounded honestly, upon this subject.

Permit me to remind the readers of The Tribune how much easier it is to ask questions than it is to answer them on all subjects. You, however, have this promise from me: when you ask me a question that I cannot answer, my first effort will be to look up the subject and try and give you a truthful reply just as soon as my information will permit; and, if I find myself unable to get the desired information, then I will frankly say so and admit that I do not know. In that way you will always get the best information I can obtain upon every subject inquired about.

A word more to the readers of The Tribune. I am called to this new field of labor suddenly and have necessarily many engagements on my hands in the lecture field, where I have been laboring for the past five years. Some of these it is impossible to cancel. If there should be seeming delay in some of my replies to your inquiries you will understand that for a few weeks I am compelled to do double work, but that as soon as former engagements can be cancelled or filled, then this work shall receive my whole time and best endeavor.

Permit me also to express the hope that the relations now entered upon between the readers of The Tribune and myself may prove beneficial to us both. One thing is certain, we all have the same object in view, and that is to render prosperous and happy the entire people of our country, a country which the Republican party did so much to save during the eventful years between 1860 and 1866, and has since done so much to strengthen and build up, securing for it a sound currency, the best of credit at home and abroad and the most marvellous industrial growth ever attained among all the nations of the world. Let us then in the outset consecrate ourselves to that work which shall promise to do the most and the best for the United States of America.

R. G. HORR.

GIVE THE TARIFF A FAIR TRIAL.

TAKE NO BACKWARD STEP TOWARD FREE TRADE.

Of course the recent elections in this country will be claimed as a verdict of the people against the McKinley bill. We insist that no such verdict has been given.

The result came from no fair, honest discussion of that measure. It was brought about by a system of trickery that would make a "heathen Chinee" blush, and by a resort to lying that was truly monumental. The country was flooded with lists of advanced prices for goods that were then, and are now, selling at old prices; and statements were made in the press and on the stump as to items contained in the bill which were simply barefaced falsehoods. The free-trade champions have never been noted for their love of truth, but their methods and statements in the last campaign were simply infamous. This is well known to the Republican members of the present House. Hence we say give the new Tariff bill a fair trial.

That bill was drawn in perfect harmony with the clearly stated utterances of our National platform, on which was fought the battle of 1888.

That contest was squarely won on that well-defined issue. At that time the question was examined from a purely National point of view, affected by no local matters or personal complications. We secured at that time the deliberate decision of the people, after the subject had been treated entirely as a National one. It was discussed and disposed of from a purely National point of view. So we repeat again, give the measure a fair trial. Let the people see how it works.

If under its provisions new industries spring up and existing industries are awakened to new life, if the crops of the farmer yield him better returns, and the laboring men of the country are furnished with more constant, well-paid employment—in short, if, with this bill fairly enforced, come better times and more widespread prosperity, then no sensible man will ask for its repeal. If it does not work well it can be easily changed so soon as the experiment shows bad results. But the only way to find out how it will work is to give it an honest, fair trial.

Of course this method will not please the manufacturers of the old world or their allies, the "revenue reformers," on this side of the ocean. They fear that it will work well, and that fear will prompt them to seek its repeal before any chance is had to test its practical working. It is not the well-being of the people of the United States that these foreigners seek to promote. They desire to get possession of the markets of this country simply to help themselves; by no means for the purpose of aiding us.

Remember that it is not the first time that Republicans have been called upon to stand by their colors when the surroundings looked dark. Immediately after the first battle of Bull Run the very men, both here and in Great Britain, who are now so full of joy were exultant at our defeat and called for an abandonment of our cause. Yes, they even declared that the contest had been decided against the Union. Abraham Lincoln answered their triumphant yell by calling for 300,000 more men. The future historian will write it down that what seemed a terrible disaster at the time was really a blessing in disguise. After five days of fearful fighting in the Wilderness, almost any other General than Grant would have advised a retreat, or at least the digging of trenches and building of fortifications. Not so with this matchless soldier. His order was: "Let the men rest to-night; we go forward to-morrow." And so they did.

Once the country went wild on the Greenback craze. The elections went badly, and the credit and prosperity of the Nation seemed to be threatened. The enemy said then: "You Republicans must yield; must back down; your resumption business will ruin the Nation." Some timid men in our own ranks recommended the heeding of such advice, but wiser counsels prevailed. Our party was right and kept steadily on in the line of duty. Resumption came, and with it not ruin but prosperity.

So say we now. Protection is right. It has done wonders for the building up of this country; it can do much more in the future. The McKinley bill is a protective measure, drawn with great care and ability, studied, revised and amended by able men. Its lines all run in the right direction. It was made for the purpose and the sole purpose of building up our own country; to help the business of our own people. That is what the men who framed that bill believed it would do. I agree with them. The records of the past teach that such must be the result. To do all these things, the bill must be put into operation, and ample time must be given to develop its merits.

Great industries do not spring up in a day. Ample factories for the making of such an article as tin-plate cannot be built in one night. The only test of such a measure is to be found in its practical workings. So give this bill a fair, honest, faithful trial. It is no time now to be talking even about amendments. To any free-trade Democrats who insist upon tinkering with this bill at the present session, one reply only should be made. Tell them to keep quiet, to take a rest. The bill as it is can be defended, if it shall need any defence. The falsehoods and mis-representations about its provisions can and will be explained. When understood it will be found that no bill was ever enacted more in the interest of our entire people. Believing that the measure is a good one, let the word be passed among the entire rank and file: "I propose to fight it out on this line if it takes all summer."

R. G. HORR.

THE ALLIANCE IN DANGER.

A WORD OF TIMELY WARNING TO SINCERE FARMERS.

CONCENTRATION UPON THE OBJECTS FOR WHICH THE FARMERS' ALLIANCE WAS ACTUALLY ORGANIZED ABSOLUTEY NECESSARY.

I desire to say a few words to the men who are just now controlling the Farmers' Alliance and other similar organizations in the United States.

No man is more ready than I am myself to admit that, for a few years past, the men who live by tilling the soil have been in serious trouble throughout the entire country. The price of farm products has been low, ruinously low. Farmers have struggled long and hard to get ahead in the world. Each year has found them no better off than the year before. Indeed, in many cases, they have run behind, in spite of all they could do. Year after year came one disaster after another, until they began to despair of ever getting relief. No wonder that, finally, they began to look about to see if they could not find some remedy for their fearful condition. Upon doing so, they found the country full of organizations formed for the purpose of protecting their members and their special interests. Many of these combinations seemed prosperous; some of them showed great power and marvellous results. Why could not farmers do what others did? What rea-

son could any one urge against their making the attempt? Hence sprang up the Farmers' Alliance, the Patrons of Husbandry, and kindred organizations, all over the country. They were all born of a deep sense of actual wrong, which, farmers believed, they were suffering from the hands of organized capital and a favored few; and they started out with the full determination to right that wrong at all hazard. The feeling was natural, and the effort to benefit their condition was commendable.

These various organizations grew with great rapidity, and seemed to be animated by one single purpose, that of securing relief for real distress. In the outset the leaders of each and every one of them declared openly and repeatedly that they were going to unite with no political party and would be controlled in the interest of no political aspirants. They further declared that they should support for office only such men as were pledged to support their needed measures, men whom they believed were in sympathy with the objects they had in view, and the members of no existing party would be shown any preference. In the early days of their organizations they seemed sincere in such utterances. But the moment their strength became apparent from increasing numbers, men began to seek membership from purely political motives. Then came the dangerous point in their existence. The cemetery of dead organizations of this kind in the past is full of graves, on the headstones of which is written one and the same inscription, "Died of political intrigue."

Just the moment the people of the country ever come to believe that such an organization is simply an annex of any political party, its purposes begin to be questioned, its integrity becomes doubtful; it loses the sympathy of honest friends and its power for doing good begins to be weakened if it does not cease altogether. Indeed, worse than that, it will soon be looked upon with suspicion for having abandoned the good work it started out to perform, and for having become the tool of mere political tricksters.

I have already admitted that there is a plenty of good, honest work for such organizations. Great good might be accomplished by them if they worked simply with an eye single to the business on hand. The recent action of the Farmers' Alliance in stepping aside from its regular work and passing resolutions, at the solicitation of partisan leaders, against the passage of the Elections bill, illustrates exactly what I mean. That is a bill for the simple purpose of securing to all the workingmen of this country their constitutional right to have a voice in the election of our Federal office-holders. Pray what is there in such a measure that should call for a protest from a body of men assembled for the purpose of benefiting the cause of agriculture? What has that bill to do with the price of grain or the transportation of hogs and cattle? How does that reach the matter of dairy products or the payment of farm mortgages? In what way does that bill tend to create monopolies and give wealth an undue advantage over men who live by tilling their little farms? Why should a body of men congregated for the special purpose of looking after the interests and well-being of farmers turn aside from its regular work to grant a request coming from a set of men who are simply trying to stifle at the polls the voice of more than one million legal citizens who live by tilling the soil?

Such exhibitions of partisan zeal as that must shake the confidence of thinking farmers in the real object of their delegates, and, in the end, must lead up to disintegration and death, because the great mass of our farmers have been noted in the past for their love of fair play and honest elections.

Another point. The farmers of the United States have also heretofore been distinguished for their conservatism, for being level headed. When other men became excited and unreasonable, they kept cool. When other men rushed off into "isms" and side-shows, the farmers kept straight ahead in old and well-beaten paths. When the country was in danger from civil foes, they were self-sacrificing and patriotic. When some men started out with hair-brained schemes for the abolition of poverty and the destruction of values, they remained true to the tradition of the fathers and stood by the experience of the ages. Of such a record our farmers have reason to be proud. The danger now seems to be that their new organizations will fall under the control of mere schemers and get into disrepute by being run in the interest of projects which have no foundation on business principles and which lack the approval of ordinary common-sense. All such schemes lead in the end unerringly to financial disaster. As an example of a body of men united for the sole purpose of benefiting their members, take the organization of Locomotive Engineers. Their history shows how possible it is for men to work together with a single purpose and still avoid all entangling alliances and disastrous combinations. No one ever accused them of favoring any political party, and with perhaps a single exception, they have never been induced to attempt the impossible. They wield a tremendous influence for their own good, and can do more to protect a member of their society from outrage and wrong than any similar organization on the face of the earth. But they keep out of the hands of political tricksters, and never allow themselves to be led away by extremists who teach that great business questions can be best solved and answered by brute force.

One danger which seems to me at this moment to be threatening the Farmers' Alliance is this: They are liable to be carried away by a lot of visionary schemes which can never bring the relief promised and which must in the very nature of things end in failure. As an example, take the idea that the general Government should go into the banking business, should loan money on farm mortgages and supply the borrowing desires of the people with cash at 2 per cent a year! Why charge them any interest? Why not include chattel mortgages, as well as those on land? People having no lands to mortgage often feel the need of ready cash quite as keenly as the men owning farms. Pray, why should not the Government relieve their pressing wants and

supply them, too, with money at a cheap rate of interest? What earthly objection can there be to the General Government also starting pawn-shops on its own account? A pawn-shop at 2 per cent a year would be a novel luxury! If not, why not? Some one might ask where is the money coming from to carry on all this new business? Is it from increased taxation? No. By selling the public domain? No. Who or what is this General Government, any way? In this country the General Government is simply the people, you and I, all of us taken together. The men who manage the General Government are our servants, not our masters. The people make and unmake them at their own sweet will. These officers of the Government have no money to loan on bonds and mortgages, as such officers. All they have is what the people furnish them for the purpose of defraying the legitimate expenses of the Government.

But these financiers tell us "Just let the Government issue money. Does not the Constitution give the National Government power to coin money and issue bills of credit?" Yes; but coining of money is not the creation of value. It is simply fixing the amount of fineness of the metal in any given piece. The Government issues no notes or bonds, except as an evidence of indebtedness. They are all "promises to pay," either on demand or at some fixed day in the future, a certain fixed sum; and the value of such promises is always determined by the ability of the holder to convert them into the money of the world. So long as they can be converted on demand they will be at par. If they can not be, their value will fluctuate with the confidence of the moneyed men in their being some day redeemed. The fact that our Government issued during the Civil War an immense sum of greenbacks as a matter of necessity, and has maintained $346,000,000 of them at par since 1879, leads some men to assume that the Government, at any time the officials deem it best, can supply itself with an unlimited amount of cash by simply printing and issuing legal-tender notes; and it is this power that these men would invoke to supply all the demands of a borrowing people. Under this theory the question reduces itself to a matter of the capacity of paper mills to supply the material, and the question of payment does not enter into the problem. Up to this time every promise of the Government to pay has been looked upon as a solemn obligation, resting upon the people, and as a first mortgage on all the property of the United States. And it will be a long time before the people will conclude to increase that mortgage indebtedness for the purpose of having the General Government go into a banking business and invest their funds in what would be only second mortgages, incurring risks and suffering losses for 2 per cent a year! The scheme is so visionary and absolutely beyond the legitimate purposes for which Governments are instituted, that no man of business sense will ever entertain it for a single moment. Yet, we find such a scheme meeting with favor in the deliberations of these new organizations. Were our Government once to enter upon any such business, we would instantly become the laughing-stock of all sensible men the wide world over.

What a notion it is that all the ills and difficulties of life can be obviated by passing statutes! The creation of value comes only through work of some kind. What Governments should be instituted and supported for is to see to it that all have a fair chance in the production of values. There is no reason in the world why a Government should go into the banking business which would not also lead it to engage in every other kind of business in the known world, and that would end in Socialism in its rankest form. My word for it, it will be a long time before you will get the able, thoughtful farmer of this country to indorse any such wild scheme.

Another effort that is being made is to lead the members of these organizations into the camp of the Free-Traders. Heretofore, a large proportion of the farmers of the United States have been Protectionists. A large majority of them still believe in Protection. As they examine the question more carefully they will see that their only salvation in the future lies in building up new industries, which will divert the stream of surplus laborers from agricultural pursuits and turn it into channels of other kinds of productive employment. They will understand that this can never be successfully done unless our laws are so framed as to give our own workmen preference over the cheaper labor of the outside world. Let me repeat, if these new organizations insist on joining hands with the cohorts of free trade, they will drive from their ranks large numbers of men who would otherwise work in harmony with them—men who have no faith in these doctrines which originate among the capitalists and manufacturers of England, and which are adopted and advocated in this country mostly by the importing agents of those foreign gentlemen.

There are many gray-haired farmers now living on the cultivated lands of the United States who distinctly remember the woe, the distress, the actual desolation among the farmers of 1857, brought about by the low tariff enacted by the Democratic party. These old men will never consent to repeat that experiment. Hence, I again say, if the members of these new organizations would be successful, would seek to secure length of days for their associations, they must rise above partisan political connections. They must devote themselves to the work they first assumed to do. Just so sure as they enter into an alliance to prevent an honest ballot and a fair count for all our voting citizens, just so sure as they adopt the wild vagaries and impracticable dreams of the believers in flat money, just so sure as they persist in an attempt to lead their followers into the camp of the English-loving, American-hating Free-Traders, just so surely will their power for doing good be destroyed and the days of their usefulness be numbered.   R. G. HORR.

NEW SUGAR REFINERIES.

Sir: I have been reading R. G. Horr's articles in your Weekly issue. You invite inquiries, so here goes a question to Mr. Horr.

Can you tell me how in the world it is, that the merchants are building sugar refineries in Baltimore now that we have free sugar, or I may say free trade in that article? Why build sugar refineries now when they would not build them under protection?   J. K. Baltimore, Md., March 12, 1891.

Our correspondent has evidently omitted to examine the law on sugar, or he would hardly have put his question in that shape.

Granulated and refined sugars are not on the free list, only sugars below and including No. 16, Dutch Standard. No. 16, Dutch standard, is a grade of sugar usually known as "Coffee C" in the markets of this country and is a nice article of common sugar for table use. The higher grades of sugar are manufactured in refineries from low-grade, dark-colored sugars which are not fit for family use. These low-grade sugars are all on the free list, but the refined article has a duty of 1-2 cent per pound, so as to enable our citizens who run refineries to pay better wages than they pay abroad and to give them the advantage over foreign manufactures in our own markets.

You are mistaken in your inference that no one under the old law built refineries in this country. There were many in the United States, and, unless I am misinformed, several in Baltimore. The reason why more are being built in that city now, is that some men, having money, have concluded that with low-grade sugar free they can make money refining sugar, even with a low protective duty of 1-2 cent a pound on foreign refined sugar.

I hope they will succeed in the enterprise and make their investment pay. Sugar, both low and high in grade, will be cheaper to our consumers under the McKinley bill than ever before. If, at the same time, we build more prosperous refineries and then still more, if the bounty on sugar stimulates the growth of beets and the manufacture of low-grade sugar at home, I will be almost happy concerning the situation on the sugar question.   What says J. K.?   R. G. H.

HENRY CLAY ON PROTECTION.

In 1824 Henry Clay, in one of his wonderful speeches, made the following statement:

It is most desirable that there should be both a home and a foreign market. But with respect to their relative superiority I cannot entertain a doubt. The home market is first in order and paramount in importance. This home market, desirable as it is, can only be created and cherished by the protection of our own legislation against the inevitable prostration of our industry which must ensue from the action of foreign policy and legislation. If I am asked why unprotected industry should not succeed in a struggle with protected industry, I answer: The fact has ever been so, and that is sufficient. I answer the uniform experience evinces that it cannot succeed in such a struggle, and that is sufficient. If we speculate on the causes of this universal truth, we may differ about them. Still the indisputable fact remains. The cause of protection is the cause of the country, and it must and will prevail. It is founded on the interests and affections of the people. It is as native as the granite deeply embosomed in our mountains.

In spite of such a declaration from such a man we have no end of the puny college striplings who go up and down our country claiming that men of brains are never protectionists, and that the great American system has in it no elements of permanency. Go and ask Henry Clay and he will tell you to go and ask the "granite hills of New England" whether they possess staying qualities. Truth may now and then receive a set-back, but in the end truth is a stayer!—(K. G. H.

ABOUT MILLIONAIRES.

A REMARKABLE LIST AND WHAT IT TEACHES.

A FREE-TRADE LIE ABOUT THE TARIFF EFFECTU-
ALLY NAILED TO THE COUNTER.

I desire to call the attention of the readers of The Tribune to the following list, which is taken from "The "New-York World" of Sunday, the 7th of December, 1890:

Men of Millions.—The Greatest Aggregation of Wealth in the World.—As fortunes go nowadays in America one of $10,000,000 is not considered particularly great. There are thirty-five fortunes of that or greater magnitude in this country. There are three men who are worth $100,000,000 or more. The list of the Americans who count their wealth at $5,000,000 and above is as follows:

John D. Rockefeller	$125,000,000
William Waldorf Astor	125,000,000
Jay Gould	100,000,000
Cornelius Vanderbilt	80,000,000
William K. Vanderbilt	75,000,000
Collis P. Huntington	40,000,000
Russell Sage	35,000,000
John I. Blair	30,000,000
William Rockefeller	30,000,000
Leland Stanford	30,000,000
Mrs. Hetty Green	30,000,000
William Astor	30,000,000
Darius O. Mills	25,000,000
Philip D. Armour	25,000,000
Mrs. Mark Hopkins	25,000,000
Charles Crocker estate	25,000,000
Henry Hilton	20,000,000
L. S. Higgins estate	20,000,000
George Westinghouse, jr	15,000,000
Anthony D. Drexel	15,000,000
J. Pierpont Morgan	15,000,000
Andrew Carnegie	15,000,000
Oliver H. Payne	15,000,000
Frederick W. Vanderbilt	15,000,000
George W. Vanderbilt	15,000,000
Mrs. Elliott F. Shepard	12,000,000
Mrs. William D. Sloane	12,000,000
Mrs. Hamilton McK. Twombly	12,000,000
Mrs. W. Seward Webb	12,000,000
George M. Pullman	12,000,000
John W. Mackay	10,000,000
Robert Goelet	10,000,000
Ogden Goelet	10,000,000
Percy R. Pyne	10,000,000
Mrs. Moses Taylor	10,000,000
David Dow estate	8,000,000
James G. Fair	8,000,000
Weld estate (Philadelphia)	8,000,000
Miss Mary Garrett	8,000,000
Robert Garrett	8,000,000
John T. Martin	8,000,000
Amos R. Eno	8,000,000
Theodore Havemeyer	8,000,000
Ives estate (Providence)	8,000,000
Brown estate (Providence)	8,000,000
Henry A. Taylor	6,000,000
Mrs. Robert Winthrop	6,000,000
Z. Leiter	5,000,000
Marshall Field	5,000,000
William L. Scott	5,000,000
George Bliss	5,000,000
James M. Constable	5,000,000
H. H. Cook	5,000,000
Mrs. R. L. Stuart	5,000,000
Mrs. Bradley Martin	5,000,000
Mrs. Anson Phelps Stokes	5,000,000
Henry G. Marquand	5,000,000
Henry Hart	5,000,000
Edward Cooper	5,000,000
Abram S. Hewitt	5,000,000
William Steinway	5,000,000
George Ehret	5,000,000
Jacob Ruppert	5,000,000
George J. Gould	5,000,000
Addison Cammack	5,000,000
Adrian Iselin	5,000,000
Henry Clews	5,000,000
Mme. de Barrios	5,000,000
John H. Inman	5,000,000
R. T. Wilson	5,000,000
E. D. Morgan	5,000,000
James M. Brown estate	5,000,000
R. Heber Bishop	5,000,000
Thomas Garner estate	5,000,000
William E. Dodge	5,000,000
D. Willis James	5,000,000
Mrs. John C. Green	5,000,000
A. A. Low	5,000,000
George W. Childs	5,000,000
John Wanamaker	5,000,000
General Samuel Thomas	5,000,000
Frederick L. Ames	5,000,000
Oliver Ames	5,000,000
Benjamin P. Hutchinson	5,000,000
Charles L. Tiffany	5,000,000
Mrs. William H. Vanderbilt	5,000,000
Levi P. Morton	5,000,000
August Belmont estate	5,000,000
James B. Colgate	5,000,000
John B. Trevor	5,000,000
Eugene Kelly	5,000,000
William Rhinelander	5,000,000
H. O. Havemeyer	5,000,000
Austin Corbin	5,000,000
Robert Bonner	5,000,000
Bayard and Robert L. Cutting	5,000,000
James and Townsend Burden	5,000,000
Edward Schermerhorn	5,000,000
J. N. L. Griswold	5,000,000
Wilson G. Hunt	5,000,000
Mrs. Josephine Ayer	5,000,000
Phineas T. Barnum	5,000,000
David W. Bishop	5,000,000
Henry A. Cram	5,000,000
Samuel Sloan	5,000,000
William Peabody Wetmore	5,000,000
Elbridge T. Gerry	5,000,000
Robert L. Livingston	5,000,000
Jesse Seligman	5,000,000
William Seligman	5,000,000
Sidney Dillon	5,000,000
E. S. Jaffray	5,000,000
John Claflin	5,000,000
Mrs. Edwin Stevens	5,000,000
Le Grand B. Cannon	5,000,000
William C. Schermerhorn	5,000,000
Rev. Charles Hoffman	5,000,000
Rev. Dean Hoffman	5,000,000
Morris K. Jesup	5,000,000
James M. Waterbury	5,000,000
Paran Stevens estate	5,000,000
Abraham R. Van Nest estate	5,000,000

Whether the amounts set opposite these names represent the wealth of these individuals accurately or not is something about which my knowledge is very limited. Nor does it matter very much for the purposes of this article. "The World" is entirely responsible for the accuracy of the figures; and as that is the leading free-trade organ of the Democratic party, we will take its statement as being correct.

One of the oft-repeated assertions of the free-trade press of the country in which "The World" has persistently joined is this: They tell us that

our tariff laws are constantly "robbing the poor
to benefit the rich," and then make the statement that the great fortunes which have been
piled up so dangerously high in this country
within the last few years are made through the
workings of our protective system: further, that
were it not for this "robbery" under our tariff
laws, wealth would be evenly distributed here
in the United States, and such colossal fortunes
would be unknown. That statement is made from
one end of the Nation to the other, on the stump,
in public debates, in private conversation. A
free-trade orator who would not close his speech
with a terrible assault on Mr. Carnegie and other
"manufacturing barons" would be considered too
tame for present use and would soon be
out of business. Indeed the effort to make
the people believe that all the riches of the day
come through the accumulations of protected industries is constant, persistent and notorious.

Right on the heels of this assertion comes this
list of millionaires published by this free-trade
organ, as a matter of news, without the slightest
idea of the lesson it teaches. Now for the lesson.

By examination you will find that the list
comprises 122 names estimated to be worth
$5,000,000 and upward each. To be more specific,
there are in the list two persons rated at $125,000,-
000, one at $100,000,000, one at $75,000,000, one
at $40,000,000, one at $35,000,000, five at $30,-
000,000 each, four at $25,000,000 each, two at
$20,000,000 each, seven at $15,000,000 each, five
at $12,000,000 each, five at $8,000,000 each, two
at $6,000,000 each, and seventy-five at $5,000,000
each. The entire list aggregates $1,552,000,000.

The wealth of the thirty-five persons first
named foots up $1,085,000,000. Among the en-
tire thirty-five there are only two who made their
money by manufacturing articles protected by our
tariff laws. One of these, L. S. Higgins, is in
the $20,000,000 list, and the other, Andrew Car-
negie, is in the $15,000,000 list.   If there is
another one among the entire thirty-five who can
be classed as among manufacturers who have made
their money by making and selling protected
goods, I have been unable to learn which one it is.

John D. Rockefeller heads the list and is rated
at $125,000,000. His fortune came through the
Standard Oil Company. But oil is exported from
this country in enormous quantities and has never
been affected in price by tariff laws.

The next two names are Astor and Gould. The
first one inherited his fortune, which comes from
merchandising and the enormous rise in real estate
in New-York City, and as for Mr. Gould, it is
well known that his wealth comes from railroad
purchases and deals in stocks and other securities.
If he ever made a dollar as a manufacturer, the
fact has been entirely concealed from the public
at large.

Go through the entire list of 122 names; and
I assert that there will not be found to exceed
twenty who made their money, or any considerable proportion of it, as manufacturers, and the
aggregate rating of these twenty is less than
$142,000,000. That leaves in the list 102 men
who made their money in other ways. Their wealth
foots up the enormous sum of $1,510,000,000.

I defy any man to examine the list and refute
this statement. Indeed, I beg of these free-trade
advocates to give it their careful attention and
then tell me if the above statement is not absolutely correct. Of course, my acquaintance with
these millionaires is very limited indeed, but my
information as to the manner in which their
accumulations were made, is, in my judgment,
most reliable. At least, my effort has been to
secure the exact facts. I believe I have been
successful.

If the foregoing statements are true, then pray
tell me what becomes of the doctrine so persistently taught by the enemies of protection, that most
of the great fortunes of this country have been
made by men who took advantage of our tariff
laws and so "robbed the people"? My opinion is
that a careful examination of all the great fortunes accumulated in the United States during the
last half a century will make about the same
showing as is so clearly made by this list. Not
to exceed one in six will be found to have been
made by men who manufacture protected goods.
This is accounted for from the fact that the benefits of a protective tariff go largely to the men
who do the work. The statement that it all goes
into the pockets of the men who manage the business is not true. Indeed, the bulk of it is ab-
sorbed in the high wages paid the men who work
in our shops and factories as compared with the
wages paid abroad in the production of the same
kind of goods.

I do not deny that very many of our manufacturers have been prosperous. It is best for the
country that they should be. Some of them have
amassed wealth, but they have risked vast sums
and managed immense institutions to do it. The
magnitude of their operations often brings wealth
on small margins. Why should not such be the
case? At the same time, many of them have
struggled hard and finally failed. It is the prosperous concern that blesses the community in
which it is located, never the failing one. Let
me state this one fact: It is always better for the
workingmen, for the merchants and the
farmers, that the men who manufacture
goods of any kind in any community
should be prosperous and successful. The fact
that they are so insures prompt payment of wages,
sure returns for the sale of merchandise and a
reliable home market at good prices for the
products of the farm. Let no farmer or merchant
or laboring man ever take any stock in the rant
of these importers of foreign goods and English
sympathizers when they attempt to make you
believe that anything which will cripple the great
manufacturing industries of this country can in
any possible manner benefit you. Hereafter, when
any of them tell you that the millionaires of the
country come mostly from men who manufacture
articles under our protective laws, call their attention to this list, and get them to explain their
statement, if they can. Then ask them to tell
you who has done more for the farmers, the merchants, the mechanics and workingmen of this
Nation than the men, like Andrew Carnegie, who
have organized immense industries, employed
thousands of men at good wages, and kept in this

country millions and millions of dollars which, except for their efforts, would have gone abroad to pay for articles made in foreign shops and factories. This whole tirade against men who build up industries in this, our own, country is wicked beyond measure, and, as a rule, is founded on false statements.　　　　R. G. HORR.

GOLD AND SILVER AS MONEY

HOW THESE METALS AND BANK NOTES CAME TO BE USED IN TRADE.

AN ENTERTAINING EXPOSITION OF THE WHOLE SUBJECT, WITH REFERENCE TO THE EFFECTS OF " FREE COINAGE " OF SILVER

To the Editor of The Tribune.

Sir: In your weekly edition of June 17, I read two articles from Mr. R. G. Horr, one on the "rice and sugar" question, the other, on the "Sub-Treasury" scheme, both of which were handled in so masterly a manner, that I am constrained (though not a subscriber) to ask, what is the meaning of "free coinage," and why do some people argue that it will be a blessing to the country, while others claim the reverse? An answer will much oblige yours respectfully,　　　　G. K. RYAN.

Barnwell, S. C., June 23, 1891.

The term "free coinage" has come to mean much more than the two words would seem to express. In order to have the subject understood, it is necessary to explain how gold and silver happened to be used at all as the money of the world. In the early dawn of civilization there was probably no kind of money in use. All commercial transactions were at first simply barter between individuals. What is meant by that is that people began the exchange of property by trading one kind of property for another. A man having a surplus of grain, if he desired a cow, hunted up some person who had a cow to spare and who needed grain, and the two men exchanged with each other. This kind of a transaction made it necessary that the man who had a surplus of grain should find a person who had an extra cow and was short of grain. Of course, after a time, the same man who had a cow to spare, learning that grain was an article of universal use, came to make the exchange, although he was not short of grain. He did it from the fact that he could more readily find persons who were in need of bread than he could those who were in need of cows; and because, with this grain, which he did not need, he could readily make an exchange for other articles which he did need. More than that, the grain being easily divided into smaller portions, he could more readily use it in exchange for a number of articles which he might need ; the cow could not easily be divided up and utilized in that way.

In this manner, no doubt, all useful articles which were easily preserved and readily divided up into smaller quantities came to be used as mediums of exchange.

As people advanced in civilization a taste for the beautiful was undoubtedly developed. There is little doubt that the first use of gold and silver was simply for the purposes of ornament, precisely as diamonds and other precious stones find a use at the present day. Gold and silver were used for ornament, owing to the brilliancy of their colors and their great durability. After the skill of the silversmith and the goldsmith had come to be established the world learned to use these two metals for the making of ornaments of various shapes and sizes, so that these metals soon came to be valuable according to the quantity of each kind. There is no doubt that the use of gold and silver was at first largely for ornamentation.

Silver, being found in by far greater abundance and being procured with very much less labor than gold, came to be considered less desirable and consequently exchangeable for very much less of other products than gold. It has always been the cheaper of the two metals, although at an early day the difference of value between gold and silver was not so great as at the present time. No doubt these metals came to be sought after as substances of real value long before they were used as the legal money of any nation.

As grain of every description was easily divided into different portions and could be used as a medium of exchange more readily than other products of the soil, so it soon became apparent that gold and silver could also be divided and subdivided with great ease, and that they were not easily destroyed by the action of the elements ; and thus people came to use them as a medium of exchange. A transaction could be made simple and definite by using an exact amount of either metal, so that all the early dealing of the human race in gold and silver came to be made by the contracting parties naming the weight of each metal that entered into each transaction. All grain came to be described naturally by measure ; and all metals by weight.

ORIGIN OF COINAGE.

After a time gold and silver, owing to their being so perfectly adapted to service as a medium of exchange, came to be used for that purpose much more extensively than any other products or any other metals. Of course it soon became apparent that to have transactions honest and fair, the purity of these metals must be carefully guarded. Thus the quantity and quality of each sample of gold and silver came to be a question of grave importance to the people. Finally a plan grew up of having the governments analyze gold and silver and form them into various shapes and sizes, determining the quality and quantity in each piece. The governments at first simply stamped upon each piece some name which indicated its exact weight. For long numbers of years no name was given to any piece of gold or silver except such as simply indicated the weight of pure metal in such piece.

At that early day the idea of a parity of value between the two metals had never been dreamed of, although each was being used in all the more civilized nations as money. Each contract in those days must have been drawn payable in so much silver or gold, and the amount of each was always designated by weight.

After a while certain pieces of gold and silver came to be called by some simple names, and the people came to talk about the value of property, as expressed by a certain number of these named pieces or coins. In that way people came to lose sight of the exact weight of metal in each piece. Different nations gave a different name, according to accident or fancy, to the piece in most common use among the people of each nation. In that way, value came to be expressed by naming the number of certain coins. That value was still really determined by the weight of pure metal contained in each coin, though not always thought of when naming them. In this way, finally, the people came to demand a uniformity of metal in each named piece, and so resorted to legislation which was simply intended to fix the exact amount of pure metal contained in each size of coin. Thus, by slow growth, the governments of the world learned to select certain metals as a standard of value with which prices could be measured and named.

By a similar slow process a definite measure of distances was long ago fixed. Originally the space between two places was designated by paces, or so many times a day's journey. Those terms were soon found to be indefinite and variable. To-day we use the terms "inches," "feet," "rods," "miles," as being something very simple and easy, yet they are the result of long ages of slow growth and careful, patient study. The same can be said of weights. So the terms "sovereigns," "francs," "doubloons" and "dollars" are the outgrowth of long and slow development. Each nation finally named how much of each metal should be contained in each of its coins; and for many centuries the unit of value has been fixed by each nation naming a certain coin as its standard, and then naming the amount of pure metal that should be contained in each coin, declaring by law that all contracts should be drawn expressing amounts to be paid with that unit as the measure of value.

The United States called its unit of value the "dollar," the same as the "foot" is made the unit of measure for distance and the "pound" the unit of measure for weight. The term "dollar," used in that way, had no definite meaning until the amount of pure metal to be contained in each piece was fixed by the same statute. It matters not what name each nation may give to its unit of value, the coin so struck off has, in the markets of the world, simply the value that is determined by the weight of pure metal contained in it. Hence, the moment any coin leaves the nation that has coined it, its value is at once determined by its weight, precisely the same as it would have been ages ago, when it had never been formed into the shape of coin or stamped by the Government.

Some nations made their standard of measure a certain amount of silver; others, a certain amount of gold. The common use of the two metals as money soon led to an attempt to fix the ratio of value between the two. In this way, in this country, it was ordered that a gold piece called an "eagle" in order to be worth ten dollars must have in it an amount of gold which would be worth exactly the same amount as the weight of silver which was first contained in ten silver dollars. It can readily be seen that if these two metals never changed at all in their relative value the value of an eagle or any other gold coin could be reached with great ease and with perfect accuracy.

GOLD THE STANDARD IN AMERICA.

The first unit of value in the United States was the silver dollar, which, according to law, must contain 371 1-4 grains of pure silver. The same act provided that 24 3-4 grains of pure gold should be the equivalent of the silver dollar of 371 1-4 grains. The amount of pure silver contained in a silver dollar has never been changed in the United States.

In 1849 an act was passed directing the coinage of gold dollars. They were issued the same year and contained only 23 22-100 grains of pure gold. The act of 1873 made this gold dollar the unit of value, instead of the silver dollar. This is the act which is said by the silver men to have "demonetized silver."

The present weight of the silver dollar is 412 1-2 grains including the alloy, and that has been the weight of the silver dollar of the United States since 1837. Previous to that time it weighed 416 grains; but the increase in weight was in the alloy and not in the amount of pure silver contained in each piece.

Since the passage of the act of 1873, silver, as compared with gold, has greatly depreciated in value. By that act our Nation became what is called "a gold standard nation." Immense quantities of silver, since the passage of the "Bland Act," have been coined into silver dollars containing 371 1-4 grains of pure silver, which was for so many years the standard of value in the United States, and hence they are commonly known as "standard" silver dollars. But the silver from which these dollars have been coined has been purchased by the Government at its gold value. Consequently while the Government issues each standard dollar as being equal in value to the gold dollar (which is now the unit of value in this country) it does not put into such silver dollar nearly as much silver as such a gold dollar will purchase. Hence we have in circulation in the United States a large amount of silver money, which can be used in this country at its face value, which in the markets of the world is worth less than 75 cents on the dollar.

The men who are in favor of the "free coinage" of silver insist that the demonetizing of silver, by decreasing its use, has cheapened silver; and that by the same act which made the gold dollar our unit of value an enormous increase in the use of gold was occasioned, and, that, consequently gold has appreciated in value. The men who believe in the gold standard claim that the depreciation of silver has been brought about by the large increase of production and by the cheapened processes of mining and smelting; and they also claim that the value of gold has been nearly stationary compared with other products of the world.

HOW PAPER MONEY CAME TO BE USED.

While, at an early day, nearly all the money of the world was either gold or silver, at a very early date people began to use as evidence of value "promises to pay" certain sums of money These written promises were undoubtedly in common use long before such a thing as a bank note was ever known. By a slow process of growth, banks were authorized by law to issue their own promissory notes as money. After another lapse of time, Governments issued the promissory notes of the nation itself to supply the needs of the Government. These, however, were always simply promissory notes, and had no other standing, with this exception, that the Government made them a legal tender for the payment of debts between individuals, something which no nation, so far as I know, has ever done for any notes issued by any individuals or by any banking institutions. Out of this power, assumed and exercised by the general Government, has grown up the notion that the Government, by its mere edict, can create value in legal tender notes.

The history of the world proves beyond all controversy that such legal tender notes can be kept at par with the coin standard of the country only when they are redeemed by the Government on presentation in hard cash. They are subject to precisely the same fluctuations as are the notes of individuals and corporate institutions. Very large sums of such paper obligations have been issued by various Governments of the world and have afterward become absolutely worthless. The assignats of France, the Continental money of the United States and the legal tender notes of the late Southern Confederacy may be given as instances of the utter absence of value in such paper money, except when constantly redeemed by the maker in gold or silver money.

The exchanges of the world to-day are very largely carried on without the actual use of either gold or silver. By the use of bank checks, sight drafts, and Clearing House certificates business to the amount of many millions of dollars is transacted every day without the counting or handling of a single coin or a paper dollar. Owing to these facts, people have come to look upon paper representations of money as the money itself. They forget that each and every one of these transactions, if genuine, can be traced to the gold or silver which is always the real, though not apparent, basis of the transaction.

THE "FREE COINAGE" IDEA.

All of these things combined have created the impression among very many people that the Government by its mere fiat power can give actual value to silver or gold without regard to quantity, and to paper promises without providing for their redemption in metal. Hence a large number of people in the United States have come to believe that if the Government of the United States would pass a law making 371 1-4 grains of silver our unit of value, and then declare that a "dollar" containing that amount of pure silver should be the equivalent of a gold dollar containing 22 8-10 grains of pure gold, the two pieces would instantly become of equal value, or nearly so, all over the world. They therefore seek to have the law so arranged that every individual on the face of the earth who shall bring to the United States Mint 371 1-4 grains of silver shall

receive for the same a coin named a "dollar" from the Government, and that such silver "dollar" shall be a legal tender for all purposes in the United States without any regard to the price of silver in the markets of the world. That is what is now meant by "free coinage of silver." If such were to be the result, if the two "dollars" would at once become equal in value, no one would oppose the free coinage of silver.

Many people do not believe that this Nation alone can produce any such result. There are those who do not believe, even if all the nations of the world should agree upon the ratio between the two metals, that all of them combined could keep the ratio the same at all times.

Those who do not desire the free coinage of silver claim that such coinage would result in driving the gold out of the United States, and that all our business would very soon be done with a cheap currency which would derange commercial transactions and work a great hardship to people who work for wages and those who have invested their means in loans.

The silver men claim that such a law would advance the price of silver and decrease the price of gold so that the two metals would be equal in value at the same ratio as in former years, and that money would become cheaper only on account of its greater abundance, and that such a result would make it easier for people to pay their debts and obtain a living.

There are those who believe the free coinage of silver would simply put large profits into the pockets of men who own silver mines, or who are holding silver bullion on speculation, and that the Government has no more right to fix the price of silver by legislation and then take all the silver at that price than it would have to fix a high price on wheat or corn and oats, and then take those articles at such advanced price, to the great advantage of those who have them to sell, but at the expense of the rest of the people.

NO RASH EXPERIMENTS.

This question of money is one so complicated in all its bearings, so far-reaching in its importance, and so intricate in its workings, that experiments with new theories and new methods should be entered upon with great caution. Any effort to do business with a depreciated measure of value must always end in disaster.

Value is something that cannot be given to an article by legislative enactment. All forms of paper money must be of necessity simply "promises to pay" in something of actual value. Any effort to make a small quantity of any article equal in value to a larger quantity of the same article must end in failure. Our Government should stand ready to join with the other nations of the world in agreeing upon some ratio of value between gold and silver, so as to keep both of these metals in use as legal money. As long as other moneyed nations refuse to enter into such an arrangement it seems to me idle for the Government of the United States, single-handed and alone, to attempt to force any fixed ratio upon the world.

If legislation is wisely taken it seems to me

that it will be confined to utilizing the silver produced in the United States, and not looking after that of the Old World. This can safely be done by enforcing our present laws. In doing this there is little risk. Why then resort to the experiment of "free coinage" for the silver of all nations, especially when such a plan is condemned by a large majority of the men in this country who have had great experience in financial matters?

I do not claim to be much of an authority on the money question. Indeed, the more I study it the less certain I am as to what will be the result of any proposed legislation For that reason, I would let well enough alone. Under no possible conditions does it appear to me best that we should make it an object for the people of the Old World to bring their silver here for coinage by offering them a chance in that way to dispose of it at much more than the value which is accorded to it in the markets of the world. How could such a law benefit our own people? I would have the laws of this country so framed as to bless, first and all the time, the people living in the United States.　　R. G. HORR.

DUTIES AND WHO PAY THEM.

QUESTIONS BY AN ILLINOIS MAN.

DO THE POOR OR THE RICH, THE FOREIGNER OR THE CITIZEN, PAY THE DUTIES ON IMPORTED GOODS?

To the Editor of The Tribune.

Sir: I, a farmer, would like to have the following questions answered through the columns of your valuable paper. Answers by R. G. Horr preferred:

1. Would a duty levied on an article produced in this country, or one not produced here, bring more money to the Treasury, a like amount being consumed?

2. What is the proportion of rich to poor in the United States? Draw the line where a poor man ends and a rich one begins that was used by R. G. H. in his article on the "Tariff of Great Britain."

3. The proportion of tariff paid by the rich and poor in the United States.

4. The amount of tariff collected in the United States for the year 1890.

5. Give the names of a few importers that you know who are compelled to contribute tariff funds to run this nation and do not get it back from the consumers.

A clear, concise answer to above questions would add much to the information of myself and others who are not informed as to the above.' Yours respectfully,

SAMUEL HOLMES.

Benson, Ill., May 20, 1891.

I am somewhat in doubt as to whether this correspondent has so shaped his first inquiry as to ask the real question he intended to. No duty is ever levied on any article produced in this country, but we do levy duties on similar articles that are produced in other countries, and such duties are paid only on such articles as come in from abroad, and never on any articles when produced in this country.

When a duty is levied on any kind of an arti-

cle none of which is produced in the United States, of course more money would go into the Treasury from that duty than would be collected from duties on that kind of goods if part of them were produced in this country. For example, if one-half the starch used by our people were made in our own country, and one-half of it abroad and a tariff duty should be levied on starch, as a matter of course only one-half as much money would be collected from the duty on starch in that case as would be collected from that same duty if we consumed the same amount of starch and made none of it here but imported it all. It seems to me he might just as well have asked me whether the whole of a thing is greater than a part of it. Such a question leads one to fear that it is not asked in good faith. In my work I am always striving to get at the truth, and it is not pleasant to have questions asked except in that same spirit. I hope my fears are groundless, and I will not take counsel of them, but will answer him candidly as one really seeking information.

In reply to the second question, will say that in the article he refers to I used the term poor as applying to those people in England who own no lands, no houses, very little of any kind of property, and who live from hand to mouth upon their daily earnings, such as they are. I used the term rich nabobs as applying to rich people—the titled nobility—the few land-owners and the wealthy merchants and bankers of England. Does Mr. Holmes dispute the statement as to the comparative number of those two classes? Now, he wants to know on the same basis what proportion of the people in the United States are rich and what poor. I have not the data at hand, so as to be exact, but nowhere near as large a proportion as will be found in England. I will venture this statement that when you get among what are usually called the common people, you will find in the United States twenty men who are in comfortable circumstances where you will find one in Great Britain. Again, you will find in Great Britain one hundred poor people born in that country—I mean people who have not a hundred dollars' worth of anything in the world—where you will find one born and living in the United States in like destitution. What says our friend Holmes to that statement? Is it true? Does it give him any information? Is he able to learn any lesson from such a fact? To me it is full of meaning. Is not this answer to his second interrogatory definite enough for all practical purposes?

As to the third question, it is impossible for me to give the exact proportion of tariff duties that are paid by the rich and by the poor in the United States. So much of these duties is paid by the foreign producers in order to get their goods into our markets that the problem is a difficult one. Then again a very large amount of our duties is collected upon luxuries, articles that are used only by the rich. We levy duties on that grade of goods even when they are not produced in this country, and when we know such duty will increase the cost of the article and will be collected from the consumers. But such consumers can afford to pay, and in such cases the duty is for revenue only. The duty on diamonds, velvet carpets, high-priced chinaware, rich laces, expensive silks and costly liquors is largely that kind of a duty, but none of it is paid by the laboring classes. Indeed, our working people use very few goods that are imported from abroad which are not either on the free list or which are not of those classes, of which our manufacturers have reduced the price, so that our people are getting them much cheaper than they would be able to had we not established the making of them in the United States. I state that as a simple fact, not as a theory. Is it or is it not true? Since sugar is on the free list very few duties are paid by our poorer people. That was a free-trade tariff, and should have been repealed long ago. A large part of that duty did come out of the laboring classes. Yet the Free-Traders and Tariff Reformers in Congress voted solidly against removing that duty. What says our correspondent, was that or was it not a good thing to do? Free sugar was one of the leading features of the McKinley bill. It has cheapened sugar for every family in the United States. Do not forget that the duty on sugar was a revenue duty, not a protective duty; and such duties are nearly always paid by the consumers.

Fourth—The duties collected on the importation of foreign goods during the year 1890 amounted to the sum of $225,428,888, of which $55,166,703 40 were collected on sugar and molasses.

Your fifth and last question is one that I am under no obligation to answer. So far as I now remember I have never claimed that any mere importers ever did much to help run this Nation. As a rule they are simply middlemen, who get all they can and pay nothing except what they can charge up to their consumers. Our own merchants often do their own importing and pay the duties themselves, and then of course they count such duties as a part of the cost of such goods and charge their consumers accordingly. But that does not prove that the duty is not paid by the foreign producer. If he has taken the duty out of his price on the goods the merchant may pay the Government the money, but it comes, all the same, from the foreign manufacturer and is not added to the cost of the articles to the ultimate consumer. Let me illustrate. I need some horses, we will say, to do work in the pine woods. The price of horses is fixed by the market in this country. The home supply is so great that the price is fixed here. I conclude to buy some horses in Canada. I go there, and do I pay the Canadian his price for a team, without regard to the duty? By no means. I compel him to put such a price on that team as will enable me to pay the duty and leave the cost for me just what I would have given him for the team if no duty was charged. If you do not think so, go over there and try to buy a pair of pure-blooded mares and see how you will come out. The Canadian farmer will ask you for the mares of the same quality for working purposes $60 more than for a span of geldings. Why? Simply because he can sell

his mares for breeding purposes, and they come into this country free of duty. It will be useless for you to tell him that you want them for work. His reply will be, "Then hunt up another team, and I will hunt up another customer. If I sell them to you simply as work animals I must deduct the amount of the duty before you will purchase them; but as 'brood mares' there is no duty." He knows very well who must pay the duty on a work team. Am I right about this or not? It seems to me so clear that I am sometimes inclined to get out of patience with a man who says he cannot see it. If such is not the case, pray why do the foreign producers care so much whether a duty is high or low? If our people, the consumers, pay the duty, then the foreign producers can get the same price for their goods, be the duty high or low. Why do the foreign producers get up mass-meetings and denounce our tariff laws if it makes no difference in the price they can get for their wares? Let me tell you simply as a matter of information why they act in the way they do; why they send up such a cry of distress the moment the duty is increased in this country on any class of goods that they have been selling largely in the United States. It is simply because they know from past experience that such a tariff will start the making of the same kind of goods in the United States; that the producers in the United States will drive down the price, and that if they get their goods into our markets after that they will have to do so by paying the duty themselves, and that the sum paid will never come back to them from the American consumer. Knowing that, no wonder they protest. There is no theory about this; it is a simple statement of facts as to what has taken place scores and scores of times within my memory. Such a result has always followed the levying of a duty on the protective plan.

If I am not correct about this, why do the foreign manufacturers all claim that these duties really come out of them? They do so claim in their public utterances and in their carefully prepared resolutions. You never hear any such claim made as to free-trade duties. Why? Because duties levied on articles that cannot be economically produced in this country do not lead to the production of any such articles over here, create no new supply, bring about no competition, and so leave the markets still open to the same vendors, and whatever the duty is it does not come out of the producers, but out of the consumers. The moment you levy a protective duty on any article that can be economically produced in this country, you instantly set our people to producing that article, and then we compel the foreign producer of similar goods to pay the duty if he would get into our markets. All of those foreign producers will tell you that the duty comes out of them. Do they or do they not know how that is? So my answer to your last question is that every foreign manufacturer who sells any article of merchandise in the United States on which a tariff has been levied, if similar articles are being economically produced in large quantities in this country by our own manufacturers, then every one of such foreign manufacturers is compelled to contribute to the support of this Government, in order to get into our markets, and he does not collect the money so paid back from the consumers. It is invariably deducted from the price paid the foreign producers by our merchants, and so there is nothing to collect back. You ask for a clear and concise answer to your questions. My answers are clear to my own mind, but it is impossible for me to tell whether they will satisfy you. I have not aimed at brevity, but have tried not to be obscure. You may not be convinced, but what I try to do is to so state my propositions that any one can readily see what I am trying to get at. I hope I have at least done that much in this instance. R. G. HORR.

THE TARIFF A BLESSING.

A CLEAN-CUT STATEMENT OF THE REAL DOCTRINE OF PROTECTION.

SOME COMPLICATED AND PONDEROUS QUESTIONS, IN THE PUREST IDIOM OF THE "HIGHER CULTURE" OF BOSTON, CLEARLY AND HANDSOMELY ANSWERED.

To the Editor of The Tribune.

Sir· Mr. Horr stated substantially April 15 in Tremont Temple that protection stands or falls with the proposition that protection has cheapened the price of our protected goods. I respectfully submit, in behalf of the Boston Question Club, the following questions for your thoughtful consideration, and hope for an early reply :

1. Why, if it cheapens things, should a tariff be put on and thus cheapen wheat and other products, which form such a large percentage of our exports? Is it desirable for us thus to cheapen for foreigners the main bulk of what we have to sell abroad?

2. While claiming, by our protective tariff, to have cheapened the price of steel rails, glassware, crockery, carpets, etc., why do Protectionists ask, McKinley-like, in the same breath, for an increase of tariff on these self-same articles, to compensate them for the greater decline of price in free-trade England? Is not the necessity of increasing our protection from being undersold by Free Traders prima facie evidence of a greater decline of their commodity prices than of ours? Is not the very asking of an increased rate of protective duty on an article an open confession that its price has declined more rapidly outside than inside our protected borders? Else why should we now need higher duties than in 1860?

3. Is not the direct primary intent and effect of tariff protection from being undersold generally been to increase the prices of these protected goods? Then, unless reaction is greater than its parent action, how can the tariff's reactionary, price-reducing effect be greater than its primary price-increasing effect?

4. Does not this primary dearness proportionally check consumption and consequent production, thus diametrically opposing that enlarged scale of the world's production which is so undeniably essential to cheapness?   D. WEBSTER GROH,
President Boston Question Club.

No. 616 Washington-st., Boston, April 18, 1891.

In answer to this letter from so high a source as the Boston Question Club, permit me first to restate just what positions I did take in the Tremont Temple debate, and what I also believe to be the positions taken by all Protectionists who have given the subject careful study. The statements which I made at that time, as clearly as was in my power, were these:

WHAT MR. HORR SAID IN BOSTON.

1. That there is no civilized nation in the world that does not levy some kind of tariff, duties and hence there is no such nation known as a purely free-trade nation. Is that statement true or not? What says the Boston Question Club? The members of that club may believe in absolute free trade ; may believe that all custom houses should be demolished. I know nothing as to where they stand upon that question, nor does it matter in this debate, because that is not the position against which I was arguing that night. What I desire to do in the outset is to see if we cannot agree, as I go along, on certain existing facts and so in the end eliminate many difficulties from this discussion.

2. I stated that among civilized nations there are two methods of levying tariff duties. One is called the free-trade method ; the other is designated as the protective system. I then stated that under the free-trade plan duties are always levied on articles which the nation levying them does not produce, and that under the protective system such articles (except luxuries) are put on the free list, and that we levy our duties on importations of those articles which our nation does or can produce. I cited the case of Great Britain, as an instance of a nation which levies its duties on the free-trade plan. I stated that she collects over $100,000,000 each year by reason of tariff duties, and that the great bulk of those revenues are levied on tea, coffee and tobacco. Am I right in those statements?

I further claimed that whenever a tariff is levied on this free-trade plan (that is to say, on goods the like of which are not produced or cannot be produced in the country where the duty is levied) that such a duty always increases the cost of the article to the ultimate consumer ; and when levied on such articles as tea, coffee and tobacco, which are in such common use, that such duties must be paid mostly by the working people of any nation which levies that kind of a tariff. Will the Boston Question Club turn itself into an answering club and tell me whether that position is correct?

England collects as I have stated very large tariff duties on those three articles. Who pays those duties? Most clearly the men who consume the tea, coffee and tobacco. As in England the poorer people number fully six hundred to every one rich nabob, and, as each one of those poor people consumes nearly the same amount of those articles that each rich person does, it follows that the great bulk of those duties are collected from the laboring classes. Is that a fact?

My next statement was, that under the protective system articles the like of which we cannot produce are placed on the free list, and that we levy our duties on foreign articles the like of which we can produce in this country for two purposes: First, to obtain revenue. Secondly, to give our own people control of our own markets and thus foster and build up industries in the United States, and secure good wages to our working people. I then stated that such duties are paid largely by the foreign manufacturers who are compelled to make these payments in order to get into our markets with their surplus goods, and that such duties are seldom added to the cost of the article to the ultimate consumers. Is that or is it not true?

3. I further claimed that duties levied on the protective plan tend to build up industries here in the United States; that under that system a very large number of manufacturing establishments have been built and run in this country for many years which never would have been established and maintained had it not been for the protection thus given. Is that a fact?

4. My next position was that when such industries are once established, they open up a field for American ingenuity, set in motion the spirit of Yankee invention, and, by large and uninterrupted operations, cheapen the actual cost of production, bring into power the great law of competition, save the enormous fees of the importers and, by all these agencies combined, result in these products being sold to the ultimate consumers at a lower price than when these goods were procured from abroad, and in all probability at a lower price than they would have been sold for had no such industries been established here in the United States. Do not the facts bear me out in that statement?

I then stated that unless, in the end, this system does result in cheapening the cost of goods to the ultimate consumers, and also in paying labor better wages than it receives in any other countries, then I would abandon my belief in protection.

I further asked that my free-trade friends should agree, if I could show that such protected articles had been constantly going down in price since we began their manufacture in this country, and that during all that time labor had been better paid than in any country which levied a free-trade tariff, then, in that event, they should stop calling the protective system "robbery" and should admit that it had worked well for the people of the United States. I now submit to the members of the Boston Question Club whether these are not precisely the positions I took in that debate.

I next stated that whether the price of such protected goods had gone down or up in the past thirty years of our protective tariff is a question of fact and not a question of theory. During all those years we had tried the plan thoroughly and knew how it worked. I then cited the cheapening of steel rails, cutlery, salt, farming implements, glassware, cotton goods, clothing, all kinds of silk goods, wire nails, paper and paper pulp, etc., etc. I closed by asking any one in the audience to name a single article, the bulk of which we produce in this country under the protective system, that has not been thus cheapened. Did

my opponent name one? The president of the Boston Question Club, who seems to have been present, did not name one; he has not named one in his letter, but has gone back to theorizing. I now ask again is that statement correct? Are such articles all cheaper now than they were before we began their production in this country?

5. I further stated that a tariff levied for revenue only always places the rate of duty at a point which will produce the most revenue for the Government, and that such a tariff, of necessity, gives foreign producers command of our markets and is to all intents and purposes a free-trade tariff; and further, that from such a tariff none of the advantages of the protective system can possibly follow. Is not that statement also true?

WHY A FEW DUTIES WERE INCREASED.

I will now turn my attention to the statements in Mr. Groh's letter, and will begin with the second question, leaving the first one for the closing of this article. The first part of the second question is as follows: "While claiming by our protective tariff to have cheapened the price of steel rails, glassware, crockery, carpets, etc., why do Protectionists ask, McKinley-like, in the same breath, for an increase of tariff on these same articles, to compensate them for a greater decline of price in free-trade England?"

My answer is that the duty in the McKinley bill on steel rails and on over 140 other articles is decreased and not increased, and that where it is increased, it is not done for the purpose of compensating Protectionists or any one else for the decline of prices in the Old World; but in every instance it is increased for the purpose of enabling our own manufacturers to carry on their business without a loss, and continue to pay the larger wages prevalent in this country. There is not an instance, so far as I am aware, of an increase of duty in the McKinley bill, where such increase was not made simply to foster and build up the manufacture of that article in this country—for the simple purpose of protecting that industry.

Pray, of what use would a tariff for the purpose of protection be if it were not high enough to protect? We have no power to determine at what starvation point the foreign manufacturer shall compel his workmen to toil; but we have the power to prevent him from driving the wages of our own workmen down to anywhere near the same point. So, wherever it was found that the tariff formerly levied on an article had not been sufficient to protect our workers in that particular industry, then it was increased simply and solely to enable our producers to keep control of our markets, to insure good wages, and to enable our factories to be run continuously so as to cheapen the cost of production.

DECLINE OF PRICES ABROAD.

"Is not," the club asks, "the very asking of an increased rate of protective duty on an article a confession that its price has declined more rapidly outside than inside our protected borders?" It may or it may not be such an admission; but whether it is or not, what has that to do with this question? What Protectionist ever claimed that the building up of our home industries did not also cheapen the product abroad? I assuredly made no such claim.

Of course the establishing of a large industry in the United States and the production on a large scale of any article of merchandise will increase the supply, and the tendency will be to drive down the price of that article all over the world. No doubt steel rails have been produced in England cheaper and cheaper, the same as they have in the United States. We soon took advantage of all their improvements. They soon took advantage of all our inventions. And hereafter, just so long as they pay only one-half as much for labor as we pay, no doubt they will constantly reduce their price of production, the same as we do ours. But what has that to do with the question? The real thing that must be decided is this: What would have been the price of steel milk, not alone in the United States, but all over the world, if we had never established the industry in this country and had never made the large quantities we produce here at home?

I assert that the history of the productions of our country demonstrates beyond all power of contradiction that in case there had been no supply here there would never have been any such decline in prices anywhere. If this is not the case, will the Boston Question Club tell me why tin-plate has not been cheapened within the last twenty years here in the United States the same as other products of steel and iron have been cheapened? The part of tin-plate which is protected by our tariff is the 96 per cent of that article which is iron or steel. If free trade in any article would lead to the establishment of an industry, why have we not been making our own tin-plate for the past twenty years? And if, on the other hand, protection does not lead to the establishment of an industry, why is it that the passage of the McKinley bill has already started so many companies into existence which are now preparing to manufacture those goods in this country?

Dare the Boston Question Club accept the result in this one industry as a test of its free-trade theories, as against the protective system? If the doctrines of its free-trade members are true, tin-plate, from this on, will be continually dearer to the consumers in the United States. If the protective doctrine is true, then when these industries are once fully established they will increase the supply, improve the methods of manufacture, dispense with the large commissions paid to the middle men, and in the end will cheapen tin-plate to the ultimate consumers of this country. I am ready now and willing to accept the result in this case as a test of the truthfulness of my position. Time will soon show which theory is the correct one. Dare the Free-Trade Question Club of Boston accept so simple a solution of this question?

I ask again, who ever claimed that the result of building up an industry, and so cheapening the article, in this country has not resulted in its also being cheapened abroad? That, of course, is always the result. The moment you take away the markets of this country, you create a glut in the Old World, and you may drive down the price faster over there than here; and yet it would

often be the case that the cheapening of the article, here or there, would never have occurred had the industry never been built up here. So if we should permit our industries to be crippled and finally ruined, the supply would be less, and the price would again advance all over the world. The simple law of supply and demand, other things being equal, would produce that result. England may always undersell us in price just so long as she gets her labor for one-half the price we pay for ours. Hence it becomes a simple question of the wages of the workingmen. What says the Boston Question Club? Are wages better in this country than they are in free-trade England? Do you believe in legislating so as to keep good wages in this country or not?

DIRECT ACTION AND BACK ACTION.

Your third question starts out: "Has not the direct, primary intent and effect of tariff protection from being undersold generally been to increase the price of those protective articles?" No, far from it. Of course the intent is to prevent foreigners from underselling us in our own markets, and that has seldom ever resulted in an increase, either primarily or secondarily, in the price of protected goods. But even should an increase take place in the price for a short season, while our manufacturers are getting the business in hand, that will very soon be made up by the decrease in price which uniformly follows. Hence, the only question of importance is whether our system results in a permanent reduction of prices.

As to the second part of this third question, I have not the slightest idea what it means. I am not posted on the great doctrines of actions and reactions, know nothing of the laws that govern double and twisted reflex action or back action, and do not at present propose to tackle that subject. I did not know, until your letter stated it, that reaction is the child of action. All this may be very profound, but it is entirely too deep for me. Life is too short to be taken up with that kind of play on words.

"PRIMARY DEARNESS."

4. "Does not this primary dearness proportionately check consumption and consequent production, thus diametrically opposing that enlarged scale of the world's production, which is so undeniably essential to cheapness?"

No; it does nothing of the kind.

In the first place, there is seldom any "primary dearness."

In the second place, the consumption of an article depends very much more on the wages of the masses, which enable them to have something to purchase goods with, than it does upon the cheapness of any articles. The consumption of articles has constantly increased under the protective system.

No doubt large and constant production always leads to the cheapness of goods. The very aim and intent of the protective system is to enable the people of the United States who produce manufactured goods to run their factories continuously month in and month out, year in and year out. That is the great factor in producing cheap goods all over the world. So important is this that a large establishment working full time the whole year round can pay a larger price for its raw material, pay larger wages to its workingmen, and then undersell to the ultimate consumer, the men who employ cheaper labor, who consume cheaper raw material, but who work with many interruptions. Is that a fact, or is it not? I say it is. What does the Boston Question Club say?

WILL PROTECTION CHEAPEN WHEAT.

I now come to your first question: "Why, if it cheapens things, should the tariff be put on, and thus cheapen wheat and other products which form such a large per cent of our exports?" Listen! It does not follow because a protective tariff, which leads up to large factories and gives constant employment to large numbers of men, and thus enables them to take the greatest advantage of labor-saving machinery and the great power of the division of labor, and so cheapens products—I say, it does not follow that the same rule will apply to the products of the farmer. Farmers' products are not manufactured in a week or a day. The price of farm products depends largely on matters entirely outside of the cheapness of labor or the continuous operation of mills. The wheat crop can be raised only once in a year. No invention, no continuity of labor, will produce a greater number of crops. The amount of wheat raised is limited by the amount of acreage. There are no such limitations upon those producing manufactured goods.

I do not claim that the tariff on wheat in the United States, at the present time, will have very much bearing upon its price, so long as we export that article largely. A tariff on that article just now has very little effect, nor was the tariff placed on wheat with a view of affecting its price materially at the present time. Such, however, was not the case with most farm products. The production of wheat in the United States, in excess of our own consumption, is growing less and less each year. There has been a decline of about 10,000,000 bushels a year for the past ten years. In a little while the entire product of wheat in the United States will be consumed by our own people. The moment that that point is reached, the price of wheat will be affected by an attempted importation of wheat from abroad. When that time arrives the farmers of this country will need protection against the cheap labor of India and Russia.

It is clear to me that the law which cheapens the price of manufactured goods by continuous operation of large factories does not apply with anything like the same force, if at all, to the products of the soil. Of course an increased price of an article like wheat or any other farm product would in a very short period stimulate the production, and result perhaps in cheapening the article; but in that case the competition would be between our own farmers paying the same price for their labor, and all contributing to the support of our Government alike. Such a competition would be healthy and should always exist in every country. That is entirely a different thing from permitting the people of every nation under the sun to dump their surplus farm products into this country, and so disturb and ruin the markets of our own farmers.

But why do you Free-Traders ask me this question, You claim that the levying of a duty on an article itself increases the price of that article. I believe the price of farm products has been too low in this country for the past five years. You will admit, will you not, that an article may be too cheap? Would you not like to do something to enable the farmers to get a better price for their grain and horses and hogs? What says your club? The McKinley bill attempts to aid these farmers by giving them control of our home markets. Are you in favor of that or not? What says the Boston Question Club? Would you like to do anything that would give these farmers relief?

The price of a farmer's products determines his wages. The constant anxiety of every Protectionist is so to manage as to keep up the price of labor in the United States. We make no exception as to classes. We would like to have all the products of this country bring a fair price. All the products of the farm are too cheap the moment they get below a point which gives good wages to the men who till the soil. The same may be said of the articles produced by all workmen. Cheapness alone does not determine the desirability of any system. We care not how cheap you make an article, so long as you do not compel the existence of cheap men and women, cheap laborers. No nation can be called prosperous that adopts any system which permanently cheapens the work of its men and women below the point of a good, decent living.

The same law which might increase the price of the product of the farm may decrease the price of manufactured goods. The same law which would raise the price of wool in the market, when applied to continuous manufacturing of wool into fabrics, might result in cheapening the fabric. Existing experiments prove this statement to be true. The result of the McKinley bill, I hope and believe, will be to increase the wool product of the United States, to give farmers a better price for their clip, and at the same time produce better and cheaper worsted goods than we have been buying in this country. This may seem anomalous to the members of the Free Trade Club of Boston, but it is clear in my own mind. Here again the result that follows will be the test of whether I am right or wrong. I would not give a fig for any theory if the facts that follow do not sustain it.

A FINAL QUESTION TO THE QUESTION CLUB.

I am perfectly satisfied that the McKinley bill will result in giving farmers better prices for their products, and also in keeping the price of manufactured goods low for the ultimate consumers of these goods; that it will insure good wages for all laborers in the United States; keep a large amount of money in this country that would otherwise go abroad; and thus, while securing prosperity to our individuals, will build up and enrich this Nation. I really believe this.

If Protection shall do this, then will the members of the Boston Question Club also rally to its support? You predict ruin to this country from the operations of that law. I promise exactly the opposite results. Time will demonstrate which of us is correct. It will then be an existing fact, not a theory.

I do so wish that I could get you Free-Trade gentlemen to agree to abide by the logic of some actual event. Visionary men are always theorizing. Practical business men are always watching results. One takes lessons from his imagination the other from experience. R. G. HORR.

IS A HIGH TARIFF NECESSARY FOR REVENUE?

NO; THAT IS NOT THE POINT AT ALL; A HIGH TARIFF IS FOR AN ENTIRELY DIFFERENT OBJECT.

To the Editor of The Tribune.

Sir: I would be pleased if Mr. Horr would answer these questions:

First, Does it not take $400,000,000 annually to pay the expenses of the general Government? Can this amount be annually raised without a protective tariff?

Second, If you decrease the present tariff 30 per cent, as the Democrats want, what amount of money will be actually collected?

Third, If we had free coinage of silver how much more money would be in circulation than we now have?

Fourth, Is not the Alliance working in the interest of the Democratic party? Respectfully,

C. R. BOSTICK.

Henry, Tenn., June 26, 1891.

1. The expenses of the General Government are fully $400,000,000 each year. They will continue to reach that amount so long as the sum paid for pensions remains as large as it is at the present time. This large amount of money could all be raised without any protective tariff by simply levying duties on the free-trade plan. Suppose our duties were levied on tea and coffee, and on other articles, the like of which are not produced in this country. Then we would obtain the revenue, only no matter how high such a duty might be, it would not be a protective tariff, as there would be no productions of that kind in the United States to protect.

2. Again, suppose that the duties were levied on some articles, the like of which are produced in this country, but that such duties were lowered 30 per cent, and levied simply for the purpose of revenue, and not with the view of protection. More money can often be raised with a low tariff than with a high one. A tariff duty levied simply for revenue will always be placed at such a point as will increase the amount of importations, and thus increase the amount of revenue collected. The objection to a duty of this sort is that it always gives the foreign manufacturers the advantage over the home producers, being levied expressly so as to bring in all the foreign goods possible and prevent the sale of our own home-made goods as much as possible. It is always the aim of men who believe in "a tariff for revenue only" to fix the duty levied at just that point which will encourage the foreign making and the importation of goods and discourage the manufacture of such goods in the United States.

The men who believe in the protective system aim to reach an exactly opposite result. They always put the duty so high as to give our own manufacturers an advantage in our markets over the foreign manufacturers, and, in that way, to increase the home production, and, as a matter of course, decrease the importations. Although the rate of the tariff may be a high one, the importations are much less, and the duties collected are also less, than if a lower rate of duty had been levied on a much larger quantity of goods.

It is at just this point that the two systems differ. The Free Traders only take into account the raising of revenue; the Protectionists look after that, also, but they never lose sight of stimulating and making possible the home production. The former plan must of necessity encourage foreign manufacturing, and discourage the making of goods here in the United States. The latter plan encourages and builds up home enterprises, enables our manufacturers to pay higher wages for work and still be prosperous and never stop to inquire whether the men who make the same goods in the Old World will be benefited or not.

Sometimes more revenue will be collected under the one system; sometimes more under the other; each case being governed by the circumstances which surround it. The Free Traders claim that nothing should be made in any country which cannot be made in competition with the rest of the world. They do not take into account the conditions as to wages, labor and capital which are known to vary so much among different nations. Protectionists claim that each nation should take care of itself; should produce the greatest possible varieties of commodities; should manage to grow and make everything that can be economically grown or made within its borders, and that, where conditions vary, laws should be so framed as to enable the men in each nation to control the markets of their own country as against the producers of the same goods in other countries.

It will be readily seen, therefore, that the result of reducing the tariff rates 30 per cent might be to increase the amount of duties collected. It would all depend on the manner of such reduction. The Free Traders are constantly claiming that the McKinley bill has raised the rate of duties; yet they all admit that it will diminish the revenues collected. Why? Because, first, it put sugar on the free list, which cut off at one stroke $55,000,000. Secondly, because whenever the duty was raised it was to enable our people to make more of those articles ourselves; and no duty is collected on the goods which we make ourselves. A Protectionist never worries about the loss of receipts from any particular duty, when it comes from having been able to supply some market with home-made goods. That is precisely what he started out to do. Why should he feel badly for having accomplished just what he hoped and desired to accomplish?

3. It is impossible to tell whether free coinage would end in an expansion or in a contraction of the money in circulation except by actual experiment. Secretary Windom claimed that

there would be less money in circulation after the passage of such a law than now. The advocates of "free coinage" claim that the volume of circulating medium would be largely increased. What seems to me to be by far the more serious question is this: "Would the money in circulation then be as good as the money we now have?" We can now convert every dollar that is in circulation among the people of the United States into a dollar which is good everywhere on the face of the earth. Could that be done after free coinage of silver has been made legal, with the same amount of silver in each dollar as our standard dollar now contains? I do not know. I am afraid not. I care not how much good money we have in circulation in this country. The more the better. I would very much dislike to have our people compelled to do business with a depreciated currency. Men who work for wages, men who consume products (and we all do), cannot afford to deal in depreciated dollars. All commercial nations are compelled in the end to settle in the money of the world. No kind of juggling can escape or avoid this final result.

4. I cannot answer your last question, because I do not know. I am not in the secrets of the Alliance. I hardly think that the originators of the Alliance had in view in the beginning the benefit of the Democratic party. That the Democrats are trying to capture the organization now is no doubt true. If they succeed, that will be the end of the Alliance. The Democratic party has always been ready to coalesce with any and every new party, but always with one and only one result. After the swallowing has taken place the Democratic party "goes right on for ever," and the new party is never again heard of among men.

R. G. HORR.

ARE NATIONAL BANK NOTES TAXABLE?

A MISSOURI READER THINKS THEY ARE NOT—MR. HORR'S REPLY.

To the Editor of The Tribune.

Sir: In your issue of May 6, Mr. Horr in answering the inquiries of C. M. Woods, says that National bank notes, unlike the greenbacks, are taxable for township, city, county and State purposes. I do not so understand it and would call Mr. Horr's attention to Sections 3,701 and 5,431 of the National Bank act.

Bethany, Mo., May 8, 1891. A. CUMMINGS.

I desire to thank Mr. Cummings for his letter. At the time I made the statement in reply to Mr. Woods I did not suppose there was a particle of doubt of its accuracy. I knew that for years, in the business world, the two kinds of currency had been treated as I there stated. He can imagine my surprise upon receipt of his letter. Upon examination of the sections of the law to which he refers I do not wonder that he has come to the conclusion he has. Yet, notwithstanding that those statutes, upon their face, seem to bear out his statement, still the conclusion is so clearly against what I know to have been the previous practice of business men, that I have made a more careful examination.

The present Controller of the Currency, under date of May 14, writes me: "In regard to whether or not National bank notes are subject to local taxation, I desire to say that that has been a mooted question for some years, and the court of last resort has never decided the question so far as I know." In a recent case, in the District Court of Jackson County. Iowa, at the April term of this year, it was decided in the case of Dunham vs. the city of Maquoketa, that National bank notes are subject to local taxation. I refer to the May number of "The Banking Law Journal," published at No. 63 Pine-st., New-York, pages 277 and 285.

Upon examining that case, I find the court uses the following language:

National bank notes are not in any just and proper sense obligations of the United States. They show upon their face that they are the obligations of particular banks, to whom they have been delivered and by whom they have been put in circulation. The Government is bound for their ultimate redemption, but this redemption is not made by the Government out of its own funds, but out of the proceeds of sales of Government bonds belonging to the banks, and by them deposited with the Government as a security for such redemption. The duty of the banks to redeem their own circulation rests primarily upon them; and it is only when a bank fails or refuses to redeem its own circulation that the Government can be called upon to make such redemption, and this, as has been stated, it does out of the proceeds of the sales of the bonds deposited with it by the bank to secure such redemption. The law of this State declares bank bills to be taxable. The circulation notes of National banks are neither more nor less than bank bills. There is nothing in the laws of this State that would exempt them from taxation and nothing in the acts of Congress properly considered that would prohibit such taxation.

Upon examination of the report of a former Controller of the Currency, made by Henry W. Cannon in 1885, on page 47, it will be seen that this question had at that time frequently been asked at his office. He states: "The question of the liability of National bank currency for taxation arose in the case of the Board of Commissioners in Montgomery County vs. Elston (32 Ind. 27) and it was decided by the Supreme Court of that State that National bank currency is not exempt from taxation by the local authorities because they are not obligations of the United States in any proper sense of that expression. In a case, however, before the Supreme Court of the State of Mississippi, Horne vs. Green, it was decided the other way. In 1873 a case was decided in North Carolina in which the court held that National bank notes are liable for taxation."

Mr. Cummings, being a lawyer, will readily see that while my former statement is not entirely beyond question, still that up to date the weight of the decisions favor the truth of my statement. Will he be kind enough to examine the case carefully and then write me his revised opinion? Nothing pleases me better than a communication calling in question any statement which I make, especially when accompanied by a reference which seems to point out my error as clearly as did the statutes referred to in the letter of Mr. Cummings. I think, however, that that gentleman, when he makes a careful examination of these cases, will come to the conclusion that he by no means had so clear a case against

me as he supposed, when he penned his brief note.
Be that as it may, I thank him for calling my attention to what seemed to him an inaccurate statement. What we should all aim at is to be right,
and never forget that we are all liable to make
mistakes.   R. G. HORR.

WAGES AND THE TARIFF.

"STEADY WORK AT LOW WAGES" NOT THE BEST, BY ANY MEANS.

WOULD THE COUNTRY HAVE BEEN BETTER OFF IF AMERICA HAD NOT BEEN SO AT- TRACTIVE TO IMMIGRANTS?

To the Editor of The Tribune.

Sir: In Mr. Horr's reply to the remark of a resident
of Lynn, Mass., that "steady work at low wages is
much better than high wages at unsteady employment," he mentions the fact that the important factor
in the labor question is a good market for the products
of labor, and that the chief disturbing element is a
glutted market. Now, will Mr. Horr answer the
following questions?

1. Do not high wages produce a glut in any certain direction, sooner than low wages, by drawing more
labor in that direction?

2. Do not the high wages of this country induce
the vast labor immigration, and is not this immigration
the chief cause of a glutted labor market?

3. Do not these immigrants, who were induced to
come to this country by high wages, now constitute
nearly the entire mass of wage-earners in this country,
largely to the exclusion of our own laborers; and do
they not form the main body of labor strikers, now
so inimical to the business of this country?

4. Would not "steady work at low wages" have
prevented undue immigration, avoided overproduction
and gluts, and warded off strikes, and would there
not have been more real peace, prosperity and happiness in this country than at present?   Sincerely
yours,   T. P. DOUDLES.

Leesburg, Penn., June 15, 1801.

In answer to your first question, I will say
that high wages are always much more attractive
to people who work than low wages; that more
people will seek work, other things being equal,
when it pays well than will try to get it where
the pay is poor; and that the greater the number
of workmen employed in any given kind of work,
the more goods of that kind will be produced;
but whether a glut will follow such increased
production depends entirely upon the quantity
of such goods consumed. It often happens that
the increased production does not keep pace with
the increased demand or consumption. One can
never tell whether a glut will follow increased
production without first knowing how many of
such articles will be used or consumed. It is
very easy to produce a glut in the market for
any commodity which people stop using and so
stop buying. It is not easy, however, to produce
a glut in the market for an article when the number who use it are every day increasing and
where the quantity used by each individual is
also daily growing larger. These all seem to be

self-evident propositions, which need no argument
to enforce their adoption as being true.

2. There is no doubt in my mind that the
high wages paid for labor in this country are one
of the main inducements which lead such vast
numbers of people to leave the Old World and seek
homes in the United States. I have stated such
to be the fact hundreds of times in the last fifteen
years, and my Free-Trade friends have denied
such is the case just as many times. I still believe
the statement to be true. No doubt this large immigration would increase the supply of workingmen in this country and would lead to a glut in the
labor market unless there should be a corresponding increase in new industries and an enlargement of old industries sufficient to absorb all the
extra help. In case there should be such an increase, immigration would produce no glut in our
labor markets. For example, with all this immigration, there is no glut in the hired-girl market;
nor do I think there is to-day any such number
of unemployed men in this country in any trade as
some people are constantly claiming. The great
bulk of our people can find work at fair prices
if they really seek for something to do. Still,
the tendency of this constant influx of laboring
people is to cheapen the price of labor. It seems
to me beyond dispute that such a result must follow such a cause. Hence I answer the second
question in the affirmative.

3. "Do not these immigrants, who were induced to come to this country by high wages, now
constitute nearly the entire mass of wage-earners
in this country, to the exclusion of our own laborers?" Very far from it. There are a large number of such immigrants, and of course the places
filled by them are not occupied by native-born
Americans. But when you say "nearly the entire mass" the statement is very wide of the mark.
If we could get an actual count of the people in
the United States who work for wages it would
be found that nowhere nearly one-half of them are
foreign-born. I know such is not the general impression. The statement of our correspondent has
been repeated so many times that it has come to
be believed without careful examination.

I find that since 1820 there have been only
15,351,009 foreign-born people landed in the
United States. True, 11,148,335 of those have
come since 1855; that is, within the last thirty-
five years. Notwithstanding that fact, I doubt
if over one out of eight of the people now in this
country were born abroad. Are there not to-day
more colored wage workers in this country than
the entire foreign wage laborers combined? Almost every one of these colored laborers is native
born. I am fully convinced that for every man
and woman in this country, working for wages,
who was born in some foreign land, there are
at least three who were born in the United States.
I am in hopes when the tables of the census are
completed that we can learn the exact facts as to
this question. While these foreign immigrants
are by no means as numerous as our correspondent
seems to think, still there are enough of them
greatly to increase the supply of laborers; and were
if not for the vast number of new works which are
being constantly organized, the labor market

would long ago have been glutted. As it is I hardly think we have a supply of workingmen greatly in excess of the actual needs of the country.

As to the other portion of the third question, my observation coincides with the suggestion of Mr. Dondles. I think a large majority of the men who engage in strikes are foreign born. At least, such has been the case with the strikes which I have myself witnessed. It may be that such is not the case with strikers on the railroads or in the cases of skilled workmen. However, these are mere impressions and not founded on sufficient knowledge of facts to warrant stating my conclusion with much emphasis.

4. Let me now repeat your fourth question as that is the one which demands a careful answer. "Would not 'steady work at low wages' have prevented undue immigration, avoided overproduction and gluts and warded off strikes? Would there not have been more real peace, prosperity and happiness in this country than at present?"

I do not see how constant work by the people in this country would have deterred people from coming here; but no one can doubt that low wages would have operated in that way, provided they were low enough. Any condition of affairs which would have made it appear that the people who work over here were worse off than the same class of people in the old world would have prevented the large majority of immigrants from coming to this country. But is it not a little strange that any one should ask, "Would not such a condition of affairs have been better for our people?"

This is really the question: "Would not low wages, constant work, poor food, bad clothes, little education and uncomfortable houses have rendered the attractions of this country so small that few foreigners would have come to seek homes among us?" I think such would have been the case. Then think of the balance of the question: "Would not our own people have been more peaceful, more prosperous and more happy with low wages and the inevitable accompaniments of low wages.?" Cholera, yellow fever, pestilence, famine and poisonous snakes would tend to keep immigrants away from a country; but one would hardly think of naming those things as sources of happiness to those living in the country. The fact that so many people seek homes in the United States is conclusive proof that they expect to better their condition. If low wages are conducive to peace, prosperity and happiness, why do not all these people stay where wages are low?

Peace, prosperity and happiness are a grand Trinity. It is difficult to think of three more desirable blessings of a material nature for the human race to seek. That continuous work and little pay will insure their possession is to me a novel idea. Is it possible that any man who is working for wages ever conceived such a notion? I have, during my life-time, labored many years for hire, beginning work on a farm for $10 a month. The fact that my work was very continuous, twelve hours and over each day, and that my wages were small has never been considered

by me as the cause of any great ecstasy at that time. Since then I have received a good deal more than that amount for each day's work in a year. The more I could earn the better I liked it. That is not all. I have never seen the time when I would not have accepted twice as much wages as I received, and willingly have run the risk of any unhappiness likely to follow.

Let me state some propositions that seem to me to be much nearer the truth.; low wages are better than none at all, better than idleness, better than vagrancy, better than want; but they are not so good as high wages. The more a man can earn, the more comforts he can procure, the more happiness he should enjoy. Constant work at low wages is far better than no work at all; it is better than high wages for a short time and idleness for a very long time, but it is not nearly as good as constant work at good wages.

Do not forget that good wages for our entire people is what increases the power of consumption and prevents gluts in our markets for products, and is what makes the markets for the 64,000,000 people living in the United States better than the markets of any other 100,000,000 of people on the face of the earth.   R. G. HORR.

ARE THE AMERICAN SCREW COMPANY GOING TO ENGLAND?

When will our opponents take to telling the truth about the industries of the United States?

A good friend of The Tribune, M. L. Imhoff, of Houstonia, Mo., writes that the Democratic newspapers of St. Louis are stating that the American Screw Company, of Providence, R. I., one of the largest companies in the United States, are about to move their factory to England, and that they are forced to do so "on account of the McKinley bill." He asks The Tribune to publish the exact facts as to this matter. Very well! Here they are:

The American Screw Company are not thinking of moving the principal part of their factory to England at all. They never even dreamed of doing so. They simply contemplate moving a small portion of it which has stood idle for some time. They had hoped to operate that portion on foreign material for their foreign trade. The McKinley bill was so drawn as to enable them to do so, not so as to prevent them from doing it. That clause in the bill which enables them to use foreign material and then allows them a rebate of the duty on all such material as is sent back into the foreign market in the form of manufactured goods was intended to aid all American manufacturers, this Rhode Island concern among them, to supply all the foreign trade possible. It was intended to enable them to obtain free raw material for all goods made in this country and shipped abroad. The Democratic journals above referred to knew that fact, or should have known it.

If the facts are as stated, then why do the Screw Company move even a small part of their factory to England? The Tribune will state the reason. It is because the managers of the American Screw Company know full well that they can obtain their labor in England for just about one-half the money they are compelled to pay for the same work in this country. An examination of the pay-roll of the company in Rhode Island and then of the pay rolls of similar concerns in England will fully prove the truth of this statement. Hence, if the McKinley bill drives these men into England with any portion of their works, it is because that bill is so drawn as to keep up the price of labor in the United States. If that is what these free-trade journals mean by the Screw Company moving the idle part of its machinery to England " on account of the McKinley bill," then I will agree with them. I am ready to admit that the result of all protective legislation is to keep good wages in this country. That is true, not merely of the McKinley bill, but of all bills that have been framed on the protective plan. The main object of all such legislation is to enable the American Screw Company and all other manufacturers in the United States to pay good wages to the men who do their work. It is owing to those laws that the laboring men in this country, of all kinds and classes, are better paid for their labor than are the workingmen of any other nation on the face of the globe.

The American Screw Company have a branch factory in Canada, and have had for some time. They contemplate putting up another branch across the Atlantic. That, however, is a very different thing from moving their great Rhode Island factory over there. The Rhode Island concern will still continue to run in the future as it has in the past.

Why cannot our free-trade friends and these Democratic journals publish the exact facts about such matters as this? It is easy to get at the truth in such cases. They have only to write the American Screw Company itself for correct information, and the secretary of that company would no doubt answer them as promptly and courteously as he has answered The Tribune. The truth, however, is not what these journals seem to care about publishing. Keep a good watch, now, and see if they do not continue to circulate the old original lie. They will do that, too, after The Tribune has pointed out that their statement is untrue and has informed them that this denial is made upon the authority of the American Screw Company itself. We took it for granted if that great concern was about to move to England that its own officers would be likely to know about it. It is always better in seeking for the truth about such a matter to make inquiries of the very persons who know about it, rather than to rely on those who do not know. At least, such is the best course to pursue where one is really seeking the truth. Where one prefers not to know the facts, then a draft on the imagination may supply a newspaper item; but the danger is that in doing so you will only add another to the batch of falsehoods which go so far to make up the entire assault on the McKinley bill. Who next?   R. G. HORR.

WHAT WORKERS REALLY NEED.

A resident of Lynn, Mass., writes to The Tribune in comment upon the McKinley bill of which he does not wholly approve) and makes a re-

mark which deserves attention. The tone of his letter is courteous, and perhaps it will be as well to omit his name from this reply to what he says; but his remark should not be allowed to pass unnoticed. He makes the following suggestion as the solution of our present business troubles:

" What the business men, farmers and laboring men need is steady employment. Now, steady work at low wages is much better than high wages with unsteady employment."

This is a remark often made nowadays by a class of men whom I meet in various parts of the country. I have no acquaintance with our correspondent, and not the least idea as to his occupation or position in the business world. His words are, however, identical with those of men I frequently meet, who think that constant toil at low prices is the desired end to be aimed at in the industrial world. My observation is, that such remarks are made only by men who are willing to get gain from the work of other people without regard to the comfort of those who do the work.

I never heard a practical farmer make such a remark for two reasons. Farmers have work enough all the time; they can always find enough to do. Secondly, because they know that low wages mean low prices for what they grow. Any sensible farmer will tell you that he prefers to pay good wages for his help and get good prices for his produce.

I never heard a workingman make such a statement, because I never met one who did not think that good, fair wages for his work was an element which entered largely into his own happiness. I never yet found a workingman who seemed to comprehend the idea that he could profit by low wages if they would only let him work longer each day and more days in each year! There may be a sort of deep significance in such a statement as "steady work at low wages" but it is so deep that it invariably escapes the observation of the average laborer. Somehow such a statement carries no real conviction to his mind.

Again, I never heard such a remark from any manufacturer who takes a broad view of this question and who has the well-being and happiness of his work-people at heart. No man should employ other men who will not guard their well-being as sacredly as he will his own. What would our correspondent think of a workingman who would assert that what the world needs is a set of manufacturers who will run their mills constantly and pay high wages whether there are any profits or not, and that it is better for manufacturers to run constantly, even at a loss, than to run on high prices only a few weeks at a time. That position is as tenable as the one he takes.

Let me state what, it seems to me, business men, farmers and laboring men need. All of them need full employment at fair wages. Good, fair prices for the products of the farm make farmers prosperous and enable them to pay their help good, fair wages. Good, fair prices for the products of shop and factory enable business men to pay good, fair wages to their workmen and should leave them a fair return for their own time and capital invested, and they should always be satisfied with a fair profit. Steady employment at good wages gives the laboring men means with which to purchase the products of the farm, the shop, and the factory, and so make steady employment possible. In short, good wages for people who work and constant employment at good wages is the key to the whole situation. It makes little difference how constantly a man labors if you keep his wages each week at the starvation point, just barely enough to keep body and soul together for himself and his family. He ceases to be a general consumer, indeed he gets no surplus of wages with which to buy ordinary comforts. Lack of consumption is as important an element in producing a glut in the markets, which leads to low prices, as is over-production.

Any economic system based on the statement of our correspondent will end, of necessity, in the degradation of labor and the ruin of the working classes. Any system that produces cheap men and cheap women must lead to misery and want. If we can so manage that the 30,000,000 of working people in the United States shall be constantly employed at good wages, then all the other conditions necessary for a prosperous people will follow as a matter of course. Constant work for little pay may be the best we can do for culprits in our penitentiaries, but it should hardly be hinted at as the thing our entire people need. R. G. HORR.

TARIFF STUDIES.

RICE AND SUGAR.

THE DIFFERENCE BETWEEN A FREE TRADE
TARIFF AND A PROTECTIVE TARIFF
CLEARLY DEFINED.

To the Editor of The Tribune.

Sir: I am a reader of The Weekly Tribune, and am pleased with all your ideas of the Tariff, but as I am almost a ricebird, I am frequently asked by Free Traders hereabouts, "Why was not rice put on the free list as well as sugar?" How much rice is raised in the United States and how much consumed here? I hope to see a reply in The Weekly Tribune. Yours, etc., L. HARLEY.

Williston, S. C., June 6, 1891.

No more pertinent question could be asked than the one suggested by this correspondent. The fact that such questions are constantly being received by The Tribune gives me great satisfaction in the work I am trying to do.

Some Free Traders in South Carolina, it seems, are anxious to know why rice should not have been put in the free list, the same as sugar. There could hardly be two agricultural articles named that better illustrate the two kinds of tariff than do rice and sugar. The duty on sugar has always been simply a revenue duty, that is, a free-trade duty, and hence was repealed by a Congress the majority of whom believed in protective duties. On the other hand, the duty on rice is most clearly a protective duty, and so was retained by the same Congress. The duty on sugar being in the nature of a duty for revenue only, was added to the cost of sugar, and had to be paid by the

ultimate consumers in the United States, for the simple reason that the producers of sugar in this country have failed heretofore to produce enough so as to sensibly affect the price. It has been found by actual experiment that unless we produce in the United States at least one-third of any given article the foreign producers control the price, and duties levied on such articles are simply free-trade duties, and are invariably added to the cost of such articles to the ultimate consumers. The growers of sugar in this country have been promising every year that if the duty on sugar should be left in force they would increase the production, and so in time would control the price; while from year to year this promise has been made, it has never been kept. The best that they have ever been able to do has been to raise about one pound in ten of the amount actually consumed in the United States, and for the last two years they have not raised even that amount.

Sugar is one of the necessities of life. It is consumed by the laboring people in enormous quantities. If our sugar producers could increase the product in this country, so as to furnish one-half or even one-third of the sugar consumed here then a Protectionist would at once restore the duty on sugar, but so long as our sugar producers can furnish only one pound in ten or twelve pounds of the amount consumed, that is too small a quantity perceptibly to affect the market price. It would afford little or no competition, and hence a tariff put upon sugar becomes a simple tax on that article, increases its price and must be paid by the people of this country who finally consume the sugar. It was on account of this admitted fact that sugar was placed on the free list. Indeed, it is much cheaper for this country to pay a bounty to the producers in such a case and so build up the industry by that direct aid. It will be cheaper to foster this industry by the aid of a bounty until the production of sugar shall be increased to a point where we will grow and market at least one-third of the sugar we consume in the United States. That point once reached, then the bounty should be repealed and the duty restored. Let me repeat again, the reason that the duty on sugar was repealed was because, after long years of trial under heavy duties, sugar-growers failed to increase their crop so as to control our markets, and hence that duty became simply a duty for revenue only. It was in no sense a protective duty. It increased the cost of sugar to our own people and was collected largely from the poorer classes of our citizens. In short, it was a simple free-trade duty and should have been repealed long ago. Then why wonder that a Congress made up of a majority of Protectionists should have repealed this duty on sugar? The wisdom of such an act is already evident. Sugar has been cheapened for every family in the United States, precisely as Protectionists predicted that it would be. Strange as it may seem, our Free-Trade friends voted against this clause in the McKinley bill and against cheap sugar for the masses. Now, after voting against this law, they "right about face" and say: "Yes, yes. Free sugar is a good thing. It is all right, but why not free rice also?"

Rice and sugar are both agricultural products, and are limited by the acreage and to the production of one crop in each year. Such productions are not controlled by the same law as are manufactured goods, where plants can be readily multiplied and where continuous running of large factories increases the supply and also cheapens the cost of production. Hence, it does not so surely follow that prices will be reduced by stimulating the production as it does in the case of manufactured products; but sugar and rice producers are compelled to compete with low wages, with cheap labor abroad, fully as much as are any industries in the land. The testimony of all the sugar-growers from the South before the Ways and Means Committee of the last Congress agreed that their labor in this country cost them fully $1 per day for each man employed. The rice-growers all said that the same price is being paid for their help. The cost of labor in Cuba and other sugarcane producing countries as sworn to by those same gentlemen is only 20 cents per day for each laborer, and the wages paid for work in the rice fields of Asia is only from 6 to 14 cents per day. So it becomes evident that if either of these industries survives in the United States, it can only do so by some method which will compensate our producers for these larger wages which they are compelled to pay to the people who do their work.

In the case of sugar, it is cheaper for our people to foster that industry by the payment of a bounty, and will be cheaper just as long as our production is so much less than our consumption of sugar. Why not then put rice on the free list; and give our rice producers a bounty the same as in the case of sugar? That is the question the Free Traders seem to be constantly asking our correspondent. The answer is not difficult. It is simply because the rice industry is a protective industry in this country. The amount of rice produced in the United States as compared with the amount imported shows conclusively that the rice industry is on an entirely different basis from that of sugar. The statements of a few facts as to rice production will show what I mean. In 1865 all the rice produced in the United States was 11,592,000 pounds; in 1870 the production had grown to 47,348,000 pounds; in 1875 the production had reached 72,360,000 pounds; in 1880 it had advanced to 111,766,000 pounds; in 1885 to 151,102,000 pounds; in 1890 our rice-growers furnished for the consumption of our own people 164,200,000 pounds. On the other hand, in 1865 we consumed foreign rice to the amount of 52,408,760 pounds, against 11,592,000 pounds produced at home. In 1870 we imported 27,000,000 pounds as against 47,348,000 raised in the United States. In 1875 we imported 47,062,414 pounds, but our own producers raised that year 72,360,800 pounds. In 1880 we imported 57,910,542 pounds of foreign rice, but we raised from our own plantations that year 117,766,000 pounds. In 1885 we imported 72,446,550 pounds, and our home production for that year was 151,102,020 pounds. In 1890 we imported 151,000,000 pounds, but we raised in this country that year 164,000,000 pounds.

I find upon careful computation that during the last ten years we have consumed in the United States, in round numbers, 1,050,000,000 pounds of foreign rice, and we have grown in this country 1,280,000,000 pounds. Thus you see, while the increase in consumption is something enormous, still, much more than one-half of the entire amount consumed is grown upon our own plantations. When the sugar-growers of this country will make such a comparative showing as that, Protectionists will proceed to drop the bounty and restore the duty on sugar. It must not be forgotten that the duty on rice, which has enabled our rice-growers to cultivate their fields, has so increased the supply of the world that rice is very much cheaper all over the world than it would be but for this enormous production in the United States. Hence it is that the consumers of rice in this country do not by any means pay the entire amount of the duty levied; indeed, a large part of that duty comes from foreign producers, who are compelled to pay it in order to reach our markets.

The rice of the United States is grown mostly in two States—Louisiana and South Carolina. It is very expensive to prepare a rice field, costing from $150 to $200 per acre. Mr. Screven, of Savannah, Ga., a very intelligent witness, said that slave labor formerly cost the Southern planter about twenty cents per day for each workman, and that with that cheap labor they could defy the world in the production of cheap rice. The same witnesses said that, being now compelled to pay $1 per day for labor, without protection no planter could raise rice a single year. Will our Free-Trade friends who are constantly declaring that labor is in no way protected by our duties on foreign products please put this statement of a Southern Democrat into their pipes and smoke it? This same witness stated that the duty on rice had not increased its cost to the consumers. If the duty was removed and no bounty were given it would at once destroy the rice industry in this country. Very likely for a little while rice would be cheaper than it now is, but our rice fields once abandoned, we would then be at the mercy of foreign producers. With an immense decrease in supply and an increase in demand, this would, of course, result in the price going up to such a point as foreign producers might demand. Besides, without either a protective duty or a bounty, our own rice planters would never open a single acre to rice culture. Should the price go up until one of our planters might conclude to try it again, the foreign producer, ever on the watch, would put down the price and ruin the business of the South Carolina or Louisiana rice-growers, and then, when he had forced them to abandon their fields, up would go the price for our consumers. Just that state of affairs has existed many times in the United States as to very many industries. In view of all these facts, would it not be simply idiotic to put rice on the free list? What true American would think of doing it?

But some one says Why not put rice now on the free list and give our producers a bounty? Because, in the case of rice, the bounty would cost our people several times as much as we would save. In the case of sugar the bounty will cost about $7,000,000 per year, but we will save eight times that amount. Of course this sum is not saved to the General Government, but to the laboring classes, who consume the sugar and are compelled to pay the bulk of such a free-trade tariff. If a bounty were placed on rice, it would compel the Government to pay an immense sum in bounty and then would save very little, if anything, to the ultimate consumers, the working people who eat rice. Rice-growers under protection have constantly increased their production, and so have held control of our market. The duty is a protective one, in the case of rice, and should be preserved, while in the case of sugar there is not enough produced in this country to make it a protective industry; yet, in order to preserve the industry, sugar was placed upon the free list and a bounty is offered to sugar producers. When sugar-growers shall do what the rice-growers have already done, when they shall have increased their product from one-tenth of our consumption to over one-half of it, then the duty on sugar should be restored and the bounty repealed. In both these cases our legislation is intended to foster and build up both these industries. Neither of them could live two years without laws favoring them. The free-trade doctrine is that all these laws should be repealed. Our free-trade friends say in so many words: if you cannot raise rice in South Carolina and Louisiana; if you cannot raise sugar in the South and pay $1 per day for labor, and compete with the slave labor of Cuba in the production of sugar, and the 14-cent per day labor of Asia in the production of rice, then stop growing rice and sugar in the United States. They tell us to go to doing something else until our working people can learn to live on 14 cents per day. It is useless to tell them that rice lands will produce nothing else; that the sugar industry is an important one for the planters of the South. It seems also useless to tell them that labor should be protected in this country; that to reduce our working people to Chinese wages is to degrade them; that such a policy will end in ruin to this country. They have a theory that each nation should attempt only what it can do cheapest, and they leave out of the problem entirely the great lesson taught by long experience, that diversified industry is what makes a nation strong and rich. They forget that constant employment at good wages is what makes a people happy and prosperous. They overlook the fact that men who work can afford to pay a fair price for what they consume, if, at the same time their own product brings a fair price, so that they get for each day's work good wages.

I now leave it to any candid Free-Trader whether my explanation is not complete. I hope and believe that the bounty on sugar will in a few years change that into a protective industry. Rice is most clearly such an industry now. My hope is that rice will stay where it is and that sugar will get there at an early date. The general activity already seen in various parts of the United States to establish the growth of sugar beets gives me great confidence in the belief that sugar in the United States in a very few years will be largely grown by our own people.

Even the Mills bill did not attack rice and sugar. If that measure, which aimed such a deadly blow at so many of the industries of the United States, omitted an assault upon rice and sugar, why should our free-trade friends worry themselves over these two industries? I hope at least that my answer to this correspondent will prove satisfactory to the "Ricebirds" of South Carolina, even though some of the sugar-producers may not enjoy my statement that a bounty is better for the people of this country on sugar than a protective duty.

R. G. HORR.

"IS THE TARIFF A TAX?"

A QUESTION WHICH WILL BE ANSWERED IF THE QUESTIONER WILL DEFINE HIS TERMS.

A list of questions propounded to The Tribune by George Huston, of Limeton, Va., are referred to me for answers. The first question reads as follows: "Is the tariff a tax? If so, who pays it? If it is not, than what is it?"

Before answering the list of questions of this correspondent, I am compelled to ask him for an explanation so as to enable me to get started on the very first question. What kind of a tariff do you mean? Some tariff duties may be called a "tax"; some may not be; some are paid by the consumers and some are not. Again, what is your definition of a "tax"? The word is used in many different senses by different persons. I have three times listened to very long and exhaustive debates in Congress on the tariff, and much time was devoted to this very question as to "whether a tariff is a tax." At the close of each debate I was impressed with what seemed to me to be the fact that a large amount of time and talk had been expended simply because the disputants did not agree in their definition of terms.

Let me illustrate. I have here on my table a letter from a correspondent which reads as follows: "Are not silver certificates money? In one of Mr. Horr's articles it seems to me he intimates that they are not money, though he does not say exactly that. If they are not money, what are they?" Is it not evident that the answer to that question depends entirely upon the definition of the word "money"? If you will examine the different authors you will find that the word money has been defined in more than a dozen different ways; and my correspondent may have still another definition as to just what money is. How is it possible to answer his question unless I know what he means by the term he uses? According to one definition, silver certificates could by no manner of means be called money; according to another they would be money, and so would bank checks and Clearing House certificates, and even promissory notes. If they are not money what are they? Why, of course, they are silver certificates.

"If a tariff is not a tax, what is it?" says Mr. Huston. It is a tariff, a duty levied on imports, all the same whether it is a tax or not. Some duties are a "tax," according to one definition of the word; some are not. Some taxes are burdens; some are blessings. A free-trade tariff is one thing; a protective tariff is quite another. A free-trade tariff may be always paid by the consumer; a protective tariff may seldom be, and when a portion of it is may still be better for the consumer, on account of other advantages. Hence my question: What kind of a tariff do you mean? What is your definition of a tax? Let us try and get started right and understand each other.

R. G. HORR.

IS AMERICAN TIN PLATE COATED WITH AMERICAN TIN?

To the Editor of The Tribune.

Sir: Will you please answer through the columns of The Tribune whether there is now any tin plate being made in the United States which is washed with tin mined in this country. The Free Traders say there are no tin mines in the United States; therefore no use of the tariff on that metal. Also state where the tin mines in the United States are located, and what estimate is placed on their value by those who are competent to judge. W. S. VAN REMER.

Rondout, N. Y., May 8, 1891.

There is to-day no tin plate coated with tin which is mined in this country. Tin plate is now being manufactured, however, in several establishments in the United States; and many more factories are being now erected. The steel and iron plates (which compose 96 per cent of all ordinary tin plate) are being already made in this country; but the tin for coating them is imported from the old world.

You state that the Free Traders say there is no tin mined in the United States; therefore, there is no use of the tariff on that metal. If they stated that, we will give them credit for telling the truth once. The fact is, there is no tariff duty on tin metal at present. Tin is on the free list. The duty about which Free Traders complain is on the tin plate. Our manufactures can buy the raw metal to-day just as cheaply as can the tin-plate makers of South Wales. And even the increased duty on tin plate will not take effect until July 1 next. Time has been given by the McKinley Bill for erecting the new machinery for producing tin plate before the tariff will take effect.

While American tin is not yet being used to coat tin plates, there are, nevertheless, at the present time, two large mines producing American tin in the United States. One is in South Dakota, a few miles from Rapid City, in the Black Hills; the other is in California; both of these mines are now being worked by between two and three hundred men. I have before me on my table a little anvil, just sent me from the Dakota mine, manufactured from pure American tin. It is marked, "American Tin, from Cow Boy Mine, Hill City, South Dakota; compliments Harney Peak Consolidated Tin Company." My information recently received from both this mine and the one in California is that the veins of tin ore are well defined, that the ore is rich, that milling plants are being erected, and that in both these mines the operators expect to be producing, in a few months, large quantities of pure metallic tin.

It is a little singular how persistently the Free Traders continue to sneer at the tin industry of the United States. It might be discouraging, were it not for the fact that the sneer is a very old one. I heard precisely the same jeering remarks, in the same sarcastic tone when we first attempted to make steel rails in the United States; also when the plate-glass industry was established, and when our crockery factories were opened. Indeed, I do not now recollect a single instance of a successful industry in the United States that has not been built up in the face of free-trade sneers. If we can judge the future by the past, the bulk of our tin plate will yet be made here in the United States, and a full supply of tin will be taken from our own mines, in spite of all these persistent scoffers. It would please me very much to have such an industry built up in the United States. I hope it will be surely done, even though it should result in breaking the hearts of our free-trade friends. Is it not a little strange that they should take such constant delight in their persistent effort to belittle every attempt to produce any new thing in this country? I would not train with a crowd which seems to consider it a duty to discourage every attempt to do anything in the United States. These men who are always sneering at what is American, and who do nothing but pour cold water on every American enterprise, ought to be ashamed of themselves. I prefer to encourage every attempt to build up a new industry in my own country, and shall always rejoice over the success of men who have the pluck and energy to start new enterprises.

R. G. H.

WHY SUGAR DOES NOT GO DOWN THREE AND A HALF CENTS.

A NEW ILLUSTRATION OF THE DIFFERENCE BETWEEN A FREE TRADE AND A PROTECTIVE TARIFF

To the Editor of The Tribune.

Sir: The tariff on sugar before the change of the law was 3 1-2 cents a pound, and it is now 1-2 a cent per pound. Can you tell me why the retail price has not changed more? It was not above 6 3-4 cents a pound at any time in March. Instead of going down three cents, it has not changed two cents. Are not the sugar Trusts getting in their fine work? Please answer and oblige. J. OSCAR TERREL.

Honesdale, Penn., April 30, 1891.

As a rule, duties levied on articles which we do not produce are added to the cost of the article to the American consumer. We do not produce sugar in this country in quantities sufficient to enable our production to enter as much of a factor into the competition of the world; and, of course, any duty levied on such an article would increase its price. But there are so many circumstances which enter into fixing the price of any commodity that the mere amount of duty paid is not of itself a statement of enough facts to determine the reason for any given price.

One might suppose that a duty of 3 1-2 cents a pound on granulated sugar would add just that amount to the cost of the article, and that when the duty was decreased to 1-2 cent a pound such sugar would at once fall in price 3 cents a pound. But the duty on the lower grades of sugar out of which granulated sugar is made only averaged about 2 cents a pound, and the balance of the 3 1-2 cents, that is, 1 1-2 cents a pound, was the duty on the manufactured article. That duty of 1 1-2 cents a pound has not been added to the cost of the article. Owing to the brisk competition among our own refiners, they have kept the price down for the manufactured article, and have not added the duty on refined sugar to the price. They have added only the 2 cents a pound that was paid on the lower grades of sugar. Hence there was no reason to suppose that refined sugars would fall in price more than about 2 cents a pound. That 2 cents duty on the low grades of sugar was, in its essential character, a free trade duty and increased the cost to the consumer about that amount. The extra 1 1-2 cents a pound was a protective duty to aid our refiners of sugar and was not added to the price to the consumer.

That sugar did not fall in price even the 2 cents a pound which was formerly paid on the low grades is readily accounted for. The families and hotels who buy in large quantities, the grocery men, both retail and wholesale, had been preparing for the change. All these persons managed to have as little on hand as possible April 1, when the law went into operation. As soon as the change took place all these persons began to call for their new supply, and that enormous demand which could not be met in a day held up the price of refined and high-grade sugars.

In such a large country as ours the means of transportation may be wonderful, yet it takes time to reach all our people with any article. It is clear that time enough has not yet elapsed to see what sugar will finally bring in this country. If our Free-Trade friends are correct in their theories, then refined sugar should soon be sold for 3 cents a pound less than it has been selling for under the 3 1-2 cents duty. I do not look for any such reduction. Sugar, it seems to me, should be about 2 cents a pound cheaper. If the 1-2 cent per pound shall prove to be sufficient to enable our manufacturers to keep their refineries in operation, then sugar will decline about the amount of the former duty on low-grade sugars and only about that amount. If the manufacturers of our country should be driven out of the business, then in a little while we will pay more for our sugar than if we had kept them running. I hope they will be able to prosper on the 1-2 cent a pound now levied on the imported article.

I do not know whether there is any Sugar Trust which can affect prices now or not. I do know that if our manufacturers of refined sugar were driven out of existence we would be in much greater danger from foreign combinations than we are now. The larger the number of operators the more difficult it is to form combinations. It was intended to place the duty on refined sugars at a point where it would give our refiners of sugar full protection against the cheaper labor of the Old World—and so also as to give them control of our home markets. If this shall prove to

be the practical result, then sugar will soon be as cheap in the United States as it can possibly be and pay fair wages to American workmen. That is as cheap as any good citizen of this country ought to desire it to be. That will be about 2 cents a pound. If it shall be much less than that then it will be owing to some outside influence which I do not now understand. If it shall be much more than that then I shall be surprised.

If the theories of Free-Trade writers are true then the decline should be 3 cents a pound. I do not believe their theories, and so do not look for any such reduction in the price of sugar. Time will demonstrate which of us is right. R. G. H.

THE TARIFF OF GREAT BRITAIN.

There seems to be an impression among many people in the United States that Great Britain is a purely free-trade nation. Such is by no means the case. The following table will show the exact amount of money collected in the United Kingdom by tariff duties for the years ending March 31, 1889 and 1890:

Articles.	Year ending March 31, 1890.	Year ending March 31, 1889.
Tea	$23,149,505	$22,432,530
Coffee	921,460	804,160
Spirits, foreign	21,483,170	23,106,125
Wine	6,052,685	6,510,800
Tobacco and snuff	41,293,905	45,309,920
Currants, raisins and dried fruits	2,897,145	2,674,153
Other articles	899,000	915,785
Miscellaneous receipts.......	159,095	144,340
Total	$99,855,955	$102,277,815

A glance at this table will show that England collected in 1889 over $102,000,000, and in 1890 nearly $100,000,000 by duties levied on foreign imports. The table further shows that nearly $70,000,000 was collected from the two items of tea and tobacco. It will be further seen that these duties were all of them levied upon articles the like of which were not produced in Great Britain. That is the Free-Trade plan of levying duties. England goes still further, and makes it a misdemeanor under her laws for her citizens to raise tobacco at all. My objections to that kind of a duty are twofold:

First, a duty levied on articles that cannot be produced in the country which levies it is always added to the price of the article, and must, of course, be paid by the consumers of such articles. The levying of such a duty cannot stimulate the production of similar articles in the country levying the duty, because no such articles are produced in that country. It builds up no industry, produces no competition, and can in no possible manner lead to the cheapening of the articles. Such a duty may always be called a tax on the consumers.

Secondly, the customs received from such imports must be paid almost entirely by the poor and laboring classes of the country. For example, take the two items of tea and tobacco. The people of the United Kingdom paid on those two articles each year over $67,000,000. Who paid that large sum? Most clearly the people who drank the tea and who consumed the tobacco. Both of those articles are in common use among the laboring people of Great Britain. No doubt a workingman consumes nearly the same amount of each of those articles each day that a rich man does. Now, as there are 600 working-people in Great Britain to every one who can be called rich, about six hundred times as much of that money was collected from the working-people as came from the rich people of that country.

Under the protective system we levy duties on articles that can be produced in the United States. In doing so, we foster and build up our own industries; the duties levied in such a case are largely paid by foreign people seeking to get possession of our markets.

However, I publish this table simply for the purpose of showing the readers of The Weekly Tribune that Great Britain is in no sense free from custom houses and custom collections. Whenever, after this, any Free Trader states that what he wants is free trade in the United States such as England has, point out this table to him, and then ask him if what he means is not really, that he would have this country levy its duties on the English free-trade plan. That plan necessarily collects its revenues mostly from the poorer classes, and we do not propose to have it adopted in the United States. We very much prefer that the tariff should be so levied that it will give good wages to our working people and compel the rich people of this country and the importers of foreign goods to supply the funds for running the Nation.   R. G. H.

WHO IS ENTITLED TO THE SUGAR BOUNTY?

A PRESSING NEED NOW FOR THE INVENTION

OF LOW PRICED AND SATISFACTORY

PLANTS FOR MAKING SUGAR.

To the Editor of The Tribune.

Sir: I am a poor farmer who raised about one ton of sugar. I want to know if I can get a bounty for that small amount. I had it boiled up in a vacuum pan. It is of a sort of yellowish color. I believe that it is of 16 Dutch standard.   ARTHUR POCHE.
Ponchatoula, La.

By a glance at the sugar schedule our correspondent will see that no bounty is paid on any sugar produced before July 1, 1891. After that date and until July 1, 1905, any person producing 500 pounds or more can get a bounty of two cents a pound on all such sugar, if it shall test not less than ninety degrees by the polariscope. If it shall test less than ninety degrees and not less than eighty degrees by the polariscope, the bounty is fixed at one and three-fourths cents per pound.

In order to obtain the bounty the producer must file with the Commissioner of Internal Revenue a notice "of the place of production, with a general description of the machinery and methods to be employed by him; an estimate of the amount of sugar proposed to be produced in the current or next ensuing year, including the number of maple trees to be tapped, and an application for a license so to produce. He must also file a bond, with sureties, to be approved by the Commissioner of Internal Revenue, conditioned that he will faith-

fully observe all rules and regulations that shall be prescribed for such manufacture and production of sugar. No bounty is to be paid on any sugar, except such as shall be produced from sorghum, beets or sugar cane grown within the United States, or from maple sap produced within the United States, at the place and with the machinery and by the methods described in the application; but said license shall not extend beyond one year from the date thereof."

All these precautions were deemed necessary to guard against the fraudulent claiming of bounties on sugars imported into this country. It is clear that the framers of this law believed that the great bulk of sugar produced from beets or sugar cane would be manufactured from the beets and cane by men who would put up machinery for that purpose, and in that way that the farmers who raise only 100, 200, 300 or 400 pounds of sugar could get this bounty by selling their beets or cane to these manufacturers.

As a rule the men who raise sugar-cane produce enough to pay them for taking out a license when they make up their own cane into sugar.

The Internal Revenue Department will no doubt furnish blanks for all persons desiring them, with full instructions just how to proceed so as to secure this bounty. Address "Commissioner of Internal Revenue, Washington, D. C."

The object of this bounty is to stimulate the production of sugar in this country. We have of late not been able to produce over one pound in ten of the sugar which our people consume. That ought not to be the case. It is believed that the raising of sugar beets will lead up to the solution of this problem in the United States. Two or three very large enterprises of this kind have already been established, notably one in Nebraska and one in California. These are mammoth concerns, and are making an immense outlay of capital. The more such institutions the better; and yet I am inclined to think that the real solution of this problem must come from the establishment of an immense number of smaller concerns. If some one can invent a process, so that for a few thousand dollars a plant can be erected which will utilize the sugar beets grown in each township or neighborhood (as cider mills now utilize and make up the "cider apples" of each neighborhood), the production of our own sugar would at once be assured.

People are fast learning how to grow the sugar beet and improve its sugar-bearing qualities. In 1829 the sugar beet yielded only 2 1-2 per cent of sugar to the weight of the beet. Ten years ago a rate of 9 per cent had been reached. In 1889 the German crop is reported to have yielded 14 per cent. Every addition of one per cent means an increase of 20 pounds of sugar per ton, and about 300 pounds increase to the acre. In Nebraska an analysis of 315 samples gave a trifle over 16 per cent as the average. Different fields vary in the amount of sugar to the ton of beets; sections of the same field also vary. It is safe to say that a fair average in this country will be fourteen pounds of sugar from each 100 pounds of beets. The quality of the sugar beet has been constantly improved by careful propagation, and selecting the very best for seed-raising purposes. It requires about twenty pounds of seed to plant an acre of sugar beets. They should be planted about eighteen inches apart, and kept clean from weeds. If well tilled an acre will produce from fourteen to thirty tons of sugar beets, depending on the kind of soil and its richness.

The plant for manufacturing sugar at Grand Island, Neb., cost $500,000. When making sugar it runs night and day, and employs 100 men on each shift, or 200 each day. It uses up 250 tons of beets a day. When the industry is fully established the factory can be run about five months in a year.

In California they report a yield of about fifteen tons per acre, and a net profit varying from $35 to $45 per acre, over and above all labor. Where the land will yield twenty-five tons to the acre of course the extra expense is small and the net profits are enormously increased.

The very large beets are not the best sugar producers. It is found that when the weight rises above about three pounds to the beet the quality becomes rapidly poorer. But the size can be readily graduated when thinning by leaving the plants nearer together.

I am largely indebted for the foregoing facts to Mr. David O'Brine, chemist of Colorado. I have given them here because, go where I will, the people are constantly asking me about the details of this new industry.

The inquiry is also becoming very general as to how small and how cheap a plant can be run with profit. I am utterly unable to answer this last question. It is a very important one, and The Tribune now invites any person knowing the facts to send a statement to this paper. We will gladly give publicity to any information which will bear upon this question, not as an advertisement, but as a matter of news which will be of great interest to many readers. Let me repeat the question: How small and how cheap a plant can be obtained, which will manufacture sugar from beets so as to insure profit for the manufacturer and a fair price per ton for the beets?

I will add that at large establishments the quality of each farmer's crop is ascertained by what seems to be a fair process, and then he is paid per ton according to the amount of sugar in his special crop.

If there is as yet in existence no plant that will meet this coming demand for neighborhood use, will some ingenious Yankee proceed to supply the needs of the country in that regard? The man who shall succeed in making such a plant need be troubled no longer after his invention with "mortgages on his farm." R. G. H.

CAN RICH MILL OWNERS COMBINE AND ROB THE PEOPLE?

A PERTINENT QUESTION SQUARELY ANSWERED
To the Editor of The Tribune.

Sir: If, under free trade, English manufacturers could obtain a monopoly of our markets and then raise prices to suit themselves, why under protection cannot the manufacturers of the United States combine and advance their prices to the consumer by the amount of duty collected on their products?

Tioc, Il   EDGAR SAMPSON.

Let me say, first, that no duty is collected on the products of American factories, shops and mills. Many people think that American products pay a duty. It may be that Mr. Sampson thinks so. But that is not the case. The only goods that pay a duty are those imported from foreign lands. Mr. Sampson's question amounts to this: Can American manufacturers combine and advance prices, and themselves virtually collect from the people and put into their own pockets a sum of money equal to what the Government collects in the form of duty on foreign goods?

If we should not produce a particular article in the United States, then the foreign producers of it would have no competition from manufacturers in the United States. They could then manipulate prices to suit themselves. They would not do this by getting a "monopoly" of our markets. There are no "monopolies" in this country, except those granted to people who secure a patent for an invention or new discovery. Our Government never grants to any one the exclusive right to manufacture or sell any article, except in cases of patent rights. The Constitution of the United States prohibits the granting of all monopolies in this country. Every one is free to manufacture and sell (limited only by patent rights), if he has the capital. Combinations are, however, found which sometimes control prices almost as effectually as if monopolies were granted. These combinations are more readily formed where the number of producers are small, and where the producers all live in foreign lands and are beyond the reach of our laws and public opinion. In no country in the world have more of these combinations been found, from time to time, than in England. American consumers have suffered from them repeatedly. They are not under control of our laws, and are beyond the reach of our public opinion. But can manufacturers in this country combine and put up prices to the amount of the duty? A combination in America to raise prices here is difficult. Combinations are frequently formed or attempted, but few of them ever succeed, and the combinations which are lasting are, as a rule, those which do not attempt to raise prices. An illustration of this is the Standard Oil Company. We often speak of that company as an immense "monopoly," and yet it is nothing of the kind. It is however, a mammoth combination which wields wonderful power. It almost absolutely controls the oil markets of the world, yet it does not put up the price of oil in this country. It may fix the price of oil in the Old World with great ease, but it has not ventured to make oils high in the United States. It has, by great skill in its management, cheapened the cost of oil to the American public greatly. It can produce oil more cheaply than any other concern in the world. Its members have amassed immense fortunes, yet those fortunes are small compared with the money saved to the consumers of oil in the United States by cheapening that article for home consumption. That corporation has been governed by men who had the sense to see that the company would be tolerated in this country only so long as it benefited our people by producing oil cheaper than that produced by any concern which made it in small quantities and which did not have the piping and other facilities for saving freights and refining at the lowest possible cost. It is clear that our people have been large gainers by the fact that that company is located here, under our own laws, where our public opinion can reach its stockholders. No doubt they have furnished oil to our people much cheaper than to any other folks in the world. That shows the advantage of having an article produced by parties living in the United States.

The moment you open up the manufacture of any article in the United States the total supply of that article is increased, and the price tends to decrease both here and in the Old World, where they are at once cut off from a portion of their markets.

But, you ask, why cannot our own manufacturers combine and put up the price to the consumer and pocket the amount of the duty imposed on the foreign articles? The answer is (1) because the duty is nearly all offset by the higher wages paid in this country; and (2) the moment the manufacturers advance the price foreign goods will come in and break down the market again. You must not forget that, when we rely on foreign manufacturers, we nearly always pay more for goods than they are really worth. We are paying to-day more for tin plate than we should pay. The foreign manufacturer, together with his agent, the importer, controls the price. We are at their mercy. Our people can make tin plate cheaper than it is selling for in this country to-day, and pay our higher price for labor; and the reason they ask protection on that article is that when they drive the prices down the cheap labor of England cannot step in and put the price still lower, so low that our manufacturers could not live and pay our better wages. If they should put the prices up as you suggest the foreigners would at once come in and undersell them and their market would be gone.

Do you not see that a combination to put up prices could not be formed so as to be effective, except by including producers in both the Old World and the New, which is not an easy thing to do? It was tried with reference to salt last year, but failed; it could not be managed. Will our correspondent learn the present price of tin plate and mark it down, and then keep a careful watch of that article, and see if we do not cheapen it by making it in this country? The Free Trader is constantly asserting that all the manufacturer in this country desires from a tariff is the power to put up the price of his goods. That is false. No tariff was ever yet levied when the object was not a double one—first, to protect the labor of this country and enable us to pay good wages; and secondly, to cheapen the price of the article for the consumers. Both objects have so far always been reached. I would like to agree upon a test case where we can soon arrive at the facts. Mr. Norton, of Chicago, states squarely that he believes in thirty-six months tin plates, which now cost $5 75 a box, will be made and sold for $4 a box here in the United States. If that shall take place, what would be the use of theorizing any longer?

Do not worry about the price of articles being put up on account of making them in this country aided by protection laws, after the protection is fairly in operation. There is no such case on record to-day. Not one. So far the price has been reduced. Do not forget my statement. One object always sought by a protective tariff on manufactured articles is to cheapen the cost of the article to our consumers. This is always done by improvements in methods of production, by the greater intelligence and skill of our workmen and by the increased competition caused by the new industry, none of which can exist until the industry has been established and built up by a protective tariff. When thus built up, I know of no instance where cheapening of the price of the goods has not taken place. It has been the case with cotton goods, woollen goods, silk goods, hardware, crockery, glass, the products of steel and iron, paper of all kinds, salt, chemicals of every description, etc., etc. If there is danger of such combinations, why have they not been formed in these cases?   R. G. H.

ARE TAXES EVER A BLESSING

POINTED QUESTIONS BY A CLEAR-HEADED MINNESOTA MAN.

MR. HORR TRIES TO GIVE THEM A FAIR AND SQUARE ANSWER.

To the Editor of The Tribune.

Sir: I am a workingman and belong to a labor organization, and am reading Mr. Horr's articles with great interest. I think he is right on the tariff. A large number of the laboring men about here believe in the doctrine of protection. We think it secures us good wages.

Just at this time the members of our society are discussing other questions. In one of Mr. Horr's articles he states that taxes may be blessings and not burdens. We plain people consider taxes burdensome and often irksome. There is a strong feeling among us also that the Government should own the telegraph lines, the railroads, and should furnish all the money needed by the people, without any banks having anything to do with the issue of the currency. Mr. Horr has several times in his articles spoken of certain things as being outside the legitimate work of the Government. I am requested to ask him a few questions and hope he will see fit to answer them as early as possible, because, I assure you, they are all questions which are being asked by the entire working people of the West.

First. What does he mean when he says a "tax may be a blessing"?

Second. Are not all taxes, of necessity, burdens?

Third. Why should not the Government own and operate the railroads and telegraph lines?

Fourth. Why should not the Government issue all the paper money needed by the people and so save the interest now paid to the National banks on the Government bonds?

I shall watch the Weekly Tribune for a reply.

OSCAR WILDER.

Minneapolis, Minn., April 25, 1891.

These questions of our correspondent are a good illustration of the fact that it is very much easier to ask questions than it is to answer them. A full answer to his four brief questions would require a book. I will, however, give my answers to them in as brief a manner as is possible in a newspaper article, and shall hope that brevity will not cause my reply to be obscure.

In reply to the first two questions, I will say that taxation is an outgrowth of civilization. Among savages there are no assessors, no tax collectors. How does it come in a republican form of government that such a thing as a tax is known? We must not forget that in this country the entire people are the government. When our forefathers landed on the American continent they found the country occupied by wild savages. They brought with them the customs of civilization.

The very first thing they did was necessarily to build houses for shelter. Each family naturally built its own domicile, one aiding the other as necessities required, on some agreed basis of labor.

WORKS OF A PUBLIC NATURE.

Probably the first work of a public nature was the building of some kind of a fortification to protect the community from the encroachments of the savages. No doubt almost every able-bodied man in the colony gave his full share of time to that work.

The next public work that followed was undoubtedly the building of a road. At first that was probably done by the voluntary work of each individual. In a little while, as the colony increased in size and wealth began to be accumulated, the needs of a passable roadway became more imperative. People began to be engrossed in their private affairs and to be absent when the needed work of repairing the road was required. Now no one will claim that the building of the street in the outset was a burden, any more than the building of the house or the tilling of the soil. It will be readily admitted by every one that the building of a passable roadway in the community was an actual blessing to every one living in the colony. It soon became evident that while some residents of the community were on hand and ready to do their share of the work, there were quite a number of others, many of them able to do, who absented themselves from this work. The entire people, coming together, formed themselves into an organized community and designated certain boundaries as constituting a township. A majority of the people constituting the township took up the question as to how the roads should be built and kept in repair. As a matter of exact justice, they finally decided upon the plan of levying a small poll tax on each able-bodied man, and then a road tax on each individual in the community, on the theory that every man would use the street more or less, hence the poll tax, and that the more property a man had the more benefit a good road would be to him. By this adjustment it was intended that each man should aid in the building of that road precisely to the extent that he should have been willing to pay had the work all been done voluntarily. If the street was a blessing to that community, then the tax for making the street was a blessing. It could not be called a burden by any man who was willing to do his full share in the enterprise. If he would share in the benefits, why should he not cheerfully pay his part of the expense? Any man who calls such a tax a burden, it seems to me, must be trying to shirk his part of the necessary work; and it is simply one form of saying that he would like all the advantages if he can only have them at the expense of his neighbors.

In a little while the people of each growing community in this country felt the need of education for their children. The first impression would naturally be that each man should provide for the education of his own children, and that schools, if organized, should be maintained entirely by private enterprise. It, however, soon became apparent in every community that poor people often have large families, and that to leave the education of children entirely to the ability and disposition of parents would result in a large proportion of these children growing up in ignorance. To prevent such a calamity, it becomes necessary to have the education of the rising generation looked after and provided for as a public necessity. The moment you admit that the entire community ought to attend to the education of all the children, then the question of establishing and supporting schools is placed upon precisely the same basis as the building of roads. That is, each individual, in every community, ought voluntarily to do his full share toward educating all the children of his district. The school tax is then simply a fair distribution of what each man in the community ought voluntarily to pay for the cause of education. Hence if education is a blessing to a community, then school houses and school teachers are blessings also, and the tax which builds up one and supports the other is a blessing, too. The man who claims that such a tax is a burden is simply declaring that it is burdensome for him to do his full duty to the community in which he lives.

As the various communities increased in number and size, it became necessary to have an organization of these various communities, and hence came the formation of counties. Within the limits of these large organizations, rivers must be bridged. The entire people of the entire county were interested in having more extended communications; and, while the bridging of a large stream might be beyond the limited means of any one township, the entire townships of the county could afford to undertake even so expensive a work as that; hence the county tax for building bridges. Are not bridges blessings to the entire people of a county? Then why should they not be built by the entire people? Here again the tax for building bridges should be exactly the amount that each person ought to pay voluntarily for that public improvement.

WHEN A TAX IS A "BURDEN."

All city taxes should be levied only for purposes that benefit the people of the city. The police tax, the water tax, the tax for lighting the streets and paving them, the sewerage tax, etc., should only be levied for the benefit of the people. Indeed, all taxes should be levied upon this one principle, that it will simply require each individual to pay just the amount for all public necessities that he would voluntarily pay if he had a proper sense of his duty toward the community in which he lives.

Taxes should be looked upon as "burdens" only when the money is expended extravagantly or corruptly, or when a large portion of the property owners evade the enlistment of their property, and by so doing throw an unfair amount on the property actually assessed.

Let me repeat: In this country, the people levy the taxes on themselves, and if they had the power to get an honest enlistment of the entire property of the country and could secure an honest expenditure of every dollar so raised, all taxes should be blessings. If such a state of affairs could be realized, then to pay taxes would not be called "burdensome" any more than one would call it a "burden" to buy the food he eats or the clothes he wears. If all property could be fairly assessed and all money raised by taxation honestly and carefully expended only for public purposes, then this outcry against taxation would cease, except from persons who desire to live at the expense of other people.

STATE CONTROL OF RAILROADS.

In answer to your third question: Just what kinds of business had better be managed by the General Government is a matter which has never been fully decided by the experience of the past ages. There has never been any uniform practice among the civilized peoples of the world upon this subject. As a general proposition, it is conceded by most thoughtful men that the primary object of every government should be to protect the lives, property and liberty of its citizens; and that no business should be managed by the nation except such of a public nature as cannot well be done by private enterprise.

As a rule, it is much more expensive for the Government to do any kind of work than it is for private individuals. The Capitol of the State of New-York has already cost the people of that State over twenty millions of dollars. The same building, by individual management, built by men working for themselves, could have been completed in just as good style for less than half that sum. As a rule, the work done by the General Government is much more expensive than the same grade of work done by private individuals. I do not believe it would be possible for the General Government to manage the railroads of the United States anywhere near as cheaply and as well as they are being managed to-day by the private corporations which own and control them. This may not be true to any great extent of the telegraph lines.

As against this theory, I am well aware that our great system of mail service is constantly quoted. I am ready to admit that this service, taken as a whole, may be named as a great success. It is by no means clear, however, that private enterprise would not have done the same work just as well with much less expense. True, we send our letters and packages at a low rate; but we send them at a lower rate than it costs the Government. In the United States, the receipts of the mail service, with the exception of a very few years, have never been sufficient to pay the expenses of the service. Several hundred millions of dollars have been drawn from the General Treasury to meet the deficiencies of that depart-

ment. Several hundred millions more have been drawn for the purposes of building postoffice buildings which have never been charged up to that account. But the carrying of mails is a matter of so much interest to almost every citizen in the United States, and must be done over all kinds of public highways, that I am inclined to think that it is, on the whole, best that it should be done, as it now is, by the General Government. I am not sure, if the telegraph business could be combined with the postoffice service, that the same might be said of that business. But even admit that and it by no means follows that the Government should also run the railroads.

I see no reason why the General Government should own and manage the great railroad systems of this country; but, if the railroads, why not all the stage lines, all the steamboats and vessels doing business in our coast trade, on the inland lakes and rivers of the United States? If all those things should be managed by the General Government, why should not the farms, the factories, the mines and the machine shops also be managed and owned by the General Government? It seems to me far wiser that all such things should be managed by private enterprise leaving power of certain limitations of them all in the hands of the people. To add to the present enormous patronage of the General Government the supervision and management of the entire railroad system would be to create such a centralization of power as would, it seems to me, be dangerous in the extreme. There are of course, now and then, enormous undertakings which can be provided for only by the combined wealth of the Nation. The improvement of the Mississippi River, the building of a railroad to the Pacific, when that was a mere experiment, may be given as instances of such enterprises. In short, my idea is that the business of any nation is always safer in the hands of private individuals than it possibly can be in the hands of everybody.

The idea of modern socialism, that the government should own everything and manage everything, that the people should all work for everybody and no one for himself, has no foundation in human organism. There is no proof in the past experience of the human race that such a plan would be possible. The whole scheme seems to be contrary to the dictates of good common sense. Legislation should be so shaped as to protect our people in all laudable enterprises and then carefully to guard the people against the encroachments and combinations of all corporate and associated wealth. With these restrictions I would give individual capacity, energy and enterprise full scope.

What the people need is not that Government should control more patronage or manage more enterprises, but rather that the efforts of each individual should be properly encouraged, so that every person shall have the same chance of success in his honest endeavor to build up some successful business. It is individual prosperity which makes up the life of a nation. People will always work more faithfully for themselves than for everybody. Give every man an equal chance and the law of personal interest will solve the problem of national growth and individual prosperity.

SHALL GOVERNMENT DO BANKING?

In reply to your last question, I will say that the length of this article prevents a very full answer. Within a few weeks I hope to publish my views as to the utility of National banks, in which this subject will be more fully discussed.

The issuing of paper money or notes payable on demand was never resorted to by this Nation until it was done as a war measure. The present greenbacks would never have been in existence had not the necessities incident to a civil war required them. They are simply demand notes of the United States, which the Government since 1879 has redeemed on presentation. Their redemption and reissue compels the Government to engage in what may be called a species of banking business. That is another kind of work which I doubt the propriety of the Government doing.

At present the National banks can not afford to accept the issue of National bank bills. Government bonds are at so high a premium that no National bank can buy and hold them for security and receive only ninety cents of circulation for each one dollar of their face value, and then make a single cent out of their circulation over and above what could be made by loaning money with which the bonds are purchased. That this is true is demonstrated by the fact that over one hundred millions of National bank circulation have been surrendered within the last ten years.

It seems to me almost nonsensical that the Government should be expected to issue its notes, payable on demand, to meet what is called the needs of private individuals. Our Constitution provides that the National Government shall have entire control of the coining of money. That is a wise provision, but that is simply done so that the people may know how much pure metal there is in each coin. That is an entirely different matter from issuing promissory notes.

In a very few years the entire bonded indebtedness of the United States will be paid. When that is done what necessity will exist which can require the Government to issue demand notes? The greenbacks were issued for the purpose of defraying the necessary expenses of the Government. Government bonds were issued for the same purpose. But at that time our expenditures were very much in excess of our revenues. To-day the revenues exceed the expenditures. It seems very clear that the Nation will be able to meet this bonded indebtedness as fast as it becomes due. The moment the bonds are all cancelled then there will be no more interest to save. If more greenbacks were issued the Government could not compel the holder of the bonds to surrender them until they are due. They will all mature in a few years and will be paid in a business-like way. With the receipts of the Government in excess of its expenditures, what object could be gained by the Government issuing more demand notes? In the end it would reduce itself to the simple proposition as to whether it would be wise for the Nation to issue circulating medium for the purpose of loaning the same to individuals. In other words, if there had been no civil war there would not be in existence to-day a single greenback or Treasury note payable on demand. Suppose that were the condition of affairs to-day. Would you then consider it wise for the Government to issue a single dollar of such money? If so, for what purpose? If it would not have been wise for them to do so except as a war measure, then why should we not get back as quickly as possible to the point from which we started?

The modern attempt of a few men to have the Government embark in the business of issuing notes, payable on demand, for the purpose of loaning them to certain individuals on time, is to me so visionary and preposterous as hardly to need any notice. Yet it seems to me that the result involved in your question must end in precisely that kind of business. It appears very clear that the whole people (that is the General Government) have the right to borrow money or even issue demand notes in order to meet the imperative needs of the Government. But that does not imply their right to either borrow money or issue such notes for the benefit of individuals. The issuing of silver and gold certificates is an entirely different business from the one your question involves. In the case of those certificates the Government receives the gold and silver with which to redeem them, and acts simply as a custodian of the precious metals. That may be a great convenience to the people and a wise plan, but that is a very different thing from issuing certificates on any kind of property which is not used as money among the nations of the world.

In conclusion, my opinion is that some plan should be devised so that the banking business of the country should all be done by banks and none of it by the General Government. As a rule the people in their individual capacities will manage the variety of business in any country much better than it can possibly be done by the General Government.   R. G. HORR.

LOANS TO THE FARMERS.

WHY THE ALLIANCE DEMAND IS AN IMPOSSIBILITY.

THE DISTINCTION BETWEEN "PUBLIC" AND "PRIVATE" BUSINESS SHARPLY STATED, WITH SOME OBSERVATIONS ON THE ROCKEFELLERS, ASTORS AND GOULDS.

To the Editor of The Tribune.

Sir: Why do you persistently misstate the Alliance demand? We ask to be allowed to borrow money on real estate alone. Land is considered to be good security. Personal property is not so good. No Alliance man expects to borrow more than he can give first-class security for. A first mortgage on real estate for a third or one-half of its selling value would certainly be as good security as any banker could give. Of course the law should be well guarded to prevent frauds in assessments, so as not to bankrupt the Government, as the Argentines have done. It is useless to object to paternalism. The General Government is endowing colleges, supporting experimental stations, distributing seeds and publishing agricultural reports. It would have been better if the Government had built and owned the railroads and telegraph lines, so as to have prevented the colossal fortunes of the Rockefellers, Goulds and others. We feel that these men have not gained their millions honestly, but have been enriched at the expense of the Nation.   M. CHESEBRO.

Mandarin, Fla., June 16, 1891.

This correspondent seems a little petulant because I have intimated that Alliance men are seeking to have the Government loan money on personal property as security. As late as June 6, during this very month, J. I. Goss, of Osceola, Fla., who states that he is now an Alliance man, asked The Tribune this question: " Would it not be safe for the Government to loan money

upon improved lands now occupied and used, and
upon wheat, corn, oats and cotton, insured and
in warehouses, at say one-half the value of the
land and three-fourths the value of the produce? Are not wheat, corn, oats and cotton personal property? I wish these two Florida Alliance men would get together, look over their
published platforms and agree between themselves
as to just what they want.

Mr. Goss very plainly advocates the loaning
of money on the warehouse receipts for personal
property; and Mr. Chesebro accuses me of mis-
representation because I took Mr. Goss at his
word. It would be so much nicer if at least
two of these modern financiers would agree upon
some one thing.

Let me suggest, however, for the benefit of
Mr. Chesebro, that such a loan on wheat, corn,
oats and cotton, insured and in warehouse, is
better and safer than loans on real-estate. Such
loans can be placed among business men and
bankers twice where one can on farming lands.
My objection lies against both of them on the
simple ground that the General Government has no
right to engage in making either kind of loans.

The money in the Treasury of the United States
and the credit of this Nation both belong to the
entire people; and neither should ever be used
except for public purposes. Loaning money to
individuals is a purely private matter, never a
public one. Our Alliance friends are constantly
talking about the loan on land being as
safe as the loan to the banks based
on Government bonds. But the Government
does not loan to the banks. That has been fully
explained already in my answer to Mr. Goss. A
National bank, a savings bank or a private bank
might own a million dollars' worth of Government
bonds each; and yet, if either of them should
need money in its business it could not get a
thousand dollars from the Government by pledg-
ing all its bonds as security. In the money centres of the country a million dollars could readily
be obtained with such security, but not one dollar from the National Treasury. The arrangement,
whereby National banks are allowed to issue their
own notes under certain conditions, and the
Government controls the amount of said notes
and secures their payment, is for the protection of
all the people and is a genuine public necessity.
That arrangement is of an entirely different nature from loaning money to these same banks for
the purpose of assisting them in the transaction of
their private business.

Will some Alliance man tell me why the whole
people of the United States (and they are the
Government) should furnish me money with which
to carry on my private business, any more than
they should loan me horses and buggies when I
want to drive, or hooks and lines when I want to
go a-fishing? The Government might perhaps do
all these things safely; but ought it to do them
at all?

But, says our correspondent, the "Government
endows colleges, supports experimental stations,
distributes seeds and publishes agricultural reports." I know it does; but only as public measures. It never gives a dollar to a Baptist or Pres-

byterian or Catholic college, as such. Experimental stations are for the benefit of the entire
country. The Government distributes seeds in
order that improved varieties of food may be
secured for the whole Nation. It will send a farmer a bunch of extra fine wheat, to see if some
better grade of wheat than is now being raised
cannot be found for the bread of the people; but
it will not furnish the farmer with seed wheat
for his regular annual crops. The Government
publishes agricultural reports, geological sur-
veys, surgical operations in the army, mining
statistics, and census reports; but they are one
and all for the public good and general use. On
that account, however, it will not do to assume
that they should also send me Milton and Byron
bound in morocco. Worcester's Dictionary in calf,
or the "latest novels" in cloth for my private
library.

It is strange that these advocates of Governmental aid and interference in the affairs of the
world cannot see the distinction between private
and public business. If the Government once
enters upon any kind of private business, will
some one tell me where it should stop? If it has
the right to loan money to private individuals for
their private and personal use, then point out
what business there is in this world in which the
Government may not engage with equal propriety in order to meet the desires of some other
portion of its citizens? Will some one of these
Alliance men, who has received new light on
these financial matters, grapple with that one
simple question and answer that first?

It is easy to see what the answer of Mr. Chesebro will be, because he informs us that "it would
have been better if the Government had built and
owned the railroads and telegraph lines." How
does he know that? Many very able, careful
and experienced business men will tell him that
it would have been infinitely worse. Does he
know that to have done what he proposes it
would have cost the Nation from twelve to fifteen
billions of dollars? In what way would the Government have raised the money in addition to
what the public needs have required? His reason
why this should have been done is also given: "So
as to have prevented the colossal fortunes of the
Rockefellers, Gould and others." Did the Rockefellers make their money in railroads? I had
supposed that their accumulations came largely
from their connection with the Standard Oil Company. Is not that a fact? If so, then following
Mr. Chesebro's course of reasoning, the Government should also have taken control of and managed the entire oil business of this country. The
Astors have become very rich in the real estate
business; hence, according to Mr. Chesebro, the
Government should own and manage that business, too. A large number of our wealthiest men
have made colossal fortunes in the mines of the
United States; therefore, the Government should
have owned and managed the mines. Mr. Gould
is supposed to have made an immense fortune in
railroads and telegraph lines. Does it follow from
that fact that the Government should have built
and owned those lines? Would the ownership
of them by the Government have prevented men

from getting great wealth in some other way?

Were there no very rich men before railroads and telegraphing were invented? Did the Rothschilds get their immense fortunes from railroads and telegraph lines? There never has been a time when a few people did not amass great fortunes, and when large numbers did not fail to accumulate at all. These fortunes may be made honestly, but are, no doubt, too often secured by dishonest methods. When honestly made, in fair, legitimate business, the owners have a right to them, and are only accountable for a wise and humane use of them. When made dishonestly, the owners of them are both to be pitied and despised.

I wish property was more evenly distributed in this world. It would be a great improvement if poverty could be entirely abolished. I wish times could always be good. It would please me greatly to have good wages for labor and good prices for the products of farm and shop at all times. If we could all manage to be happy and prosperous without giving any mortgages at all, that would be better than to borrow money at ever so low a rate of interest. But such is not the condition of affairs in this world at the present time. We are all compelled to meet life as we find it. I have but little of this world's goods. Had I been more saving of my earnings, such might not have been the case. The Government is in no way responsible for my misfortunes.

The members of the Farmers' Alliance, as a rule, have seen hard times for a few years past. My sympathies are all with them in their struggle to better their condition. What pains me is to see them rush into such wild schemes and follow off after a set of leaders who have as yet never organized any genuine reform. Men who are always grasping at every new-fangled notion, and who are ever on the alert to abandon any principle and form any combination, for the simple purpose of self-aggrandizement seldom help any one except themselves. Of all the methods mentioned to enable the people of this country to bring about better times and greater prosperity, the most dangerous is the attempt to draw the Government from its legitimate public work and to put under its control the private business of the people. Such business should always be managed by individuals, having individual interests at stake and feeling personal responsibility. Let the Government confine itself to public duties, and let the business of this Nation be managed by private skill and individual enterprise. R. G. H.

HOW CAN THE KANSAS FARMER PAY HIS DEBTS.

Sir: The celebrated Alliance "man," Mrs. M. E. Lease, spoke here last Tuesday night. Below are some of her statements. Are they true?

She said that the National debt is as large now (compared with present prices of labor and produce) as it was at the close of the war.

Also, that in 1850 the common people owned three-fourths of the property of the country and paid one-quarter of the taxes; but that now the common people own a fraction less than one-quarter of the property and pay three-quarters of the taxes.

She also said that there are 60,000 Union soldiers in the poorhouses of the United States; that the amount of money in circulation amounts to only $8 per capita; and that the recorded indebtedness in Kansas is several hundred dollars per capita.

She wanted to know how the people of Kansas could ever expect to pay their debts under such circumstances.
W. K. DAVIS.

Nortonville, Kan., March 6, 1891.

In reply to this correspondent, I will say that the National debt has been reduced since the war from about three thousand millions of dollars to about eight hundred millions at the present time. If calculated on a gold basis, wages are higher now than they were in 1866. We were then using a largely depreciated currency, and wages and prices seemed much higher than they actually were.

The statement about taxes is absolutely false. No one can tell what is meant by the term "common people." Who does it include? Who does it exclude? In this country we have no titled classes. We are all common people in the United States. Wealth is no more concentrated now than it was in 1850. The poor people pay no different rate of taxes now than then. Taxes are paid in this country on precisely the same basis as they have been from the foundation of the Government. It is a rate on each $100. It always has been. Some rich people lie about their property and cheat in the amount of taxes they pay. They did the same thing in 1850.

Did the speaker tell in what poorhouses the 60,000 old soldiers are? It is easy for any one to stand up and utter such a slander upon our people; but where is the proof? The people of this Nation have stood by the old soldiers grandly. Our immense pension rolls prove that. The Dependent Pension bill was intended to place every soldier out of reach of the poorhouse. It has substantially done so. Such statements as you refer to are simply disgraceful. If there are 60,000 old soldiers in our poorhouses, why not tell us where they are? Then they can be removed. I have never yet been able to get the names of the poorhouses where it is alleged that these old soldiers are held. Until they name the locations and substantiate the statement I shall refuse to believe it. Tell us where these old soldiers are; then we will have them removed to better quarters. To do that would be a grand work; and to be telling such a tale, if it is not true, is infamous. Next time you hear this assertion made, call for the proof.

The statement as to there being only $8 of money per capita in circulation in this country is absolutely untrue. On the 1st day of February last there was more than three times that amount, not less than $24 60 for each man, woman and child. My statement is taken from the official reports of the Government and can be verified by the figures.

I do not know how much the indebtedness per capita is for each person in Kansas. It is more than I wish it was; but it is only such an amount as her people have voluntarily assumed. They created their debts in their efforts to better their condition.

How can they be expected to pay them? is one

of your orator's questions. Sure enough! I answer: By honest work and careful, good management. How else can any one get out of debt? Raise crops; live frugally; pay as you go; and in a little time the load will be lifted. Kansas has great resources. Her people are full of pluck. Two good years will put her on her feet. Remember this! Any one who goes about your State teaching that there is any way to discharge your debts, except by paying them, is no friend of Kansas or her excellent people. Good, honest work will help your people out. Nothing else ever will.

These may not be pleasant words to listen to, but, before condemning them, please examine them and see if they are not true. R. G. H.

DO FARMERS BEAR BURDENS WHICH MILL-OWNERS DO NOT?

NONE WHATEVER—NOR ARE THEY MORTGAGED ON ACCOUNT OF THE TARIFF—THE WAY TO PAY A MORTGAGE.

To the Editor of The Tribune.

Sir: I am a farmer, and would like to have the following questions answered in The Weekly Tribune:

First—Why should not the American farmer have the same right to trade his surplus farm products for European manufactures that the American mill-owner has to trade every production of mill-goods for South American and Asiatic products?

Second—Can you give some reason why the American mill-owner should be protected against this trade of the American farmer?

Third—Please explain why the trade of our surplus farm products should not be as free as the trade of our surplus mill products?

Fourth—Why should farmers bear burdens that mill-owners do not?

Fifth—Why has real estate in Delaware County, N. Y., depreciated nearly one-half in value within fifteen or twenty years?

Sixth—If the American farmer has been protected, why does the record of the Clerk's office of Delaware County, N. Y., show that two-thirds of the farms of that county are under mortgage?

Respectfully, R. C. HODGES.
East Sidney, N. Y., May 15, 1891.

In answer to your first question, I know of no reason in the world why the farmers of the United States should not have precisely the same right to sell all their products in Europe or Asia that the mill-owners have. I know of no law that gives the slightest advantage to the one over the other.

I am not certain as to what you mean by your second question. I am not aware that the American mill-owners are in any way protected against the American farmers. The policy of the protective tariff is to take care of and build up every American industry, whether it be in the factory, in the shop, in the mine, or on the farm. I know of no discriminations in favor of the one against the other.

Your third question implies that there is some disadvantages placed upon the surplus products of the farm that are not placed upon the surplus

products of the mills. I supposed that all products of this country were treated precisely alike.

Your fourth question also intimates that certain burdens are placed upon farm products which are not placed upon other products of the United States. I know of no such burdens. If there are any, they certainly should be removed. Every kind of industry in the United States should have a fair chance, and be equally protected. The real object of levying duties on the protective plan is to give our own manufacturers and farmers the advantages of our superior markets. The late tariff law was drawn in the spirit of that system. From beginning to end, it favors the farmers more than any tariff bill ever before enacted in the United States. If there is any discrimination in that bill, it is most surely in favor of the farmer, and not against him. I am at a loss to imagine just what it is of which you complain.

In answer to your fifth question: I am not familiar enough with the condition of the various agricultural industries in Delaware County to state why farms have thus depreciated. Indeed, I am not sure that the depreciation is anywhere near as much as you state. It would seem from your question, however, that these lands brought a good price, fifteen or twenty years ago. The same tariff was in existence then as for the past five years. Was it the same tariff that made them high then that makes them low now? Is it not possible that the depreciation of real estate has taken place on account of conditions entirely outside of and foreign from tariff legislation? To make your comparison of value, you should go back to 1856 and 1857, and take the price of farms in Delaware County at that time, when we were living under a low, free-trade tariff, and compare prices then with prices now. I will guarantee that you will find no such difference in prices as you now mention. The distress of the farming communities for the past five years has been nothing as compared with the terrors of 1857. For proof of this statement, ask any of your neighbors whose hair, like mine, is white with age.

In reply to your last question: Let me suggest that you may have taken the number of mortgages from mere hearsay. If you will examine the records of your county carefully, I will venture the assertion that not one in five of those farms are under mortgage. I doubt, if over one in ten will be found in that condition. The same statements have been repeatedly made for the last three years about the farming lands of my own State of Michigan, and of Iowa; and yet the census returns just completed show that only about one farm in nine in the State of Iowa, and only about one in eleven in the State of Michigan, is under mortgage at all. The reports from both States show that those mortgages have been largely reduced in the last few years. The same reports further show that the very largest portion of those mortgages were placed on these farms for the purpose of buying more lands, or building new houses on the same. And in each State it was found that less than 2 per cent of such mortgages were given to pay the running expenses of the farmers. It is such an easy thing to claim that everything is going to ruin, and to assume that everybody is mortgaging his home, but it is quite a different thing to count up the instances and get at the exact facts. I make this prediction that when the statistics shall be fully reported, the property in the cities of the United States, the property owned by manufacturers, the property owned by the great corporations, including the railroads of the United States, will be found to be more deeply mortgaged to-day than are the farms. I am not sure that I cannot almost count on the fingers of my hands every railroad in the United States that is free from a mortgage; and yet we seldom hear those mortgages mentioned.

The mortgage is a device used by people for the purpose of obtaining money with which they hope to better their condition. The great mass of farm mortgages are no exception to this rule. Farmers, like other business men, have borrowed money for the purpose of doing more business, and have given mortgage security for the payment, rather than seek personal indorsement. In some instances they would perhaps have done better not to have made the loans. That is undoubtedly often the case with large numbers of other people who borrow money; but having made the loans, having done it according to their own best judgment, why should so much be said about these same mortgages? I know of no way honestly to discharge a mortgage except by paying it, and I can see no possible advantage that could accrue to the farmers who owe these mortgages by decreasing the number of shops and factories, and thus sending more people who now consume the food of the farmers out on the farms and set them to raising food, which would simply increase the glut of the farmer's market.

I have a little mortgage on my own farm. I am quite sure that the best method for me is to try and earn the money to pay it off, and that such a procedure will be much more to my benefit than the spending my time in finding fault with myself for having borrowed the money. I thought at the time I gave the mortgage I could better my condition by purchasing another small piece of land adjoining my own. I think the investment was a good one, even now, but whether good or not, it was my own doing. The mortgage was put on the place by the exercise of my judgment. No outsider induced me to enter upon the enterprise in any way, and it seems to me that the manly thing is to stand by my own head and make the best of the situation.

To listen to the clamor about mortgages, one would think that some hobgoblin had been through the country putting mortgages upon farms without the consent of the owners. Such is not the case. As a rule, these mortgages were all made to secure money for what seemed at the time to be a good scheme. Hard times followed and payment has been impossible. Times are better now. Farm products are bringing a good price once more. And this is the time to stop grumbling and go to raising crops. The wheat all over the West looks promising. The hard work of the farmer will

bring him a better reward. In my judgment the way to solve this mortgage trouble is to plant and sow and reap and hoe, harvest, dig and sell. In time that will dispose of the problem. Not a single farm has been mortgaged on account of the tariff laws. Not one. More than that, if you should adopt free-trade in this country to-morrow, the mortgages would still be there; and you would cripple the manufacturing industries and destroy your own home markets. My word for it, the mortgages would then surely remain there unpaid.   R. G. HORR.

A FARMER'S TARIFF.

PROTECTION TO THE HOME PRODUCT.

The Tribune is asked to reprint the table below repeatedly for the benefit of all concerned.

Not one article of farm produce which can be raised in the United States in quantity sufficient to supply the home market failed to receive protection in the McKinley bill. Upon most of the articles which the farmers of the United States produce in large quantity an increased protection has been given by raising the duty on the foreign articles imported in competition with our own produce. The following list speaks for itself:

	Old duty.	New duty.
Barley	10 cts. bush.	30 cts. bush.
Buckwheat	10 per cent.	15 cts. bush.
Corn and oats	10 cts. bush.	15 cts. bush.
Wheat	20 cts. bush.	25 cts. bush.
Hops	8 cts. lb.	15 cts. lb.
Butter and cheese	4 cts. lb.	6 cts. lb.
Hay	$2 ton.	$4 ton
Straw	Free.	30 per cent.
Eggs	Free.	5 cts. dozen.
Broom corn	Free.	$8 ton.
Peas and beans	10 per cent.	40 cts. bush.
Nursery stock	Free.	20 per cent.
Apples, fresh	Free.	25 cts. bush.
Apples, dry	Free.	2 cts. lb.
Bacon, hams	2 cts. lb.	5 cts. lb.
Beef and pork	1 ct. lb.	2 cts. lb.
Mutton	10 per cent.	2 cts. lb.
Poultry, live	Free.	3 cts. lb.
Poultry, dressed	10 per cent.	5 cts. lb.
Horses worth over $150	20 per cent.	30 per cent.
Horses, others	20 per cent.	$30 head.
Mules	20 per cent.	$30 head.
Cattle, yearlings	20 per cent.	$2 head.
Cattle, over a year	20 per cent.	$10 head.
Hogs	20 per cent.	$1 50 head.
Sheep, yearlings	20 per cent.	75 cts. head.
Sheep, over a year	20 per cent.	$1 50 head.
Milk	10 per cent.	5 cts. gallon.
Onions	10 per cent.	40 cts. bush.
Potatoes	15 cts. bush.	25 cts. bush.
Other vegetables	30 & 35 p. c.	45 per cent.
Tobacco, not stemmed	75 cts. per lb.	$2 per lb.
Tobacco, stemmed	$1 lb.	$2 75 per lb.
Fruit brandy	$2 gall.	$2 50 gall.
Peppermint oil	25 per cent.	50 cts. gall.
Flax, hackled	$40 ton.	$67 20 ton.
Hemp, hackled	$25 ton.	$50 ton.
Wool, Class 1. Unwashed	10 & 12 cts. lb.	11 cts. lb.
Washed	20 & 24 cts. lb.	22 cts. lb.
Scoured	30 & 36 cts. lb.	33 cts. lb.
Class 2. Unwashed	10 & 12 cts. lb.	12 cts. lb.
Scoured	30 & 36 cts. lb.	36 cts. lb.
Class 3. Under 13 cts.	2½ cts lb	32 per cent.
Over 13 cts.	5 cts. lb	50 per cent.
Bounty on American sugar	None.	14 & 2 cts. lb.

This by no means covers the whole subject, however. The McKinley bill in full (printed by The Tribune in pamphlet form, old and new rates compared; price, 10 cents a copy) alone gives full particulars.   ...—1

FOREIGN FARM PRODUCTS

More than $213,000,000 worth of foreign farm products in the natural state was imported into the United States during the calendar year of 1890, all of which should have been raised by the farmers of this country and been a source of income to them. The McKinley bill was framed with a view to enable the farmers of America to get possession of this large business and themselves supply the bulk of the $213,000,000 of farm products imported. The following will show how much American agriculture is interested in this feature of the McKinley bill (the figures representing the net imports—that is to say, the total imports, less the small quantity of each kind of goods re-exported during the year):

Animals, etc.:	Quantity.	Value.
Live cattle, No	26,284	$187,007
Horses, No	40,703	4,145,709
Sheep, No	356,820	1,199,141
All other, including fowls		350,597
Feathers, natural		1,981,149
Hair		2,910,437
Hides and skins		25,836,098
Bristles, ℔	1,282,271	1,277,250
Provisions:		
Meat products		688,013
Butter, ℔	76,522	12,013
Cheese, ℔	9,431,826	1,395,662
Milk		130,528
Eggs, dozens	12,194,506	1,094,812
Fibres:		
Cotton, raw, ℔	10,928,963	1,570,346
Flax, tons	7,303	1,950,182
Hemp, tons	25,529	4,591,384
Wool, ℔	105,890,747	13,057,748
Cereals, etc.:		
Barley, bush	9,365,614	5,044,573
Barley malt, bush	281,030	194,478
Corn, bush	2,135	1,480
Oats, bush	13,015	6,197
Rye and wheat	All re-exported.	
Other breadstuffs		326,775
Oatmeal, ℔s	1,005,671	27,433
Linseed, ℔s	2,570,284	2,939,658
Other seeds		1,513,399
Rice, ℔s	76,707,202	1,802,986
Rice flour, meal, etc., ℔s	64,922,264	1,102,560
Vegetables:		
Beans and peas, bush	1,569,060	1,703,889
Potatoes, bush	3,990,502	1,046,323
Pickles and sauces		514,578
Other vegetables		972,015
Vegetables, preserved		606,772
Tobacco, ℔	26,792,809	17,505,180
Molasses, gal	29,546,017	4,584,540
Sugar, ℔	3,008,761,690	60,002,511
Fruits, etc.:		
Lemons		3,789,006
Oranges		2,047,121
Plums and prunes, ℔	61,908,200	2,803,901
Raisins, ℔	43,077,097	2,227,838
Other fruits		1,353,019
Preserved fruits		1,375,787
Almonds, ℔	7,333,096	973,560
Hay, tons	99,314	844,582
Hops, ℔	5,320,579	1,546,502
Volatile oils, ℔	1,172,031	225,087
Hemlock bark, cords	46,231	215,330

Total $213,003,321

It ought to be mentioned that, in addition to the articles referred to above, there were also imported into the United States during 1890 about $97,000,000 worth of manufactured goods, made out of the raw materials of agriculture, the raw materials for which were not but might have been supplied by American farmers namely:

Manufactures of hemp, flax, etc	$26,892,310
Manufactures of hair	102,773
Leather and manufactures of	12,538,550
Manufactures of tobacco	4,160,619
Manufactures of wool	53,663,022

Total $97,417,208

Are not the farmers interested in the success of the McKinley bill?

FARM PRODUCTS EXPORTED.

Sir: Will you please state in Weekly Tribune upon what authority Mr. Horr, among others, makes the statement that we are using in this country 90 per cent of all the wheat produced, while the Agricultural Department asserts that for nine years preceding 1880 the average exports were 128,000,000 bushels. Such assertions as that of Mr. Horr have been numerous the last year. A. WARD.
Clyde, N. Y.

Let me say, in reply to Mr. Ward, that I have no recollection of ever making such a statement. If I did make it, it was done inadvertently, and is not true.

We have a class of people who are constantly claiming that the price of wheat is absolutely fixed in this country by the price in England. That proposition I have frequently disputed, and have stated that Great Britain does not purchase 10 per cent of our wheat, and that such 10 per cent hardly controls the price of the other 90 per cent. The agricultural reports show that we have exported an average of 128,000,000 bushels of wheat each year for nine years, but the same reports show that Great Britain bought only about 40,000,000 of bushels each year for five years past. In 1890 we raised of wheat 399,262,000 bushels. That year Great Britain bought of us only 38,240,523 bushels. That, you see, is less than 10 per cent of the entire yield.

An average yield of wheat for the past twelve years has been about 445,000,000 bushels per year, and of late England has not taken one-tenth of it; but Great Britain and the rest of the world have together consumed about one-fourth of it.

Does Mr. Ward suppose for a moment that I would purposely misstate the facts about such a matter? I may have said that we consume in this country fully 90 per cent of all the products of our farms—that is, taking them all together, wheat, corn, oats and all the rest. That is a statement I have often seen; and one very able and careful statistician asserts that we do not export over 8 per cent of all four products. Is not that the statement of Mr. Ward has so often seen? More than that—is not that true? Will our correspondent devote himself to its examination?

From the best data that I can find that statement is absolutely correct. If it be true that over 90 per cent of all farm products find a home market in the United States, is not that even more significant than it would be of wheat alone? But has not been true of wheat for ten years past. I predict that it will be true of wheat in less than five years. In 1880 we exported over 186,000,000 bushels of wheat; in 1889 only about 88,000,000 bushels. It is easy to see where we will soon bring up. It will be but a few years when our own people will eat all the wheat we raise.
R. G. HORR.

WHO WAS IT THAT "ROBBED" FARMER BRANCH?

EVIDENCE OF GUILT ON THE PART OF MERCHANT KNOX—AN OBJECT LESSON IN THE STUDY OF THE TARIFF.

To the Editor of The Tribune.

Sir: I inclose herewith a clipping from "The Wisconsin Agriculturist," published without comment, as an object lesson to instruct farmers how they are "fleeced" by the "robber tariff." Will Mr. Horr aid in undeceiving those of us who would be glad to be wise in such matters? V. N. LESTER.
Ottawa, Kan.

The following is the entire clipping sent by our correspondent:

"The Buffalo Courier" says that some time ago Senator James K. Jones asked C. R. P. Breckinridge, of the House Ways and Means Committee, to prepare for W. L. Terry, of Little Rock, a statement of the amount of tariff duties on a bill of goods bought by a representative farmer. In reply Mr. Breckinridge furnished an exhibit based on actual transactions between R. M. Knox, a merchant of Pine Bluff, Ark., and D. W.

Branch, a farmer, who bought the goods. Mr. Breck-inridge explains that "this is calculated upon the basis of cost from the books of Mr. Knox and upon the rate of taxes actually paid upon competing articles at the ports as provided by law." The bill as it appears in Mr. Knox's books is subjoined:

1887. Article.	Cost.	Tariff.
Jan. 20—To cassimere suit of clothes	$11 00	$1 00
2 pair brogans, $1 65 ...	3.30	75
Feb. 5—1 bell collar	1 50	75
2 pair plow lines	70	10
1 pair boys' brogans	1 25	29
Feb. 17—1 box axle grease	10	
Feb. 21—1 A very plough	3 50	1 00
2 buckboards, 50c.; 9 pounds nails at 6c. 55c. ...	1 05	29
1 bushel salt, 75c.; 1 pair miss's shoes, $1 25	2 00	62
Mar. 6—3 pair shoes, $1 75; 1 pair of bing's, 25c. ...	2 00	50
1 yard waterproof	75	30
Mar. 26—1 pair brogans	1 60	37
2 yards calico, 10c.	20	5
1 water bucket, 25c.; 1 spool thread, 5c. ...	30	9
April 9—11 pounds nails, 6c.	66	14
April 22—2 hats, 05c.; 1 yard lawn, 50c.; 20 yards calico, 12½c.; 3 yards jeans, 50c. ...	1 50	70
½ dozen thread	40	13
32 yards ticking, 25c.	3 00	1 25
1 set cups and saucers	75	29
May 9—1 knife	75	25
June 8—2 pair men's shoes	4 00	47
2 pair suspenders	75	20
June 24—10 yards bleached domestic, 12½c. ...	1 25	54
July 26—2 suits clothes, $7 50, $9 ...	16 50	5 79
2 yards oil cloth, 40c.	80	12
10 yards gingham, 10c.	1 00	5
1 curreycomb and brush	10	6
Aug. 13—35 yards bagging, 9c.	3 15	75
1 bundle ties, $1 50; 12 pounds nails, 5c., 60c. ...		
Sept. 8—14 pounds nails, 5c.	70	21
1 box axle grease, 10 pounds soda, 10c. ...	20	6
Sept. 16—95 yards bagging, ½ pound, 8c. ...	2 80	95
1 bundle ties	1 00	39
10 yards Osnaburgs, 11c. ...	1 10	34
Oct. 24—1 suit jean clothes	7 50	2 67
2 wool hats, $1 and $1 50 ...	2 50	1 02
1 boy's wool hat	75	32
10 yards worsted, 20c.	2 00	97
13 yards worsted, 17c.	2 20	95
1 set plates	65	24
1 set goblets	65	21
1 set knives and forks	2 75	91
1 dishes, 40c. and 60c.	1 00	36
35 yards bagging, 8c.	2 80	99
1 bundle ties	3 13	95
Total	**$101 50**	**$33 80**

I give this clipping in full because it is a fair specimen of the rubbish which the free-trade press is constantly putting forth on the tariff question. It is amazing that as able a man as Mr. Breckinridge is acknowledged to be should resort to such a trick to deceive the people. Let us examine the statements of this clipping.

I point out first that the bill of goods was sold four years ago, and a new Tariff bill has been passed since then. However, the previous tariff was a protective one, and, in substance, the situation was the same as now.

It seems that Mr. Breckinridge was asked by Senator Jones, of Arkansas, to prepare a statement of the amount of tariff duties on a bill of goods bought by a representative farmer. In reply Mr. Breckinridge sends a bill of goods actually purchased by a Mr. Branch from a merchant by the name of Knox, at Pine Bluffs, Ark. Mr. Breckinridge then makes out and places opposite each article "the taxes actually paid upon competing articles at the ports as provided by law."

Now, to begin with, to make such a table of any value one must assume that, if a duty is levied on a foreign article when imported, the same duty is added to the price of competing articles produced in this country. But such is never the case. No man should have known this better than Mr. Breckinridge. I doubt if there is an article in the whole list on which one cent of duty had ever been paid. The bill is made up almost entirely of articles produced in the United States, many of which can be bought in this country to-day as cheaply as in the Old World.

To get at this question intelligently, we need not consider just what Mr. Knox charged Mr. Branch for the goods. The actual amount charged has no bearing whatever on the question. The real question is, Did Mr. Knox himself have to pay for those goods more money on account of the duties levied on foreign goods of the same class imported than he would have been compelled to pay had no such duties been levied on the foreign goods, and had no such articles been produced in this country, or, if produced in this country, had they been manufactured without the protection of the tariff? Just how much Mr. Knox swindled Mr. Branch may be an important side question, but it has no bearing whatever on the real issue.

Let me illustrate. There are several charges in this bill for nails at 6 cents per pound. Take this eleven pounds of nails at 6 cents per pound, 66 cents; tariff, 14 cents. That is 1 1-4 cents per pound tariff on each pound of nails—or $1 25 tariff on each keg of 100 pounds. When you come to look at the price of nails quoted in the various cities where they are made in the United States and find that Mr. Knox could have bought them for $1 75 a keg, then you will see how dishonest the statement of Mr. Breckinridge is, that Farmer Branch had paid 14 cents tariff on those nails. Merchant Knox only paid 19 3-4 cents for the eleven pounds, to which should be added freight, which would leave only 5 3-4 cents for the real cost of the eleven pounds of nails, that is to say, if they could be produced for $1 75 a keg, less the tariff, $1 25. In other words, if Mr. Breckinridge tells the truth, then nails can be made for $10 a ton, which is less than the price of pig-iron.

Again, here is another item: One bushel of salt, 75 cents, on which the tariff would be a trifle over 6 cents. What can Mr. Knox buy that bushel of salt for? In Michigan it would cost him only 6 cents; in New-York, 7 cents; in Kansas, 9 cents. To this must be added freight, in order to find out how much he robbed Farmer Branch; still, that is not to be considered in determining how much of that price should be charged up to the tariff. If he had bought foreign salt, he would still have had to pay the freight. In short, salt is selling to-day in Michigan for less than the tariff on the foreign salt and is cheaper than it is produced abroad. Why, then, does Mr. Breckinridge claim that the tariff robbed Mr. Branch on salt? He knows better. The robbing was done by Merchant Knox, and not by the tariff. The fact is, salt is one of the cheapest articles produced in this country to-day; and it has been cheapened by our own producers, since the tariff law of 1861 protected the industry.

The next article I name is calico. Here the charge is, two yards of calico at 10 cents, 20 cents; tariff, 9 cents, or 4 1-2 cents a yard. Again, how much did Mr. Knox pay for that calico? No one can tell who robbed Farmer Branch until after that question is answered. Judging from what Merchant Knox charged for nails and salt, he did not pay more than 4 cents a yard for the calico. But calico is quoted as low as 3 cents a yard at wholesale. We doubt if Merchant Knox paid over 4 1-2 cents for it at the outside; and that is just what the duty would be. Does Mr. Breckinridge claim that the tariff on foreign calico raised the price on those two yards 9 cents, when that is all the calico cost? Can they make calico in the Old World and give it away as a paying business?

Again twelve yards of ticking is charged for at 25 cents per yard, total $3; tariff $1 25. The same question again: How much did Merchant Knox pay for that ticking? How can you tell how much Farmer Branch was cheated, or who did the cheating, until after you get at the whole transaction? Suppose, Mr. Breckinridge, it should turn out that Merchant Knox paid only $1 25 for that identical ten-yard piece of ticking! You would hardly claim, in that case, that the tariff robbed Farmer Branch of $1 25, will you? It surely cost something to make the goods.

I might take up the entire list, had I time to look up the actual cost of these articles, so as to be able to state whether any money was paid out by Farmer Branch on account of the tariff. So far as I am able to recall the facts, there is not a single article named where the American-made product has not been cheapened by manufacture in this country. I now invite Mr. Breckinridge to an honest examination of that bill of goods. Will he please take up each item and state what its cost was when bought from the manufacturers in the United States. Then will he please tell us what the same article cost before we started the industry in this country, and how much less it can be bought for abroad to-day than it can in the United States. When all those facts are given we will have some data from which can be ascertained just how much the price of that bill of goods was honestly affected by the tariff. Let that be fairly done. I will notify Mr. Breckinridge that the facts will show that Merchant Knox could have sold that bill of goods at a fair profit, and that they would have cost Farmer Branch much less than he would have been compelled to pay for them had we not made them under the protective system in the United States.

I am inclined to think that this bill of goods does clearly prove that Merchant Knox is imposing upon the Arkansas farmers. I do not wonder at his being able to do so, when a man of Mr. Breckinridge's position and experience lends himself to the claim that it was the tariff which raised the cost of these goods to Farmer Branch.

One word with Farmer Branch: After this, before you take the word of Mr. Breckinridge, or any one else, as to the tariff making your bill too large, you will do well to find out whether you are charged 75 cents for a bushel of salt which cost Merchant Knox not to exceed 15 cents, and other articles in the same ratio. Then, do you "go" for Merchant Knox, and not the protective tariff.

                         R. G. HORR.

FINANCIAL ISSUES.

MORE MONEY NOW THAN EVER

THERE IS NO SUCH DECREASE PER CAPITA IN THE CIRCULATING MEDIUM AS IS FALSELY CLAIMED.

To the Editor of The Tribune.

Sir: Our Alliance wishes Mr. Horr to answer through The Tribune the following questions:

First—What was the largest amount of greenback money in circulation at any one time, and when?

Second—What, approximately, was the population of the United States at that time?

Third—How much of that money was withdrawn from circulation and destroyed by the Government?

                CHARLES STODDARD.

Woodland, Iowa, Feb. 24, 1891.

Previous to answering these questions I have taken the trouble to procure the exact facts, as nearly as they can be ascertained, from the officials at Washington, as well as the facts upon some other questions which are being put to me daily, both as I meet the people and in letters.

The greatest amount of United States notes, commonly called "greenbacks," in existence at any one time cannot be exactly stated from any report now in print. The amount outstanding July 1, 1864, is probably within a small fraction of the highest amount ever in existence at any one time. The amount outstanding at that date was $447,300,203, but of that amount there was in the United States Treasury $32,184,213. That left in actual circulation $415,115,990.

There were in circulation at the same time other forms of paper money amounting to $239,347,864, making an aggregate paper circulation of $654,463,854.

July 1, 1864, there were in existence of paper money formerly issued in the United States the following amounts:

State bank notes	$179,157,717
Compound interest notes	6,060,000
Fractional currency	22,894,877
Greenbacks	447,300,203
National bank notes	31,235,270
Total	$686,648,067

Of this money there were in the United States Treasury $31,235,270 of greenbacks, leaving in circulation, as before stated, $654,463,854. The population at that time is estimated to have been 34,046,000, which made an average of $19 22 of paper money for each man, woman and child at that time in the country. It must be borne in mind that at that time neither gold nor silver was being used as currency in the United States. Both were then at a high premium and were bought and sold simply as commodities. Gold was used, though, in payment of customs duties, and the Government paid the interest on its bonds with gold. There was estimated at that time to be of gold coin in this country the sum of $203,000,000. There was in the Treasury at that date $18,653,580, which left in the hands of the people $184,346,420. There was also estimated to be $10,000,000 of silver in the United States at that time, of which $625,366 was in the Treasury of the Government, leaving of silver owned by the people $9,371,634. If these amounts of gold and silver were added to the paper money then in circulation, the sum would be increased to $848,184,908, which would have been $24.91 for each person living in the United States at that time.

There were also outstanding on July 1, 1864, one and two years' notes of 1863 to the amount of $153,471,450. These notes were not included in the estimate of paper money because they were interest-bearing obligations of the Government, were at that time at a premium, and were being rapidly funded in 5-20 and 10-40 bonds. Of course such obligations could in no sense be called currency; but if treated as circulating medium and added to the paper money then in circulation it would have raised the amount of paper money to $807,935,304, which would give $23.73 for each individual then living in the United States. If again to that sum be added the gold and silver not in the Treasury at that date, it will make $1,901,656,358, or $29.42 per capita. I repeat that as these notes were not money, and as gold and silver were not then circulating as such, the real amount of circulating medium at that time for each person was the sum first named—$19.22.

The amount of greenbacks was decreased from year to year up to 1873, and then there was a new issue of $26,000,000, so that on the 1st day of July, 1874, there were outstanding $382,000,-000. From that date there was a gradual reduction in the amount up to May 31, 1878, when the sum outstanding was $346,681,016. At that time the law was approved which forbade the retirement of any more of these United States notes; and that is the amount of greenbacks now in existence.

From these statements it is evident that there is now $100,619,287 less of greenbacks in existence than were outstanding July 1, 1864, when the highest point was probably reached.

The total amount of money outstanding and in circulation July 1, 1878, is shown in detail by the following table:

ISSUED.

Standard silver dollars	17,509,079
Subsidiary coin	65,778,328
Silver certificates	1,462,900
Greenbacks	346,681,016
National bank notes	324,514,284
Total	$751,705,807

At that date there were in the Treasury of the United States the following amounts of the various kinds of currency above referred to:

IN THE TREASURY.

Standard silver dollars	$15,039,827
Subsidiary coins	6,809,305
Silver certificates	1,455,320
Greenbacks	25,775,121
National bank notes	12,759,923
Total	$61,940,830

Deducting that amount from the entire sum issued, and it leaves $692,764,911, which was the amount of money in circulation July 1, 1878. Gold is not included in this estimate, because it was still at a premium and not in general use as money. The estimated population at that time was 47,598,000, which shows that on that date there was in circulation as money only $14.56 for each man, woman and child in the

United States. But on July 1, 1878, there was estimated to be the sum of $213,200,000 of gold coin in this country. Of that amount $128,-460,203 were in the Treasury of the Government; so that among the people would be left $84,739,797. Add that amount to the $692,764,-911 above and it gives $777,504,708, which is $16.33 per capita of every possible kind of money in 1878.

I will now give the amount of circulating medium in existence and the amount in actual use among the people February 1, 1891.

ISSUED.

Gold coin	$639,384,021
Standard silver dollars—Act of Feb. 28, 1878	377,246,880
Standard silver dollars—Act of July 14, 1890	14,319,125
Subsidiary silver	77,696,840
Gold certificates	175,731,499
Silver certificates	307,062,874
Treasury notes—Act July 14, 1890	24,864,600
Greenbacks	346,681,016
National bank notes	175,021,739
Total	$2,142,547,994

IN THE TREASURY.

Gold coin	$229,912,085
Standard silver dollars—Act of February 28, 1878 and act of July 14, 1890	302,747,050
Subsidiary silver	15,973,211
Gold certificates	19,892,050
Silver certificates	3,218,738
Treasury notes, act of July 14, 1890	3,202,964
Greenbacks	6,995,508
National bank notes	6,820,151
Total	$610,791,749

Deduct the amount in the Treasury from $2,142,547,994 and it leaves the quantity of money in actual circulation among our people on the 1st day of February, 1891, at $1,525,756,251. The census just taken shows that we have a population of 63,000,000. So that to-day there is in actual circulation for every man, woman and child in this country the sum of $24.80, as against $14.56 in 1878 and $19.22 in 1864, provided you include as money at those dates only such currency as was in actual use as money at the time.

Are not these figures significant? Let me state frankly that they have been a surprise to me. I have heard the statement made so frequently from day to day that we lacked circulating medium; that the volume of currency had been constantly contracted for many years past, that I came to take it for granted there must be some foundation for the statement. It now turns out that we really have vastly more money in circulation per capita than in 1864 and half as much again as in the good times from 1878 to 1885. These statements are from documents in my possession under the official signature of my acting Secretary of the Treasury.

The advocates of free coinage may dispute this estimate as to 1864 and claim that there was really then in use $29.42 per capita, which I deny for reasons formerly given, but how can they successfully refute the figures as to 1878? What do they say as to the amount shown to be in circulation then including every possible kind of money? Prices were good and times were then prosperous. Does it not force thoughtful men to look somewhere else for the cause of business depression than to the amount of circulating medium? Is it not possible that it is a cheap dollar these men are seeking much more than the number of dollars? When a depreciated dollar is used for the measure of value, prices may seem to be high, but there must always come a day of settlement; when that day arrives the people are compelled to settle in good money. To do that always hurts, and sometimes hurts terribly. Men who sell their crops, men who sell their day's works, are always injured by the use of poor money. Good, honest dollars are always best in the long run for the entire people of any nation. So long as our currency is all convertible without expense to the holder into the best it will all be good. The moment you enact a law that will compel us to take a cheaper dollar and pay for it with one more valuable, that moment the more valuable dollars will begin to disappear from among us, and the cheaper money will hold possession of the entire field. I see that to-day in the Argentine Republic gold is quoted at a premium of 219. Does any one imagine that gold is being circulated in that country as money? Go there and you will find that the people are using as their medium of exchange only the depreciated paper money of that nation. It may be the best they can do under the circumstances, but admit that it is, no one will claim that any nation which can avoid such a condition of affairs should plunge into the same vortex, simply because that Republic has been hurled into the whirlpool. We have to-day as good money as any nation in the world can boast of; let us all resolve to keep it good.   R. G. HORR.

QUESTIONS AS TO SILVER.

To the Editor of The Tribune.

Sir: As a patron of The Tribune, I submit a few questions with the expression of my best wishes for its success:

First—If we should adopt the British monetary laws, which regulate prices with gold by excluding all bills less than £5, and silver, too, except the necessary small change, would not our prices naturally fall about as low as theirs, and so make Protection useless?

Second—Or, if they should adopt our monetary laws, and so ply their trade with all the small bills and cheap silver coins they could press into circulation, would not their prices naturally rise about as high as ours, and so make Protection useless?

Third—But if we inflate our circulation and prices above other nations, will not every unprotected advance in our prices insure to the advantage of foreign trade, and to the disadvantage of the home trade, which would be compelled to procure labor and materials at the higher prices?

Fourth—Since prices depend upon the circulation, and an advance in prices inures to the advantage of foreign trade and the disadvantage of the home trade, are we not rationally bound to prevent a rise in price or protect it from foreign spoliation by an adequate tariff?

Fifth—In the past many lines of trade may have suffered severely by stress of foreign trade, and prices have been too low to comport with prices in other lines; but does the "McKinley bill" now afford just and adequate protection? Would it not become totally inadequate under a "free coinage" of cheap silver dollars?

Sixth—Is it presumable that they who prate about the "high prices" protected, though not engendered, by the McKinley bill really want lower prices in all

lines of business; and think the economic way to reduce prices cannot be found in our money, but in our tariff?   J NORTON.

Farmer Village, Jan. 16, 1891.

In addition to these questions, we have received two long letters from Mr. Norton which throw light on his views, but our lack of space prevents their publication in full.

The foregoing questions, while constantly applied by Mr. Norton to the tariff, really involve the whole controversy as to money, currency, banking, promissory notes, the issuing of circulating bills, etc., etc. I have never claimed to be an expert on these matters, though I have some well-defined "notions," such as a man must have formed who has been hearing such questions discussed constantly for twenty years past.

In answer to the first question, I will state that, as I understand it, we are regulating prices with a gold standard right now in this country. All the various kinds of money used in the United States to-day can be converted into gold by any holder of them with very little effort, and at no expense for exchange. What the silver men complain about is that we are a gold-standard nation. I cannot see how our money is inflated so long as we keep it all redeemable in or convertible into gold. If the gold dollar is not the measure of value in this country to-day, pray what is? When we buy an ounce of silver or a bushel of wheat, do we not pay for it in precisely the same money that England does? What do we buy in the United States to-day which we do not pay for in gold or its equivalent? I do not mean that our present silver dollar is the equivalent of our gold dollar in value intrinsically, but that the Government owns the silver to make up the difference, and so long as it remains convertible into gold the gold standard will stand.

The second question is the same in substance as the first. In fact, it is the same question turned around. I cannot see how the size of the bills has any bearing on the question of inflation. Suppose the Bank of England issued 18,000,000 notes five pounds sterling each, or 90,000,000 notes one pound sterling each, or 360,000,000 notes of five shillings each, would there be any more inflation in the one issue than in the other? The amount outstanding is the same in each case. There may be some quality about a small bill that does not belong to a large one. If so, it is beyond my knowledge. It cannot be that Mr. Norton uses the term "inflated" in the sense of the word "depreciated." I can readily see how a depreciated currency always seems to raise prices, and have no doubt that a resort to the free coinage of silver would lead to the troubles he fears as to an inflated currency, but only because it would end in placing gold at a premium, and we would be doing business with irredeemable money. In that case the gold dollar would cease to be the unit of value and the cheaper silver dollar would become the standard in this country; and we would no longer be able to convert our currency, all of it, into gold, except by paying the difference between the silver dollar and the gold one.

In answer to the third question, I would say

that a resort to a depreciated currency would seem to raise prices and would result in an advantage to foreign traders.

The fourth question assumes that prices depend on the amount of circulating medium, which I doubt, so long as you keep all the money at a gold standard. Of course the moment you do business with a depreciated currency then there are at once two prices for articles, the one in the cheap money, the other in the money of the business world.

In reply to the remainder of the questions, I will say that the enactment of a silver bill such as has just passed the Senate will, in my judgment, injure the business of the country, and will, in many instances, deprive the McKinley bill of its protective features, because it will permit the payment of duties in the cheap money. During our era of inflated, irredeemable money, this trouble was avoided because duties were all made payable in gold. That increased instead of weakened the protection of the Morrill bill.

These answers may seem very inadequate to Mr. Norton. He and I will agree, no doubt, that our country will suffer from a plunge into the use of cheap, depreciated money. It will hurt in more ways than one. It will also weaken the protection now given to our own industries by our tariff laws. Just what should be done with the currency question is a hard problem to solve. I do not pretend to be fully satisfied on all points. The history of past efforts in that direction convinces me beyond all doubt that a resort to the use of irredeemable, cheap money will most surely not better the situation. It must lead to unhealthy speculation and to final disaster.

No nation can for any length of time do business up in a balloon. It is sure to come down to hard pan in time; and the fall usually hurts. Still, this money question is so far-reaching in its results, so complicated in its workings, that my conclusions may be wide of the mark. These hints are thrown out with no idea of placing this subject beyond all doubt. It may be all clear to Mr. Norton. It is not to me.—(R. G. H.

HOW DO NATIONS PAY THEIR DEBTS WHEN THE BALANCE OF TRADE IS AGAINST THEM?

THE SILVER QUESTION IN THE MINDS OF EVERY ONE.

To the Editor of The Tribune.

Sir: Please answer the following questions:

First—Are silver certificates used in trade with countries that have a silver basis, or is silver bullion ever used?

Second—In our trade with Brazil, where the balance is against us, what part, if any, is paid in silver?

Third—With the balance of trade in our favor and free coinage of silver, could there be a scarcity of gold in this country except by speculation?

Fourth—If silver was not used in any country as a circulating medium, would not its value largely depreciate?

Fifth—Is not over two-fifths of the world's production of silver mined in the United States?

Sixth—With iron and the metals generally protected

should silver be debased? ROBERT CARTWRIGHT.
Sidney, N. Y., Feb. 23, 1891.

The silver certificates of the United States are not used as money in any nation except our own. Very few of them are ever seen in any foreign country.

In our trade with all foreign nations, if silver is used in payment of a balance, it is always used as bullion; never as anything else. It makes no difference whether the nation is a silver standard or a gold standard nation, silver sent there would be credited up by weight without regard to its coin value in the country where it came from. For that matter the same is also true of gold. It is the amount of pure gold in a sovereign that fixes its value in Germany or France or the United States. The stamp of the Government of Great Britain does not add one particle of value to the coin.

In answer to your second question, I will say that no one can tell how much or how little silver is used in our settlement with Brazil. Our balances are so seldom settled by the shipment of coin of any kind that there are no data upon which to make a calculation. All such accounts are usually settled by some American bank giving a draft on some bank in London. That draft is taken by the Brazilian merchant to a bank in Brazil which also has an account in London, and the holder of the draft gets credit for it in Brazil or gets the cash, as may be. If the draft calls for gold, and there is a difference in the value of gold and the currency of the country, the bank adjusts that difference and pays the merchant in such currency as much as his gold draft is worth. The American merchant has calculated upon the same basis and the amount of the draft sent is only the amount required after taking into account the kind of money in which his bill must be paid. The banks adjust these matters and most of the shipments of gold and silver from one country to another are made between the banks of the world.

In reply to your third question, I will say that if money were only sent from one country to another in payment for food or manufactured goods, there would be little danger of getting any kind of money out of a country that sent more of these articles abroad than it brought back. But if you pass a law that permits men owning silver to bring it here, and for what they can get only 80 cents at home, compel our mints to pay them 100 cents, how long could you keep the gold in this country, which would be required to pay for the silver which such profits would send to this country? If by the passage of such a law the value of the silver dollar would at once advance so as to be equal to that of the gold dollar all over the world, then the calamity would not follow. Does any sane man think that such would be the case? The moment our laws permit the people of other nations to pay us with cheap money and compel us to pay them with money that is more valuable, the question as to the balance of trade in ordinary commodities will have little to do with the scarcity of the good money that will follow in this country. As a rule, water runs down hill in this world.

If silver was not used in any country as a circulating medium its value would depreciate immensely. You might as well ask if the human race should stop eating potatoes would not that lower the price of potatoes? It would nearly destroy their production. Is there any nation in the world that does not use silver as money? Is there any nation that proposes to stop its use as money? I have never known an instance where silver was driven out of circulation, except in countries that were compelled to resort to depreciated paper money. Cheap paper money will stop the use of silver in any country. I well remember ten years of my life during which I did not see a single silver dollar, and that, too, before silver had been demonetized by law.

In reply to your fifth question I will say that you name the amount of silver raised in the United States as compared with the rest of the world about as it is stated by men who are giving the subject great attention. It does not seem to me possible that we produce almost as much silver as does the balance of the world; but it has been recently estimated at about two-fifths of the entire output. It is, of course, a matter somewhat of guess work.

"With iron and other metals protected should silver be debased?" Of course it should not. Silver should be treated fairly, whether the other metals are misused or not. Do you know of any people who are attempting to fix the price of iron by statute? Why debase iron, or steel, or tin, or lead, or zinc, or copper? If the price of an article can be fixed by law, why not arrange a schedule of fair prices for everything, and so hereafter always know just what each article will bring? It would be attended with some difficulties, perhaps, but it certainly sounds well. The blessings that would follow such an arrangement, if it worked, seem to me simply immense. Would it work? I fear not. There are so many things in this world that seem desirable that do not come through legislation. Silver is not debased in this country now. It is performing its own good work. We are utilizing nearly, or quite, the entire product from our own mines now. Why should we attempt to do more than that? Why not go slow, and see how the new law works? Experiments are often educational, but they are sometimes expensive.—(R. G. Horr.

A STRING OF QUESTIONS ON SILVER.

AN EFFORT TO EXPLAIN A FEW POINTS UPON WHICH A GOOD MANY FARMERS ARE PERPLEXED.

To the Editor of The Tribune.

Sir: Will you please answer the following questions:

1. When was the silver dollar deprived of its legal-tender quality?

2. Would the demonetization of silver tend to reduce or increase its value as a commodity?

3. If, as a commodity, during a period of large production, silver has depreciated only 18.6 per cent, measured by a gold standard, how much inflation of the circulating medium will free coinage produce?

4. Did the demonetization of silver increase the value of gold as compared with the value of all other commodities?

5. If so; did it not disturb contracts in favor of the creditor?

6. With United States bonds at 25 per cent premium, is it any longer necessary to strengthen the public credit by the continued demonetization of silver?

7. Will restoring to silver the legal qualities it once had make a greater difference between the value of the silver and gold coin than now exists?

8. Would it be any more than just to make the silver dollar the laborer receives for his day's work a full legal tender and equal in purchasing power to the gold dollar of the bondholder?

9. You state that free coinage of silver "will in many instances deprive the McKinley bill of its protective features." Silver certificates are now received in payment of duties. Would payment in silver be any less protection than payment in that which is exchangeable for silver?   W. C. WHITEHEAD.

Pataskala, Ohio, Jan. 30, 1891.

In answer to our correspondent, I will say that the act which he refers to as demonetizing silver was passed in 1873. At that time neither gold nor silver was in circulation in the United States as currency. That bill simply made the gold dollar our standard of value and deprived the silver dollar of that place. That is usually called the "demonetizing" of silver, but it did not "demonetize" that metal. Silver and gold were used as money, long before any Government passed laws as to their use. Their value as money in the markets of the world does not come from legislation, but is owing to their being better adapted to that purpose than any other product of labor known to the civilized world. At the time the bill of 1873 became a law it did not affect the price of either gold or silver one iota, although it may have had some effect on the price of silver since the resumption of specie payments.

Your second question is based on the supposition that silver is now used as money, which is true. Any new use to which you put any article which is the product of labor increases the demand for that article and tends to increase its value. My opinion is that no product of labor should ever be given any value, which it does not possess as a commodity. The use of gold and silver as money could not be except for their recognized value as products of human labor. The use of each as money adds to that value, because it adds an extra use to the article; but the value of the commodity must also keep pace with the value as money.

Your third question cannot be answered, because you do not give terms enough on which to base a mathematical calculation. A moment's thought will show any one that free coinage involves the silver product of the world. So there is no basis for any calculation that can be expressed in any per cent statement. If you coined a silver dollar which was of the same value as the gold one, there would be little effect from the numbers coined. But suppose you should coin a silver dollar of less intrinsic value than the gold one. Then, if the Government coining such dollars should make them the standard of value in that country, they would of course drive out of circulation the more valuable dollars, because persons paying out money will always use the cheap money in making payments. Gold might still be a legal-tender; but no one would make a tender of gold, when he could sell his gold and get more dollars (silver) with it which would answer the same purpose. If by any legal enactment you could make 412 1-2 grains of silver actually of the same value as 25 8-10 grains of gold, then "free coinage" would lose all its terrors. Not believing that such a feat is within the reach of human possibilities, I fear the results of making our Nation a silver standard nation. We are now using both metals as currency, but with a gold standard; and the people, who are the Government in this country, always have in the possession of the Government the difference between the value of the silver and the gold dollars coined. Free coinage, which puts that difference into the pockets of the holders of silver, would no doubt please them; but, would it not be at the expense of the people?

My answer to your fourth question is: that the demonetizing of silver in this country had little effect on the price of gold. Several other nations also demonetized silver. The united action of all of them may have appreciated the value of gold somewhat. But do not forget this, that all these nations changed from the silver standard because silver itself had depreciated in value before it was demonetized. If all the great Powers of the world should combine and agree on a ratio between gold and silver, they might keep the two metals at pretty nearly that ratio, provided they fixed the value of each metal at near the cost of production; but all of them together could not prevent the fluctuations in either metal which come from causes higher and more powerful than all legal enactments.

Fifth. Of course, if any legislative enactment could raise the standard of value, such change in value would benefit the creditor class and would injure those who owe money and must pay in something more valuable than it was when the debt was contracted. It also follows that if they are permitted to pay in a less valuable dollar than the one in legal use when the debt was contracted such a law would benefit the debtor and wrong the men who loaned the money.

In answer to your sixth question, I will say that there is now no need of further legislation to strengthen the public credit. It is as strong as it can be now. That, however, does not imply that it would be right to do anything to weaken or impair that credit. If our credit is high, so high that there is none better on the face of the globe, that can hardly be given as a reason for doing any foolish thing. It is better to examine carefully and learn, if possible, the wisdom of the action which has given us this proud position, and then profit by the lesson.

In reply to your seventh question, I would say that if you mean the making of 412 1-2 grains of silver our standard of value, I do not think that making that dollar a legal tender will change the relative value of the two metals for any great length of time to any great extent. It would probably increase the value of silver a few points for a time. In the end, the value of each metal would be determined by weight and purity and not by legislation.

In answer to your eighth question, let me say that the laborer should always be paid in the best money there is in any country. To-day the silver dollar of the workingman is precisely as valuable as the gold dollar of the bondholder. They are interchangeable, the one for the other, without expense to the holder. Our silver dollars

are now, for all practical purposes, a legal tender for all debts. All the money circulating in the United States to-day is of equal value, not because all of it is a legal tender, for it is not, but because it is all readily convertible the one into the other at the option of the holder. It matters not what money you have. If, with certainty, you can convert it into the best, it becomes at once as good as the best. But if you change the law so that you cannot get the best, but permit all payments to be made in the cheapest, then you will of necessity drive out of use the better money, and gold will be bought and sold as a commodity, to be paid for with the cheap money.

In your ninth question, you seem to think that because silver certificates are now used to pay duties this somehow militates against my former statement that free coinage would enable importers to pay their duties in cheap money. The silver certificates are now as good as gold. The Government paid gold price for the silver, and you can get gold for the dollars by stepping into any bank in the country. But we are now living under a gold standard. Your question implies that the Government can make 412 1-2 grains of silver worth as much as 25 8-10 grains of gold by the Free Coinage bill. That I do not believe. If they can, why not make 200 grains do the business? I admit that the lawmaking power can change the standard of value. It could make a dollar consist of 200 grains of silver; but I deny the power of any Government to make a silver dollar with only 200 grains of silver in it worth as much as one with 412 1-2 grains. The Government might compel the creditors of the country to take such small dollars and cancel its obligations; but that would not change the fact that one dollar is cheaper than the other and actually worth less. Indeed, your last question shows that you understand this principle. Of course, as I have already stated, as long as silver and gold dollars are exchangeable the one for the other, it makes no difference which ones are used. But, do you not see that involves the assumption that they will be exchangeable the one for the other when you have made 412 1-2 grains of silver our standard of value for a dollar? If they will still remain interchangeable after such a change of standard, then you are right. My fear is that silver dollars would then be much cheaper than gold ones, and the world would know that fact and would instantly pay us entirely in silver and compel us to pay them in gold, which could work nothing except ruin to our Nation in the end. We need both gold and silver as the basis of circulation in this country. We need, in my judgment, the entire output of our own mines for that purpose. That end can be easily reached without changing our standard of value, and without giving the rest of the world power to buy from us with cheap money and compel us to pay them in the money of the world (which is and always has been so much metal, either gold or silver, at a price which depends entirely upon weight and purity, and not in the least upon its legal-tender value in any country).

This whole question turns on the power of government to create value. It can be decided perhaps only by experiment. Good men differ with me as to what the result would be. I do not claim that the question is free from doubt. I have answered these questions in view of the knowledge I now possess. If I am wrong, then experience with free silver may show me my error. If I am right, then the free-silver experiment will have been a costly one, but the experience will be none the less instructive. I believe that silver is cheaper to-day than it was a few years ago for the same reason that wheat is, and that no legislation can permanently fix the price of either. The price of each will always be governed by the cost of production and the great law of supply and demand.   R. G. HORR.

A CHALLENGE ON THE TARIFF

MR. HORR PAYS HIS COMPLIMENTS TO A RIGHT HONORABLE K. C. B.

A SPEECH AT LEEDS EFFECTIVELY ANSWERED.

A Democratic ex-member of Congress, who is also an ardent free-trader, has sent me a speech delivered by the Right Hon. Sir Lyon Playfair, K. C. B., M. P., in Leeds, England, November 13, 1890. This American friend has taken pains to mark many passages in this wonderful production, showing his glee, as is usual with all free-traders, over everything "English, you know"; and he has suggested that I try my pen in reply, if, indeed, any reply is deemed possible.

Bear in mind that the speech of Sir Lyon Playfair was made to the manufacturers of the great manufacturing town of Leeds, and is devoted entirely to a discussion of the McKinley bill. The speaker informed his audience that he was in America during the passage of the bill and gave great study to the measure. There can be little doubt that his statement on that point is true; for, after reading the speech with care, I fail to find in it a single argument (indeed, hardly a single utterance) which was not repeated over and over again by the free-trade opponents of that bill during the debate in Congress. So marked is this similarity that I am left in a painful perplexity as to whether this member of the British Parliament furnished the ammunition for our free-trade members of Congress, or whether, at Leeds, he supplied his English audience with a mere repetition of what he had heard from their tried-and-true friends here in America.

One thing certainly can be truthfully said of the speech. It does not contain a single new idea or suggestion; and, while as an argument it is somewhat better than Mr. Mills or Mr. Springer can make, it is not as well done as one would expect from Mr. Carlisle. It is somewhat significant, however, in this regard. It does show that precisely the same nonsense which is dealt out by our free-trade speakers in this country is fitted to please the men who manufacture goods in England. Mr. Playfair did not feel called upon "to change the dot of an i or the cross of a t."

He was kind enough to admit in the outset that Mr. McKinley is an honest man. He then adds that Mr. McKinley "thoroughly believes that a wall of protection built around his country is needful for the prosperity of his Nation, and he has erected this wall in as good faith as the Chinese made their great wall as a defence from foreign foes." This Chinese wall illustration is growing extremely stale on this side of the water, though it may be fresh at Leeds. Taking into account the enormous increase of the exports and imports of the United States since the tariff law of 1861, when a man over here begins to talk about a "Chinese wall" he becomes a laughing-stock for well-informed men; there are those who are so lacking in dignity or diction that they would call such a statement "mere rot."

This English free-trader makes another statement which has been refuted so many times as also to be out of date. Hear him: "Never during the history of the United States was there so much prosperity as during the low tariffs from 1847 to 1860." A man must have lived in this country and known about 1857 to understand what an unmitigated falsehood that is. I lived and labored in the United States during all those years, and no man need ask me to believe such nonsense.

His next utterance is worse yet: "There is no intimate connection between the tariff and wages. As a whole, wages have gone down under the new tariff, and there seems to be no tendency to rise." Just think of it. The new tariff law went into effect October 6, and this wonderful man is making this wonderful speech November 13—in less than forty days—and telling his audience how the law has "on the whole, lowered wages"! How he must have presumed on the ignorance or gullibility of his hearers! What data could he have had on which to make that announcement? None in the world. It takes more than six weeks to learn what has happened to wages "as a whole" in this large country of ours. But I notice that in order to prove both these propositions—the one as to the growth of our country and the one as to wages—he launches off into the unlimited field of "per cents." In the hands of an earnest, sincere and well-informed statistician, who knows to what percentages properly apply and to what they properly do not, this method of comparison has its merits. On the other hand, the statement of a per centum loss or gain may mean absolutely nothing. It is sometimes a term used to hide the actual condition of affairs. The trouble is that it gives no information as to the surrounding circumstances. If the starting-point is not disclosed, what value is there in stating "per cents"?

Let me illustrate. A man who has just finished a comfortable supper, and who has had before that on the same day a good dinner and a good breakfast, says: "Well, I have fared well for food to-day. It contrasts so with my experience one day in my army life that I can but feel thankful for my present happy condition."

"Hold on a moment," say Mr. Mills, Mr. Springer, Mr. Carlisle and the Right Hon. Sir Lyon Playfair, K. C. B., M. P., "we are not so sure about that. Tell us, what did you have for breakfast that day in the army?"

The old soldier answers, "About half of a hard-tack biscuit, which I soaked in some tough-looking water, but it was the best I could do."

"Very well; what did you have for dinner?"

"I did not have any dinner that day. We were too busy to look after rations."

"All right; now what did you have for supper?"

"I had a whole hard-tack biscuit, a piece of bacon and a tin cup full of coffee—about half a meal, but not half a one for a man as hungry as I was."

"Now, then, tell us, what did you have for breakfast this morning?"

"Oh, let me see! Some ham and eggs, some baked potatoes, some bread and butter, some griddle cakes with maple syrup and two cups of excellent coffee, with cream."

"Just so. Now, what for dinner?"

"We had an old-fashioned boiled dinner—corned beef and cabbage and other vegetables—and ended up with a suet pudding boiled in a bag."

"Exactly; and what for supper?"

"Rather a light supper. Just some tea-biscuits with fresh creamery butter and honey, and a bit of cold goose left over from a swell dinner my wife had given some friends a day or two ago, and a cup of tea."

"Now, you wait just a bit," says the English spokesman, "while we four intellectual giants retire and make the necessary mathematical calculations, and we will then report to you whether you have any cause to feel happy or not." The four Free-Trade wiseacres then go by themselves. They cipher and study, and study and cipher. They agree on a fair estimate of the food properties in half of an army hardtack biscuit and add to that "no dinner," and then get at the amount of food properties in a whole hardtack biscuit, a piece of bacon and a tin cupful of coffee. Mirabile dictu! It turns out that the old soldier's condition improved at least 300 per cent during that day in the army. Then they go through the careful estimates of his breakfast, dinner and supper that day and those at home and find that there is no "per cent" in his favor. If anything, the "per cent" is against him. They are now ready to report, and the whole four immediately attack the old man for his stupidity.

"See here," says the Right Honorable Sir Lyon Playfair, K. C. B., M. P., "you are rejoicing, old man, over your condition here at home to-day, whereas you should rejoice over your real condition that day in the army." "Of course you should," chime in the three American allies. "How is that?" timidly inquires the old veteran. "Why, we find that you had an improvement of fully 300 per cent that day, while to-day the per cent is against you! It is a matter of mathematical demonstration."

The old soldier with "a sort of dreamy, faraway look in his eye," says to himself, "Per cent, per cent; I don't remember eating anything of that kind. Yet, it must be some kind of victuals, else these big men would not mention it."

All of a sudden he espies the buttonhole bouquet in the lapel of Mr. Springer's coat and mistakes him for a military man, and sidling up to him, asks: "Did we have any 'per cent' issued among our army rations?"

"I am not an army man," says the Congressman from Illinois. "Colonel Mills, here, is the military chieftain of this band of economic heroes."

The veteran then turns pleadingly to the Congressman from Texas: "How is it, comrade; did we ever have any 'per cent' among our rations in the army?"

"Don't you comrade me," Mr. Mills retorts; "I am no comrade of yours. I am a Free-Trader, and was in the Confederate Army."

"Very well; but the 'boys in gray' had rations, did they not? Please tell me; did they ever have any of this 'per cent' which this gentleman tells me I had 200 of that day, when it seemed to me I would starve?"

"Old man, go and put your head in soak," is the classical and customary reply from the Texas statesman.

So the old soldier would leave these four great teachers of free-trade sorely perplexed, and would wonder still what this "per cent" could be over which he ought to have rejoiced that day in the army, and which really had in it more cause for rejoicing than belonged to the day he had just passed, which seemed to him so full of blessings.

Our Leeds orator then grapples with the question as to who pays the duties, the foreign producer or the home consumer. He concludes, after the manner of all Free-Traders, that these duties come out of the consumers; and he then states that the McKinley bill will cost the people of the United States, in addition to old rates on metal, woollen, cotton and linen goods (all of which are largely made in Leeds), about $32,-000,000 each year. If this money is all coming out of the people of the United States, what were the men in Leeds grumbling about? They will still get the same price for their goods. If not, why not? Why did he tell them that the bill would prove most disastrous to England or more disastrous to her than to any other European Nation, if the duties are all paid by our consumers?

He then asserts that American Protectionists well understand that the bill will raise prices, and in support of that assertion he says: "Jay Gould, a millionaire, is stated to justify the rise in prices because it will teach a workingman thrift, for while he now buys a suit of clothes once in the year, in the future he will make it last him two years. Why should he not go further and recommend the workingman not to buy clothes at all? But decency reminds me that I ought not to mention what the result would be." I never saw Mr. Gould in my life. I know nothing about what his views on the tariff are; but I will wager a big apple (and apples are scarce) that he never made any such remark. How do I know? Let me tell you. Some one said to Andy Johnson: "They tell me, Mr. Johnson, that you are a Spiritualist. Is that so?" "Yes," was his instant reply; "but I am not a —— fool!" It will be readily gathered from that answer of Mr. Johnson's why I am sure that Jay Gould never made any such remark as the one attributed to him. More than that, if the Right Honorable Sir Lyon Playfair, K. C. B., M. P., will be honest, I will wager another apple that he will admit that he had no idea that Mr. Gould ever uttered such a sentiment when he made the statement to his audience at Leeds. If his devotion to decency were anywhere near as strong as he intimated, why did he attempt to bolster up his cause with such an absurd freak of some dishonest Free-Trader's imagination?

Not satisfied with such an indecent imputation upon the common-sense of an American citizen, who, say what people may of him, has never yet been classed among the "fools," this orator then says: "All this kind of justification of the tariff by leading men is quite inconsistent with the general assertion that the effect of protective tariffs in America has been to lower the prices of commodities. They point to steel, which, in 1874, sold at twelve pounds sterling per ton, and has now been lowered to about five pounds sterling." That is, that this statement of Mr. Gould (which Mr. Gould never made), and similar statements of other leading men, not one of which was ever made, is inconsistent with what these leading men actually do claim! If any one can surpass that statement for indecent impudence, it will please me to watch the attempt. This gentleman tells us that he was present, and so of course heard the arguments on the McKinley bill. He knows then, very well, that every Protectionist in this country claims that the final result of our protective system has been to cheapen all articles manufactured here. He should know that the facts bear out this inference. We do not confine the statement to steel. We simply name that as one article among all the rest. It is just as true of salt, cutlery, earthenware, glass goods, silks, cotton goods, starch, nails, paper-pulp, etc., etc.,—every one are cheaper now than when we trusted to the foreign manufacturers for our supplies. Why did he not name one single article of which this is not true? He would not be slow to do it if he could. Instead of doing that, he rushes off into tin plate before we have had time to try that.

Listen to him: " Neither have I alluded to the monstrous tax on tin plates, which may restrict consumption, as the tax is likely to amount to four millions sterling. It will certainly raise the price on domestic utensils and canned provisions; but South Wales need not fear that tin plates will be made in the United States in any quantity. I could give good reason for this belief, but time fails me." It is very plain what reason was running in the gentleman's mind. Want of time was not really what caused his failure to name it. He could not have named it without betraying some of his coadjutors in this country, who had thus early informed him that capital already had been frightened out of the tin-plate industry here in the United States.

I am very glad, however, that we have finally one straight prediction from a Free-Trader as to what will be the result of this tariff on even on one article, to wit, tin plate. I now propose to match this prediction of the Right Hon. Sir Lyon Playfair, K. C. B, M. P., Free-Trader, etc., with one from a Protectionist, who has no very long tail at either end of his name. First, domestic utensils and tin cans will not rise in price for any great length of time, if at all, but, on the contrary, inside of two years, tin plate will be cheaper, and we will get a better article for less money than we are now paying for the foreign product. Second, it makes no difference whether South Wales fears or not, tin plate will be made in the United States, not only in considerable quantities, but in large quantities, and that too within a few months. Dare this English Free-Trader agree to submit the question of protection and free trade as to prices to this test? I know my predictions are as unequivocal as his. Come, now. What can home competition do to cheapen the price of an article? That question can be settled by this one experiment, at least, as between us two individuals. I am ready to risk the result. Is he?

I cannot close this article without warning the good people of South Wales against being mis'ed by the predictions of this distinguished gentleman. Tin plate is, to-day, being made in no inconsiderable quantity in this country. Several large works for its manufacture are already being built. The plates, both of iron and steel, are being manufactured now and laid aside for use when the tariff on tin plate goes into effect, and the people of this country propose to make large quantities of this article right here in our own mills and by the aid of our own workmen. We have never yet started a new industry in this country without having met this same cry of "Wolf! wolf!" from these same Free-Traders. Our people have learned not to be frightened at this clatter of tongues. The noise has become familiar to us all. Then permit me to assure you that our business men certainly intend to make our own tin plate in the near future, not because they love South Wales less, but the United States of America more. That they may succeed in this laudable undertaking is my hope and earnest prayer.　　　　R. G HORR.

IN AMERICA the PEOPLE RULE

WHAT GOVERNMENTS ARE FOR AND WHY THEY EXIST.

AN ENTERTAINING ACCOUNT OF THE WHOLE MATTER FOR AMERICAN VOTERS TO READ, ESPECIALLY THOSE WHO ARE FOREIGN BORN.

It is well for people living under any form of government to stop at times and examine the question as to how it happens that there are any Governments among men, and also try and learn the fundamental principles upon which Governments are founded, and more especially the principles which underlie the government of the Nation in which they are living themselves. A study of this sort, while good for all, is especially desirable for that large number of our fellow-citizens of foreign birth who have come among us to live.

Nations have come into existence only after a slow growth for ages. An individual, solitary and alone, could simply make a struggle for life, without being helped or hampered by any other of his species; and when he died, that would be the end of him. His end would be mourned by no one. Nature ordained that the human race can be continued in existence only by the commingling of the sexes. Hence the first form of government on the face of the earth must have been the family. The father and mother, their children and their children's children, constituted an organization of persons who had interests in common, and their interests being mutual, they soon came to make common cause of the rights or wrongs of each person in the family. The oldest man of the family came naturally to assume the highest authority, and just as naturally received the completest homage. The entire household, from youth up, became accustomed to obey him, to look up to him for aid and counsel. His word soon came to be law, and his decisions, of necessity, final. This family relation came in time to be considered sacred, and the authority of each patriarch, that is, of the oldest man in each family, became supreme at a very early day in the existence of the human race.

Thus, in the very dawn of civilization, obedience to the commands of one person came to be considered a duty, and the right of such person to exercise power was fully established, and has never since been questioned by any civilized people. That same power is exercised to-day by the head of every family, and the same obedience is required among all the civilized descendants of Adam.

As population increased, as families became more numerous, as the fight for a living became more severe, families which had intermarried with each other began to form clans, or tribes, for purposes of defence and common protection. Thus small bands of men with a common interest learned to make a common cause with each other. The patriarchs and their followers united to form a community larger than the family, but Nature had made no provision for a leader of the tribe. His selection must of necessity have been made by those constituting the tribe. They naturally chose some man among them noted for his physical strength, for his cunning and courage, and he became the chief of the tribe. Having been selected, what would be more natural than that he should be given the same power over tribal matters which the patriarch had long possessed over the family? This was the second step in the formation of all governments. This chosen chief at once became a ruler of men, but his place and power were given to him by the people composing the tribe.

In the outset, no man could have been born a chief. He had to prove himself worthy of the place, and the office must have been given him by the consent of those who constituted the clan or tribe.

REPUBLICS AND MONARCHIES.

After a lapse of time clans and tribes became more numerous and they finally banded themselves together into still larger communities and formed nations, also for purposes of mutual protection and profit. These combinations soon discovered the need of some supreme authority, some person vested with the right to command and receive obedience. To meet such a necessity they selected, no doubt at first always from among the chiefs, a ruler; and he was placed at the head of all the clans or tribes in settling national questions. In this case, too, he must have received his place from the choice of the men constituting the tribes or clans. So it is very clear that in those early days there could have been no such thing as a man being born a king or a ruler. In those early times all rulers must have been selected or chosen to their place.

As the ownership of property came to be understood and agreed to, the right of inheritance also came to be insisted upon and recognized; and thus, property came to be held in the same family from generation to generation. Out of that idea, no doubt, afterward grew up the notion that families could also inherit the right to rulership. When a man possessed great strength, courage, capacity, and did great things for his people, why should he not impart to his children the same power to dare and to do? Religious notions may have aided in the work at an early day, and helped to form the idea of the divine rights of kings and princes. In my judgment, however, the notions that people had about their rulers had far more to do with the shaping of their idols than their ideas about their deities had in determining the character they attributed to their rulers. It was no doubt a long time before any man claimed the divine right to rule or even the right to do so on account of his birth. The idea that kings received their right to govern from on high came from theology; it was resorted to on account of the constantly recurring claim, which has been stated over and over again from time immemorial, that rulers got their power from the people. The world has never been free from people somewhere who were asserting that the right to govern could not be inherited and did not come from above, but that

it was a right which came only from the consent of the governed. Kings and princes have of late never ceased claiming that their right to rule comes from on high; and that human agencies have no right to interfere with them in their exercise of a power bestowed upon them by the Almighty.

Those people who believed that the power to govern could come only from the consent of the governed formed republics and chose their own rulers. Other people recognized the alleged "divine right" of certain families to rule; and they submitted to be governed by monarchs and kings.

The nation in which Americans live has been managed for over a century now upon the old, primitive plan that the people are the source of all civil power. A little examination will show how completely we have preserved all the ancient divisions and landmarks.

EACH DISTRICT SUPREME IN ITS OWN WAY.

We still have the original form and power of the family. In the great bulk of the duties and transactions of life, the family is still supreme. In the management of the household, in the gaining of a living, in the training and management of children, in nearly all there is of ordinary daily life, each family manages its own affairs, submits to dictation from neither priest nor potentate, and is seldom interfered with by the officers of Church or State. Families are seldom meddled with by the rest of the world. It may seem strange, but it is true, that nearly all the ordinary transactions of life are controlled and managed under the unwritten law of the household. Each family is a law unto itself; and no two are governed precisely alike in any nation. This is as it should be. The family, the home, is the natural unit of power with which the world has been civilized. It is the first, the natural organization of human beings. Its precincts should always be held sacred; its prerogatives should be abridged as little as possible.

In the place of the ancient clans and tribes we now have school and road districts, towns, cities, counties and States, and all these together make up the Nation. Certain minor matters are left to small districts. These were organized, not as the result of any theory, but as a matter of growth.

The school district is as small a portion of the country as can maintain a school. As the population increases, the district is made smaller, so as to save the children travel.

A road district is fixed by the distance within which people can readily go to work on the road.

These small districts have certain duties to perform, and in matters pertaining to those small districts they are supreme. In hiring a district school-teacher, the town, or the county or State have no voice; nor would they be permitted to interfere any more than the directors of a school district would be permitted to meddle in the management of any family in that district except their own.

The townships and cities are still larger organizations than the school districts. They take charge of matters of a wider scope than those intrusted to these small districts. They, too, are supreme in matters intrusted to them; and in such matters the counties and States are not permitted to interfere.

Again, in matters which pertain to the counties the latter are also supreme. They have charge of large bridges, building and furnishing court houses, recording of deeds, probating of wills, etc., etc. The State never thinks of interfering in any way with the duties which belong to the counties.

The States are still larger organizations and have charge of broader and weightier affairs. In matters which belong to them, the States also are supreme. They have absolute control; the Nation has no right to meddle in any way with purely State matters.

Last of all comes the Nation, the Government of the United States, with National powers and National rights. In all matters that are National the Nation is supreme, and its laws are final

Let us now go back again to the unit of power, the family. While it is supreme in so many of the transactions of life, still the moment a school district is formed and the members of the family have become members of that organization, then the family ceases to have the right, as a family, to interfere with the management of the school. Even the right to control and correct their own children while in the school-room has been delegated to the larger organization, and that body is clothed with full power to do whatever is best and proper to secure a good school. The rights of the family over its children must give way to the rights of the larger organization in its efforts to perform its duties. So it is all the way up the ladder. While the larger organizations have no right to meddle with matters which pertain to the smaller ones, the smaller ones are equally bound to yield to the larger in all matters pertaining to the peculiar duties of the latter.

All the talk about the "supremacy and sovereignty of the States" has no special significance. It would be just as sensible to talk about the "sovereignty" of the family, the school district, the town, the city or the county, as of that of the State. Each of these organizations is supreme in its own special department, one no more than another.

At the top round of the ladder is the Nation, supreme in all National matters, and from whose decision there is no appeal. Its courts are those of last resort, its laws the supreme laws of the land. Its jurisdiction is hemmed in by no State lines. It takes notice neither of districts nor towns, nor counties. Its only question is where is the boundary line of the United States, and everywhere within those lines it is equally at home. Failure to recognize this principle led to civil war. The people of the South constantly talked about being "invaded" by the Federal Army. The Army of the United States is never an invading army so long as it remains within the boundaries of this Nation. A nation cannot "invade" itself. In an attempt to enforce National laws, the Nation never stops to inquire about State lines or other local lines. I know the Constitution provides that the Government may send the National troops into a State, after having been requested to do so by the Governor of that State, but that is when the Governor desires help to enforce some State law. There is no such provision as to the enforcement of National laws. Such a provision as that in reference to sustaining National authority would be simply ridiculous.

From what has gone before, it is evident that the people are the source of all power in this country. Our officials are expected simply to carry out the will of the people. It then follows as a matter of necessity that to have a wise and intelligent Government our people must be wise and intelligent themselves, because they are, in fact, the Government.

No man is born to any civil or political office in the United States. Rulers are made and unmade at the will of the people. Our theory is that the people will select the best men for place and power. They often fail to do so, but they hit it right more frequently than is done when these offices are filled by the accidents of birth.

A RULER'S FIRST TRAINING.

In a Republic like ours, the Nation rests upon the intelligence, virtue and honesty of the individual men and women living within our borders. Cultivated, pure, honest people give pure, happy homes, and good homes secure good rulers, good lawmakers and a good Government.

In the very outset, men being physically stronger than women, being free from the duty of nursing the young, it naturally fell to their lot to provide food for the families and to bear the burdens of protection and defence. Women had other duties which fell to them naturally. In this way, from time immemorial, the duty of managing Governments and defending them from foreign foes has been considered the proper work for men. When one recollects that the family is the unit of political power in this world, it will be seen that so long as the families are represented the entire people are also represented. It is too true that man has often been a tyrant in the exercise of the power given him in the organization of the family. But in very many more cases he has been an affectionate husband, a kind father, a hard-working provider and a genuine protector for his family. A man who does not manage his household on the principles of love and kindness is one of the worst of rulers among men. He is causing misery at the very threshold of human society. The first duty of every human being is to learn to govern himself. Then he will manage his family well. That will prepare him to do well in managing a township. He will soon be valuable in the affairs of the State, and will be fitted for a place among the Nation's rulers.

When once understood, I believe our form of government will be admitted to be the best ever yet devised. The system of local management being left with the people of each locality for themselves, is as perfect a plan as has ever yet been formed. If our people could only always agree on what is best to be done, there would be little friction in the management of affairs. Here comes the trouble. Good men often differ as to what policy should be pursued. They cannot agree as to what is best. Selfishness and ignorance also mix up in the solution of the problem, and sometimes wickedness and bad motives are not wanting. A decision must be made. In an absolute monarchy the question would be settled by the will of the monarch. In a republic, we leave the decision to the vote of the majority of the people. Our theory is that the majority will be more likely to be right than the minority, and certainly more likely to be right than any one man.

Thus it becomes evident that the intelligence of the voter, which will enable him to decide wisely, and then an honest count of the ballots, so as to learn where the majority stands, these are the two safeguards of this Republic. Intelligent, well-informed people and an honest, fair election are the substratum on which rests this great American Nation. Pure homes, well regulated families, good common schools, an untrammelled press, and honest ballots honestly counted will keep this Nation among the best and wisest Governments on the face of the earth. R. G. H.

THE RECIPROCITY POLICY.

EXCHANGES OF NON-COMPETING PRODUCTS PROMOTED BY THE TREATIES.

ENLARGING EXPORT TRADE

RESOURCES OF RECIPROCITY.

The Reciprocity treaties which have been negotiated are the beginning but not the end of a great policy. If it had been impracticable for the State Department to make commercial arrangements with any Southern countries, all would have remained on equal terms after the 1st of January. Not one of them would have been placed at a disadvantage in comparison with the others, if the free market for coffee, sugar, molasses and hides had been withdrawn from all. In order to convert the Reciprocity amendment into a lever for opening many foreign markets for American exports it was necessary to bring it to bear upon the two chief sources from which coffee and sugar were derived. As soon as Brazil and the Spanish West Indies were drawn into commercial union a basis was established for future discriminations against competing countries, which might be reluctant to comply with the requirements of equitable Reciprocity.

Herein lies the potential efficiency of the Aldrich amendment. The free market for coffee, sugar, molasses and hides is offered on equal terms to all the Southern countries. Those willing to pay for their privileges by making reasonable concessions to the American export trade will retain that free market permanently. Those accepting it only as a gratuity will be deprived of the benefits of unrestricted trade in these tropical staples. The Reciprocity amendment will operate after the close of this year as a discrimination in favor of those countries which comply with the conditions of the offer of the free market, and against those which neglect their opportunities. The language of the act is explicit respecting the President's obligations to enforce a fixed schedule of duties whenever the conditions of trade are inequitable and unreasonable. It is as follows:

That with a view to secure reciprocal trade with countries producing the following articles, and for this purpose, on and after the first day of January, 1892, whenever and so often as the President shall be satisfied that the Government of any country producing and exporting sugars, molasses, coffee, tea and hides, raw and uncured, or any of such articles, imposes duties or other exactions upon the agricultural or other products of the United States, which in view of the free introduction of such sugar, molasses, coffee, tea and hides into the United States he may deem to be reciprocally unequal and unreasonable, he shall have the power, and it shall be his duty to suspend, by proclamation to that effect, the provisions of this act relating to the free introduction of such sugar, molasses, coffee, tea and hides, the production of such country, for such time as he shall deem just, and in such case and during such suspension duties shall be levied, collected and paid upon sugar, molasses, coffee, tea and hides, the product of or exported from such designated country as follows: (The schedule follows.)

Nothing can be clearer than the President's duty to impose the schedule of duties and thereby to place a premium upon the produce of countries entering into commercial union, and to discount the industries of those which do not conform to the requirements of reciprocal trade. On the basis of the coffee importations of 1890 a duty of 3 cents a pound will make in favor of Brazil the following discriminations against the countries named: Venezuela, $1,722,614 13; Central America, $923,363 94; Mexico, $620,009 25; Hayti, $201,049 50; British West Indies, $146,181 08. To these discriminations will be added the duties on hides, and in the case of the British West Indies the duties on sugar. There will be sufficient force in this discrimination in favor of Brazil to compel Venezuela and the other coffee countries to make Reciprocity treaties. As for the British West Indies, they will be ruined without Reciprocity. The schedule of duties, if imposed on the basis of recent importations from Jamaica alone, will amount to $466,000; and for the entire group it will be not less than $1,500,000. If the Home Government allows the interests of the islands to be sacrificed to those of Brazil, the Spanish West Indies and Santo Domingo it will be wantonly indifferent to their fate.

The more closely the Reciprocity question is studied the larger and more practical appear the results of this great policy. Congress has armed the President with tremendous power in opening the Southern markets to American trade. Determined as he is known to be to make Reciprocity and the enlargement of the Nation's exporting interests the crowning issue of his Administration, he can be depended upon to employ the resources of the act to their full extent during the last fifteen months of his term.

RECIPROCITY AND FREE TRADE.

For a week "The World" has been asking questions like this: "Are foreigners better than Americans that they should be untaxed and our own people left burdened?" "If the tariff be not a tax on consumers, why are these foreign people congratulated on getting American products free of duty?" "If it be a benefit, as all concede that it is, to relieve South American and Spanish American people from tariff taxes on universal necessaries, it would be a boon to the people of the United States to relieve them of similar burdens, as these treaties do not." "The placing of coal upon our free list would without doubt have an important effect upon the manufactures in New-England that are being forced to the wall by the tax-enhanced cost of their fuel and raw materials."

The common answer to all these questions is that the tariffs in Spanish-America are not protective, but revenue tariffs. Take, for example, coal in Cuba. There are no coal mines in the island; there is no industry, as there is in the United States, that has been protected by the duty; it has been a revenue tax imposed in the interest of the Spanish administration. In the same manner the heavy import duties on flour have not been levied in the interest of the agricultural classes of the island. There is no wheat raised in Cuba. It is a country which produces sugar, tobacco, coffee and tropical fruits. When wheat flour has been taxed, it has been for revenue purposes, but not in the interest of protection of home industries. The same remarks apply to all the South American tariffs. Not one of them is protective and based upon the principles of our own economic system. All these tariffs are modelled after the Spanish system of taxation and are designed to produce revenue, and very largely from the taxation of food products. Venezuela, for example, taxes flour over 100 per cent, and does it for revenue only, without protecting in the least its agricultural population.

When, therefore, our inquisitive Free-Trade neighbor asks such questions as we have quoted

it leaves Protection out of the case. Take the Reciprocity offer in detail, and what do we find? The abolition of revenue taxes on articles of common consumption which cannot be produced in the United States. If coffee and sugar were taxed, no home industries would be benefited. These sources of revenue are given up for the sake of cheapening the necessities of life. In return, Brazil, Cuba and Santo Domingo place on the free list food products which are necessary there but cannot be raised by home industry. Reciprocity in the main involves an exchange of non-competing products at a loss of revenue on each side, but without sacrifice of the principle of Protection as it is understood in the United States. Such manufactures as are included in the free lists and reduced schedules obtained in payment for free sugar and free coffee are those which are not carried on in Southern countries. The revenue tariffs are lowered, but home industries and productive interests are not sacrificed either North or South.

We are glad that "The World" is taking the line that it does respecting Reciprocity. It is bringing out in the strongest way the Free-Trade tendencies of the Democratic party. The Republican party in its tariff legislation and Reciprocity policy does not stand for revenue taxation, but for the development of National industries and the employment of home labor. It is not asking Southern countries to do more than the United States is doing, and that is to give up for the benefit of consumers purely revenue taxation on non-competing products. When Democrats find fault with Reciprocity because it is not English free-trade, they show what it is they really want, and why they are hostile to the system of Protection, under which American prosperity has become the marvel of the modern world. Our neighbor is forcing the Free-Trade issue. Republicans are ready for it. By all means let it be made the decisive issue of the next Presidential canvass.

DEVELOPMENT OF RECIPROCITY.

Reciprocity is no longer to be regarded as a theory or as an experiment. It is a policy which is producing large practical results. Three commercial agreements have been negotiated with coffee and sugar countries and three foreign markets have been opened to the products of American farms, mines and factories. These advantages for the export trade have been secured without the sacrifice of the principles of Protection. A free market is offered to Southern countries producing staples belonging to a different zone. The value of that free market, which is the best in the world, entitles us on strict business principles to have certain privileges in exchange in disposing of our surplus products. The United States, as the heaviest purchaser of Brazilian coffee and Cuban sugar, is allowed by the Reciprocity agreements discriminating advantages over England in selling its exports. It is a good business trade with countries having a large surplus of staples which cannot be produced in the United States. Competing American industries, like tobacco, are protected, but tropical produce which we want but cannot raise is admitted without restrictions; and since the consumption of that produce is so large as to create an overwhelming balance of trade in favor of Southern countries, the conditions are equitably readjusted by concessions to the surplus of American breadstuffs, meats and manufactures.

A good many of our Democratic friends the enemy are seeking to prove that Reciprocity is essentially a Free-Trade policy. If they really think so, why are they sneering at it as a delusion and a trick? Until they can succeed in demonstrating that any competing industrial interest in the United States has been sacrificed they will fail in convicting a Republican Congress and the Harrison Administration of inconsistency in connecting Reciprocity with the tariff policy. All that has been done has been to facilitate the exchanges of different zones and to get something like its full value for the privilege of free entry into a market of 63,000,000 of consumers. Before the Reciprocity policy was put into effect, the United States gave away its free market without securing any compensating advantages. It put coffee on the free list, and left Brazil free to impose an export duty upon it. Now there is a reversion to common-sense business principles. Consumers have the full benefit of a free market for coffee and sugar, and exporters of farm and factory produce receive special advantages in trading with Southern countries. The results will be apparent when the following table is examined:

TRADE WITH SOUTHERN COUNTRIES IN 1890.

	Exports from United States.	Imports to United States.
Spanish West Indies	$15,381,953	$57,855,217
Brazil	11,072,214	59,318,756
Santo Domingo	926,651	1,951,013
Total	**$28,280,818**	**$119,124,986**
Venezuela	4,028,583	10,956,745
Mexico	13,285,287	22,690,915
Central America	5,650,940	8,239,375
Hayti	5,101,464	2,421,221
British West Indies	8,288,786	14,865,018
Guiana	2,546,797	4,918,730
Other West Indies	3,498,368	911,672
Plate Countries	12,239,351	7,156,600
West Coast States	7,905,703	7,645,287
Total	**$90,886,105**	**$198,940,575**

This table shows at once the results of Reciprocity, the necessity for it and the promise of its future potency. Out of a total importation of $198,940,575 from Southern countries, treaties have been made with three which supply considerably more than one-half. While selling $119,124,986 of their produce to the United States, they have purchased only $28,280,818 in return. Under Reciprocity these countries

will become larger buyers, as in justice and common-sense they ought to be.

Venezuela, Mexico, Central America, the British West Indies and Guiana also find the best market for their staples in the United States. Reciprocity is necessary in order to secure an equitable readjustment of trade. The President is armed by Congress with power under the Aldrich amendment to close the free market for coffee, sugar and hides against those nations which fail to enter into commercial union with the United States. The scope of the Reciprocity policy includes all the countries which we have named. When the resources of the amendment have been fully employed we believe that all these republics and islands will be united with the American market by the bonds of fair and reciprocal exchange. Then there will be a large development of the American export trade in compensation for the privilege of a free market for non-competing tropical produce. All this will be accomplished without the sacrifice of any American interest.

ATTACKS ON RECIPROCITY.

Partisan attacks are continued upon the Reciprocity treaties, and mainly without knowledge of the facts. Certain Democratic journals have made a sharp outcry against the convention with Santo Domingo on the ground that wheat flour is not on the free list nor on the reduced schedule of duties. The reason for its exclusion was a financial one. The Dominican Government is wretchedly poor, and has pledged its customs revenues to secure a loan from a Dutch syndicate. This syndicate has been allowed to exercise supervision over the collection of duties. The duty on flour is $4 20 a barrel, and it is the chief source of revenue. The negotiators made an earnest effort to obtain free flour, but were met with the despairing assertion that the treaty would have to be abandoned if this were made an absolute condition, as it was impossible to give up the revenue and fulfil financial obligations. They were offered a much larger list of articles in which American exporters now have very little trade with the island, such as cottons, hats, shoes, furniture, iron goods and papers. They accepted these concessions the more readily as every barrel of flour now imported by Santo Domingo comes from the United States. There is no competition in the flour trade with any other country, as there is in Brazil and Cuba.

Another ground for captious criticism is raised by Democratic journals in the South. They assert that Reciprocity may help the trade in Northern breadstuffs and manufactures, but that it does not promote the interests of the South. Their attention apparently has not been directed to the large favors obtained by the Spanish treaties for the products and industries of the Southern States. One of the most important of these gains is the addition of "fish, live, fresh," to the free list. Fifteen years ago the entire consumption of fish in Cuba was supplied from the Florida coast fisheries. It maintained a large fleet of fishing vessels. It was not only a profitable trade, but it also recruited a useful body of sailors available in time of war. The industry was either destroyed or transferred to Spaniards by the imposition of a prohibitory tariff. Reciprocity will restore a most remunerative coast trade.

Rice, moreover, will have a preferred market under Reciprocity, and it is a staple article of consumption in Cuba. Southern lumber, already a large industry with short lines of communication with the island, will be greatly benefited. Coal, which is now a great Southern product at the very door of Cuba, will be free under the treaty. The low-grade cotton fabrics of the South are already heavily exported to Brazil and South America. A large market for them will be created in the Spanish West Indies by Reciprocity. Cotton-seed oil will have no competition in the Cuban market. The iron products of the South are also favored by the recent treaties and several other industries. Reciprocity is not a sectional policy. It promotes the interests of all the productive interests of the Nation, South as well as North.

A FEW COLD FACTS.

The Free-Trade press, when it ventures to say anything about the Reciprocity treaties, makes the wildest misstatements. One journal, for example, has remarked that the United States already supplies three-fifths of Cuba's total consumption of flour, that we had the best of her commerce without Reciprocity, and that our exporters "would do better to rely upon their natural advantages than to count too much upon this defective Reciprocity agreement." Now let us see what are the facts about flour. Before July 1, 1890, our exporters did send to Cuba about one-half of the flour which it consumed. This was done even with a discrimination of about $4 50 a barrel in favor of Spanish flour. But at that date Spanish flour not only became absolutely free under the sliding scale of reductions which had begun about 1883, but 20 per cent was added to the existing duties on American flour. This brought the discrimination against American flour up to $5 62 1-2 a barrel. The effect of this increase of duties is shown in the following table made up from information furnished to us by the Bureau of Statistics of the Treasury Department:

EXPORT OF FLOUR TO CUBA.

Period.	Barrels.	Value.
Year ending June 30, 1889.......	243,153	$1,190,494
Year ending June 30, 1890.......	253,920	1,104,538
Half-year ending June 30, 1891....	40,764	214,503

Instead, then, of having three-fifths of the flour trade of Cuba when the Reciprocity Treaty was negotiated, we were rapidly losing the market, only a small amount of the highest grade being used by the bakers to mix with Spanish flour. In place of having the best of the commerce in breadstuffs without Reciprocity, we were going from bad to worse. The discrimination of $4 50 not sufficing to bring in Spanish flour in competition with American, the duty was raised to $5 62 1-2 in order to drive us out of the market altogether. What is true of breadstuffs applies equally to all other imports of the island. Twenty per cent was added on July 1, 1891, to the duties on all imports from other countries than Spain.

In the face of these facts how preposterous is the Free-Trade journal's statement that our exporters "would do better to rely upon their natural advantages than to count too much upon this defective Reciprocity agreement." If they had been forced to do that, they would have been driven out of the market. Reciprocity has intervened, and the duty on American flour is reduced from $5 62 1-2 to 90 cents. That will give our exporters absolute control of the market. If $4 50 did not avail to keep out American flour, 90 cents will be merely a revenue duty imposed on a largely increased importation into the island. Reciprocity will cheapen enormously the cost of living in the island and double the consumption of all food products. As the treaty contains a long free list and reductions of 50 and 25 per cent on large classes of manufactures, it will add materially to the volume of the American export trade.

THE MARYLAND PLATFORM.

The Maryland Democracy at its State Convention recently put into concrete expressions all the current Democratic falsehoods concerning the so-called surplus and the "billion-dollar Congress." These falsehoods are as ingenious as they are knavish. We quote them here exactly as they were put in the Maryland platform:

President Harrison and a Republican Congress found in 1889 a large surplus in the Treasury, left by an economical Democratic Administration. That surplus told a plain tale to the people of the United States. It demonstrated that the taxes which had been imposed by Republican legislation were in excess of the actual needs of a Government economically administered, and were therefore unnecessary and unjust. The people supposed that the evil would be remedied by a sufficient and well-considered reduction of these taxes and by the strict application of the surplus to the payment of the public debt. They were disappointed. The finances of the country were mismanaged and wild speculations and commercial disasters followed in the train of such mismanagement. The surplus was wasted by extravagant expenditures. The unjust and unnecessary taxation of the people continued. The Last Congress appropriated in the money and credit of the people more than a billion of dollars. It would seem to have been the deliberate purpose of the managers of the Republican party to maintain and create an amount of public indebtedness which would consume any surplus which might accumulate under the existing tariff and make a further increase in the taxation of imports necessary for the support of the Government.

Now, what are the honest facts as to this business? The Rebellion left the United States with a burden of debt amounting in 1867 to $2,678,126,103 87. From that time until to-day it has been the policy of the Government to collect more revenues than were required for the actual expenses of administration, applying the surplus revenues to the reduction of this debt. On March 4, 1885, when Grover Cleveland entered the White House, he found an available surplus of exactly $21,631,381 67. He found that during the eighteen years of Republican Administration from 1867 to 1885 the outstanding principal of the public debt had been reduced from $2,678,126,103 87 to $1,863,964,873 14. The annual interest charge had fallen from $138,892,451 39 in 1867 to $47,014,133 in 1885, and the per capita debt from $69 26 to $24 50. In the four years preceding Grover Cleveland's term of office, that is, from March 4, 1881, to March 4, 1885, the face of the bonded debt had been reduced in the sum of $479,983,280, an average annual reduction of $120,000,000! This was done, as any Democrat may see, by collecting just that much more money than was needed for the current operations of the Government, on the theory that an honest people wished to pay their honest debts as rapidly as they could.

But Mr. Cleveland and his party had a tariff plan that was not in harmony with this theory. They were deadset for Free Trade, and, as a means of working up public sentiment in support of their scheme, they stopped paying the public debt except as they were absolutely compelled to. They hoarded these surplus revenues, and summoned the country to witness how grievously it was being taxed by the Republican tariff, urging as the remedy for that iniquitous state of things their plan of Free Trade. But even in their statement of the size of the so-called surplus they were dishonest. By juggling with the debt statement they were able to make the surplus at one time fifty millions, at another a hundred. They even got it up as far as a hundred and twenty. But, although the receipts of the Government during Cleveland's term grew larger each year, and although he reduced the bonded debt only $341,396,980, or exactly $138,586,300 less than it had been reduced by Arthur with smaller revenues at his command, yet so extravagant were the appropriations of Cleveland's two Democratic Congresses that his surplus on March 4, 1889, when he gave way to Harrison, was only $48,096,-158 50, or only $26,464,876 83 more than the sum left him by President Arthur! In other words, if he had paid as much of the debt as Arthur did he would not have had a surplus at all, but a deficit of $90,000,000.

This, then—$48,096,158 50—is the boasted Cleveland surplus, left in the Treasury, according to the Maryland Convention, "by an economical Democratic Administration," telling a plain tale of over-taxation, etc. Now, say the Maryland Democrats, the people supposed that this shocking condition would be remedied by Mr. Harrison and his Republican Congress; but the people were disappointed; the surplus was not spent in reducing the public debt as it should have been, but was wasted in the extravagant expenditures of a Congress which appropriated more than a billion of dollars; the revenues were not reduced, but unjust over-taxation was continued. These charges are the current Democratic allegation, and they constitute the capital on which the Democracy proposes to contest the next National election. And every one of them is a falsehood! The surplus and six times the surplus has been paid under Harrison in the liquidation of the public debt. The surplus, as Cleveland left it, was $48,-096,158 50. The amount of the bonded debt discharged under Harrison up to June 30, 1891, was $234,009,640. In two years and four months he has reduced the per capita debt from $24 50, where Cleveland left it, to $12 87, where it is to-day. This is the financial management which the Democrats claim has caused commercial panics and disasters. As every schoolboy knows, the distress of last year was mainly caused by failure of crops and the Baring failure in London, and was relieved and dissipated here by just the policy that the Maryland platform attacks. The Llst Congress did not appropriate "over a billion of dollars," but just exactly exactly $988,410,129, or $170,-446,269 more than the Lth Congress. Of this excess $25,321,907 was for a pension deficiency which the Democrats of that Congress dishonestly left unpaid; $22,667,343 58 was for post-office bills, three-fourths of which will be returned to the Treasury; $7,307,146 70 was for the purchase of Indian lands that will sell for three times their cost; $14,042,344 69 was to meet contracts for naval vessels theretofore authorized, and $62,668,536 99 to pay new pensions under the new act authorized by the people in 1888. The balance went in census expenses, harbor defences and improvements and World's Fair appropriations. As to the revenues, they were reduced, and unjust taxation was not continued. As we have already demonstrated in these columns, the people are enjoying under the McKinley bill a greater volume of trade than ever before while they are paying less taxes.

It is thus that the honest truth disposes of Democratic outcry. The figures we have given are every one official, and they prove that the Democratic lies about the wasted surplus, the billion-dollar appropriations and the continued over-taxation are utterly reckless.

NEW TREATIES.

RECIPROCITY WITH SPAIN.

TEXT OF THE TREATY.

THE PORTS OF CUBA AND PORTO RICO OPENED
TO AMERICAN PRODUCTS—SPAIN MEETS THE
UNITED STATES HALF WAY—TOBACCO
TO BE CONSIDERED SEPARATELY.

Washington, July 31.—The Spanish Reciprocity
Treaty and the diplomatic correspondence in regard to it were made public to-day. The following is the President's proclamation:

RECIPROCITY WITH SPAIN.

BY THE PRESIDENT OF THE UNITED STATES—
A PROCLAMATION.

Whereas, pursuant to Section 3 of the Act of Congress approved October 1, 1890, entitled "An act
to reduce the revenues and equalize duties on imports, and for other purposes," the Secretary of State
of the United States of America communicated to the
Government of Spain the action of the Congress of the
United States of America, with a view to secure reciprocal trade in declaring the articles enumerated in
said Section 3, to wit, sugars, molasses, coffee and
hides, to be exempt from duty upon their importation
into the United States of America;

And whereas, the Envoy Extraordinary and Minister
Plenipotentiary of Spain at Washington has communicated to the Secretary of State the fact that, in reciprocity and compensation for the admission into the
United States of America, free of all duties, of the
articles enumerated in Section 3 of said act, the Government of Spain will, by due legal enactment, and as
a provisional measure, admit, from and after September
1, 1891, into all the established ports of entry of the
Spanish Islands of Cuba and Porto Rico, the articles
or merchandise named in the following transitory
schedule, on the terms stated therein, provided that the
same be the product or manufacture of the United
States and proceed directly from the ports of said
States:

TRANSITORY SCHEDULE.

Products or manufactures of the United States to be
admitted into Cuba and Porto Rico free of duties:

1. Meats, in brine, salted or smoked, bacon, hams,
and meats preserved in cans, in lard, or by extraction
of air: jerked beef excepted.

2. Lard.

3. Tallow and other animal greases, melted or
crude, unmanufactured.

4. Fish and shellfish, live, fresh, dried, in brine,
smoked, pickled; oysters and salmon in cans.

5. Oats, barley, rye and buckwheat, and flour of
these cereals.

6. Starch, maizena and other alimentary products
of corn, except corn meal.

7. Cottonseed, oil, and meal cake of said seed for
cattle.

8. Hay, straw for forage and bran.

9. Fruits, fresh, dried and preserved, except
raisins.

10. Vegetables and garden products, fresh and
dried.

11. Rosin of pine, tar, pitch and turpentine.

12. Woods of all kinds, in trunks or logs, joists,
rafters, planks, beams, boards, round or cylindric
masts, although cut, planed and tongued and grooved,
including flooring.

13. Woods for cooperage, including staves, headings and wooden hoops.

14. Wooden boxes, mounted or unmounted, except
of cedar.

15. Woods, ordinary, manufactured into doors,
frames, windows and shutters, without paint or varnish, and wooden houses, unmounted, without paint
or varnish.

16. Wagons and carts for ordinary roads and agriculture.

17. Sewing machines.

18. Petroleum, raw or unrefined, according to the
classification fixed in the existing orders for the importation of this article in said islands.

19. Coal, mineral.

20. Ice.

Products or manufactures of the United States to be
admitted into Cuba and Porto Rico on payment of the
duties stated:

21. Corn or maize, 25 cents per 100 kilogrammes.

22. Corn meal, 25 cents per 100 kilogrammes.

23. Wheat, from January 1, 1892, 30 cents per 100
kilogrammes.

24. Wheat flour, from January 1, 1892, $1 per 100
kilogrammes,

Products or manufactures of the United States to be
admitted into Cuba and Porto Rico at a reduction of
25 per centum:

25. Butter and cheese.

26. Petroleum, refined.

27. Boots or shoes in whole or in part of leather
skins.

And whereas, the Envoy Extraordinary and
Minister Plenipotentiary of Spain in Washington has further communicated to the Secretary of State that the Government of Spain
will, in like manner and as a definitive arrangement, admit, from and after July 1, 1892, into
all the established ports of entry of the Spanish
Islands of Cuba and Porto Rico, the articles of merchandise named in the following schedules A, B, C and
D, on the terms stated therein, provided that the same
be the product or manufacture of the United States
and proceed directly from the ports of said States:

SCHEDULE A.

Products or manufactures of the United States to be
admitted into Cuba and Porto Rico free of duties:

1. Marble, jasper and alabaster, natural or artificial, in rough or in pieces, dressed, squared and
prepared for taking shape.

2. Other stones and earthy matters, including cement, employed in building, the arts and industries.

3. Waters, mineral or medicinal.

4. Ice.

5. Coal, mineral.

6. Rosin, tar, pitch, turpentine, asphalt, schist
and bitumen.

7. Petroleum, raw or crude, in accordance with the
classification fixed in the tariff of said islands.

8. Clay, ordinary, in paving tiles large and small,
bricks and roof tiles unglazed, for the construction of
buildings, ovens and other similar purposes.

9. Gold and silver coin.

10. Iron, cast in pigs, and old iron and steel.

11. Iron, cast in pipes, beams, rafters and similar
articles, for the construction of buildings, and in
ordinary manufactures. (See repertory.)

12. Iron, wrought and steel, in bars, rails and
bars of all kinds, plates, beams, rafters and other
similar articles for construction of buildings.

13. Iron, wrought, and steel, in wire, nails, screws, nuts and pipes.

14. Iron, wrought, and steel, in ordinary manufactures and wire cloth unmanufactured. (See repertory.)

15. Cotton, raw, with or without seed.

16. Cottonseed, oil and meal cake of same for cattle.

17. Tallow and all other animal greases, melted or crude, unmanufactured.

18. Books and pamphlets, printed, bound and unbound.

19. Woods of all kinds, in trunks or logs, joists, rafters, planks, beams, boards and round or cylindric masts, although cut, planed, tongued and grooved, including flooring.

20. Wooden cooperage, including staves, headings and wooden hoops.

21. Wooden boxes, mounted or unmounted, except of cedar.

22. Woods, ordinary, manufactured into doors, frames, windows and shutters, without paint or varnish, and wooden houses, unmounted, without paint or varnish.

23. Woods, ordinary, manufactured into all kinds of articles, turned or unturned, painted or varnished, except furniture. (See repertory.)

24. Manures, natural or artificial.

25. Implements, utensils and tools for agriculture, the arts and mechanical trades.

26. Machines and apparatus, agricultural, motive, industrial and scientific, of all classes and materials, and loose pieces for the same, including wagons, carts and hand-carts for ordinary roads and agriculture.

27. Material and articles for public works, such as railroads, tramways, roads, canals for irrigation and navigation, use of waters, ports, lighthouses, and civil construction of general utility, when introduced by authorization of the Government, or if free admission is obtained in accordance with local laws.

28. Materials of all classes for the construction, repair, in whole or in part, of vessels, subject to specific regulations to avoid abuse in the importation.

29. Meats, in brine, salted and smoked, including bacon, hams, and meats preserved in cans, in lard, or by extraction of air: jerked beef excepted.

30. Lard and butter.

31. Cheese.

32. Fish and shellfish, live, fresh, dried, in brine, salted, smoked and pickled; oysters and salmon in cans.

33. Oats, barley, rye and buckwheat, and flour of these cereals.

34. Starch, maizena and other alimentary products of corn, except corn meal.

35. Fruits, fresh, dried and preserved, except raisins.

36. Vegetables and garden products, fresh and dried.

37. Hay, straw for forage, and bran.

38. Trees, plants, shrubs and garden seeds.

39. Tan bark.

SCHEDULE B.

Products of manufactures of the United States to be admitted into Cuba and Porto Rico on payment of the duties stated:

40. Corn or maize, 25 cents per 100 kilogrammes.
41. Corn meal, 25 cents per 100 kilogrammes.
42. Wheat, 30 cents per 100 kilogrammes.
43. Wheat flour, $1 per 100 kilogrammes.
44. Carriages, cars and other vehicles for railroads or tramways, where authorization of the Government for free admission has not been obtained, 1 per centum ad valorem.

SCHEDULE C.

Products of manufactures of the United States to be admitted into Cuba and Porto Rico at a reduction of duty of 50 per centum:

45. Marble, jasper and alabaster, of all kinds, cut into flags, slabs or steps, and the same worked or carved in all kinds of articles, polished or not.

46. Glass and crystal ware, plate and window glass, and the same silvered, quicksilvered and platinized.

47. Clay in tiles, large and small, and mosaic for pavements, colored tiles, roof tiles glazed and pipes.

48. Stoneware and fine earthenware, and porcelain.

49. Iron, cast, in fine manufactures or those polished, with coating of porcelain or part of other metals. (See repertory.)

50. Iron, wrought, and steel, in axles, tires, springs and wheels for carriages, rivets and their washers.

51. Iron, wrought, and steel in fine manufactures or those polished, with coating of porcelain or part of other metals, not expressly comprised in other numbers of these schedules, and platform scales for weighing. (See repertory.)

52. Needles, pins, knives, table and carving, razors, penknives, scissors, pieces for watches and other similar articles of iron and steel.

53. Tin plate in sheets or manufactured.

54. Copper, bronze, brass and nickel, and alloys of same with common metals, in lumps or bars, and all manufactures of the same.

55. All other common metals and alloys of the same, in lumps or bars, and all manufactures of the same, plain, varnished, gilt, silvered or nickeled.

56. Furniture of all kinds, of wood or metal, including school furniture, blackboards and other materials for schools, and all kinds of articles of fine woods not expressly comprised in other numbers of these schedules. (See repertory.)

57. Rushes, esparto, vegetable hair, broom corn, willow, straw, palm and other similar materials, manufactured into articles of all kinds.

58. Pastes for soups, rice, flour, bread and crackers, and alimentary farinas, not comprised in other numbers of these schedules.

59. Preserved alimentary substances and canned goods, not comprised in other numbers of these schedules, including sausages, stuffed meats, mustards, sauces, pickles, jams and jellies.

60. Rubber and gutta-percha, and manufactures thereof, alone or mixed with other substances (except silk), and oilcloths and tarpaulin.

61. Rice, hulled or unhulled.

SCHEDULE D.

Products or manufactures of the United States to be admitted into Cuba and Porto Rico at a reduction of duty of 25 per centum:

62. Petroleum, refined, and benzine.

63. Cotton manufactured, spun or twisted, and in goods of all kinds, woven or knit, and the same mixed with other vegetable or animal fibres in which cotton is an equal or greater component part, and clothing exclusively of cotton.

64. Rope, cordage and twine of all kinds.

65. Colors, crude and prepared, with or without oil, inks of all kinds, shoe-blacking and varnishes.

66. Soap, toilet, and perfumery.

67. Medicines, proprietary or patent, and all others, and drugs.

68. Stearine and tallow manufactured in candles.

69. Paper for printing, for decorating rooms, of wood or straw, for wrapping and packing, and bags and boxes of same, sandpaper and pasteboard.

70. Leather and skins, tanned, dressed, varnished or japanned, of all kinds, including sole leather or belting.

71. Boots and shoes in whole or in part of leather or skins.

72. Trunks, valises, travelling bags, portfolios and other similar articles in whole or in part of leather.

73. Harness and saddlery of all kinds.

74. Watches and clocks, of gold, silver or other metals, with cases of stone, wood or other material, plain or ornamented.

75. Carriages of two or four wheels and pieces of the same.

It is understood that flour, which on its exportation from the United States has been favored with draw-backs, shall not share in the foregoing reduction of duty.

The provisional arrangement as set forth in the " transitory schedule" shall come to an end on July 1, 1892, and on that date be substituted by the definitive arrangement as set forth in schedules A, B, C and D.

And that the Government of Spain has further provided that the laws and regulations, adopted to protect its revenue and prevent fraud in the declarations and proof that the articles named in the foregoing schedules are the product or manufacture of the United States of America, shall place no undue restrictions on the importer, nor impose any additional charges or fees therefor on the articles imported.

And whereas, the Secretary of State has, by my direction, given assurance to the Envoy Extraordinary and Minister Plenipotentiary of Spain at Washington that this action of the Government of Spain, in granting exemption of duties to the products and manufactures of the United States of America on their importation into Cuba and Porto Rico, is accepted for those islands as a due reciprocity for the action of Congress as set forth in Section 3 of sa'd act:

Now, therefore, be it known that I, Benjamin Harrison, President of the United States of America, have caused the above-stated modifications of the tariff laws of Cuba and Porto Rico to be made public for the information of the citizens of the United States of America.

In testimony whereof, I have hereunto set my hand and caused the seal of the United States to be affixed. Done at the City of Washington, this 31st day of July, 1891, and of the Independence of the United States of America, the 116th.   BENJAMIN HARRISON.

By the President: WILLIAM F. WHARTON,
Acting Secretary of State.

THE SAN DOMINGO TREATY.

IT PROVIDES FOR RECIPROCAL TRADE WITH THAT REPUBLIC.

SUCCESSFUL OUTCOME OF MR. FOSTER'S MISSION

—THE PRESIDENT'S PROCLAMATION

Washington, Aug. 1.—The San Domingo reciprocity treaty and the diplomatic correspondence concerning it were made public to-day. The following is the President's proclamation:

Whereas, Pursuant to Section 3 of the Act of Congress approved October 1, 1890, entitled " An act to reduce the revenue and equalize duties on imports, and for other purposes," the Secretary of State of the United States of America communicated to the Government of the Dominican Republic the action of the Congress of the United States of America, with a

view to secure reciprocal trade, in declaring the articles enumerated in said section 3, to wit, sugars, molasses, coffee and hides, to be exempt from duty upon their importation into the United States of America.

And whereas, The Envoy Extraordinary and Minister Plenipotentiary of the Dominican Republic at Washington has communicated to the Special Plenipotentiary of the United States the fact that, in reciprocity and compensation for the admission into the United States of America, free of all duty, of the articles enumerated in Section 3 of said act, the Government of the Dominican Republic will, by due legal enactment, admit, from and after September 1, 1891, into all the established ports of entry of the Dominican Republic, the articles or merchndise named in the following schedules, on the terms stated therein, provided that the same be the product or manufacture of the United States and proceed directly from the ports of said States:

SCHEDULE A.

Articles to be admitted free of duty into the Dominican Republic:

1. Animals, live.

2. Meats of all kinds, salted or in brine, but not smoked.

3. Corn or maize, cornmeal and starch.

4. Oats, barley, rye and buckwheat, and flour of these cereals.

5. Hay, bran and straw for forage.

6. Trees, plants, vines and seeds and grains of all kinds for propagation.

7. Cottonseed oil and meal-cake of same.

8. Tallow in cake or melted, and oil for machinery, subject to examination and proof respecting the use of said oil.

9. Resin, tar, pitch and turpentine.

10. Manures, natural and artificial.

11. Coal, mineral.

12. Mineral waters, natural and artificial.

13. Ice.

14. Machines, including steam engines and those of all other kinds, and parts of the same, implements and tools for agricultural, mining, manufacturing, industrial and scientific purposes, including carts, wagons, hand-carts and wheelbarrows, and parts of the same.

15. Material for the equipment and construction of railroads.

16. Iron, cast and wrought, and steel in pigs, bars, rods, plates, beams, rafters and other similar articles for the construction of buildings, and in wire nails, screws and pipes.

17. Zinc, galvanized and corrugated iron, tin and lead in sheets, asbestos, tar paper, tiles, slate and other materials for roofing.

18. Copper in bars, plates, nails and screws.

19. Copper and lead pipe.

20. Bricks, firebricks, cement, lime, artificial stone, paving tiles, marble and other stones in rough, dressed or polished, and other earthy materials used in building.

21. Windmills.

22. Wire, plin or barbed, for fences, with hooks, staples, nails and similar articles used in the construction of fences.

23. Telegraph wire and telegraphic, telephonic and electric apparatus of all kinds for communication and illumination.

24. Wood and lumber of all kinds for building, in logs or pieces, beams, rafters, planks, boards, shingles, flooring, joists, wooden-houses, mounted or unmounted, and accessory parts of buildings.

25. Cooperage of all kinds, including staves, head-

ings and hoops, barrels and boxes, mounted or unmounted.

26. Materials for ship building.

27. Boats and lighters.

28. School furniture, blackboards and other articles exclusively for the use of schools.

29. Books, bound or unbound, pamphlets, newspapers and printed matter, and paper for printing newspapers.

30. Printers' ink of all colors, type, leads and all accessories for printing.

31. Sacks, empty, for packing sugar.

32. Gold and silver coin and bullion.

SCHEDULE B.

Articles to be admitted into the Dominican Republic at a reduction of duty of 25 per centum:

33. Meats not included in schedule A and meat products of all kinds, except lard.

34. Butter, cheese and condensed or canned milk.

35. Fish and shellfish, salted, dried, smoked, pickled or preserved in cans.

36. Fruits and vegetables, fresh, canned, dried, pickled or preserved.

37. Manufactures of iron and steel, single or mixed, not included in schedule A.

38. Cotton, manufactured, spun or twisted, and in fabrics of all kinds, woven or knit, and the same fabrics mixed with other vegetable or animal fibres in which cotton is the equal or greater component part.

39. Boots and shoes in whole or in part of leather or skins.

40. Paper for writing, in envelopes, ruled or blank hooks, wall paper, paper for wrapping and packing, for cigarettes, in cardboard, boxes and bags, sand paper and paste-board.

41. Tin plate and tin ware for arts, industries, and domestic uses.

42. Cordage, rope and twine of all kinds.

43. Manufactures of wood of all kinds not embraced in schedule A, including wooden ware, implements for household use and furniture in whole or in part of wood.

And that the Government of the Dominican Republic has further provided that the laws and regulations adopted to protect its revenue, and prevent fraud in the declarations and proof that the articles named in the foregoing schedules are the product or manufacture of the United States of America, shall place no undue restrictions upon the importer, nor impose any additional charges or fees therefor on the articles imported.

And whereas, the Special Plenipotentiary of the United States has, by my direction, given assurance to the Envoy Extraordinary and Minister Plenipotentiary of the Dominican Republic at Washington that this action of the Government of the Dominican Republic in granting exemption of duties to the products and manufactures of the United States of America on their importation into the Dominican Republic is accepted as a due reciprocity for the action of Congress as set forth in Section 3 of said act:

Now, therefore, be it known that I, Benjamin Harrison, President of the United States of America, have caused the above stated modifications of the tariff laws of the Dominican Republic to be made public for the information of the citizens of the United States of America.

In testimony whereof, I have hereunto set my hand and caused the seal of the United States to be affixed. Done at the City of Washington, this 1st day of August, 1891, and of the Independence of the United States of America the 116th.

                                    BENJAMIN HARRISON.

By the President: WILLIAM F. WHARTON,
                        Acting Secretary of State.

A CANADIAN FLIRTATION.

WOOING THAT WILL NOT LEAD TO JAMAICA'S UNDOING.

A POOR RELATION THAT WAS ONCE FLOUTED ARDENTLY COURTED — THE UNITED STATES THE RICH COUSIN IN THE RECIPROCITY PLAY.

Kingston, April 17.—Mr. Froude describes the British West Indies as the children of an unnatural mother, who has cast them off and allowed them to shift for themselves as poor relations. Emancipation instead of being gradually introduced was brought on with such precipitate haste as to be ruinous to the colonial planters. When protection was demanded against rival cane producers in countries where slavery existed, it was refused on the ground that the British workman must have a cheap breakfast. When the beetroot industry was established in Europe under a liberal system of Government bounties, another appeal was made to the mother State for aid in rescuing the cane planters from destructive competition. The islands had ceased to have a marketable value as possessions of the Crown and the Home Government was indifferent to their necessities and interests. Despairing of receiving encouragement from the United Kingdom the islands turned for assistance to the United States. Meeting with cold shoulders everywhere else, they found there, as Mr. Froude says, a hand held out to them. The Americans were willing, though at a serious loss of revenue, to admit the poor West Indians to their markets. A commercial treaty alone was necessary; but it could not be made without the sanction of the British Government, and this was coldly and wantonly refused; to use Mr. Froude's phrase, "on some fine-drawn crotchet, to colonies which were weak and helpless."

As a last resort, when the American treaty was disallowed, a delegation was sent from Jamaica to Ottawa and an urgent appeal was made for more intimate trade relations with the West Indies. The Dominion Government sent a commission to Kingston to find out if anything could be done and Mr. Froude met him there wholly out of humor with Canada's poor relations. "The Jamaicans did not know what they wanted," remarked the commissioner. "They were without spirit to help themselves; they cried out to others to help them, and if all they asked could not be granted, they clamored as if the whole world was combining to hurt them. They had a fine country; soil and climate all that could be desired; they had all that was required for a quiet and easy life. Why could they not be content and make the best of things?" "Unfortunate Jamaicans!" exclaims sympathetic Mr. Froude. "The old mother at home acts like an unnatural parent and will neither help them nor let their cousin Jonathan help them. They turn for comfort to their big brother in the North, and the big brother being himself robust and healthy gives them wholesome advice."

That was before Canada itself was hurt and crippled by commercial competition and the pressure of economic law. Now the attitude of the Dominion has changed. It is wooing and caressing the West Indians and fairly embarrassing them with the warmth and intensity of its affection for them. The flirtation began about the time of the passage of the McKinley Tariff bill, which, while a generous relief measure for the Southern countries, involved Canada in material loss and serious hardship. When the West Indian delegation was sent to Ottawa, a few years ago, to solicit reciprocal trade relations, Canada was enjoying large commercial privileges in the American market. Then her Ministers considered West Indian trade to be one of very little account. Jamaica then seemed to them to be a long way off, and to have an impoverished, non-consuming population of ignorant blacks. They treated the delegation with scant courtesy and did nothing for the island. It was not until the McKinley tariff bill was passed and Canada was deprived of many of its privileges in the American market that the Ministers began to take any interest in the West Indies. When they perceived that the Dominion was badly hurt by tariff legislation in the United States, they cast about to find some other market for their surplus produce. Then the once-despised Jamaica loomed up in their imagination as a thrifty and prosperous island tenanted by loyal Britons, and the West Indian archipelago, from Trinidad to Barbados, from Grenada to Dominica, and from Antigua to the Bahamas, assumed the importance of a commercial empire held by the Queen's worshipful subjects of the same breed as themselves. Then it seemed the most natural thing in the world that brethren should dwell together in unity and be wholly independent of the United States, which, after all, was not a larger market, at least in extent of territory, than British North America!

The Jamaica Exhibition opened at an opportune time for this Canadian demonstration. It was organized primarily for the purpose of displaying the industrial resources of the British West Indies and attracting European capital and immigration to a neglected quarter of the Empire. The invitation to the United States was mysteriously delayed and finally extended with so little tact and with such bungling irregularity that it could not be accepted with dignity. Canada voted a large appropriation and made extensive preparations for loudly advertising itself as the chief industrial State in North America. Its exhibit was the largest and most pretentious in the main building, and not only occupied the lion's share of the space on the floor and in the galleries, but also called into requisition several structures and side-shows outside. It was a complete and very creditable display of the Dominion fisheries, manufactures, and produce of field, mine and forest. It was under the charge of an active and intelligent staff, which ceased not, day nor night, to glorify

the Dominion and to depreciate the value of the American market as a base of exchange for West Indian products. For six months there has been a most determined effort made to draw Jamaica and the Windward and Leeward groups into a specious scheme of commercial union by which Canada will have everything to gain and the West Indies everything to lose. In this remarkable propaganda "The London Times" has lent aid, for it has recommended that Her Majesty's possessions in North America and the West Indies should follow the example of the South African and Australian colonies, and form a customs union for mutual advantage.

The Canadian Minister of Finance, Mr. Foster, has taken an active part in this commercial raid upon the United States. Several months ago he visited Trinidad, and boldly advocated a British Colonial trade bund. Canada, he announced, would be willing to discriminate in favor of West Indian products, if preferential advantages were offered in return. It could supply everything that was imported from the United States, and if allowed preferential advantages in the West Indies it would put differential duties on the coffee, sugar, logwood and fruit produced in the islands. The same programme was unfolded at Barbados, where he proposed a differential of about 25 per cent "as a first go off" on duties enforced in Canada upon West Indian sugar, and a corresponding discrimination in favor of oranges, bananas and other fruits. In return he modestly pleaded for an equivalent differential —" only this and nothing more"—by which the products of Canadian seas, mines, farms and herds could be placed on a preferential footing in Jamaica, Barbados, Trinidad and the remaining islands. When he arrived at Kingston he was less explicit in his proposals for commercial reciprocity, but even more grandiose and impassioned in his tributes to the industrial resources and commercial potentiality of Canada. He enlarged upon the imperial domain of the Dominion, its magnificent continental line of railway and its subsidized steamers which were speedily to whiten every sea. He contended that Canada was entering upon an era of emigration and wonderful growth, and that its consumption of sugar, coffee, oranges and bananas was capable of enormous expansion. There might be a good deal of ice well toward the North, but it was a country of boundless extent and enormous resources, and could produce cheaply and abundantly nineteen-twentieths of the merchandise that comes from the United States to these islands. So this statesman's elastic argument ran along until he reached the conclusion that the Jamaicans as loyal Britons and practical men of business ought to make heavy differential reductions on the duties levied on Canadian merchandise, and to be content to receive in return a corresponding "go off" on sugar and fruit.

In order to appreciate the humor of this extravagant and inopportune agitation on behalf of Canadian trade, it is necessary to examine the commercial statistics of the island and to ascertain the comparative standing of the United States and the Dominion as buyers and sellers for this market. For this purpose I have condensed with the following result the latest figures printed by the Government and supplied by the courteous and efficient American Consul, Mr. Estes:

FOREIGN TRADE WITH JAMAICA.

	Buys.	Sells.
Great Britain	$2,625,500	$1,422,220
United States	3,906,550	2,722,050
Canada	183,775	721,765
France	104,795	2,150
Germany	197,565	4,690
Other States	503,015	114,515
Total	$7,533,230	$7,987,990

Hence it appears that Mr. Foster's ambitious Dominion has been selling to Jamaica four times as much as it has been buying, yet has the assurance to demand differential advantages by which its sales may be increased to the detriment of the United States. He has had the coolness, moreover, to bid for an exclusive arrangement for supplying the Jamaica market with breadstuffs, fish, lumber, coal and various classes of manufacture, when the United States buys from Jamaica twenty-one times as much as Canada, and sells less than four times as much. He makes this overture on the extraordinary assumption that a population of 5,000,000 can offer as large a market for coffee, sugar and fruit as a population of 63,000,000. The absurdity of this claim is revealed by the following exhibit of the exports of Jamaica:

EXPORTS OF JAMAICA—HOW DISTRIBUTED.

	United States.	Canada.	Great Britain.
Coffee	$832,410	$15,510	$321,145
Sugar	881,705	138,160	164,960
Fruit	1,500,0 5	7,015	12,105
Logwood	422,470	6,880	903,750
Rum	18,720	2,910	0 8,005
Various	231,480	13,270	350,635
Total	$3,906,550	$183,775	$2,625,500

The United States supplies a market for nearly $4,000,000 of a total export of something over $7,500,000. It takes one-half as much again as Great Britain, and would be still further in excess if that country did not take almost the entire surplus of Jamaica rum. It buys nearly three times as much of the sugar as England and Canada together, and 98 1-2 per cent of the fruit, leaving to them the beggarly remnant. Yet Mr. Foster and the Canadian contingent, who have been clamoring for a differential reciprocity based upon the Dominion's future consumption of sugar and fruit, invite Jamaica to discriminate against the United States, their best market, in the expectation that a population which now takes $7,045 worth of fruit will suddenly acquire an appetite for $1,580,005 worth of it. They ask the Jamaicans to adopt this policy of incredible folly at a time when President Harrison has been empowered by Congress to impose discriminating duties on tropical produce from countries which continue to trade with the United States on inequitable terms. The adoption of the Canadian differentials would not affect the export of fruit and logwood to the American market, but it would inevitably shut out the sugar and coffee. If Jamaica does not accept the reciprocity proposals of the United States, and President Harrison imposes duties after January 1, 1892, under the schedule provided in the Aldrich amendment, the amount of differential taxes on the coffee, sugar and hides exported from the island will be as shown below, on the basis of the latest commercial statistics:

OPERATION OF RECIPROCITY AMENDMENT.

Export.	Duty.	Amount.
23,327,230 ℔ sugar	1½c. per ℔	$420,749 00
4,832,254 ℔ coffee	3c. per ℔	114,967 02
18 001 ℔ hides	1½c. per ℔	£79 91
		$105,997 19

In the face of this menace, which would at once be carried into execution, it would be an act of sheer madness if Jamaica were to favor an insignificant customer, such as Canada is, at the expense of a nation of 63,000,000 consumers that has been buying freely everything produced on the island with the single exception of rum. The Canadian delegation has made a great noise over the thousands of samples of bread baked from the choicest grades of Canadian flour which have been peddled about the island during the Exhibition period; but the Jamaicans know that they cannot live by bread that is cast upon the West Indian waters to be returned to the Dominion in the form of exclusive trade privileges. Their bread has been poor because they have persisted in importing cheaper and inferior grades of American flour; but they are well aware that they could have better bread if they were willing to pay $8 a barrel for their flour, or if the Government would remove the import duty of $2. If they were to lose the American market for their produce, they would not be able to buy flour from any quarter, duty or no duty.

The Canadian unreciprocal trade proposals have not been taken very seriously. Sir Henry Blake was grateful to the delegation for furnishing so fine an exhibit at his West Indian Fair, and has entertained the visitors with expansive rhetoric and hospitality; but when the show comes to an end he will follow his sober judgment, and be very careful to avoid openly challenging President Harrison to convert a generous offer of commercial reciprocity into a menace of retaliation. That offer comes from a nation which has been the salvation of Jamaica and the West Indies for many years. Behind that offer is a market that is essentially free. With the exception of oranges and tobacco everything produced in Jamaica enters a free market in the United States. In return the products of American factories, farms and forests are heavily taxed. The following exhibit, which Mr. Estes has prepared for me, illustrates the inequitable conditions of trade between Jamaica and the great free market where a large share of its exports are sold:

IMPORTS FROM THE UNITED STATES.

		Valuation.			Specific duty.
Quantity imported.		£.	s.	d.	
141,268 bbls flour		56,507	4	0	8s. per bbl.
1,536,981 ℔ bread		4,010	18	10	6d. 100 ℔.
567,890 ℔ butter		4,732	5	0	2d. per ℔.
212,135 ℔ cheese		1,770	5	10	2d. per ℔.
86,911 ℔ ham		724	5	2	2d. per ℔.
68,104 ℔ refined sugar		563	0	8	2d. per ℔.
9,501 ℔ bacon		54	3	6	2d. per ℔.
18,427 bbls salt meat		13,820	5	0	8s. per bol.
2,861 M. shingles		856	6	0	6s. per M.
4,009,419 feet white pine		1,804	4	8	9s. per M.
3,475,380 feet pitch pine		2,250	0	0	13s. per M.
523,819 gal. oil		19,643	4	3	8s. per bbl.
19,931 ℔ tallow		62	5	8	2d. per ℔.
108,584 bush. corn		1,609	14	8	4d. per bush.
5,216 bush. oats		86	18	8	4d. per bush.
5,785 bush peas, beans		90	8	4	4d. per bush.
		109,800	10	0	

The United States, while offering a very large

measure of free trade to the West Indies and the unrestricted advantage of selling in the largest and best market in the world, has an equitable right to demand substantial concessions in return. Jamaica not only levies an export duty on the sugar, coffee and logwood shipped to the United States, but claps a tax of $2 on every barrel of American flour, and restricts all other importations of farm produce and manufactures by high specific duties. Sir Henry Blake during the last six months has been listening with a rapt air to the Canadian cuckoo song, and has scouted the idea of making concessions to the United States. Sometimes he has seemed almost willing to be convinced that there were millions of fur-traders in the barren stretches of Hudson's Bay territory athirst for Jamaica rum with sugar in it, and that in the regions toward the north pole there were other millions of Esquimaux who were hungering after Jamaica bananas and oranges to eat with their icecream; but he is a practical statesman, and will inevitably be released from his illusions when the necessity for being polite to his exhibition guests and patrons passes. Nothing can be plainer than the superiority of the American market, with its 63,000,000 consumers. Practically it is a free market for tropical produce, and if any differentials or discriminations are offered the United States ought to have the advantage rather than Canada, which already sells to Jamaica far more than it buys. Canada's successful wooing would be Jamaica's undoing. The Dominion may come sighing like furnace and writing sonnets to the Queen and the dusky maidens of the tropics, but the islanders know that it is only a desperate attempt to raise the wind. As "The West Indian" has expressed the case; "What object is there in making common cause with a big brother who flouted us when we were out of favor with a rich cousin, but who comes and knocks at our door and wishes to hang his hat in our hall and put his walking-stick in our umbrella-stand when he knows that the rich cousin now smiles upon us and frowns upon him?"

                                        I. N. F.

A RECIPROCITY STUDY.

TRADE OF THE BRITISH WEST INDIES.

WITH COMMENTS UPON CANADIAN ASSURANCE
AND THE DEVELOPMENT OF AN ENLIGHT-
ENED AMERICAN POLICY.

Kingston, May 1.—Port Royal is the key of the West Indian Empire, for which England made great sacrifices and won imperishable prestige on the ocean in her historic battle for supremacy with Spain and France. That Empire seemed to have been lost after Yorktown, when the powerful French fleet was supreme among the Leeward and Windward islands, but Rodney's genius and pluck rescued it from conquest and delivered Jamaica from invasion. As the Empire was left after that great sea fight off the mountain-peaks of Dominica, it has remained to this day, save that its colonial population has been im-

poverished, brought to the verge of ruin and driven out in the face of increasing swarms of blacks. With the Bahamas in the north, Belize on the west, and the Lesser Antilles in the east, curving from Puerto Rico for 600 miles toward the mouth of the Orinoco and British Guiana, Port Royal is the geographical and strategic centre of this once prosperous and highly prized Empire. With the exception of the mahogany and logwood clearings of Belize, it is essentially a black Empire. The whites were ruined by emancipation, for which grants of $100,000,000 from the British exchequer were an inadequate compensation. Their great industry was cheapened and well nigh destroyed by the competition of European beet sugar, and for this there was no compensation in bounties, upon which the rival industry was fattening. Immigration from England ceased long ago; the whites are rapidly disappearing; and the future of the British West Indies is largely dependent upon the negro's lack of ambition and the increasing market for tropical produce in the United States.

Nine British Governors are employed to direct the destinies of this West Indian Empire. They draw their salaries, respect the traditions of the Colonial Office, entertain the officers of Her Majesty's navy, and strive to conciliate in every possible way the black constituencies, which are already conscious of their growing political power. In the Bahamas there is a Governor of genuine creative impulses, who is bent upon supplying the impoverished islands with a new industry; in Jamaica there is another who has organized an exhibition and encouraged rash speculations in hotel building; but in the main these functionaries are content to wind and unwind the red-tape spools of the Colonial Office. They are drawn helplessly along in the drift of West Indian tendencies. There has been constant experimenting with constitutions and franchises. In Jamaica there is a legislative council of nominated and elected members, in equal voting strength, with a veto power vested in the Governor, and with a low franchise practically permitting every negro to vote. In Grenada, Dominica, and other islands there are large communities of negro free-holders invested with political power. In Barbados the whites still control the ownership of the land, but everywhere else the negro is becoming a peasant proprietor and a politician. The general trend of events and tendencies is in the direction of negro rule. The whites, disheartened by the economic conditions, are selling their plantations and emigrating. In Jamaica there are 700,000 blacks and 15,000 whites, and in other islands the preponderance of black blood is ever greater. Coolie labor has proved a failure, and the industries of the islands are dependent upon the indolent blacks, who are already impressed with the conviction that the islands are theirs, and that they are destined to govern them. The English Church has failed to leaven this mass of ignorance, because it is the white man's church. The Moravians have done the best missionary work, but even they have been powerless to enforce the necessity of marriage and to repress the shocking immorality prevailing in the islands.

The population of the British West Indies numbers 1,600,000 in round numbers, and its foreign trade aggregates $75,000,000, divided almost equally between exports and imports. Trinidad has the largest trade, nearly $20,000,000, and Jamaica and Barbados rank among the islands, with $17,000,000 and $10,000,000 respectively. British Guiana has a foreign trade equal to that of Jamaica. St. Kitts, the Bahamas, St. Lucia, Antigua, St. Vincent and Dominica form the next group in importance, but their trade is of small volume. Out of a total export of $39,000,000 of produce of all kinds, $13,235,500 represents sugar shipped to the United States, where it forms about 13 per cent of the entire importation of cane and beet sugar. In 1889 the British West Indies furnished to the same market 14,083,710 pounds of coffee, worth $1,689,217, but in 1890 a smaller quantity, worth $803,281. In 1888 the importation of hides from the islands was $465,777. In round numbers about $15,000,000 of the export trade of the islands and British Guiana will be covered by the reciprocity amendment to the Tariff act. Of this aggregate the main entry is sugar. The British West Indies and British Guiana supply about one-third as much cane sugar to the American market as Cuba and Puerto Rico.

The light-fingered Canadian gamblers who have been seeking to draw the British West Indies into a quiet little reciprocity game of their own, wherein they would have all the aces, kings and knaves in their sleeves, have been greatly demoralized this week by the announcement of the successful negotiation of a treaty between the United States and Spain. This treaty confers upon Cuba and Puerto Rico the advantage of a permanent free market for their sugar. The question which British West Indian planters are now asking is whether they can afford to be deprived of the free market for their sugar by the operation of the retaliatory clause of the reciprocity amendment. They are selling $13,235,500 of their sugar in the United States, to say nothing of coffee and hides. Cuba and Puerto Rico are selling in the same market $39,099,670, and are preparing to increase very largely their production. If a discrimination be made against British West Indian sugar and a duty be imposed upon it, it will be shut out of the American market. What then will they do with it? Europe has its own supply of beet-sugar, which is increasing at an enormous rate every year. It cannot be forced to take the surplus of cane-sugar produced in the West Indies. What then have the Canadian diplomats to say? They have been talking about the advantages of a preferential arrangement by which sugar and fruit will be admitted into Canada with a discrimination of 25 per cent, and the products of their fisheries, farms, mines and forests favored in the same way in return. Can they guarantee a market for $13,000,000 of sugar? That is what they cannot do. Indeed, from the first, they have not been interested so much in Canada's purchasing power as in its increased facilities for selling a surplus of its own which is no longer marketable in the United States.

Several years ago, when the British West Indies could not enlist sympathy and support for their shattered industries in England, the United States offered to give their sugar an advantage in its markets over competing sugars. The islanders were overjoyed and pleaded earnestly with the Home Government for the negotiation of a treaty. The Colonial Office intervened with a veto. England refused to allow the United States to go to the aid of the colonies. The new offer of the United States is for a free market for sugar, but that is an advantage to be shared equally by Brazil and Cuba. It is not so generous as the first preferential proposal, but it is made by the best customer which the islands have. If it be rejected they may lose that trade, and that would be something serious. The British West Indies may not be willing to enter into reciprocity arrangements with the United States, but they will be certain to avoid giving offence and thereby subjecting themselves to the loss of the free market by supporting Canada's demand for preferential trade. Any special concessions which might be made to Canada would involve the enforcement of the amendment and the imposition of duties on their coffee, sugar and hides in the American market. It may be possible for them to have the free market permanently without paying for it in compensating concessions to the United States. They may consider it safe to trust to the indulgence of the great Republic; but they will not venture to challenge it to lose its markets against them.

The answer to Canada's importunate and unreasonable demands for a one-sided reciprocity profitable only to its own interests has come already from British Guiana. Mr. Foster asked for differential treatment of Canadian coal, wheat, fish, meat, lumber and manufactures in return for preferential reductions of duties on sugar and fruit. The Governor has replied that British Guiana cannot adopt a course which would exclude the sugars and fruits of the colony from admission to the markets of the United States upon the most favored terms. In order to appreciate the good sense of the Governor it is only necessary to compare the trade of the United States and Canada with the leading colonies.

EXPORTS FROM WEST INDIES.

	To United States.	To Canada.
Guiana	$3,744,620	$147,260
Trinidad	3,235,027	73,278
Barbadoes	2,082,408	768,132
Jamaica	3,966,550	183,775
	$13,629,205	$1,172,451

IMPORTS TO WEST INDIES.

	From United States.	From Canada.
Guiana	$1,500,185	$410,146
Trinidad	1,693,337	292,622
Barbadoes	1,926,334	383,380
Jamaica	2,722,650	721,765
	$7,902,456	$1,817,919

These figures disclose the inherent weakness of the Canadian case for reciprocity. The United States buys twelve times as much as Canada, and sells only four times as much to the islands. Trade, so far as the United States is concerned, is unreciprocal, but Canada has no reason for complaint so long as it already sells more than it buys. When Canada asks for differential advantages in West Indian markets at the expense of the United States, which is a much larger purchaser of coffee, sugar and fruit, its assurance and coolness are almost grotesque. The sober judgment of the West Indian planters will inevitably reject this specious appeal to obtain a larger export trade on the strength of inferior purchasing power. England has neglected the colonies, and by allowing them to shift for themselves is gradually converting them into commercial dependencies of the United States. The colonies cannot help feeling that they have been cast off by an unnatural mother; but that fact does not predispose them to accept Canada's services as a wet-nurse. Their real interests lie in the direction of commercial union with the United States, on equal terms with Cuba and Puerto Rico. Loyalty to the Crown and fraternal feeling among British dependencies are excellent in sentiment, but the commercial exchanges of the world are regulated by economic laws of demand and supply, and are strictly business relations. The British flag may be at Halifax and Montreal, but the best market for West Indian produce is New-York. If reciprocity be brought to bear, the commerce of the islands will inevitably be drawn toward the market as a magnet superior to the flag. The rapid development of trade with the United States during recent years, as illustrated below, demonstrates the efficiency of the attractive force of a great market:

TRADE OF BRITISH WEST INDIES AND GUIANA.

Year.	Exports from United States.	Imports into United States.
1886	$8,668,425	$11,718,276
1887	7,888,241	14,309,652
1888	9,101,729	15 373,292
1889	8,197,094	20,511,749
1890	10,180,778	19,191,983
	$44,036,866	$81,104,936

The latest year for which I can obtain statistics of the entire trade of the British West Indies and Guiana is 1888, when the exports from the islands amounted to $39,803,276, and the imports to $35,579,436. Nearly one-half of the exports sent abroad went to the United States, and the proportion has increased during the last two years. The islands have a large trade with Great Britain in rum, sugar, cocoa, logwood, dyewoods and spices, but it is not a growing trade. Sugar and fruit are the staple exports from the islands, and the markets for those products are in the United States. Mr. Foster, when he was in the West Indies, offered on the part of Canada to establish two steam lines—one a monthly service between St. John and Demerara, touching at the principal Leeward and Windward Islands, and the other a monthly service between Halifax and Kingston. These lines will undoubtedly enlarge the trade between Canada and the West Indies, but the service will not be better than that already existing between the islands and New-York, although that ought to be improved. Even with these new transportation facilities, for which subsidies will be paid at both ends, 5,000,000 Canadians cannot hope to compete with 63,000,000 Americans.

Undoubtedly the British West Indies are hoping to make practical use of the Canadian overtures for the control of their trade. Now that

the United States has concluded reciprocity arrangements with Brazil and the Spanish West Indies, and may be expected to follow up the same policy with Santo Domingo, Hayti, Venezuela, Mexico and other countries, it is a matter of pressing importance to the British West Indies to retain the free market for their sugar. If they have a standing offer from Canada to enter into a preferential arrangement they have at least a resource upon which they can depend in preventing the closing of the free market. They will not accept Canada's proposals, but they will hold the offer under consideration and subsidize its new steamship lines. This they will be likely to do in the hope of being allowed to retain the free market on sufferance without paying for it in concessions to American exports. They will trade upon their neutrality in this commercial rivalry between Canada and the United States, and ask to have their unwillingness to favor the one at the expense of the other accepted at Washington as an equivalent for the large advantages which they enjoy in the American market.

What course the Administration will take in this matter next January it would be, of course, premature to forecast. The President is empowered to close the free market if, in his judgment, the conditions of trade are inequitable. He will have no alternative if preferential treaties are made with Canada; but if the islands, as is probable, reject these overtures from the Dominion, his course will largely depend upon his judgment as to what are to be considered equitable conditions of Southern trade. The following exhibit will illustrate the question:

TRADE OF SOUTHERN COUNTRIES WITH THE UNITED STATES IN 1890.

West Indies.	Exports from United States.	Imports into United States.
Spanish	$15,381,958	$57,855,217
British	9,288,786	14,865,018
Guianas	2,546,797	4,918,736
Santo Domingo	926.651	1,951,019
Hayti	5,101,461	2,421,221
Danish	791,203	588,739
Dutch	609,693	194.036
French	2,094,382	129,997
	$35,744,019	$82,922,977
Brazil	11,972,214	59,318,756
Venezuela	4,028 583	10,909,705
Central America	5,650,916	8 139,273
Plate countries	12,239,951	7,156,600
West Coast States	7,965,709	7,645,287
Mexico	13,285.287	22,090,915
Total	$90,886,103	$198.910,575

Judged by the practical standard of the exports and imports, the British West Indies and the Guianas are in less unfavorable relations of inequality and inequity than Brazil, the Spanish West Indies, Venezuela and Santo Domingo; but in comparison with Mexico, Hayti, Central America, the Plate countries and the west coast States of South America they are at a disadvantage. Reciprocity under the Aldrich amendment applies mainly to Brazil, the Spanish West Indies, Venezuela, Santo Domingo, the British West Indies, British Guiana and Central America. With Mexico and the remaining countries the conditions require special treaties outside of the range of the amendment.

Reciprocity is a great policy which will readjust the present inequitable conditions of trade and enlarge the foreign markets for American exports.

The fact that the United States receives $200,-000,000 of produce from the South and sells less than $01,000,000 in return is a complete demonstration of the necessity of more equitable conditions of exchange. Under fair relations of reciprocity the United States, instead of having $300,000,000 of the $1,200,000,000 of foreign trade of the countries included in the foregoing table, can reasonably expect to have $600,000,000. But this tremendous gain will require something in addition to the enlightened diplomacy of the Harrison Administration. There must be a restoration of the American commercial marine and a development of mercantile energy on land and sea. The flag must be carried into foreign ports and wholesale houses established in the chief centres of population. Reciprocity will be a great gain, but it is only a condition for the development of American enterprise. The way to compete is to compete.   I. N. F.

OPENING FOREIGN MARKETS.

HOW TO ENLARGE THE EXPORT TRADE.

FREE RAW MATERIALS ALREADY AVAILABLE— THE TARIFF NOT AT FAULT—PRACTICAL SUGGESTIONS FROM A SUCCESSFUL MERCHANT—WHOLESALE HOUSES REQUIRED.

Kingston, April 20.—When the question of enlarging the export trade of the United States was raised by the Harrison Administration our free-trade doctrinaires condemned the movement with fine irony. How could Southern countries, they asked, be expected to buy their imports in a market from which their own products were shut out by a Chinese tariff wall? Commerce is barter, they were good enough to explain, and a nation which hopes to sell its surplus stock must show its readiness to buy freely from foreign customers. Long before the Pan-American Conference was closed the country knew that it was buying more freely than any European nation in Southern markets. So large was the margin between its imports from that quarter and its exports sent in exchange that there was broad ground for the reciprocity policy which is now one of the leading issues presented to the American people by the Harrison Administration.

The doctrinaires, having been forced to abandon their first line, fell back upon what they have considered impregnable ground. They admitted reluctantly that the United States has established what is virtually a large measure of free trade with Southern countries; but they contended that without free raw materials it would be impracticable for American manufacturers to compete with European rivals. Spanish-America and Brazil, they reasoned, would continue to sell their coffee, sugar, rubber, hides, dye-woods and fruits wherever there was a market for them; but when they had anything to buy they would avoid the dearest and go to the cheapest market. Until raw materials were cheapened, they added, Americans could not hope to manufacture on even terms with England, France and Germany. The tariff must first go; and then all things would be fulfilled.

One position can be turned as easily as the other. Of the imports received in Southern countries, at least 75 per cent are manufactures which have free raw materials in the United States. Those manufactures which are heavily protected there are not those which come to these countries in large quantity from Europe. Jamaica, for example, imports $1,536,438 of cotton goods and only $137,456 of woollen goods, and the proportion is even larger for Brazil and other countries. Blankets, carpets, upholstered furniture, felts, heavy cloth and linens are imported sparingly. The bulk of the manufactures required in these markets are those which are most lightly protected in the United States, and for which free raw materials are available, even without the rebate allowed for the export trade. When, therefore, the doctrinaires lay stress upon the necessity of having free raw materials before active competition can be successfully conducted in Southern markets, they make a concession which virtually opens the greater part of the field to American manufacturers and exporters. Few of those goods which are heavily protected in the United States are wanted here at any price. What are wanted are cottons, boots and shoes and manufactures of paper, leather, hides, skins, glass, rubber, iron and steel, for which free raw materials are furnished already, or which have been so greatly cheapened in price by competition under the protective system as to be on a level with European goods. Americans are not compelled to wait for an era of free trade before making a vigorous effort to supply these markets with what is needed. It is not their tariff that is at fault and stands in their way. It is ignorance of the requirements and conditions of Southern trade that is the chief obstacle to the development of their export trade. Maritime energy, by which a commercial marine can be brought into existence under the national flag is also lacking; mercantile energy has been confined to the home market and the foreign field surrendered to foreigners; and Southern countries have been allowed to receive as gratuities commercial privileges of tremendous magnitude which ought to have been made the basis of equitable reciprocity.

An ounce of practical experience is worth a pound of theoretical statement. During my stay in Jamaica, I have conversed frequently with Captain D. F. Murphy, an enterprising American merchant, who, in a short period, has established a large and profitable trade not only with the island, but with Hayti and Central America. A New-England manufacturer of boots and shoes, he has succeeded in displacing, to a large extent, English goods of this class in Jamaica; and has demonstrated the practicability of opening a large market in the South for a wide range of American manufactures. Before making Kingston his headquarters for wholesale trade, he travelled through Nicaragua and other portions of Central America, and convinced not only himself, but also a syndicate of New-England manufacturers, that Americans were neglecting a field for enterprise that was white already for harvest. I have taken pains to run over with Captain Murphy a schedule of exports from the United States and to note down his comments upon the chances and opportunities for largely increasing their volume. His judgment, being based upon experience and marked success in establishing a profitable business, is entitled to great weight.

Beginning with his own specialty, Captain Murphy says that while shoes of English and German manufacture below 75 cents are cheaper than American goods; the condition is reversed for all above that price. At 75 cents and up to $1 25, a pair of American shoes will average 10 per cent less than foreign goods; from $1 25 to $1 75 the average cost will be 15 per cent less ; and from $1.75 to $3, English, German, French and Austrian shoes will cost 20 per cent more than New-England shoes. When Captain Murphy arrived in Jamaica there was a strong prejudice against American shoes. Now every retail dealer is compelled to sell them because the goods are cheaper, and at the same time superior to those of foreign make. Of harness, trunks, valises and other manufactures of leather there is a large consumption in Southern markets and there is nothing in the way of the introduction of American goods, since European goods can be undersold. American leather is now exported to Germany in large quantities and shipped to Central America to be sold at high prices. American merchants have only to make the effort in order to sell their leather themselves in that market.

The sale of American furniture, Captain Murphy asserts, can be trebled in Southern countries if large stocks can be displayed in wholesale houses. Rubber goods, for which free raw material is supplied from Brazil, Colombia and Central America, can be sold at prices fifteen per cent lower than English importations. There is a very large demand for rubber blankets, overcoats, waterproofs, hosepipe and many other manufactures in which the United States excels.

American tinware is preferred, although the prices may be higher than English prices. American stationery and paper are ten per cent cheaper than English and more desirable in styles. American clocks and watches are without competition when once introduced. Small iron castings from the United States are largely in demand and are the cheapest in the market. American nails, from Wheeling, are often imported from England for Southern markets. Fencing-wire from the United States is 5 per cent cheaper than European wire. There is a marked preference for American horseshoes, locks, hinges, builders' hardware, kitchen utensils and housekeeping goods, which are often cheaper than competing articles. Iron-pipe for gas and water is found to be greatly superior to European stock when imported from the United States, and is sold at the same price.

Notwithstanding the marked superiority of American agricultural implements, their introduction has been attended with great difficulty in Southern countries. In Mexico this class of farm machinery is coming into use, but in Central and South America primitive methods of agriculture are still in vogue. Captain Murphy maintains that the American goods will inevitably displace European competition, since they are already cheaper. The sale of American carriages, street-cars and railway rolling-stock can be greatly enlarged if facilities are afforded for seeing them in wholesale warehouses. American pianos have no sale because the European manufacturers put them into the market at a reduction of 25 or 30 per cent in cost. English sewing machines of inferior quality are also sold in preference to American on the score of cheapness, but are generally found to be unsatisfactory. American patterns are slowly coming into the market. Belgian boilers are in common use, but are short-lived, the tubes being badly set. If American boilers were once fairly in the market, a slight difference in price would not operate against them. There are large classes of wood manufactures in which the United States does not need to fear competition. Shooks, hogsheads and barrels; mouldings, picture frames, sashes, blinds, doors and other house furnishings and many other articles can be sold at lower prices in the South than European goods. Brooms and brushes are already largely imported from New-York. American lamps and stoves are also in demand. Norwegian and German matches are without competition. American paints are often called for and not supplied with energy and enterprise.

American cottons are imported in increasing quantity in the face of strenuous competition from England. This is a great field for enterprise, for which the system of manufacturing in New-England is well adapted. The cotton manufacturers there are, to a large extent, specialists, like the shoe manufacturers, and they have a marked advantage over European rivals, who employ less labor-saving machinery and produce a larger variety of stock. Wholesale houses in which the great specialties of American manufacture can be collected and exhibited in stock are indispensable for the development of the export trade in cottons and shoes. A single specialist cannot hope to sell his goods in this market, although he may undersell all competitors. Wholesale merchants dealing in all the leading specialties and prepared to furnish goods from stock actually in hand can alone be depended upon to open a market for many classes of manufacture unrivalled in cheapness and excellence. For woollen goods there is little demand in hot countries. Only in the lighter grades will it be practical for Americans to introduce goods of this class.

It is most invigorating to meet an American merchant in these countries who can speak confidently, and yet from personal experience, of an immediate prospect of an expansion of the export trade and active competition with industrial Europe. Captain Murphy's wholesale business has been so successful that he and his financial supporters in Boston are contemplating the establishment of similar houses on the west coast and elsewhere. He ridicules the idea that the American tariff prevents competition with Europe, and contends that the long-credit system, of which so much has been said and written, is of far less importance than has been represented. The credits given by American houses are long enough for securing remunerative trade. He has found the conditions of business integrity good wherever he has traded in the West Indies and Central America, and does not think that exporters need to be afraid of running up bad debts in the South. He attaches less importance to the necessity of building up an American commercial marine than other merchants whom I have met in Spanish-America. This, I think, is because he is more familiar with the West Indies than with South America. Here there is no lack of steam communication with the United States. There are always fifteen, and sometimes as many as twenty-five, steamers a month between the island and American ports, and not more than six to and from Europe. Freights, consequently, are favorable here for United States exporters. In South America the transportation conditions are very different.

In order to be quite just to Captain Murphy, I must also add that he is not an enthusiast on the subject of reciprocity. He does not consider it necessary to have special commercial arrangements in order to develop the export trade of the United States. I think he is wrong in that matter, but let that pass. The main obstacle, he contends, is ignorance on the part of manufacturers and merchants. They do not know how to make goods for southern markets; nor how to ship, pack and sell them. When duties are levied upon gross weight, to pack goods in heavy boxes is to add 20 per cent to the cost. Southern merchants never know what American goods will cost until they have them on their counters, for they cannot forecast the blunders in invoicing and packing which inevitably are made. Here comes in the great advantage of American wholesale houses established at the centres of Spanish-American population. Merchants on the ground will be familiar with all the details of customs law, interior transportation, invoicing, and the requirements of public taste and convenience. They can carry large stocks from which retail dealers can replenish their shelves whenever they choose to order goods, and there will be no delay in filling orders and no blunders in packing. They will not antagonize the local retail merchants, but will enable them to buy American goods from stock on the ground as they want them.

To American merchants and manufacturers who are aspiring to take advantage of the reciprocity treaties and to sell them goods in southern markets, I recommend a careful consideration of the plan of establishing wholesale houses in Havana, Matanzas, Cienfuegos, Santiago, Kingston, Barbados, Para, Pernambuco, Bahia, Rio, Montevideo, Buenos Ayres, and all the important ports of the west and north coasts of South America. A shoe or a cotton-print manufacturer cannot open a market by writing letters to American Consuls, by sending samples by mail, by soliciting orders through commercial travellers, or by spasmodic dealing with commission houses. A few groups of a dozen such manufacturers, co-operating in the establishment of a series of wholesale houses by which all classes of American goods can be handled, will solve the problem of the extension of the export trade.   I. N. F.

WHAT PROTECTIONISTS IN CANADA SAY.

There is an association in Canada called the Canadian Manufacturers' Association. Here is what they say of the object of their organization:

To secure by all legitimate means the powerful aid both of public opinion and governmental policy in favor of the development of home industry and the promotion of the interests of Canadian manufacturers generally. To enable manufacturers in all branches to act together as a united and organized body whenever action on behalf of any particular interest or of the whole body is necessary. To promote direct trade with such countries as may offer profitable markets for Canadian manufactures and productions.

The inception of this association dates back to 1874; when a number of manufacturers, many of them reformers in politics, met together and discussed the then industrial situation. With a tariff for revenue only, such as at that time was in force, it was impossible to build up a diversity of manufacturing industries in Canada; and it was resolved that, unless a policy of protection to home industry was adopted as a National policy, the country would continue in the future with even more certainty than in the past a purely agricultural community, raising grain and farm products for such other nations as could buy from us more cheaply than elsewhere.

So it seems that there were some business men in Canada, who had sense enough to discover " that with a tariff for revenue only, it was an impossibility to build up a diversity of manufacturing industries" in the country. Australia years ago made the same discovery. Why do not the free traders of England train their guns upon the colonies of Great Britain for a while? New-Zealand is almost the only one among them all which has not a protective tariff. Indeed, if there is another first or second class Power on the globe, outside of England, with perhaps the exception of Switzerland, which has not a protective tariff, will some one name it? How long is it since the people of England secured a monopoly of the intellect and business sense of the world? Again, if free trade is such a self-evident blessing, why cannot these English teachers of the doctrine make it appear plain to the English speaking colonies of their own country? They have utterly failed to do this. The civilized nations of the world pronounce the theory, in fact, a humbug, and, as a rule, each of them that has ever tried its practical workings of free trade, has been compelled to abandon it and return to the protective system. England alone survives the general catastrophe, and clings to her idol; but so far she has been unable to delude even her own colonies.—(R. G. H.

NEW ENTERPRISES, AND WHAT THEY MEAN.

We clip from the " Bulletin of the American Iron and Steel Association" of December 31, 1890, the following item:

Contracts have just been signed between the Oxnard Beet Sugar Company and Richard Gird, millionaire, of

Chino Ranch, San Bernardino County, Cal., for building a big sugar factory and refinery, which will work 500 tons of beets and turn out over fifty tons of sugar daily. Henry T. Oxnard, whose company will expend $1,000,000 for buildings and machinery, said recently that the success of his beet-sugar factory at Grand Island, Nebraska, induced him to enter into this work. He added: " We will begin on Monday to erect at Chino one of the largest and most perfectly equipped beet-sugar factories in the United States. The success of our company is a brilliant example of the wisdom of the Republican party when, true to its doctrine of protection to home industries, it gave a bounty to manufacturers of home-grown sugar. The machinery has been ordered from Cologne, Germany, which could not be secured in this country, but the greater part of the plant is of American make. The factory will be ready for operation next November." Richard Gird is under contract to plant 2.500 acres in sugar beets this season and 5,000 acres every year thereafter. He will employ from 300 to 500 men on his ranch, while the factory will employ 2,500. This is the largest beet-sugar enterprise in California, and is due directly to the McKinley bill.

We wish that every farmer, mechanic and workingman in the United States would read that item and then reflect upon its significance. To us it is full of meaning.

For many years there has been a duty levied on sugar, ranging from 2 to 3 1-2 cents per pound. The growers of sugar in this country have kept promising that they would increase the acreage and in a short time produce sugar enough to give us home competition, and in that way to aid in regulating the price of that article. After long years of trial they have utterly failed to do this. So great has been that failure that last year they did not produce one pound in ten of the sugar actually consumed in the United States. That condition of things caused the tariff on sugar to become simply a revenue tariff and deprived it of all the elements of a protective duty.

As a rule, a free-trade tariff, or a "tariff for revenue only" (and they are one and the same thing) is simply a tax on consumers. Hence this duty on sugar had to be paid mostly by the poorer people of the country, because sugar is an article universally used, and the rich people comprise a very small portion of the population when you come to consider the number which consume this article; and our own raisers of sugar failed to produce enough to enable them to affect the price.

Now, in view of these facts, the McKinley bill put all the cheaper grades of sugar on the free list. But, in order to stimulate the production of sugar here in the United States, the bill offered a bounty of 2 cents a pound for sugar produced in this country to be paid to any person producing 500 or more pounds in any one year from sorghum, beets, sugar-cane or maple trees This payment of a bounty to stimulate and encourage home production is no new experiment in this country. The State of Michigan did that for the salt industry, when it was new and undeveloped in that State. Almost every free-trader in Congress voted against putting sugar on the free list, and also against the bounty for encouraging its growth and production here at home. That clause of the McKinley bill alone will save to our sugar consuming people $60,000,000 each year over and above the

$3,000,000 that will at first be paid in bounties; and that saving will be felt at almost every meal eaten in the United States.

That the bounty will continue to increase in amount is what we all should desire, because that will show that the legislation was in the right direction. The contract named in the item above quoted is proof of the wisdom of this very provision of the bill. Here is one new enterprise that will employ 3,000 men at the very start in a new kind of labor , and this is only one of half a hundred just like it which we hope to see within the next ten years.

Examine, also, the statement of Norton Brothers, of Chicago, in The Tribune of last week. These large manufacturers of tin cans tell us that they are already making their own tin-plate from imported iron sheets, but that before long they intend to make even their tin-plate sheets at their factory in Chicago. One portion of their statement is quite remarkable, and that is that they did not go abroad for a single workman. This is what they say: " We found a good many workmen scattered about the country who had worked for years in Welsh tin-plate works, and gathered force enough in this way to man our plant with experienced help. Since it became known that we are at work we have applications from more men than we can employ at present, and we anticipate no difficulty in getting all the skilled help we shall require "

Only think up to what these two items lead! First, the making of all the tin-plate we need right here in our own factories, and thus keeping in this country for our own people $20,000,000 heretofore sent abroad each year for the purchase of this one article. Secondly, the raising in a few years at least one-half of all the sugar we consume, and, at a day not very far distant, all we need from our own soil, and having it manufactured ready for the table in our own mills, thus keeping for the use of our own people $260,000,000 that must otherwise be sent abroad for sugar alone! Think also of the assured fact that, while these two industries alone will employ at good wages an immense army of workers, sugar will be cheapened to every one who must buy and eat it. In a little while, tin-plate also will be furnished here at home, of a better quality than we now get, and at a cheaper price than the foreign manufacturer now compels us to pay. Watch the results. This is no theorizing. It is simply predicting something that seems to us sure to follow. If these things do follow we will all know it, and for one I expect to live long enough to call the attention of the free traders of this Nation to both these results.

One of my self-imposed duties will be to watch for these new enterprises, and report their existence to the readers of The Tribune. My faith is very strong as to the workings of this new tariff law. My veneration is very great for all people who do honest work, who live by honest toil, for every man who drains a swamp or fertilizes a barren spot, and for any man of means who will build up any enterprise that will give employment at living wages to our own people. Such men, all of them, bless humanity. Let us make more tin-plate, raise more sugar beets, do more of everything that builds up our country and makes it a desirable place in which to live. That is what protection means.   R. G. HORR.

LABOR AND IMMIGRATION.

IS THE AMERICAN WORKINGMAN REALLY PROTECTED?

WHY IMMIGRATION RENDERS A PROTECTIVE TARIFF ABSOLUTELY NECESSARY.

In the issue of The Semi-Weekly Tribune of January 2 we published portions of a letter written by W. B. Stickney, of Ann Arbor, Mich., and gave our answer to two of his inquiries. The same letter also contained a question which seemed worthy of a separate reply, namely: "How does Protection benefit the wage-earner in this country if our country is constantly supplied with Hungarians, Poles, Italians and the cheaper kind of labor from Europe to meet the demand for the same?"

That is a question which has been constantly asked by all the free-trade speakers of the United States for the last five years. Let us examine it with some care and see if any solution can be reached.

In the first place, it might well be claimed that this question has very little direct bearing upon the general question as to whether we should have a high or a low tariff, or none at all, on products imported from foreign lands. Our tariff laws deal with the people who are here. The moment these Hungarians, Poles and Italians land on our shores, they instantly become a part of our people and must be provided for the same as the rest of our population. If not, where would you draw the line? How long would you have a man here before he should be entitled to the full benefits of our institutions? One day? One week? One month? One year? Ten years? Or should it be twenty years?

However, this must be admitted. Our tariff laws make plenty of work at good wages in the United States, and the high wages induce the workmen of the Old World to seek our shores; and this tide of immigration causes an increased supply of workingmen. So that the real question of Mr. Stickney is this: "How does a protective tariff benefit our laborers, if a supply of workingmen comes from across the water to meet every new demand?" That is a pertinent inquiry, but the answer is easily given.

Protection benefits labor in the United States by supplying an abundance of work for, not only all who are here, but all who come, by maintaining wages at a high level, in spite of the continual immigration of foreign workmen, and by promoting the general prosperity of the whole country.

Mr. Stickney assumes that the demand for more workmen in America is constantly supplied by an influx of "Hungarians, Poles, Italians and the cheaper kind of labor from Europe." This is not strictly correct. A certain percentage of the 500,000 immigrants who come here every year have, indeed, been accustomed in Europe to work for starvation wages; but the majority are Englishmen, Germans, Scotch and Irish. It is undoubtedly true that all of them have worked for lower wages than workmen in the United States receive, otherwise they would not come here; but it is not true that the ranks of Labor in the United States are being constantly recruited from the cheapest-paid labor of Europe, which said foreign labor goes to work in the United States at correspondingly low wages, and thus undermines the wages of American workmen. These immigrants as a rule, do not work for the low wages they left behind them in the Old World. On the contrary, they instantly demand the highest wages, and they are usually noted for their vigorous desire to get the highest pay possible for their work. Until it can be proved that the constant influx of foreign labor actually undermines wages in the United States, protection will be absolutely necessary for our workers, because, whether or not they need protection against the vast throngs of workers who come to America annually from Europe, they certainly do need protection against the low-paid workers who remain behind in Europe, and who, if they could flood America with the low-priced products of their cheap labor, would throw our own people out of work by the thousands.

After all, the point involved in Mr. Stickney's question has little to do directly with the subject of a high or low tariff. Whether it would be wise to put a stop to the coming of these half a million of foreigners each year or not is one question. The kind of laws that we should have to provide for the well-being of all our people, including these very immigrants, so long as our laws permit them to come, is another question. It may be that the time has come when this immense tide should be checked. If so, let us examine that question carefully, honestly, courageously, and decide it upon its own merits. So long as we permit them to come (and in the past we have invited, even urged them to do so), it is our duty to look after their welfare the same as we do that of the balance of our people.

Is it possible that our free-trade friends would claim that we should adopt a tariff for revenue only in order to reduce the wages of our working people to so low a point that it would remove all inducement for immigration? I will say this, that up to date I have never met a Free Trader who had the courage to take that position. Permit me to ask this question: "Is there a single argument that could be urged against the coming here of these Hungarians, Poles and Italians that would not be just as potent and appropriate if we had a free-trade tariff, as it is under our present protective system?" If there is one, what is it? If there is none, then pray why ask the question at all in a debate on the tariff?

I can see a much stronger reason for the protective system so long as we permit this immigration to continue than would exist if we had only to deal with that increase of population which comes from the normal birth-rate of our own people. So long as this influx of foreign-born people is permitted, there will be all the more need of that system, so that we may keep up the standard of wages here in the United States.

Let me illustrate. We all admit that our system of common schools is a good thing for our people. We all agree that it should be maintained for the purpose of keeping up the standard of education here in the United States. What would you think of the suggestion that there is no use of trying to do this so long as we permit many ignorant immigrants to land on our shores, and so bring down the standard of education here? The reply would most certainly come, without the least hesitation, that in that event there would be more need than ever to keep our schools running, so as to prepare these newcomers for the duties of intelligent citizenship.

The people who are constantly being born in this country, when grown to womanhood and manhood, also compete with other laborers and increase the supply of workers, and, if the country were stationary, would tend to cheapen wages as much as the immigrants would. If you were to consult one Malthus, who has written a book on the dangerous increase of the human race, he would tell you that the arrival of these enormous numbers should also in some way be checked. What says our correspondent to such a proposition as that? Because these constantly increasing new-born citizens supply the demand for labor would hardly be given as an argument in favor of any special view of the tariff question, unless it was that the tariff should be maintained. Whether anything should be done to lessen the natural increase of the human race is a question that should be considered by itself. Mr. Malthus takes one side of that question and Henry George the other side, but neither of them claims for a moment that the question has any bearing on the theories of protection or free trade.

The problem that every one of our statesmen who makes any pretensions to a knowledge of political economy should strive to solve is this: How best to provide for all our people as he finds them here, without asking where they came from, how they got here or how long they have been on the ground.

I am not sure but the time is near at hand when we ought to take up this question of immigration in dead earnest and decide it. The Republican party has been legislating in that direction for several years. Laws have been passed restricting Chinese immigration, preventing the landing of criminals and paupers on our shores, and also to stop the bringing of laborers here from abroad under the contract system. The writer of this article voted for each of those measures and believes in their wisdom now. Whether we should not also, at the present moment, put some restrictions upon the throngs of ignorant people that are daily reaching this country, lowering the standard of intelligence and morality in our large cities, and taking the place of so many of our own citizens in shops and factories, in the mines and upon our farms, is a very grave question; but it should be examined and settled by itself.

What I protest against is this constant effort to attach it to a debate on the tariff, as if it could be settled in a discussion of that question, whereas it should be met and determined on great principles of public policy, and can only affect the question of tariff legislation by making the demands for protection all the more imperative.

My experience is that no free-trade debater who mentions this matter of immigration ever has the courage to state where he stands himself on that subject. Never does he dare to intimate that he is in favor of preventing or even restricting it. But he is constantly asking why Protectionists do not do it. My answer is this: "If you, Mr. Free Trader, think that immigration is a bad thing for our country, why do you not say so? Why do you not take hold of the question yourself, and try and put a stop to the evil? It will never be decided by innuendo or by any attempt to hitch it to the tail of your free-trade kite."

Protectionists are not called upon to take sides upon this question, as Protectionists, at present; because their problem is to deal with the great questions of wages, markets, home industries, the products of shops, mines and farms, and they need only to take into account the people as they find them. Their aim is to adopt that system which will be most beneficial to all the people of the United States without regard to where they were born or how long they have resided in our Republic. So long as these people are here with us and are of us, our duty is to make the best possible provision for their well being. Nothing would please me more than to see the Democratic Free Traders of the United States set their faces against this influx of foreign labor and foreign voters. They can get plenty of help in such an undertaking.

From this time on for the next ten years there will be so many children born in the United States that our increase in population will be fully one and a quarter millions of people each year without counting a single immigrant. Is not that as fast as we ought to grow? Will it not tax all our energies to provide well for ourselves and our own children? What answer will our free-trade friends make to these questions? Come, gentlemen, speak up and let us know where you stand. We know what you are trying to do as to the tariff. Your aim to break down the American system of protection is well understood. You work for that purpose early and late, in season and out of season, with means that are fair or foul, it makes little difference to you which. At the same time, you are constantly wondering why Protectionists do not stop this incessant flow of cheap labor into our country. Yet there is not a single soul among you all who will tell us squarely where he stands upon that same question. Let me ask our correspondent: "Do you know the position of a single Democratic Free Trader in the entire United States on that subject? Can you in any way learn where any of them do stand on the simple separate question of checking or stopping immigration?" If you can find out and will let The Tribune know, we will do our best to spread the information. They seem always so anxious to have us Protectionists stop this tide of foreign labor, that they really must have some notion about what ought to be done. If you can learn what that notion is and are at liberty to use your knowledge, please let us know, too. It would be difficult to tell you just how anxious we are to find out, and that anxiety is increased by the fact that, so far, all our efforts to ascertain the real opinion of a single one of these gentlemen, upon a question that always seems to be present with them have been flat failures.

R. G. HORR.